Baggage Claim

BAGGAGE
CLAIM

HOPE AGAIN SERIES BOOK 1

CATHE SWANSON

Dedication

For my parents, Paul and Gayle Nyberg,

because they teach and demonstrate love

to their children,

their grandchildren,

their great-grandchildren,

and generations to come

Prologue

"Someday, I'm going to be rich." A skinny blond woman with two black eyes and a missing tooth held a fussy baby against her shoulder, absentmindedly patting its back.

Teresa Cooper glanced up from the book she was reading to the baby's brothers. Wounded pride and embarrassment kept her apart from the other women, but she sat on the floor with the children, playing hand games, drawing pictures with them, telling stories and encouraging their responses. She felt useful, and she didn't have to socialize with the adults.

"And you," the young mother continued, "can come and be my nanny."

A hoot went up across the room. "You ain't gonna be rich. You're gonna keep having babies, and babies are expensive. You can't get a job because you can't afford day care!"

"I will! I'm not going to live like this forever. I'm going to college. They said I can."

Teresa wanted to tell her that going to college wouldn't protect her from an abusive husband, but why discourage the woman if she still had dreams?

Derisive laughter and rude comments started the endless cycle of sniping. It would deteriorate, as always, into tears and slammed doors. The drama would last for days.

Teresa took the boys with her when she left the room.

Their mother wouldn't remember to tuck them into bed. Most of the women weren't emotionally or physically able to provide the comfort their traumatized children needed, so she helped when she could. A college-educated, healthy, single woman with no children shouldn't be taking up space in the shelter, using their limited resources.

She resented being forced into the humiliating role of victim. Leo had no right to do this to her. She'd divorced him while he was in prison, but he hadn't accepted that. He'd stalked her, calling her, following her on the street and riding the same buses she used to get to and from work. He hung around the preschool, talking to the children through the fence, telling them he was Mr. Cooper. He told them to ask her if her arm still hurt.

That was when she ran. She'd worked at Kinder Academy since graduation and liked her job, but her presence—no, Leo's presence—put the children in danger. Leo had been mean when she sent him to prison two years ago, after he broke her arm and left her bleeding on their kitchen floor. When he got out, dressed in gang tattoos and whispering revenge, he was crazy, and she was terrified. Terrified and angry.

Katie would give her a good reference, but she couldn't work at a school anymore. Patty's words hummed in her head. A nanny. She'd gone to school to be a teacher, not a babysitter, but Leo had taken that from her.

Maybe there was more to nannying than she thought. She'd seen a television show about nannies who turned spoiled brats into well-behaved children. She could do that. Rich people might pay well for a professional preschool teacher, and most wealthy families lived in the suburbs. She would feel safer outside of the city. She wouldn't have to go back and forth to work on a bus. Her expenses would be low; she could save money for the future if the pay was good. If it wasn't, at least she would be safe.

Teresa closed the door of her small room and sat on her bed in the dark. This might be the perfect thing for her. Protection, anonymity, privacy. Safety. Leo would never find her. She wouldn't even have a personal address or phone number. It might be glorified babysitting, but she was willing to do it for a year or two until she had a better plan.

Marcia Phelps groaned at the sight of the letter Teresa threw on her desk. "Is that one from the Greers?" As career adviser for the shelter, Marcia had been enthusiastic about Teresa's idea, but every rejection letter brought fresh disappointment.

"No, this one's the Willises. I thought they liked me." Teresa dropped into the chair opposite Marcia. "Actually, I think Mr. Willis liked me, and his friendly conversation sent up red flags for his wife."

Her educational credentials and job experience landed her several interviews, but no sensible wife wanted to hire a young and pretty girl to work and live in her home. Teresa didn't blame them. She didn't have a high opinion of most men, and if their own wives couldn't trust them, she didn't want to live with them.

"It's not fair," declared Marcia. "I don't think it's legal for them to reject you based on your age and appearance."

Teresa turned up her hands in a shrug. "It's not like they list that as a reason for not hiring me. Usually, they just hire someone else. And it's their marriage, their kids, their home. No one should be forced to hire someone they don't want in that situation."

"I suppose not." Marcia picked up a stack of papers and handed them to Teresa. "All we can do is keep on trying. There's a couple more here, and one is for a single woman."

"Mmhmm." Teresa leafed through the papers and handed one back to the adviser. "I already applied for this one. You remember. . . it turned out Leslie Samson is a man."

"Oh, right." Marcia picked it up by one corner and dropped it in the trash. "Not going there."

A knock sounded on the door, and Marcia called out, "Come in."

"I'm sorry to interrupt." The woman who entered wore a denim skirt and a cream-colored sweater that must have been hand-knit. She had glossy brown hair, cut in a fashionable bob. "Do you have a key to the basement gate? John needed the car today, and he took my keys by mistake."

Marcia took a large key ring from her top drawer and held it out. "It's the blue one. Have you met Teresa Cooper? Teresa, this is Betty Mitchell."

"Yes, we've met." Both women spoke at once and then laughed.

"We've been looking for a nanny position for Teresa," Marcia said. "She has a degree in early childhood education and experience as a preschool teacher, but we haven't had much luck placing her."

Betty studied Teresa for a few minutes. "You don't look like a nanny." A call from the hallway summoned her away before she had time to elaborate.

Marcia looked at Teresa. "What should a nanny look like?"

"Old and ugly, I think. Did you ever see that Nazi nanny show?"

Marcia looked blank for a minute and then laughed. "Super Nanny?"

"Something like that. Those women looked like something out of a gothic novel. Grim, and a lot older. Jane Eyre was young, but that didn't work out very well."

"True. Rochester was single, right?"

"Actually, no," said Teresa. "That was a train wreck."

"What about that hoochie, New York Jewish one on that sitcom?"

"She worked for a single man. A fictional single man in a fictional comedy." Teresa set the papers on the desk. "Anyhow, it seems like the Nazi ones worked out better, at least on TV."

"Did you see the Nanny McPhee movie? She was really creepy looking." Marcia shuddered dramatically, and then her eyes opened wide. She sat upright. "Oh, Teresa. Did you see Mrs. Doubtfire?"

"I don't think so. It sounds familiar."

"Look." Marcia pulled her computer monitor around and opened the IMDB website. She scrolled through pictures and described the movie. "I'm not saying you should go that far. You don't need an actual disguise, but. . ."

"Good makeup. You can't even tell it's him." Teresa scrutinized the familiar actor in his role as an elderly nanny. "Maybe I should try that."

The comment was lighthearted, but as she gazed at the page, she wondered if it would work. She'd been trying to look smart and professional in her interviews, with enough enthusiasm and energy to keep up with little children. Those qualities were instrumental in landing her the job as a preschool teacher, but if she wanted to be a live-in nanny, maybe it would be better to look older, more serious, and less attractive.

The other women at the shelter entered into her transformation with giggles, and Teresa caught glimpses of the girls they ought to have been. They helped her dye her hair a drab, dark blond color and offered advice as she applied black eyeliner. Laughter filled the room when Patty said, "That's perfect! It looks terrible!"

Calls of encouragement and farewell followed her when

she left for her interview with the Harts. Teresa had spent an hour on her makeup and pulled her hair back tightly, securing it with a dozen black bobby pins. She wore a shapeless jumper over a white blouse, tan nylons, and a pair of brown lace-up shoes that Marcia found at the thrift store. At the last minute, one of the women produced a pair of reading glasses on a silver chain and draped it around her neck like a gold medal.

Breathlessly nervous at the audacity of her masquerade, she answered all of Miranda Hart's questions in a tight, eager-to-please voice, clutching her beige vinyl purse in her lap. Polite but obviously bored, Mr. Hart left the room halfway through the interview, and Teresa knew she had the job.

CHAPTER 1

The door slammed shut in Ben Taylor's face as he stammered out the awkward introduction. He stared at the scratched and dented metal door that separated him from Linda Hawkins—his biological grandmother.

He knocked again.

"Go away!"

"I just want to talk to you." So much for his rehearsed lines.

"If you don't leave, I'm calling the cops." Her voice was shrill, clearly audible through the door. "Right now."

"Please! I don't mean you any harm. I just want to talk." She didn't answer, and he continued. "We could sit out here on the steps if you prefer." She didn't answer. He knocked again. "Hello?" Would she really call the police?

"I said to go away."

He hadn't come this far to be chased off now. "I won't stay long. I just want to meet you."

She wrenched the door open to the limit of the heavy chain bolt. "I don't want to meet you."

His mother had told him to be gentle with this unknown grandmother, reminding him that Linda Hawkins was probably still grieving the loss of her daughter. He tried to sound soothing. "Just for a few minutes? Please." That tone sounded more like one of his children, but it worked. She closed the door and wrenched the bolt back, yanked open the door and stepped back to let him in. The woman glared at him, resentment set in sunken, hooded eyes. Thin, pale lips almost disappeared in her mottled complexion, and the tank top she wore with Tinkerbell sleep pants revealed an uncomfortable amount of loose skin draped over prominent bones. More creased skin hung from her cheek and jaw, the evidence of age incongruous with her long blond hair. Despite the suspicious stare, she seemed to have trouble focusing on him; every few seconds she swayed and then righted herself.

Ben took a deep breath and resumed his prepared introduction. "Like I was saying, I'm Benjamin Taylor, and I was adopted as an infant. . ."

She turned abruptly, interrupting—or ignoring—his clumsy explanation, and lifted the telephone receiver from its wall mount. She punched in a number and stood with her back to him, apparently waiting for someone to answer. "I need you to come over here now." She waited. "No! There's a man here and you need to talk to him." Another wait. "Just get over here." She hung up the phone and disappeared through a doorway.

Ben gaped after her. What was the matter with the woman? He didn't expect her to fall all over her long-lost grandson, but it was pretty rude to walk out of the room without a word. She was surprised, of course. He should have written ahead of time instead of just going there without warning, but he didn't write many letters. He hadn't been able to find her on Facebook, and all the phone numbers he found online were out of date. It had seemed easiest to just show up. She couldn't ignore him face-to-face.

He grimaced. He had wanted the truth about his birth, and that's what he was getting. His parents had encouraged him to seek out his birth family, but they had urged him to be cautious, for everyone's sake. Once he made contact, it couldn't be undone. He would have another family. He'd forged ahead and regretted it already. Was it too late to abandon the whole project? Apparently, someone was coming to talk to him, but if he left now, they'd never find him. The old woman probably wouldn't even remember his name.

Ben prowled through the room, rubbing his nose as it reacted to the cigarette smoke permeating the apartment. A large television was housed in a laminated entertainment center across from a dumpy couch, and empty beer cans stood in a neat line down the center of the cluttered coffee table between them. Maybe he should just leave.

He pushed a curtain aside and looked down into the narrow alley. Small garages and wooden fences crowded the pavement, leaving no shoulders. Maybe that's why most of the cars were parked out front. Had his mother grown up here? He watched a group of girls walk down the middle of the alley, laughing and dancing around, smoking cigarettes. She might have been like that. They looked happy.

Two men strolled by, stopping to peer into garages and trash cans. They slid away between houses when a police cruiser turned into the alley. A slim teenager in a black leather vest bounced on the balls of his feet, turning frequently as if watching for someone. He ignored the police car. Ben wondered why his pants didn't fall down.

Across the alley, a woman leaned out of a garage apartment window. She and a man in the alley below engaged in a furious argument, complete with vulgar gestures and obscenities loud enough for Ben to hear through the glass. He tried to imagine his nanny, Mrs. Cooper, living in such a place. Her apartment over his garage was light and spacious, with a view of the back yard and a tree-shaded park. The alley there was wide and clean, paved smooth enough for the neighbors' kids to play basketball.

Ben took out a business card and wrote his cell phone

number on the back. He'd waited long enough. "Mrs. Hawkins? I'm leaving now."

The woman came back in such a rush that she staggered against the door frame. He caught her arm and steadied her. "Are you okay?" Close to her, he could smell the strong liquor. Not beer this time.

She concentrated on his face, as if trying hard to remember who he was. "Rhonda's coming."

"Okay," Ben said, "will she be here soon?"

On cue, a hard, double knock rattled the door before a sturdy woman opened it and strode in. She wore ripped jeans and a red sports jersey. Her thick black hair stood up in spikes. She looked at Ben and Linda. "What's up, Mom?"

For one confused moment, Ben thought this woman must be his mother. Were the records wrong? No, his mother was Shari, and she was dead. Rhonda must be a sister.

That was all he had time to process before things fell apart. Linda threw herself at Rhonda, wailing and shaking. The younger woman tried to reason with her at first, but their interaction rapidly turned antagonistic, quarreling about Linda's drinking and Rhonda's neglect, as if they had forgotten he was there.

Ben gave up trying to be polite. "Excuse me!"

They both stopped suddenly and turned to him. Linda crumpled, rolling into a ball on the floor. Rhonda yelled at her. "Mom! Knock it off. Enough drama already. What's the problem?"

Ben started the explanation over again. It came more easily this time, but she stopped him as soon as she understood who he was.

"Oh no. No! That's over. Finished. We don't need you, you don't need us, so just go!"

"I just want to ask you a couple questions!"

"No." She stood in front of him, hands on her hips. "You

leave."

Linda was still sobbing, but she was sitting upright. "Go away!" She waved him away, her hand flopping out of control.

He was getting angry. "I have a right to know about my birth."

That set Linda off again, wailing and moaning. Rhonda marched over and slapped her mother sharply.

Ben was horrified. "Hey!"

But the older woman stopped crying and allowed her daughter to help her to her feet. She moved to sit on the couch, watching Ben as if he was a coiled rattlesnake. Rhonda returned to Ben. She was exasperated. "You don't have any rights. Just leave. She doesn't need you here, messing with her mind. You're not family."

Ben didn't want to be related to the crazy old lady. He didn't want to be related to anyone except his parents—his normal parents—and his children. But he'd started this and still had to find his father. Hopefully, the man wouldn't be drunk or insane.

"I need to know more. I'm not going until I get some answers."

Rhonda glowered at him through eyes smudged with two-day-old makeup. "I can call the cops."

"Just a few questions—*please*."

Ten minutes later, he sat in his car and rested his forehead on the steering wheel. Rhonda didn't know who his father was. The inference was that it could have been just about anyone. His grandfather, Gary, was long gone. Probably dead, according to Rhonda. Linda and her children had lived with their grandmother, who died shortly after Shari did. Rhonda was currently unmarried; his uncle Hawk was in prison. She didn't say why, or for how long, and Ben didn't ask.

"If you want to know anything else about Shari," Rhonda had snapped, "you'll have to talk to Connie Price."

CHAPTER 2

Ben bit into the cold pizza and used his free hand to help Benjie drag the coffee table to the center of the room. "Why not leave it where it is?"

"It's too close to the couch." The boy adjusted the position of the table.

"It's supposed to be close to the couch." Ben regarded his son with suspicion. "So you can sit on the couch and set cups and things on the coffee table. What are you doing with it?"

"We're playing that TV show game we saw last night."

"American Warrior?" They had been enthralled by the show, commenting on the contestants and challenges through the handfuls of popcorn they shoved into their mouths. It wasn't something they usually watched, but traumatized by the afternoon's events, Ben had turned it on and collapsed on the couch. He hadn't felt up to parenting.

"Yeah. American Warrior. Do we have any rope?"

"I don't think so. What do you need rope for?"

"We can hang it over the light and swing from the coffee table to the couch." Benjie eyed the distance between the two pieces of furniture.

Ben looked up at the ceiling. "No, you cannot hang from the chandelier. Mrs. Cooper would kill me."

"I've got pillows," Jack called from the top of the stairs.

"Throw 'em down and I'll catch them!" Benjie clambered over the table and reached the staircase in time to be hit with a flying pillow. "Ooph. Get as many as you can find."

Jack threw the other pillow at his brother and turned back toward the bedrooms. "Dad's got three of them on his bed."

"Whoa! Why do you need the pillows down here?" Ben picked up the second pillow and handed it to his son.

Benjie dropped it on the floor and gestured toward the opposite wall. "We're gonna line up all the kitchen chairs and low crawl underneath them, then jump on top of them and run back across as fast as we can and jump into a big pile of pillows. Maybe if there's no rope we can find a board and make a bridge between the couch and the coffee table and use the pillows underneath in case we fall off." He twisted up his mouth, considering his options.

"It's really close to the ground. We don't need pillows for that." Jack pitched two more pillows down the stairs as he spoke. "I think we should make something to jump from one to another—like stacks of books or boxes—in a row from the coffee table to the couch."

"That sounds dangerous, guys, and I don't think Mrs. Cooper would like it if you trashed the house."

"Will you help us make a climbing wall?"

Something youthful flickered in Ben, but he shook his head. "We can't nail stuff into the walls."

"Da-ad!" Jack stretched the name to two whiney syllables. He descended the stairs in a series of hops, his blond hair bouncing with each step.

"And we need a box way up high, like on top of the refrigerator, and that's the last thing you have to do—shoot the basketball into the box. Once you do that, we stop the clock." Benjie pantomimed slamming down on a buzzer.

"We need a tunnel, too," said Jack, "and some old tires

to run through."

"I don't have any tires. Isn't the kitchen chair thing like a tunnel?"

"Yeah, but it would be more fun to have a real tunnel. Hey! We could do it outside, and then we could just dig a tunnel."

Benjie ran to the window. "If we did it outside, we could have more things. We could do a lot with the swing set."

"You'll have to settle for chairs." Ben held up a hand for silence. "I think Annie's awake."

"Good!"

Good? Taken aback by their unprecedented enthusiasm, Ben followed the boys as they charged up the stairs. Annie stood in her crib, blue eyes wide, apparently as confused by her brothers' attention as Ben was.

"Good morning, Annie Banannie!"

She cooed at him and patted his cheek. "Eat."

"Good idea." He turned to the boys. "Aren't you guys hungry?"

"We want to use Annie's mattress." Benjie stepped up onto the side rail and rolled himself into the crib. Apparently realizing that he couldn't lift it out while standing on it, he rolled out again. "How do you lower the side?"

"You're not taking her mattress downstairs!"

"Dad!"

The nanny had mentioned Jack's whining to him. He was supposed to stand firm. "No. You'll have to come up with something else."

"We could use our mattresses," said Benjie, "and Mark's, if he ever gets up."

Ben stood back, letting the boys exit the nursery. "No mattresses downstairs. It's time for breakfast."

"Can we have waffles?"

In other words, Jack wanted a plate full of syrup and

enough waffle to wipe it up with. Ben couldn't blame him. "Sure. I saw two boxes in the freezer. Mrs. Cooper must have gone shopping."

He set Annie on her feet. "Don't move, baby. You need some dry clothes." He unzipped and peeled down the pink sleeper, helping her step out of it and keeping hold of one small arm so she didn't escape before he could get her dressed again. "Mrs. Cooper says you get to wear big girl underwear during the daytime now. Look! This one has Dora the Explorer on it! No more diapers! You are such a big girl!" He taped up the soggy diaper and shot it into the wastebasket. "Score!" Annie doubled over with laughter and clapped. He blew a raspberry into her neck. Their silly weekend ritual was short, but it was important. Five minutes alone with his daughter. What would he do when she was potty-trained? He hoisted her to his shoulder and kicked aside the sleeper so he wouldn't trip over it.

Mark was supposed to be potty-trained, but Ben didn't count on it. He slid Annie to the floor and shook the boy's shoulder. His youngest son was wrapped up in a cocoon of blankets. Wet. Ben sighed and started the long process of getting Mark out of bed and dressed.

"Come on, buddy. It's time to get up. Everyone's hungry." He took hold of the end of a blanket and pulled. Mark clutched it.

"Get up. It's morning."

Annie tried to climb onto the bed, and Ben barred her path with an outstretched leg. He didn't want to have to change her clothes again already. As soon as the sleepy boy emerged from the nest of bedding, Ben tugged the fitted sheet off the mattress, rolled it all up together and tossed it into the corner of the room.

Annie laughed and clapped. "Score!"

"Yeah, baby, Daddy scored. You sit over here and play

with Mark's blocks."

Mark lunged toward his toy box. "She'll break them!"

"She can't break blocks, Mark." Ben wrinkled his nose. "You need a bath. Put your pajamas in the hamper, and I'll start the water. Watch Annie."

They were fighting when he returned thirty seconds later, and he scooped them up, one under each arm. "Which of you goes in the bath? Oh, yeah. The naked one." He kicked the door shut so Annie wouldn't run out and started washing Mark in the shallow water. "You've gotta stop wetting the bed, buddy.

"I was asleep."

"Did you go before you went to bed?" Ben knew he had; he hadn't had anything to drink after eight o'clock. Mrs. Cooper had reminded him.

"Yes!"

Ben caught the movement in his peripheral vision just before Annie launched herself into the tub. He caught her before she hit the water. "Hey! You don't need a bath!" But maybe she did. That diaper had been pretty wet. She'd already stripped off her clothes, so he let her play while he finished Mark. He draped a towel over the boy and gave him a gentle shove toward the door. "Go get some clothes on."

Ben turned back and saw his daughter's gleeful expression for one second before she dashed a cup of water at his face. He shook his head like a dog and made menacing sounds at her. She giggled and nearly fell as she scooped up more water.

"Oh, no you don't." He lifted her up and swaddled her in a towel, confining her arms at her sides. She kicked and squirmed. He blew a raspberry on her neck. "Aren't you hungry? Don't you want to eat? Waffles!"

He'd ace the parenting thing today. Two clean kids with no yelling or crying from any of them. He spun her free of the towel and rubbed her head until the wisps of hair stood out like dandelion fluff. "Where did you put. . .? Oh. Okay, let's get you some dry clothes." No yelling. He grabbed the sodden bundle of clothing without releasing her and threw them into the empty tub. Another score. He'd have to remember to hang them up to dry later.

His saintly forbearance was wearing thin by the time he followed Mark down the stairs. Annie stretched upward, trying to touch the ceiling, confident in his grip on her ankles. He bounced a bit, to make it more fun for her.

They reached the bottom of the stairs before the shriek of the smoke detector filled the house. Ben lifted Annie from his shoulders and carried her, pulling Mark behind him, toward the kitchen. "Benjie! Where are you?" The back door slammed. "Benjie? Jack?" Annie clutched his neck, wailing into his ear. "Stop, Annie. I need to find your brothers."

CHAPTER 3

He nearly ran over them in the kitchen doorway. They stood side-by-side, defensively, as if to block his path.

"Where's the fire?" He knew he should be getting them all safely out of the house. Stop, drop, roll, and get out of the house. But the boys didn't look afraid—they looked apprehensive. They didn't want him in the kitchen. He strode into the kitchen.

The noise intensified. There was no fire, but smoke hung in the air, wafting a burnt stench through the room. He reached up and yanked the cover off the smoke detector. The alarm stopped instantly with the removal of the battery. Annie did not. He pried her loose.

"Annie. Stop. Stop crying. It's okay." He tried to set her down, but she clung to him. "Stop, Annie." He dragged the highchair to the living room and buckled her into it. She fought, arching her back and causing the chair to rock. "Stop that! Benjie, come here and hold the highchair." The boy complied instantly—a sure sign of a guilty conscience. Ben grabbed the bag of candies Mrs. Cooper kept for potty-training and emptied it onto the tray. Annie's hysteria evaporated.

Silence. Ben scooped up some of the candy and set it on the coffee table. "Here, Mark, have some breakfast." The boy dropped onto one of the pillows and started sorting through the pieces.

The two older boys watched with open mouths until they realized their father was looking at them. He ushered them back into the kitchen. "What got burned?"

"Waffles."

Ben looked at the counter where the toaster should have been. The butter dish was there, and a bottle of syrup, but the toaster was missing. "Where's the toaster?"

"We threw it outside," said Benjie. "But we were really careful. I used potholders and carried it by the cord."

"By the cord." Ben's stomach hurt. It used to do that when he was a child and something scared him. "Did you burn the waffles?" It didn't smell like burnt waffles. "Why did you throw the toaster outside?"

"It was on fire." Jack didn't look up.

"On fire! It was on fire and you carried it outside? By the cord?" He was going to be sick.

"I was really careful. The fire went out after I unplugged it, but the smoke detector went off." Benjie's blue eyes, so like his own, filled with tears.

There must have been an electrical short, or a defect in the toaster. Ben reached out and caught both boys in a hug. "Never do that again. If something catches on fire, you yell for me or Mrs. Cooper and then get out of the house. Don't try to put out the fire yourself." He closed his eyes and squeezed them tighter. "It's my fault. I shouldn't have let you make the waffles by yourself while I was upstairs. I'm just glad you're okay. We can buy a new toaster, but I can't replace you guys." Both boys were shaking, and Ben wanted to kick himself. The boys could have been seriously injured. He looked over at the electrical outlet. It didn't appear to be scorched, so the problem was probably with the toaster and not the wiring, but maybe he should take the kids to his parents' house until they had it checked out by an electrician.

After a minute, he released them and peered out the

door. The toaster was burnt black, crackled and shiny. The pain in his stomach flared up again. He stepped outside and crouched down to touch it. It still stank, but the chilly morning air had cooled it. The remains of waffles filled all four slots. His negligence had nearly killed them, and they hadn't even got their breakfast. Annie and Mark were eating candy. Major parenting fail.

He wiped his fingers on his jeans and picked up the toaster. It was sticky. Ben sniffed it. It wasn't an electrical odor—at least, he didn't think so. This wasn't soot or a stain from heat. It was sticky, and the black stuff was something that had burned onto it. He stood up and turned to look back at the house. He saw a flash of color as his sons raced back inside.

"Benjie? Come out here."

No response.

"Jack, Benjie, get out here now!" Anger crowded out his guilt and fear. He carried the toaster back into the house and set it on the kitchen table. The boys were nowhere in sight. Annie and Mark looked up quickly when he entered the living room, as if afraid he'd changed his mind about the breakfast menu, and then went back to their candy.

"Benjie? Jack?" He started in the basement and worked his way upstairs. They were just making it worse. Hiding from him, disobeying him by not coming when he called, and setting the toaster on fire. Ben slapped his hand on the door frame. The day had started out so well, and they had ruined it. He opened and closed doors, calling their names. They wouldn't do this if Mrs. Cooper was here. She would have had answers and apologies out of them already. But if Mrs. Cooper were here, they wouldn't have been using the toaster without supervision.

A twitch of the skirt under Annie's crib was followed by sounds of a skirmish. Muffled quarreling. The crib rattled and knocked against the wall, and then Jack came rolling out, obviously propelled by a solid shove from his brother. He came to a stop at his father's feet, looked up, and tried to scurry back under the crib.

Ben lifted the hem of the skirt. "Get out here."

The boys emerged and scooted back against the crib, cowering as if he was in the habit of beating them twice a day. It annoyed him.

"Downstairs." Annie must have run out of candy by now, and he was afraid to think of what Mark might be doing. At least Annie was confined to the highchair. He followed the boys downstairs. They continued their impersonation of death row inmates, and the injustice made him even madder. He'd hardly ever even spanked them. He didn't often yell. He did fun things with them. He bought them treats. In fact, they usually saw him as a pal. He didn't deserve to be treated like a monster.

"Mark! What are you doing?" He rushed past the older boys to snatch Mark from the top shelf of the pantry.

"Annie wants more candy." The guileless stare of the little boy didn't fool Ben. He dropped Mark on the couch, twisted Annie's highchair to face the television and flipped through channels until he found something animated. Hopefully, it was a kids' show.

"Sit down. At the table."

The boys complied, averting their gaze from the toaster. They looked at their hands, the floor, the walls. . . everything but their father and the toaster. Ben knocked on the toaster. "What happened?"

No answer.

"Look, guys, I want to know what happened. Just tell me the truth. Man up." Ben grimaced. Man up. Benjie was seven, and Jack was only five and a half. If they were lying or not confessing, it was because they were afraid. He knew what it was like to be afraid. "I know the toaster didn't just catch fire on its own. Did you put something other than waffles into it?"

Jack stole a look at his stubbornly silent brother and spoke up defiantly. "Benjie said it would work."

"Said what would work?"

"You know how Grandma's syrup is always warm?"

"Yes."

"Well, we wanted to have warm syrup, but the bottle didn't fit in the microwave. So, we took frozen waffles, put butter on them and then poured syrup over them and down into all of the holes. Then the waffles would cook, and the syrup would get warm at the same time." Judging by Jack's triumphant tone, he still thought it was a brilliant idea.

Benjie blew out a long breath. "We weren't adding anything different. It was just waffles and butter and syrup, but we put the other stuff on first." He looked more dejected than guilty. "But then the toaster started on fire, so we don't know if it worked or not."

Ben blinked. They didn't know if it worked. He spun the toaster and used a finger to pry out a bit of the waffle. "You can't put butter or syrup in the toaster. You can't put anything but bread or waffles in the toaster. Otherwise, it catches on fire. And next time, it might burn down the whole house."

"It was just syrup and butter," said Benjie.

"The butter and syrup caused the fire." He was talking to a brick wall. And apparently, they weren't as afraid as he thought they were. "From now on, you don't touch the toaster without an adult in the room. Or the stove. Or the microwave."

"Not even for popcorn?" Jack protested.

Ben wavered. Popcorn was a healthy snack, right? "If we have popcorn, I'll make it."

"Because we're going to watch American Warrior again tonight, and we need popcorn while we watch it." Benjie pushed his chair back and jumped down. "Can we have one mattress?"

There was that brick wall again.

"No. In fact, no popcorn. No TV for the rest of the weekend." He tried to think of something more punitive. Banishment to their shared bedroom, with its boxes of toys and books, would be no hardship for them. They didn't have any upcoming events he could cancel. The garage didn't need to be cleaned. "And no video games or computers." That was annoying, because he enjoyed those things, too, and now he would have to wait until they were all in bed.

"Daddy!"

"And you stop whining." He stood up. "You guys are lucky you didn't burn the house down. Go keep an eye on Annie and Mark while I make breakfast."

He was perfectly happy with cereal, but the waffles were supposed to be a treat. And now what? No toast to go with eggs, so it would have to be cereal. How was he going to explain this one to Mrs. Cooper?

CHAPTER 4

Ben really just wanted to go home and forget about the biological family thing. It was a train wreck. His parents had expressed compassion for Linda Hawkins, but they hadn't seen her. They weren't related to her. If this was a dead-end, he was finished. He'd happily spend the rest of his life grateful that he'd been adopted.

He tried to pull up some optimism as he hurried toward Connie Price's front door, hunching his shoulders and bending into the wind. It was a single-family home, not littered with the extra mailboxes and outside staircases of a multi-unit dwelling. The aluminum siding was a little rusted, but the broken cement walk was free of graffiti. All the windows had curtains. Upscale for this neighborhood.

The door swung inward before he could ring the doorbell, and his hostess stood before him. Connie Price was solid and tenaciously blond, wearing blue eyeliner, sticky mascara and opaque makeup that failed to conceal an acne-scarred complexion, but her black leggings and blue sweatshirt were clean, and she appeared to be sober.

"Hello?" The inquiry, more like a telephone greeting than a welcome, cut off his polite introduction. It irritated him. She knew perfectly well who he was and was reveling in the drama, forcing him to make the awkward explanation all over again before she would invite him inside. He twitched as a stream of cold rainwater rolled down the back of his head and soaked into his shirt.

"Hi. I'm Ben Taylor. Rhonda Hawkins sent me."

He thought she looked a little disappointed, but she bustled him through the door under a flow of chatter.

"Come in. Please take off your shoes. I like to keep the carpet nice. So, you're poor Shari's baby." She clucked her tongue. "That was just so awful. I cried for weeks. My mother thought I'd go into a depression. She wanted me to see a psychiatrist, but with one thing and another it never happened." She held out her hand. "Let me take your coat. It seems like it was just yesterday, or maybe a thousand years ago. I tried to go to the funeral, you know, but I had to leave. They actually had an open casket! I just kept imagining all the blood and poor Shari dying in agony. It was awful."

Stunned, Ben shrugged off his coat, and she hung it carefully on a hook.

"And then they didn't know what to do with the baby. With you, I guess." She chuckled. "It's just so strange to have you here. You can put your shoes over there." She pointed at the rubber mat to the left of the door. "I've never gotten over it, and then Rhonda's call brought it all back to me. It was awful. No one knew what to do. Linda was hysterical. Rhonda was just a kid. They didn't even know she was pregnant. A social worker came and asked me questions about who the father might be. My mother had a fit. The thing is, without a father, no one knew who had custody of you. Linda—your grandmother—was the next of kin, but she was just a mess. At first, she didn't even want to see you. Then she wanted to take you home with her, but then she didn't. My mother said the social worker told her that Linda was an unfit mother. Anyhow, you went into foster care right from the hospital, and eventually Linda signed the paperwork for you to be adopted."

Ben stood stupidly, one shoe in his hand and one on his

foot. In thirty seconds, this intense stranger had dealt him a series of blows, revealing more information about his personal history than he'd uncovered in weeks of research.

She continued before he could recover. "Rhonda said you wanted to know about it. She was a lot younger than us, of course, so she probably doesn't remember much herself. She didn't even know her own sister was pregnant!" Connie rolled her eyes. "Shari was a little plump, so she was able to hide it a long time. Not fat," she assured Ben, "just plump. Curvy. And you were early, of course, so she wasn't even showing yet when she went into labor. You had to stay in the hospital for a while. I don't remember all the details. I just know you went into foster care when you were released. And after that," Connie said apologetically, "we never saw you again. I was just devastated by Shari's death. It was such a shock. Awful. Come on in." She gestured toward a couch and sat down in the matching chair across from him.

Ben perched on the edge of the couch. "But you knew she was pregnant? Rhonda said you and. . . Shari were inseparable."

Rhonda had told Ben that Shari and Connie skipped school during the day and ran wild at night, drinking, and chasing boys. Her spiteful attitude had shocked him at first, but it hadn't taken long to realize that Rhonda was still living with the fallout from the tragedy. After Shari's death, Linda had made her into a saint and martyr, lighting candles and leaving gifts on the girl's grave. Rhonda and their younger brother had been emotionally abandoned—their own confusion, fear and grief ignored, while their mother wallowed in self-pity and alcohol.

Connie bristled. "Of course, I knew. She was my best friend. We took the bus to the Planned Parenthood clinic and they tested her. She cried all afternoon. They signed her up for an abortion, and we went back to the clinic, but she chickened out at the last minute. Just jumped up and ran out. I followed her, of course, and we ended up back here. This was my parents' house before they died. We got so plastered that night! I thought for sure she'd go back to the clinic in the morning, but she wouldn't. She said she was going to have the baby." She looked around the room. "Do you see an ashtray?"

Ben found one on the end table and walked over to hand it to her.

"Thanks. She said the baby's father would marry her."

Ben stopped. "Rhonda said her sister didn't know who the father was."

"Rhonda's a cat. She didn't even know Shari was pregnant!" She paused to light a cigarette. "Well, I wasn't sure, either, but Shari was totally convinced it was this Joe guy who took her to his prom."

Ben dropped onto the couch, staring at her. A name. Joe. He'd talked to a few people, but no one had offered any names. They all seemed to think that it could have been any one of a number of men.

"Did you believe her?"

She turned up her hands in a shrug. "Oh, I don't know. Maybe. The boys really liked Shari, and we didn't know much about cycles back then. You just waited to see if your period was late, and then you knew you were pregnant. Shari had just started having periods, so she didn't have a regular schedule. That's why she didn't realize she was pregnant for so long."

TMI. "What can you tell me about this Joe?"

"His name was Jonah. That's why I remember it. Not Joseph. And I've been trying all day, but I just can't remember his last name."

"Was he local?"

She perked up at the question and launched into another tale. "No, he was from some other town. But it wasn't really far away. South side, or maybe one of the western suburbs. He had a black car with a sunroof. Shari just loved that car. She liked him, too, of course—not just the car. We met at a wedding reception. Shari and I hadn't been invited—didn't even know the bride or groom. We just saw the party and walked in. That was a riot. There was an open bar. We ate a meal and then there was dancing. I picked up one of the groomsmen and Shari met Joe. The four of us went out for coffee after the reception ended. I don't really remember what happened after that." She smiled wistfully. "It was a long time ago. But Shari got a phone call from this Joe guy, and he invited her to a Valentine's party. She wore an entirely pink outfit, right down to her underwear. They got together a few times, I think, and then he asked her to the prom at his school. Can I get you a cup of coffee or something?"

Ben shook his head, not wanting to distract her from the story. "I'm good, thanks."

"Anyhow, she got herself a really nice dress and we fixed her hair. He gave her a corsage. All the usual prom things. I never went to one, myself. That was the last time she ever saw him."

Ben blinked at the abrupt ending to her monologue. "She never saw Joe again?"

"I don't think so. I was trying to remember. . . we went to summer school that year, in the morning, for drivers ed. We spent the afternoons on the beach and the nights riding around in muscle cars with the guys we met on the beach. Then we went back to school in the fall, so it must have been September that we went to the clinic. You were born around Thanksgiving, and that's when she died." She stubbed out her cigarette in the ashtray and tapped a new one out of the pack. She lit it and inhaled deeply before blowing a long stream in the direction of the front door.

Ben wondered how she had the lung capacity to talk so rapidly. He waited, willing her to continue.

"That's about it."

But it wasn't enough, now that he had a name. "But what makes you think this Joe was the father?"

"She just said he was. She seemed really sure about it. She went to get his address from his mother, but his mom said he wasn't allowed to have letters during boot camp. Shari didn't want anyone to know he was the father, though, because she didn't want him to get in trouble. She was a minor, and I think she was nervous because she'd told him she was seventeen. She was only fifteen. He'd have gone to jail if anyone found out."

"Fifteen?" His voice squeaked.

"She looked older, and we wore a lot of makeup back then. And, like I said, she was curvy. She didn't want to tell him her age until she had the baby, because she'd be nearly sixteen by then and they could get married."

"So, he never knew there was a baby." Ben grasped at that redeeming fact. At least his father hadn't abandoned a pregnant, young girlfriend.

"Not as far as I know. That was it. I never saw him again, either."

"Can you think of anything else that might help me find him?"

"I don't think so, but the name Jonah shouldn't be too hard to trace around here. He graduated from high school and went into the military the year you were born."

"Do you know if he had a job?"

"Well, he must have, to support that car, but I don't remember anything. I do remember that Shari said he was really interested in computers."

"I guess that should get me started." Ben stood up. "Thanks for talking to me. May I come back if I have more questions?"

"Sure." She watched him put on his shoes and then

opened the door for him. "Your mom wasn't a bad girl. She was just young and dumb. We all were. And you can't really blame your dad, either. He never even knew. It was just a casual relationship. It only became important to Shari when she found out she was pregnant. Otherwise, she'd pretty much forgotten him already."

Great. Was that supposed to comfort him? She'd given him a clear vision of his mother. A wild child. A tramp.

As he climbed into the van, Connie called after him. "About the computers. . . that was 1990. Computers were still pretty new then. Schools had clubs for them. If you can find the high school he went to, you might be able to look in the old yearbooks."

Ben ignored the rain on his face. "You don't remember where he lived?"

"No, but it couldn't have been too far away. He drove here. It was one of the suburbs. I'm sure of it." She retreated into the warmth of the house, waving goodbye over her shoulder before she closed the door.

He went through the motions of buckling his seat belt, starting the engine, flipping on the headlights and turning on the windshield wipers. The rain was pouring down from darkening gray skies, as it had been the night Anneliese died. The van had good tires, of course. That was important. He never forgot that he had to drive cautiously, for the kids' sake. They were with his parents—his real parents. His mother would have fed them by now, so he could take them home, give them baths and read them stories until they fell asleep. All children should have that—safe homes with loving grandparents and daddies who tucked them in at night. Mothers, too, but even without one or the other, there should still be families. He inhaled deeply and sat up straighter, fending off tears that might blur his vision and memories that would distract him in the dangerous driving conditions.

Maybe he would track down this Jonah. If he'd gone into the military, he could be anywhere, and maybe he'd be glad to meet his son. Ben wasn't sure anymore. Right now, he wanted to get home to his own sons and his daughter—to *his* family.

CHAPTER 5

Ben's mother opened the front door before he was out of the van. The sun had emerged in time to set, and its lingering rays limned her apricot-gold hair like a halo. It revealed lines of weariness, too, and he suspected some of them might be new. A day with four energetic children would exhaust even the most doting grandparents. They made him tired, and he was nearly fifty years younger than his mother.

"How did it go?"

"It was fine. They played in the rec room most of the day. I gave them hot dogs and French fries for dinner, and now they're watching a video with your dad."

"Thanks." Ben hugged her. "You're amazing. I would have given them frozen pizza." He pulled the door closed behind them. "Then I'd pray Mrs. Cooper didn't find out. She's trying to cut down on junk food."

"Teresa just wants to cut down on the sugar. They had milk and carrots, too, so it wasn't all that bad. And apples and raisins for a snack earlier." She examined his face. "How did it go with you?"

"Pretty rough. Thank you for adopting me."

She smiled up at him. "Our pleasure."

Ben followed her through the house to the kitchen. "It wasn't as bad as Friday. She knew I was coming, so she was ready to talk about it. She was Shari's best friend."

He poured himself a glass of milk and walked into the living room. The boys lay on their stomachs absorbing a loud cartoon. Annie was curled up on her grandfather's chest, her whiffly little breaths harmonizing with his soft baritone snores.

"Oh, I'm sorry." His mother sounded flustered and apologetic. "I didn't realize he'd gone to sleep. I thought he was watching them."

"They're fine. They probably wore him out." He flopped down on the floor next to the boys. "Did you guys wear out Grandpa?"

"Daddy!" Mark rolled over and Ben tickled him, enjoying his son's squeals, comforted by the normalcy of his own family. When the movie reclaimed Mark's attention, Ben drank his milk and returned to the kitchen to scrounge for food.

His mother followed like an anxious hen. "Did you learn anything new today?"

When he was younger, she had asked him that question every day after school. Now, she asked because she was worried. He understood his parents' concern. They'd adopted him through the government agency with no information about his origins except that he was a ward of the court, and they'd given him a good life. They didn't want him hurt now. Maybe they also felt a little jealous, or hurt, as if he thought they weren't his "real" parents. He didn't know how to address that.

"It was informative. This woman, Connie Price, talked faster than Aunt Sarah does." Ben opened the pantry door and surveyed the shelves. "She talked nonstop, from the time I got there. I'm not sure I got everything. The important thing is that I may have a lead on my father." He gave up on his search and closed the door. "Well, not a real father. More like a sperm donor. He doesn't seem to have played any other role in the situation. Connie said it was just a casual relationship."

"But his name wasn't in your birth records. Your. . .

grandmother said no one knew."

They'd learned that when the record was unsealed: mother deceased, father unknown. Ben tried to make an orderly presentation of the information. "No. He never knew she was pregnant. Connie said Shari lied to this guy about her age, and then when she found out she was pregnant, she didn't want him to get in trouble. She thought he'd marry her when he got back from his military training. She didn't even tell anyone she was pregnant, except for Connie, and she went into premature labor. She died in childbirth." He took a deep breath. "She was only fifteen."

"Fifteen?" His mother's voice broke on the word. She squeezed her eyes shut. "That poor girl. No one knew she was pregnant? Where were her parents?"

Drunk, Ben thought, or just wrapped up in themselves. He suddenly hurt for the girl—the young girl—who had died giving birth to him. She'd been wild and rootless, living only for temporary enjoyments. Connie had made it sound exciting, but it wasn't. It was heartbreaking. What would his own life have been like if she'd lived? Would his father have married her? Would he have been raised like she was? Instead, because she had died, he'd been raised in the most stable and loving of homes. Guilt and shame stabbed him. He couldn't be glad Shari had died.

It was impossible to think of her as his mother. This woman, crying over the tragic death of a fifteen-year-old girl, was his mother. He was grateful for that, however it came about. He put an arm around her shoulders and gave her a squeeze.

"Connie said Shari was certain this guy named Jonah was the father. He lived in a nearby suburb, was interested in computers and joined the military after high school. Jonah's not a common name, so he should be pretty easy to track down. Connie thought high school yearbooks might help. He graduated in 1990. It's a place to start."

Eliza stepped away and wiped her face with one hand. "Can you find old yearbooks online?"

"I'm sure." He hesitated before confessing, "He may not be the father. Even Connie didn't seem convinced that Shari could be sure. She was. . . Connie said the boys liked her."

"She was a child!"

"It was like she didn't even have parents. She did whatever—" Ben's hot words were cut off by the eruption of three little boys from the living room doorway.

Jack was in the lead. "Grandma, do you have any cookies? Or crackers, or anything?"

"Grandpa said you have cookies." Benjie sounded accusatory. He didn't like carrots.

"I said we would ask if she has any—no promises." The oldest Benjamin Taylor passed the sleeping girl to her father. "I think she's wet."

"Thanks." Ben accepted the child and clutched the edge of the counter so he wouldn't drop her when the boys hurled themselves at him. His dad skills were improving; he was getting better at anticipating and preventing disaster. Except for the toaster, of course, and that was a lesson learned. No more cooking without supervision.

He listened to the recounting of their day, only interrupting to respond to his father's inquiry. "It was productive. Mom can tell you about it; I'd better get these rug rats home to bed."

When Annie had been changed and the boys refilled, Ben started loading up his family for the trip home. "Thanks for watching them."

"No problem," said his dad. "We had a good time."

Both of his parents looked tired. Or were they just old? He knew it wasn't only the babysitting that wore them out. They were the ones with parenting skills; he was an amateur.

"I think I'm going to take a break from the family search. It's just depressing."

"You don't want to track down your father?"

The question sounded wrong coming from his dad's lips. Ben shook his head. "Not right now. He's probably in jail or something. I'll have to make do with just one of you. It's worked so far."

He gave his father an awkward hug and slid into the driver's seat. The older man still looked troubled. Ben wished he could fix it.

The children fell asleep almost immediately, leaving the van an oasis of quiet in the drizzling rain. They slept, limp in the bulky car seats, secure in the safety harnesses. What would they think someday of their parents? They would have hard truths to face, too, just as he did, and it was hard enough at twenty-five. Until they were ready for that—if they could ever be ready—he'd give them a secure life like he'd had. And then, they'd just have to accept the truth. Life was like that. Everyone had some kind of baggage, and they all had to learn to manage it.

His genetic roots didn't affect his life now. A teenage girl got pregnant. He was given up for adoption and had great adoptive parents. The baggage was outweighed by the happy ending.

He and Anneliese had been seventeen when they realized she was pregnant. They'd been horrified, but not desperate. If Anneliese had considered an abortion, she hadn't told him. They got married right after graduation. Ben found a job and started at the community college. Money was tight, but they'd never been afraid as Shari must have been. His parents helped out, too. It wasn't bad.

Why hadn't Shari gone through with the abortion? It

must have seemed like the easier option, but she'd decided to carry the baby. To carry him. Was that courage? She hadn't been brave enough to tell her mother about the pregnancy, but she'd protected the man she'd put in jeopardy. Fifteen years old. Ben shuddered.

Ben wondered about his father, this Jonah. He'd escaped the dismal city that trapped the rest of his biological family. The Army could have taken him anywhere. He probably didn't even live in Illinois anymore. He might have a wife and other children. Ben did the math. The man would be about forty-four now—younger than his parents had been when they adopted him. It was skipping a whole generation. What would Jonah think of having a pack of grandchildren at forty-four years old?

The children didn't wake as he unbuckled and carried each one upstairs to bed. Benjie was getting heavy. The boy jerked awake and called out before dropping back onto the bed. Ben waited a minute, holding his breath, before cautiously removing his son's shoes and covering him with a blanket. Benjie wasn't a good sleeper.

He went through the nightly routine of locking doors and turning out the lights. Mrs. Cooper had been awake when they got home, the lights in her little apartment over the garage filtering through the lace curtains. They were out now. Sometimes he wondered if she waited up for him, as if she was his nanny, too, or yet another mother.

Despite everything, it was still sad to go to bed alone in the quiet house. He and Anneliese had been in love, at least for a while. Now she was gone, never coming back. Except for Benjie, the boys hardly remembered her anymore. The counselor had said it was important to talk about their mother and encourage the good memories, but Ben couldn't do it. Not yet. For now, they had Mrs. Cooper and Daddy and their grandparents and each other. They had love and security. It was enough. It had to be. As he drifted into sleep, he heard the ghost of Anneliese's mocking voice. "No one is promised a normal family, dear, and we all grow up anyhow."

CHAPTER 6

Jonah Campbell carried his coffee outside and was relieved to see that it was still winter. In late February, it *should* be winter in the western Upper Peninsula. Last week's unexpected thaw had set him back, but it would snow today from a smoky white blanket of clouds. He needed a few more inches, to freshen up the landscape. Rabbits and deer had made a mess of the smooth surface of the creek bed. He wanted unblemished snow on the ground when he photographed the frozen creek, with its chunks of ice and debris trapped in it, as if captured unexpectedly by a sharp freeze. Like fossils, caught instantly, but these bits and pieces would be released with the thaw and flow with the current, high and fast with the melting snow.

"'He gives snow like wool; He scatters the frost like ashes. He casts forth His ice as fragments; Who can stand before His cold? He sends forth His word and melts them; He causes His wind to blow and the waters to flow.'"

Jonah rolled out the words dramatically. It was his favorite Scripture passage, from Psalms, and one of the few he could recite accurately. He rather liked the sound of his voice in the wakening woods. Birds of every variety were greeting each other, wondering if their return was premature, and the wind was brushing through the trees, sloughing off soft snow, but those sounds were native to the forest and part of the stillness.

He hoped it would be cold enough for a dry snow. He didn't want mush. Most of the month had been unseasonably warm, but this week's forecast promised a return to normal temperatures. He'd become a true Yooper since his retirement four years ago. People up here weren't fooled by spring's occasional peek-a-boo games. Or maybe it was more like Whack-a-Mole. The daffodils popped up and were buried under a dumping of snow or ice. They tried again and were promptly crushed. The trees would bud out and a hard frost would blow in and freeze them solid.

The year-round residents of the Upper Peninsula—Yoopers—were realistic about their challenging climate, but Jonah had noticed that they became more restless and watchful as they waited for winter to go away. They talked about the ice breaking up on the rivers and lakes, denouncing the fools who tried to snowmobile across the melting lakes or left their ice shanties out too late. They announced robin and fawn sightings. They waited. Anticipation was part of the pleasure of springtime.

Anticipation of Spring. He set down the coffee cup, went back into the house and made a note on a paper napkin. It would make a good photo series, or maybe even watercolor sketches. Probably photos, he decided, because there just wasn't enough color in the winter for good painting. The pine trees were supposed to be evergreen, but they were mostly just dark or covered with white snow. Only the night sky had color—gaudy sunsets or incredible northern lights. Jonah enjoyed the blue winter evenings, but he hadn't managed to capture them successfully in any medium. Like the flaming pink-orange of autumn leaves or vivid green of new grass, winter blue was only found on God's palette and couldn't be duplicated in man-made pigments.

Mulling over nature's improbable colors, Jonah crossed the living room and climbed the spiral stairs to his sleeping loft.

He liked the steep, twisting climb upward, but he'd descend on the more practical one off the kitchen, favoring his stiff knee.

He stripped off his cargo shorts and pulled on jeans and a Green Bay Packers sweatshirt. He needed to walk down to the mailbox today, or maybe he should drive. He hadn't started up the truck in a few days. He tossed a pair of wool socks onto the bed. No need to shave today.

Back downstairs, he looked around for his coffee, but he'd lost it. It would show up later. Yesterday, he'd found a cup of coffee on the seat of the snowplow, frozen solid.

"Oh—it's on the porch." Pleased with his recall, he collected the cup, took a sip, and dumped the cold liquid down the drain.

Jonah ambled through the rest of his morning routine, periodically diverted by ideas for his spring theme. There was no hurry to get to the mailbox. Packages were delivered to his door. Most of his business was transacted online, so he didn't get much regular mail. With no stores nearby, he didn't even get advertisements.

Before Cindy died, the isolation had been one of the cabin's best qualities. They'd only been married a few months when Uncle Jake passed away and left the property to his favorite-and-only nephew. Jonah did his enthusiastic best to describe it to his town-bred bride, but his boyhood memories consisted of fishing and campfires instead of domestic arrangements. There had been a wood-burning stove and an outhouse; the rest he had forgotten or never noticed.

They flew into Chicago, that first time, and rented a car for the drive up north. As soon as they crossed into the Upper Peninsula, Wisconsin's smooth, beautiful highways, designed to attract tourists, gave way to Michigan's rough, cracked, pitted roads.

"There sure is a lot of trash," said Cindy. "I'd expect it in the cities, but you'd think it would be better out here in the middle of nowhere."

Jonah focused on driving. The last stretch of the obscure county road sucked the compact rental car into its muddy ruts, making him clutch the steering wheel and hover over the brake pedal. Unwilling to believe the map, they drove back and forth in the appointed place before accepting the truth that the barely-discernible path on the south side of the road really was their driveway.

Jonah cast a glance at his wife. Her happy chatter had dwindled away to silence in the last hour. "It looks like that shrubbery has kept the road from getting too muddy."

"Road."

He decided to accept the word as conversation. "The driveway. It probably hasn't been plowed or mowed since Uncle Jake went into the nursing home."

"The road hasn't been mowed." She enunciated the words clearly.

He wasn't even tempted to make a joke about her cute little poem. They jolted along the overgrown track that snaked through the forest, keeping them enclosed by the looming trees. It was a surreal, claustrophobic drive. Jonah turned on the headlights.

"Are you sure this. . .?"

Jonah interrupted her. "Look! See that red thing?" He pointed straight ahead of them, beyond a sharp turn in the road. "It's a bike reflector Uncle Jake nailed to the tree. There were more of them, but we didn't see them without the lights on."

The drive became less stressful after that. They were forced to stop several times to remove obstacles, including a small tree that had fallen across the driveway, but they made steady progress. Even in the approaching dusk, Jonah became increasingly confident as he recognized landmarks, and Cindy laughed at his Paul Bunyan act. Darkness settled in the woods as they pulled up to the door of their new vacation home.

Cindy, the most cheerful and flexible person he knew, had thrown a fit. The "cabin in the Northwoods" turned out to be a shack, as cold and dark inside as it was outside, filled with spiders and other wildlife. Squirrels, or something else, had chewed the corners of the building, and even though the windows were boarded up, the door was broken.

And Jonah couldn't locate the outhouse at all.

They slept in the car that night, and the next day they made the drive back to the nearest city large enough to sell brooms and shovels. They worked on it for years, eventually getting electricity brought in, but rejecting telephone service. Their military careers often kept them apart, but whenever they were able to get leave at the same time, they came up to this hidden place to be alone together.

The memories still made his throat ache, but he had settled in. The rhythm of this place brought him peace. He was free here to do as he liked. The Internet kept him as connected as he chose to be to the outside world. The graphic art skills he had used in the army were still useful for commercial work, and the security of his military pension allowed him to do more creative work, marketing his paintings and photographs to tourists as well as online.

He could be alone or drive into town for coffee at the diner. Most Sundays, he attended the small Baptist church in Ewen. Cindy had insisted on it from the start. She said it made her feel like a normal married couple to dress up and go to church together on Sunday mornings. They made friends there. When Jonah came back alone, the community brought him comfort. They were quiet, kind people who lived as he did, close to God here in the wilderness. They were his family.

CHAPTER 7

He knew that song. Ben groped for his cell phone and blinked against the bright screen in the darkness, trying to focus on the answer button. No one called this late. The clock brought him to full wakefulness. No one called this early.

"Hello." His voice was rough with sleep. He coughed to clear it. "Hello?" Noises on the other end of the call confused him. A prank call? Wailing music overrode a thin voice that rose and fell in pitch, the words unintelligible, punctuated with gasps and sobs. Linda.

"Is this Linda? How are you?" That was a stupid question. She was hysterical and probably stoned out of her mind. "Are you okay?" He squeezed his eyes shut, listening intently, trying to understand the slurred words. "Now? I could come in the morning." Morning, in his world, began after seven o'clock—not at three a.m.

She became more agitated, her jumbled words rising in pitch. She didn't want to wait until morning. He wasn't about to tell her he couldn't leave the children. In a more sober moment, she might want to meet them. Ben shivered. If he could get Mrs. Cooper to come over, he might as well go now. He hit the mute button on his cell phone—Linda didn't seem to require a response—and used the land line to call his nanny.

She sounded as calm at three in the morning as at three in the afternoon. "Yes, Ben?"

"Hi. I hate to bother you, but I need to run out for an hour or two. Would you mind coming over here and sleeping on the couch until I get back? It's... um... kind of important."

Traffic moved faster in the middle of the night. Lights glazed the wet streets and buildings of Calumet City, transforming the drab grays to slick reflections and blackness that concealed the shabbiness and broken buildings. People, singly and in groups, occupied the city. Even in the residential areas, at four in the morning, people stood or strolled, appearing and fading out as silhouettes and shadows.

By the time he reached Linda's house, Ben's jittery fingers twitched on the steering wheel. To his relief, the small parking lot was well-lit, bright in the oppressive surroundings. A woman smoking outside the building watched him get out of his car but didn't respond to his nod as he passed.

Linda hadn't left a light on for him, and she didn't respond to the doorbell. The door was locked. Music and a yellow glow emanated from the window; maybe she couldn't hear him. He hoped she was still awake. She might have passed out in the hour since her call. A quick look over his shoulder told him that the woman with the cigarette had been joined by two men. They watched him with interest. Just what he needed... an audience.

He pounded on the door and called her name. Almost instantly, the door flew open and Linda stood before him, extending a wine bottle in one out-flung hand. He took the bottle instinctively and tilted it to measure its level.

"It's all gone!" She mourned. "Do you have any?" She peered at him through tangled hair.

Ben wished he pitied her, but his revulsion was stronger. The woman must be nearly sixty years old, sloppy drunk and maybe on drugs, too.

"No. I don't. Too bad the stores are closed." He tried to sound casual and friendly. "Can I come in?" Their interchange was probably fascinating the observers.

She waved him inside. "You might as well. It's getting late." She glared at him. "Why did you come here?"

Ben stopped in the doorway, indignant. "You asked me to!"

"No!" She shook her head several times. "Why did you come now, talking about my sweet Shari?" She stepped backward, further into the apartment. When he followed, she moved toward him and stared into his face. "She's dead." The hollow voice was terrible. "She died having a baby. A baby!" She drew out the word. Blue and green lightbulbs, filtering through the haze of cigarette smoke, lit her ravaged face without mercy. "Having a baby."

To Ben's horror, she burst into howls of agony that somehow harmonized with the sad ballads pouring from unseen speakers. He hoped the music drowned out her weeping, so her neighbors wouldn't feel compelled to investigate. Maybe that wasn't a concern; they hadn't looked like a neighborhood watch committee. He steered her toward the couch and got her seated before closing the door.

"Linda, it's me, Ben Taylor."

"I know who you are."

The triumphant accusation relieved him. "Good. Here I am. I came as soon as I could. What can I do for you?"

"Not for me." Linda jabbed her finger in his direction. "For you." She leaned close to his face. "I have a boksh." She licked her lips after the juicy sibilants and then dried them with the back of her hand. "Shari's boksh. You can see it, but you can't take it away. It's mine now."

It took him a few seconds to understand the word. "Box? You have a box that belonged to your daughter?"

"It's mine now." She pulled a shoebox from under the end table and held it on her lap.

"I understand completely." He forced himself to be

gentle in spite of his vibrating desire to snatch the box away. If she fell apart, he might not be able to resist the urge to grab it and run. He kept his voice low and soothing. "It must be very special to you."

She clutched it to her stomach and rocked slightly. "It was under her bed. I never saw it until after. . . later." She inhaled, sat up straight and held out the box with both hands. "You can look at it."

Ben took it reverently and crouched to set it on the coffee table. There were unicorn stickers on the lid, and her name in uneven cursive handwriting, embellished with curlicues and flowers. She had used a flower to dot the I at the end of her name. Shari had liked unicorns. Like a little girl. An unexpected ache welled up in his throat.

The box was full. It looked like a little girl's treasure chest. Personal. Ben felt like a peeping tom or a stalker as he picked up a glittery velvet pouch and poured the contents into his hand. The pathetic assortment of trinkets gleamed in the colored lights of the room. There were some cheap rings, a charm bracelet, one large hoop earring and a fine gold chain that was probably her first "real gold" jewelry. He returned all of it to the bag and set it on the table. He lifted out a tiny china cat, a silk rose and a third-place ribbon for a fifth-grade spelling bee. Like the stickers, they summoned images of a child. Wallet-size school pictures of boys, and one of a girl who might have been Connie Price fifty pounds ago, rested on top of a pile of snapshots. Shari. The girl in these pictures did look much older than fifteen, posing in front of cars and on the beach, hugging her friend and one of Shari alone, in a prom dress that would have made Anneliese blush. No wonder the guy believed she was seventeen.

One item remained in the bottom of the box, so flat that he almost missed it. Ben carefully peeled up the flimsy paper and turned it over. The old newsprint was as fresh as the day it came off the press. He glanced at Linda, but she had picked up Shari's prom picture and was crooning to it. He shifted the newspaper clipping so he could see it better in the eerie light. It was an announcement that Jonah William Campbell, recent graduate of Raynor Park High School, was leaving for army boot camp. The brief paragraphs gave his address, the names of his parents and details of his high school career. Connie had been right; Jonah was a member of the computer club. And there was a picture. Ben squinted at it. It was black and white and grainy, not clear enough to see if there was a resemblance to himself. The man's hair was dark. His jaw appeared to be more square than his own. Ben felt light-headed. This was the man—the boy—Shari had identified as the father of her baby. Of Ben. This man might be his father.

"Could you turn on a brighter light, please?"

When Linda didn't respond, he looked over and saw she'd tipped over sideways on the couch, hiccupping in a miserable sleep. Suddenly, finally, compassion flooded him. Ben stood and pulled the afghan over her, removing the prom picture from her fist and smoothing it out on the coffee table next to the newspaper clipping. She wouldn't want it creased.

He couldn't find a light switch, and it took him a few minutes to notice the string hanging from the overhead fixture. It didn't occur to him to look away when he pulled on it, and the flash of the bright light momentarily blinded him. Linda didn't awaken.

Ben looked at his grandmother. He could pick up the shoebox and walk out of the apartment. He wanted to. It would be safer to take just the newspaper clipping, though; she might never notice it was missing. He packed the rest of Shari's treasures back into the box and set the decorated lid on top. The sparkly unicorns still capered around her name.

He couldn't do it. Linda might have been an unfit parent, but she was Shari's mother, and she grieved. The box was precious to her.

He laid the newspaper clipping under the light and took pictures of it with his cell phone. That would serve the purpose, and the digital format might even be more useful than the paper copy. He had a name. An address. He hoped it was the right one. A military man might be more stable than the family members he had met so far. Ben's pride had taken a beating since he started the search. Maybe Jonah, if the man was his father, had escaped this depressing environment and found a better life, not lost to drink or in jail. There had to be at least one healthy branch on his family tree.

CHAPTER 8

"Hey, Ben. Tom wants you to meet him in the big training room in ten minutes. Looks like you've got your first solo client."

"Great!" He set the box on his desk. A real desk of his own, in a real office. "Do you know who it is?"

"A new one. Pretty girl." Lauren glanced at the picture of his parents, face-up on top of the contents of the box. "It's about time you settled in. Two months, and you don't even have a plant."

"It would probably die," Ben said. He took in her appearance. "Are you leaving?"

She pulled the strap of her purse higher on her shoulder. "Yeah. If the phone rings, it'll roll over to Tom. I have a parent-teacher conference in half an hour. They couldn't schedule it in the evening. I guess other parents take priority."

"That stinks. How old are your kids?"

"Four, eight, and fourteen. So, they're all in different schools, which is really a pain, especially at conference time." She rolled her eyes. "You'd think I'd asked for a week off with pay. Tom doesn't like it when his employees have an outside life. I had to call in sick when my youngest one had strep throat last year, and I thought he'd fire me."

"For calling in sick? Once?" Ben was startled. At the nursing home, the staff called in regularly. They were never fully staffed.

"I think it had more to do with the kids. He wants

employees with no other priorities. You're his ideal employee. No wife or kids." She pointed at the picture. "I hope your parents are in good health and won't distract you from your duties here."

Her acidic comments made him pause, and she continued, "You aren't married, are you?" She nodded at his left hand. "No ring."

"No." His all-knowing father had done it again. Benjamin Sr. had been adamant about keeping his personal life separate from work, telling him frankly that, whatever the law said, an employer would be hesitant to hire a single dad with four young children. Ben didn't want to discuss his situation, anyhow, especially the circumstances of Anneliese's death. He steered the conversation away from his personal life. "I'll get ready."

She waved on her way out the door. "Good luck!"

Ben put the box on the floor by the coat rack and dropped his jacket on top of it. So much for personalizing his office. He made sure his polo shirt was tucked in before heading out to meet Tom and the new client.

She was pretty. The girl perched on the edge of the examination table, swinging a booted foot and inspecting him with interest.

"Here he is," said Tom. "Ben, this is Kendra Ross. She tripped over a bicycle and twisted up her leg. Kendra, this is Ben Taylor. He'll be helping with the exercises and monitoring your progress. You'll have to come back here every couple of weeks for a full evaluation. Can you get a ride?"

"Oh, yeah." She smiled at Ben, displaying a dimple and expensive teeth. "But please don't tell people I tripped over a bicycle. It makes me sound like such a klutz. It was dark out, and it shouldn't have been laying on the sidewalk."

Ben shook her hand. "Accidents happen. That's what keeps us in business."

Tom chuckled. It wasn't convincing. Ben straightened and picked up her folder.

"Are you a physical therapist, too?" She tucked a strand of long blond hair behind her ear and gazed at Ben with obvious approval.

Tom responded quickly. "Ben is a licensed physical therapist assistant. I design the rehab plan and he does the work. He's fully qualified to help you."

"That's awesome!"

Her enthusiasm made Ben nervous. He was trying to impress Tom with his professionalism, and Tom didn't look enthusiastic at all.

"If you're ready, Ben and I will go over the plan with you now." Tom led them through the series of exercises, explaining the purpose of each and pointing out the markers they would use to measure her progress.

"What should I wear?" Her question interrupted Tom's parting remarks.

"Pretty much anything but jeans. Ben needs to be able to feel the muscles and joints." Tom handed her the crutches as she prepared to hop off the table. "Don't forget these. Don't go anywhere without them."

That got her attention. "Nowhere? Not even when I'm out with my friends?"

"Nowhere. Use them every time you leave the house."

"My apartment is up a flight of stairs!"

"Especially on the stairs. I'll take you out front, and you can wait in the reception area while I print out your paperwork."

Ben couldn't decide if Tom was irritated by the girl's attitude or because he had to do the receptionist's job. He wondered if Tom would really fire Lauren if she had to miss work because her kids were sick. Good thing he had a nanny.

Just a drive-by to see the house. Ben didn't plan to introduce himself to anyone. His recent attempts—and this morning's email from his functional anatomy professor—already had him depressed. Neither Linda nor Rhonda had been happy to meet him, and this time he didn't have any documentary evidence of relationship. It would be an awkward conversation at best. He wasn't about to set himself up for more rejection today.

In late February, the black and gray cityscape had little color to break up the soggy gloom, and he could taste the air; heavy metals and bitter smoke tried to invade his mouth as well as his nostrils.

Ben slowed as he entered the Campbell's neighborhood. At a glance, Truman Street looked the same as miles of other residential streets in the area. The red brick houses stood close together, with small front yards and alley garages, but the absence of junk cars, discarded furniture, and loiterers lent it a more spacious atmosphere. Grass was starting to grow in some of the yards. Most of the front porches had chairs on them, and lights shone behind curtained windows as the evening fell.

He stopped the car and gazed at Jonah's house. Had this been a good neighborhood twenty-five years ago? What had Mr. Campbell done for a living? Was Mrs. Campbell a housewife, or did she have a job? Was Jonah an only child, or were there others? Were they still there, inside the house right now?

A young Black man opened the front door of the house to collect the mail. That answered one question. Ben unbuckled his seat belt and clambered out of the car.

"Excuse me." He walked a little closer, and the man waited for him. "I'm looking for some people who used to live here. Their name was Campbell, and they had a son named Jonah. Do you know what happened to them?"

The man came out and closed the door behind him,

shivering theatrically in the cold air. "No, we bought the house from some people named Newbury, and they said they got it from the bank. I think it was a foreclosure. I never heard of any Campbells."

"They were here in 1990, and I lost track of them after that." Ben looked around. "This is a nice neighborhood, especially compared with the rest of the city."

"It used to be pretty run down. The whole street got in on an urban renewal grant right after we moved here. Some people fixed up their houses and then sold out, but we like it here." He glanced back as a dog barked inside the house. "We have a neighborhood watch program." The man's attitude abruptly changed to wariness. "Why are you looking for these people?"

"They're distant relations, but we've lost them. Do you have any idea where I can find the Newburys, or the bank that sold them the house?"

The man shook his head. "No." He began easing his way back toward the warmth of his home.

Ben didn't try to keep him. "Thank you. Have a good evening."

"No problem."

Ben rolled with the rest of the cars on the bypass, resigned to the usual congestion. It shouldn't be hard to find the family online. A foreclosure didn't sound good, though. Didn't he have any responsible relatives?

The impulsive trip to Joliet had taken longer than he'd expected. Mrs. Cooper would have fed the kids by now, and they'd be playing while she cleaned up the kitchen. He looked forward to going home these days to a clean house, hot meal, and happy children. Safe children.

Anneliese had been younger, of course, with no experience at managing a home and four children. He'd worried about them as he worked and attended classes, and he never knew what kind of situation he'd come home to. Sometimes, he'd been afraid.

Mrs. Cooper always had things under control. She didn't scream at him if he came in late. At 6:00, she'd set aside a plate for him and stay until he returned. He mourned the loss of his wife, but it really was much easier now.

His phone rang as he neared home, and he tapped the Bluetooth button on the dashboard. "Hello?"

He reflexively stomped on the brakes when a string of ripe expletives filled the car. The driver behind him laid on her horn, and he missed part of the rant. Not Linda. This hysterical woman wasn't crying; she was furious. "What did you say to my mother?"

"Rhonda?"

"You had no right to come snooping around and upsetting her. She's in the hospital, you know. She took a whole bottle of sleeping pills and drank herself into a coma. And it's all your fault! If she dies, I'll come after you with the best lawyer I can find! Don't you ever come around her or me again. Just stay out of our lives. Do you hear me?"

Ben pulled over and stopped the car. "Yes, but. . ."

The strident voice went on without waiting for him. "We don't want you. You are not part of this family. All you've done is cause grief."

"She called me and asked me to come over! I didn't mean to upset her!"

"It doesn't matter what you meant, but you've nearly killed her, just like you did your mother! Stay away from us. We don't want you."

The call ended with the crash of a receiver being slammed home. He sat perfectly still for a few minutes. Logically, he knew he hadn't killed his mother. Did they believe that? He felt sick. No one had ever hated him before. It wasn't his fault. All he'd done was try to track down his family.

He hadn't asked anything of them, not even acceptance. He'd just wanted to know who they were. Now he was sorry he did.

CHAPTER 9

Teresa Cooper had mastered the art of minding her own business. During her brief foray into embroidery, she made one sampler. Instead of a sentimental passage about home and hearth, she had stitched her then-favorite piece of Scripture: "Make it your ambition to lead a quiet life, work with your hands and mind your own business." She hadn't bothered with the rest of the passage; it was a small sampler and that was the pertinent line.

In return, she expected others to respect her privacy. Her business was none of theirs. Few people had the nerve to inquire about her personal life; if they weren't deterred by her serene reserve, a gentle snub usually silenced them. The attitude precluded close friendships, but she was universally liked and respected in instinctive response to her main rule for human interaction: everyone needed dignity. That policy was why Ben was allowed—encouraged—to believe he was in control of the household while she held it all together. She never neglected the small courtesies, like knocking on the back door before letting herself into the house, even when they were all waiting for her.

"Good morning!"

No one responded. She set her bag on the table, hung up her coat and tugged off her galoshes.

"Hello?"

Were they all asleep? Ben was usually dressed and waiting for his breakfast when she arrived. The man was always hungry. Teresa pulled out a pot and dumped in two cups of oats and one of cracked wheat. She didn't hear anyone moving around upstairs. She cut up an apple and a banana and set them aside. Walnuts and dried cranberries, too, she decided. The cranberries had added sugar, but they were still fruit, and the kids loved them. It was very odd that no one was downstairs yet. She poured water over the grains and set them on the stove to heat. It was an easy breakfast.

She hovered at the foot of the stairs. She wasn't going to yell. She never yelled. If Ben was still sleeping, though, he would want to be awakened. He had to get to work. Teresa stepped up the stairs with resolution, concern overcoming her qualms. While Ben had a right to his privacy, theirs was an odd relationship. She felt more like his mother—or his nanny—than an ordinary employee, and his recent behavior alarmed her. At first, she had wondered if Ben had found a girlfriend. Teresa hoped he wasn't in love; if he was, the relationship didn't appear to be a healthy one. Ben was increasingly tense and unhappy, and he had never called her in the middle of the night before or come home as late and distraught as he had yesterday. He'd babbled a meaningless apology and then disappeared into his bedroom instead of waiting for her to leave. She'd turned out the lights, locked the doors and gone home worried. And this morning, the house was silent.

Sunlight blazed down the hallway, revealing a series of open doorways. Even the linen closet door was ajar, with a loose pile of sheets on the floor in front of it. Teresa walked over and scooped up the sheets, replacing them automatically as she considered the situation. The doors to the children's rooms were always closed to a six-inch gap at nap time as well as bedtime. Ben shut his door at night.

She closed the closet door, turned around and gasped at

the sight in front of her. Blood smeared over the bathroom floor and sink. She moved into the room, unease flaring into panic. Wads of red-stained toilet paper overflowed the wastebasket and onto the floor, with more in the toilet. Bloody handprints on the door and the wall by the light switch looked like something from a slasher movie. Teresa took a deep breath. Smears, not pools. It wasn't really that much blood. Probably a bloody nose. She whispered the phrase several times before rushing to the boys' room.

It was empty. All three beds were rumpled; Mark's was stripped, and his pajamas and linens—probably wet—were in a heap on top of it. More blood had splashed, in big drops, onto the rug near Jack's bed. She hadn't noticed the trail on the dark wood of the hallway floor, but it was there, leading back to the bathroom. Across the hall, she could see Annie's empty crib.

They had to be with Ben. All of them. A few long strides brought her to the master bedroom. They were there, miraculously asleep with the boneless relaxation of the very young. She could see Ben's head, one bare shoulder and arm, and part of a flannel-clad leg. The rest of him was buried under children. Annie sprawled under the arm, taking up more than her fair share of the bed. Benjie snuggled up on the other side of her. Mark, dressed only in his Spiderman underwear, pressed against his dad's back. Jack draped over all of them. They looked like a litter of puppies.

Teresa leaned against the door frame. "Thank you, God." Her words didn't disturb any of them; it must have been a hard night. She pulled the door closed as she backed away. If Ben was late for work, he'd have to deal with it himself.

Twenty minutes later, the boys plunged down the stairs, announcing their arrival with a loud discussion of their plans for an obstacle course. She heard Ben talking as she scooped hot cereal into bowls, and he appeared a minute later, stuffing his shirt tail into his waistband and dangling Annie over his shoulder in her favorite "sack of potatoes" hold. Teresa averted her gaze and bit her tongue.

"I have time for breakfast," said Ben. "That looks good." He swung Annie around and plopped her into the highchair. "There you go, cupcake." He buckled her into the seat and snapped the tray in place.

"Do you want some coffee?" She'd already drunk two cups.

"No, thanks. That stuff is nasty. I'll grab an energy drink on my way in."

"Can you get one for me, Daddy?" Benjie thought energy drinks were the ultimate in adult beverages. Teresa shuddered.

"Sorry, buddy. You stick to orange juice." Ben spoke around a mouthful of cereal, directing his next comments to Teresa. "We had quite a night. Benjie had a bad dream."

Teresa knew what that meant. Eliza told her that Benjie occasionally woke in the night, crying hysterically and calling for his mother. It could take an hour or more to get him calmed down and back to sleep. In the morning, he only remembered that he'd had a bad dream. She smiled at the boy sympathetically.

"I'm sorry, Benjie. Did you get back to sleep okay?"

His father answered for him. "Well, it was kind of a domino effect. Benjie made a lot of noise, and he woke up his brothers. Jack jumped out of bed and landed on his face, so he got a bloody nose."

"It bled a lot," Jack remarked with satisfaction. "Maybe it's broken."

Ben continued his tale. "And Mark had a little accident, and in all the excitement, Annie woke up. In the end, we all just slept in my bed."

"That was quite a night," Teresa agreed. She'd already cleaned up the evidence of the night's events, as Ben must have noticed.

Ben straightened and met her eyes. "I think Benjie can stay home from school today." Teresa suppressed a grin at his effort at a masterful tone. He must have promised Benjie already.

"That's a good idea," she said promptly. "He should probably stay in bed and rest after his wakeful night."

The boy's face fell.

"Or," she said thoughtfully, "he could play quietly with his Legos and read for a while and then take a nap later in the afternoon when everyone else does."

Ben looked relieved at the compromise. "Sounds good." He stood up and distributed hugs in preparation for his departure. "You guys be good for Mrs. Cooper. Do what she says."

CHAPTER 10

He couldn't ask for an extension—or even reschedule—after missing the last one. Ben raced across the parking lot, clutching his messenger bag to his side. Even if he made it to this lab on time, Dr. Wick would dock points for not having the notes prepared in advance.

She was the strictest teacher in the program, and he'd been messing up all semester. He had to pass this class.

But he couldn't lose his job, either. Would Tom be mad if Ben asked him to make the appointments earlier in the day? Of course, he would. He didn't even like Lauren's kids. Ben yanked the door open and let it fall shut behind him as he headed down the hall.

"Mr. Taylor." The crisp voice stopped him like a leash. "You seem to be running late. Again."

"I'm sorry." That was usually a safer option than excuses.

"Are you working?" The professor sounded surprised.

He glanced down at his Great Lakes Therapy Services polo shirt. He hadn't even realized he was still wearing it. "Yeah. I work as a PTA at this place." He flicked toward the logo. "I'm sorry I'm late. I need to see if I can get my boss to change some appointments. I came straight from the client's house out in Maywood."

"Would it work better for you to come on Saturdays?"

"Maybe. I don't know."

She raised her eyebrows and waited.

"The afternoon labs should work out. There's only a few left this semester, and my boss knows I have to be done by three o'clock Monday, Wednesday and Friday. He just scheduled right up to that time, all the way across town, and then the client wasn't ready."

"But we do have Saturday labs."

"Could I. . . well, could I keep that option open in case I get stuck at work again? I'd rather not do it unless I have to." Ben sighed. He hated making the excuse. "I have kids, and they're with the nanny all week. I don't have anyone to watch them on Saturday unless I drive them out to my parents' house in Palatine. But I will if I have to."

The woman regarded him with interest. Despite the cropped white hair and bifocals, she looked like a child playing dress-up in her over-sized white lab coat with her hands pushed into the pockets. "You have a nanny? How many children do you have?"

"Four." The admission was always embarrassing. He could practically see her doing the math in her head. "But I'll do whatever I need to so I don't miss any more work. Work here at school, I mean."

"Four!" Everyone got stuck on that number. "You do have your hands full."

Actually, his hands were full of work and school. Mrs. Cooper's hands were full of the children, and she could probably manage a dozen.

"Well, it won't last forever." At her scandalized expression, he rushed on. "School. I should be done soon. Another two years at the most." He hoped.

"Okay," she said. "Get in there and I'll be around to see your lab notes."

"They're not done." Might as well get that out in the

open.

"Get them done." The woman turned and stalked back into her office. "That's a ten-point deduction."

Ben entered the capacious gymnasium and found his name on the station list. Would he ever finish this? Physical therapy assistants made decent money. Once all the kids were in school and didn't need a nanny, he could probably make ends meet. Maybe. Or he could just finish the program and become a real physical therapist and be able to support them properly. He'd rather not give up the nanny if he didn't have to.

The PTA certification had taken twice as long as it should have. He'd gotten the nurse's aide certification right after high school, because his dad said it would make a good work path—CNA to PTA to PT. Ben liked working with the old people at the nursing home. Observing their therapy sessions reinforced his commitment to his career plans, keeping him going when things got hard at home.

In the early, hopeful years, Anneliese and he believed it would all happen quickly, and they would be living comfortably within a few years. Ben worked full-time split shifts while taking classes online and at the community college. Spare moments were spent rocking babies and studying.

He figured he got as much sleep as his unmarried friends in their college dorms. As far as he could tell, most of them spent their college years partying. Some had even worked or played sports, and some had girlfriends, which was more expensive and time-consuming than all the rest of it combined. But those guys were all done now, graduated and in real jobs. He didn't even have Anneliese anymore.

They'd both been left behind when all their friends went away to college, but Ben had adult conversation at work and school. Anneliese stayed home and changed diapers. He tried to give her opportunities to get out whenever he could, but in the end, that caused even more problems.

Perhaps he should have been tougher. Maybe he should have been more loving. He just didn't know, and it was useless and painful to let guilt trample his head and heart. She was gone, and he was moving forward, picking up the rubble and making a future for his kids.

"Daddy, Daddy!" Small rockets of denim hurled themselves against his legs. The boys latched onto his neck and legs so he could drag them into the kitchen, groaning loudly about the weight. The daily assault never failed to lighten his mood, reminding him, in a perverse way, of the need to keep moving forward. The kids weren't a heavy burden; they were his purpose. No matter what his life was, theirs were just beginning. They could do anything, and he was going to make sure they had the opportunity.

Mrs. Cooper smiled at him as she buckled Annie into the highchair. "The boys have already washed their hands, so as soon as you're ready, I'll serve dinner and be on my way."

"It smells good." He rubbed Annie's wispy head, shook off his other offspring and went obediently into the bathroom to clean up.

The boys' rapid conversation didn't slow down their consumption of Mrs. Cooper's delicious chicken casserole and bread. Annie kept her father's attention by playfully tapping his elbow with her spoon and eating her meal with her fingers. He was fine with that but glad Mrs. Cooper wasn't around to witness it. At least the spoon was clean.

"Can we play American Warrior after dinner?" Benjie forked up another mouthful of casserole.

"I told you guys we can't do that. If you don't break your neck, you'll break the furniture."

"No! Mrs. Cooper said it's safe. She made it."

Ben raised his brows. "Mrs. Cooper made American Warrior?"

"Yeah. She set it up in the basement and outside," Benjie said. "Can I have some more bread?"

"May I, please," said his father. "What did she set up?"

"In the garage, too," Jack said. "It's really big. We worked on it all day."

"Really?" Ben was skeptical. "With tunnels and ropes and tires?"

"Not all of that," Benjie admitted, "but it's really good. Do you want to see it?"

"Yeah! Finish up your food and we'll go look."

Ben took the spoon from Annie and scooped up some casserole. She took the spoon, scraped off the food and ate it with her fingers. Oh, well. He'd tried.

Occasionally, Mrs. Cooper surprised him. Or rather, he was surprised by the boys' reports. He never actually saw her playing baseball with them or engaging in a squirt gun fight, but they insisted it was true. He almost believed them, until they claimed she was an excellent jump-roper. Right. She wasn't really old enough to break a hip, but it still sounded dangerous. He should ask his dad if they had workman's comp on her. Probably. Dad bought insurance for everything.

The boys stacked their dishes in the sink and Ben carried his daughter to the bathroom for a quick bath. A wet washcloth would be insufficient. When she was clean, dry and warm in a fluffy pink sleeper, he joined the boys in the living room.

"More American Warrior? You guys aren't supposed to be watching TV by yourselves." Who knew what they would see while channel surfing cable television. . . Ben picked up the remote to shut it off.

"No, it's a DVD!" Both of the older boys spoke at once. Benjie continued. "Mrs. Cooper recorded it for us. She says it's a good show for boys."

"Mrs. Cooper recorded it?" Ben considered the unlikely idea. "Why would she think that?"

"She said it's exercise for the body and the imagination." Jack spoke solemnly, as if repeating the nanny's words. "She said it's better than cartoons or movies."

"Hm. Well, let's see this obstacle course." He slung Annie over his shoulder and followed the boys down the basement stairs.

They hurdled the baby gate at the bottom of the steps, but Ben stopped to stare. It really was an obstacle course. She must have purchased some of the elements—the inner tubes and expandable toy tunnel were new. The boys jumped and ran and crawled through the tunnel and then raced back along a series of activities outlined in blue painter's tape.

"Look at these!" Jack held up a tin can with bungee cords attached to it. "You stand on them and hold onto the cords, like walking on stilts. Mrs. Cooper said they're Romper Stompers." He rolled out the R in a growl and rocked with laughter. The two older boys demonstrated. Stomping was a good word for it.

Mark and Annie ran around the room, jumping over the inner tubes. She'd connected pool noodles to make hoops. Clever. There were baskets of bean bags and something that looked like a ring toss with the goal high on the wall near the ceiling.

"And look at this part!" Benjie pointed at a web of bungee cords blocking the entrance to the laundry room. He plucked at one of the cords and bells jingled. "See—there are bells on the top string, and you have to get through without making them ring. And when you get inside, you throw a ball into a laundry hamper on top of the dryer and ring a bell!"

"She said it has to come down tomorrow so she can do laundry," said Jack regretfully. "But we can put it up ourselves with the step stool."

"Mrs. Cooper did this?"

"We all did it! And did you see the garage?"

"No, and I parked in the garage." He hoped he hadn't broken anything.

They pounded up the stairs and stopped at the kitchen door to put on shoes.

"Mrs. Cooper's in her apartment, so we have to be quiet in the garage," Ben cautioned them.

"We will. We won't be able to set it up with the car in there, anyhow," Jack said. "There's no room."

"You have to walk up the stairs, and through the kitchen," Ben instructed. "and sit on a chair to put on your shoes."

"And lace them up and double tie them," Jack interrupted. "I can do that now, Dad!"

"High five!" Ben held up his hand and the boy jumped to slap it.

"Score!" Annie bounced, and Ben gave her a high five, too.

"After you get your shoes on," Benjie continued loudly, "you go through the yard. We haven't done much there yet because of the rain, but there's gonna be a balance beam and a see saw thing that you run over, and then the monkey bars and stuff on the swing set. Then you go in the garage."

Ben hushed them as they entered the garage. He didn't see anything in the dim space until Jack pointed upward. A sturdy rope was looped over the rafter, but tied back out of the way now, presumably so he could park.

"You swing on that?" Mrs. Cooper must have lost her mind. The boys would crack their heads open on the concrete floor. Then he saw the helmet and started laughing.

"Yeah! We have to put on the helmet first and then swing from that box to that one. But we put them out in the middle of the garage first."

The boxes weren't very big. Ben looked around. "Then what?"

They were already tugging a pallet away from the back wall. "It opens up and you climb over it. Then you take the helmet off and put it back in the basket and go back outside."

The contraption was two pallets hinged at the top. It would open to make a tent-shaped frame, just the right size for the boys. Mrs. Cooper put this together? He replaced the pallets and followed them outside. It was already getting dark.

"The rope will go over that tree." Benjie indicated a sturdy branch. "And the climbing wall will be out here, too, when it warms up and it's not raining all the time."

"We're getting some blocks to jump from one to the other, too," said Jack. "It's gonna be really fun."

"It looks like it's already fun," Ben said. "You can show me more tomorrow, because it's the weekend!" He pumped a fist in the air and the boys copied the action, jumping up and down.

"Weekend! It's the weekend, weekend, weekend!"

Mark ran in circles and then straight toward the swing set. "Weekend, weekend!" His feet slid in the wet grass and he fell face-down in the mud under the swing. Ben reached the boy while he was still inhaling, so the howl sounded directly into his ear as he helped Mark to his feet.

"Hey, buddy. You okay?" Mark might not be ready for an obstacle course. He scooped up Annie and held Mark's wrist—not the muddy hand—as they all returned to the warm house. This was the life children should have, he thought. Active play to burn off energy, plenty of food and a safe bed to sleep in at night. Parents—or at least one parent—and other people who loved them.

If he hadn't been adopted. . . Ben shied from the thought. He wasn't glad his biological mother was dead; he was just glad he hadn't grown up as she had.

CHAPTER 11

With regret, Ben signed out of the game and tracked down his messenger bag. He hadn't meant to play for so long on a Sunday night. Monday mornings always came earlier than the rest of the workdays.

He could probably get away with doing Carmichael's and Sorensen's reports in the morning, but Kendra's couldn't wait. He'd expected to do it on Friday morning, but that day had filled up quickly, and Ben just couldn't get back to the office to do reports after late afternoon appointments. Tom knew he had school.

Home visit documentation was going to be a pain. Tom wanted him to make notes by hand while he was there and enter them into the computer as soon as he got back to the office. He'd made a point of that: do them immediately and shred the paper. In the office.

Ben opened up his email and launched Kendra's spreadsheet. He didn't mind doing it this one time, but he didn't want Tom to start expecting him to take work home. Afternoon clients could be documented the next day. Kendra's report, however, should have been done four days ago.

The situation worried him. He had the notes from Tom's initial assessment, and he'd been with them for the first therapy appointment at the clinic. He knew what muscles and joints they were treating, but he couldn't pinpoint her injury. If

Kendra would stop flirting long enough to answer sensible questions and let him examine the leg, maybe he could understand it better. He still had a lot to learn. Maybe there was some secret yet to be imparted about diagnosing from vague and inconsistent descriptions. Or maybe he just wasn't cut out to be a physical therapist.

Kendra's flirtation made him nervous. Her laughter and sideways glances—wasn't it hard to see through all that mascara? —distracted him. Instead of paying attention to his instruction, she asked questions about his job, his school, his personal life. He tried to return to the topic of her therapy, but the girl was tenacious. She leaned against him just a little more than was necessary. In return, he had to be scrupulously professional and polite while not hurting her feelings or offending her.

Ben scowled at the computer. He'd be doing her therapy twice a week for at least a month—probably more—and some girls were unpredictable. Most physical therapy assistants were women, and they could report harassment by male clients, but they didn't have to worry about accusations of inappropriate behavior. If Ben claimed that he was uncomfortable in private therapy sessions with women, he would be a laughingstock.

Tom didn't appear to have a sense of humor.

"Might as well do the others," his voice sank into the sleeping house, absorbed by the carpet and overstuffed furniture. When the boys and Annie were awake, the house wakened, too. An odd thought, but Ben liked it.

With the reports finished and emailed, he checked the locks, peeked in on each child, and got ready for bed. Before setting the alarm, he scrolled through the pictures on his phone until he found the newspaper clipping. He could probably track down the Campbells. There were public records of bankruptcies and foreclosures. The thought made him tired.

He'd look into it later.

"Nothing says morning like the smell of coffee!"

"Daddy!" Benjie set a stack of plates on the table. "You don't like coffee!"

Ben ruffled the boy's hair. "Even people who don't like drinking coffee like the smell of it. The bacon smells even better."

Annie walked around the table with napkins clutched to her chest, distributing one to each chair. Mark followed, transferring the napkins to the table. Ben didn't quite understand the reasoning behind that division of labor, but if Mrs. Cooper thought it was a good idea, it was good enough for him.

"Bacon and scrambled eggs, Daddy," said Jack. "Your favorite."

"Well, now, if there were pancakes, too, that would really be my favorite, but bacon and eggs will have to be good enough for today." He took an energy drink from the refrigerator and popped the tab. "Bacon and eggs and pancakes and hash browns. And toast with grape jelly."

A brief silence filled the room before Jack spoke quickly. "And oatmeal. And orange juice and cereal."

"And yogurt," agreed Ben, "with chocolate cake for dessert."

The boys played the game with enthusiasm. As they continued the list, he picked up Annie and blew raspberries into her neck. "Good morning, Annie Banannie."

After a brief hug, she wrestled away from him. "Eat!"

"Yes, ma'am!" Ben dropped her into the highchair and latched the tray. "You're getting kind of big for this thing." He turned to his nanny. "Will she be graduating to a booster seat soon?"

He continued quickly at her irritated expression. "Or she can use the highchair for a while yet." It had been useful the other day when he needed to confine her while he dealt with the toaster.

"I'll pick up a booster seat for her after I drop the boys off at school." Mrs. Cooper set two dishes on the table. "There you go. Just bacon and eggs. No chocolate cake today. There's orange juice in the refrigerator or they can have milk."

"Thanks. I should be home a little earlier today."

"Daddy, did you know today's leapfrog day?" Benjie interrupted.

"Leapfrog?"

"It's February twenty-ninth. My teacher says it only happens every four years." The boy jumped to the floor, landing in a squatting position, poised to spring into a series of hops. Ben caught him by the arm.

"Sit down and eat. I didn't know it had a name." He looked for Mrs. Cooper, not wanting to agree with 'leapfrog day' if it was wrong. The woman had disappeared. She seldom stayed in the kitchen while they ate. "Are you doing something special in school to celebrate?"

"Probably," said Benjie. "Maybe we should bring treats."

Ben spoke around the food in his mouth. "You'll have to talk to Mrs. Cooper about that one. She's the boss."

He started at the sharp sound of a slammed door. Mrs. Cooper never slammed doors. "You okay?"

She returned to the kitchen—probably to set an example of not shouting across the house—and smiled at him. He'd never noticed her teeth before. She had a lot of them. Were they dentures?

"I'm fine, thank you."

He wasn't convinced. Maybe she wasn't feeling well. She'd never been sick before. Did they have a backup plan for that?

She interrupted his anxious thoughts. "It looks like we're all running a few minutes later than usual today. Lunches are on the counter. You still need to brush your teeth and get your coats on."

Ben almost complied before he realized she was looking at the kids. He'd wait until they were done.

The sun was shining, he had a good breakfast, and he wasn't late for work. Ben swung the car door shut and sauntered across the parking lot. No school today, either. He could go home and play with the boys on the obstacle course after work. He wondered if Mrs. Cooper had thought about climbing up the slide instead of going down it. They could climb up the wavy slide and down the straight one. Or maybe up the straight one.

"Ben!"

"Good morning!" Even before he completed the phrase, Ben realized his own morning had just crashed. Tom's expression was dark. Lauren, behind the desk, looked apprehensive.

"Where's the home visit report for Kendra Moss?"

"I just finished that last night. Want me to email it to you or print it out?" Ben hoped he sounded casual. He hoped he didn't get fired.

"Last night?" Tom stared at him. "You did it at home? On your own computer?"

"Yeah, and I emailed it to my work address so I'd have it here." He looked from Tom to Lauren. "Is that a problem?"

Tom rubbed the back of his neck. "I guess we should have covered that. For HIPAA compliance, all reports have to be done here, on our computers. You can't have copies of these things on your personal computer. We can get in a lot of trouble if we get caught. Did you delete the information from your hard drive? And your email outbox and then the trash folder?"

"I'll do that as soon as I get home." No need to mention the other two reports.

"Thanks, Ben." Tom clapped him on the shoulder. "You know what red tape is like. I swear it gets worse every day."

"Should I print it out?"

"No, just enter it into the computer like usual." The forced pleasantness in his boss's voice sent alarm bells ringing in Ben's head. After an awkward silence, he continued. "You don't need to take work home with you, Ben. You should have plenty of time to get it done here. If you can't, we'll see what we can do about rearranging your schedule."

"I'll get it done. I'm sorry."

Ben inched toward his office, but Tom spoke again. "There are security issues, too. We have an obligation to protect our clients' insurance numbers and payment information."

None of that had been on Ben's report. "That makes sense. It won't happen again."

"It can even leave us vulnerable—and you personally vulnerable—if there is any question of fraud."

Fraud? A dozen of Kendra's dance teammates saw her trip over the bicycle someone had left lying just outside the apartment building. She told Ben at length about the embarrassment she'd felt at her clumsiness. As a dancer, she said, she was normally more graceful, but the parking lot light was burned out. They were coming in late, a little high but sober enough to call 911. It seemed pretty straightforward to him.

He entered the reports immediately, hoping no one would ask about the Carmichael and Sorensen visits. It was perfectly reasonable to be writing those up today. If Tom had a problem with it, Ben would have to remind him of their agreement—no late clients on school days. His sense of injustice grew as he typed out the reports with emphatic keystrokes. He had a life of his own, outside of work.

Like Lauren. Being a single mom was hard enough without having to worry about losing your job. Tom probably didn't pay her all that much, either. Ben had help from his parents and Mrs. Cooper. What would he do if he had to support his family on a receptionist salary? He just couldn't.

"Another new one for the traveling therapist." The words came before the double rap on the door.

Ben jumped. "I didn't see you coming!"

"It's the shoes." Lauren kicked up the hem of her long black skirt to display clunky sandals. "Rubber soles."

She dropped a blue folder in his inbox. "Mrs. Melkin, right after lunch. Then Carmichael and Sorensen. All in different directions, of course. You'll be driving back and forth all afternoon."

Ben leaned forward and lowered his voice. "Do I need to get reports done the same day as the appointment?"

Lauren raised her brows above her rectangular eyeglasses. "Is that a problem?"

"Yeah, at least on Monday, Wednesday and Friday. I have school at four o'clock, out in Naperville."

"Does Tom know that?"

"Yes, he knew it when he hired me. He said I could be done by three o'clock on those days."

"Sorry. He didn't tell me. I do most of the scheduling, so I'll watch that."

"What about the reports? I have to be out of here by three o'clock."

She shrugged. "Well, if you don't get them done on the day of, finish them in the morning. In the office. He's a real stickler for that kind of thing."

"He's right about the HIPAA." Ben grimaced. "I didn't think about that."

"You can't win. He was looking for that Ross file on Friday afternoon. You would've been in trouble if it wasn't done, too." She turned to leave the room and said over her shoulder, "Just keep your head down for a while."

Ben sank back in his chair. What was that supposed to mean? Was he really in trouble? He'd only been here two months, but he thought it was going okay. He was beginning to think he might actually like being a physical therapy assistant better than being a physical therapist. As an assistant, he was able to work with people. The 'real' therapists spent ninety percent of their time doing paperwork. Of course, the pay was better, and with four kids to raise, he needed to be thinking about that.

Four kids kept a guy busy. What if they hung some kind of target from a tree branch and got a Nerf gun or bow and arrow set? It would be something to do between bigger challenges, so they'd run up to it, shoot, and then run on to the next thing. He squinted at the opposite wall, trying to picture the back yard. Maybe it would be good to have something that would make a noise when you hit it, like a gong. Yeah, that would be awesome.

"Can you tell me exactly where it hurts?" Ben squatted next to Kendra's chair. He'd reread Tom's initial report, but his inability to diagnose the problem for himself frustrated him. He should be able to do this by now.

"Well," she said, "if I roll my foot outward like this, it hurts my knee here."

"Your knee?"

"My shin, anyhow. And my ankle." She twisted her foot around. "Mostly the ankle."

"Have you been doing the exercises according to the schedule?"

Her sincere gaze was almost a parody. "Oh, yes. Just like you said."

"Have you noticed any difference—good or bad—in the pain level or flexibility?"

"Umm. . . I'm not sure. Don't you have to measure it?"

He was careful to not roll his eyes as he began the process. "Hey, your range of motion is much better than it was on Thursday. Good job!"

She seemed to hesitate. "Well, I was pushing a bit. It kind of hurt when you straightened it."

"Okay, let's try it again. This is just a measurement, not an exercise, so it shouldn't be painful."

"There. After that, it gets painful."

He looked at her. "There?"

"Yes."

"Are you sure? That's a big difference from the first measurement."

She bit her lip. The lipstick stuck to her front tooth. "I don't know. This is all new to me. I've never had physical therapy before."

Maybe the problem wasn't him. Maybe Tom had just guessed instead of making a real diagnosis. Ben leafed through the folder. He'd do the exercises, record the numbers, and get back to the office to write up the report. In a week or so, when Tom was in a better mood, he'd ask him about it.

CHAPTER 12

"Unbelievable." Teresa glared at the woman in the car ahead of her. Did she really think honking her horn would make traffic move faster? She looked in the rearview mirror at a squeak from Annie. "Don't wake up, baby. Please don't wake up." Mark didn't stir. She hoped Jack would fall asleep, too. She'd put their most boring movie on his tablet, but so far it was still holding his attention.

This event was important to Eliza, but the organizers were obviously not stay-at-home moms. Stay-at-home moms scheduled their lives around afternoon naptime. Didn't the nursing home residents take afternoon naps? It wouldn't be a problem if it were local. The kids could have taken their nap a little earlier and been ready by 2:30. But they weren't her children, and Eliza paid her good money to take care of them. She'd have time to meet her at the nursing home, change Annie into her most be-ruffled dress and slip a bow on the girl's head before leaving again to pick up Benjie.

The other driver laid on the horn again. Tension crawled up Teresa's spine and gripped the back of her head. Was this road rage? "Oh, God, keep me sweet. Please don't let the kids wake up."

She'd appropriated Lila Rose's favorite prayer the first time she heard it, and she definitely needed a sweeter spirit today. Teresa loved the children dearly, but she was not their mother. She was not Ben's mother. He was all too happy to hand off authority to her, not because of her responsibilities as nanny, but because he didn't want to worry about anything.

"Sweet. Keep me sweet, God."

"What?"

"I was just talking to myself, Jack. If you want to close your eyes for a little while, this would be a good time to do it. We still have half an hour before we get to the nursing home to meet your grandma."

"I don't want to go to the nursing home. Why do I have to go?"

The boy needed a nap. She crisped her voice. "Don't whine, Jack. Your grandma is looking forward to seeing you, and it makes the people at the nursing home happy to have company. They don't get company very often."

"I don't like it there."

"Sorry, kiddo. Sometimes we do things to make others happy instead of worrying about making ourselves happy."

The silence from the back seat was probably sulking, but she decided to ignore it. She was feeling a bit sulky, too. Ben needed to step up and make some decisions on his own, or at least give some input. He needed to learn to manage his household, or he'd be dependent on other people forever. She wouldn't be there forever, and she didn't think any other nanny would be as flexible as she was. And she was not the boss. It wasn't her job to train him. Every once in a while, she wanted to smack him alongside the head and tell him to "man up."

"Keep me sweet, God. I'm not feeling very sweet."

"What?"

"Sorry, Jack. Close your eyes and take a little nap."

It wasn't working. Her foul mood was exacerbated by

the sight of Eliza greeting the children with hugs and lollypops. Lollypops. Really? That would make a sticky mess for her to clean up later, and the kids would be bouncing of the walls while she did it.

Teresa started the van and flipped down the sunshade to look in the mirror. The only natural part of the image scowling back at her were the roots growing out in her over-processed hair. She wore makeup like a mask: matte foundation one shade too light, frosted pink lipstick, penciled brows, black eyeliner, and gray eyeshadow that made her look like she hadn't slept in a week.

The navy calico dress, with its elbow-length puffed sleeves and satin bow tie, was fashionable twenty years ago, but not retro enough to be trendy. It would *never* be trendy. At least she hadn't paid much for it; the woman running the garage sale let her have it for fifty cents when Teresa pointed out the coffee stain on the collar.

The math ran through her head. Nine years ago, she was twenty-five and trying to look forty. At thirty-four, in her daily uniform, she looked fifty. She didn't have to do this anymore. Leo was dead, and she was old enough to qualify as a respectable nanny in any household. She could gradually ease back into a more youthful style—normal, attractive clothes that fit and were right for a not-yet-middle-aged woman.

If she let her hair go back to its natural copper color, people would assume she'd colored it to make it red instead of the other way around. She would willingly give up cosmetics forever. Under the pancake makeup, her complexion was still clear, with a Milky Way of freckles sprinkled over her nose and cheeks. Woodsy brown eyes that turned nearly olive green in warm lighting, turned flat and small with the heavy, black eyeliner she applied with a liberal hand.

Four more years. Would there be anything left of the real Teresa by then?

CHAPTER 13

"Huh." Ben brooded in the computer's blue light. Once he worked up the courage, it had been all too easy. After procrastinating with an email to Dr. Wick about the lab schedule and paying the cable bill, he took the plunge and did a fast google search for Jonah Campbell.

Other than a professional hockey player and obscure genealogy reports, most of the search results were about an artist. He added the word 'army' to his search. The artist was the top of the returns. Ben took a deep breath and clicked on the official link. The man did wilderness photography and painting in Bruce Crossing in the Upper Peninsula of Michigan. Interesting.

Ben clicked around the site until he found a profile. It was short and impersonal, but the information was right. No mention of a family or his age, but the artist grew up in Illinois and worked with computer systems in the army. It had to be him—the Jonah Campbell who took Shari to his senior prom.

Why didn't a photographer have a profile picture? Ben explored the website. There were pencil drawings, too—all outdoor scenes, nothing with people or buildings. How did a man go from Joliet to being an artist in the Upper Peninsula? He did commercial artwork as well as creative work, so he must be fairly normal, and he was sufficiently educated to have a professional website and make a living with art and photography. That was encouraging. At least he wasn't in jail.

Excitement flickered in him. He'd stalled out on the family history project, dreading the discovery of more problematic relatives. It was depressing. He hadn't expected to be greeted with open arms, but so far, he'd only seen hostility and a suicide attempt. This situation was different, because the man didn't even know he might have a son. There was no guarantee he'd welcome a connection, but he probably wouldn't fall apart at the idea.

Ben realized that he was already thinking of the man as his father. Could he locate him? The Upper Peninsula was pretty remote but not too far to drive. Some of his friends used to go there for hunting and snowmobiling, and it was a popular place for summer homes. Or was that northern Wisconsin? His parents had preferred warm vacations.

He tapped it into his phone's GPS. Six and a half hours. That was a long way to drive without some guarantee that Jonah Campbell would talk to him. Showing up on his doorstep and saying, "Hello, you don't know me, but I might be your son", seemed too blunt. The man might have a heart attack. Or he might close the door in his face and call the police to take away the lunatic. Did they have Mounties up there?

Showing up unannounced hadn't worked so well with Linda. Should he write? Telephone? Email might be too impersonal, but it was easy, and the man's email address was on his website.

An hour later, Ben studied the final draft.

Dear Mr. Campbell,

My name is Benjamin Taylor. I would like to talk to you about something that happened 26 years ago in Calumet City, IL. If it is convenient to you, I will stop by on Saturday afternoon. I will not take much of your time.

Sincerely,

Benjamin Taylor

He added a postscript: *I'm not selling anything and I'm not a police officer.*

He clicked on the send button and shut his eyes. No going back now. If it failed, he'd give it up. He had a perfectly good father already.

A reply came within minutes.

Dear Mr. Taylor,
Very few good things happened in Calumet City 26 years ago. I do not often have guests up here. Communication by email is usually more convenient.
Sincerely,
Jonah Campbell

Ben was stung.

Dear Mr. Campbell,
This is an extremely personal matter. I would prefer to talk to you in person.
Ben Taylor

Dear Mr. Taylor,
Although my youth was far from blameless, I can recall nothing so personal that it can't be shared by email. Can you give me a hint?
Jonah Campbell

Dear Mr. Campbell,
This matter is very personal to both of us, and I believe you will want to hear what I have to tell you. If Saturday is not convenient, I can come at another time.

Dear Mr. Taylor,

I appreciate your discretion and am now wild with curiosity. I will look forward to meeting you on Saturday afternoon and hope you will stay for dinner.

Ben's elation ebbed quickly when he realized he didn't have the man's address. How embarrassing.

Dear Mr. Campbell,
Thank you. If you tell me your address, I'll be there by 2pm.

The next email was a string of numbers on a county highway and didn't seem to require a response. Ben felt breathless with the speed of it. The man didn't sound antagonistic, in spite of his initial response. He might even have a sense of humor.

CHAPTER 14

Ben turned his back to the rubberneckers and held the phone close to his head, cupping his other hand over it to block out the wind and street noises. The day had started badly. He'd been one minute late for work, and Tom delivered a nasty lecture about courtesy to clients. An hour later, Ben had to call him to explain that he'd be late for his next appointment. It would be a miracle if he kept this job much longer.

"Okay, I'll call Martin Carmichael and tell him you'll be a little late. Then you're going to Sorensen, right? If you take a short lunch, you can get to your afternoon appointment on time."

"We're waiting for the police now. It's going to be at least half an hour before I get back on the road." Ben hoped he didn't sound as pathetic as he felt, but some of it must have shown, because his boss's tone was sympathetic.

"Are you sure you're okay?"

"I'm fine. I was barely moving. We were just starting to go when the light turned green." Despite the woman's accusation that he had stepped on his brakes for no reason, there was really no question of his being at fault in the accident. He hoped she had good insurance.

"You know, Ben, I think you should stop by the ER and get checked out. You never know with neck injuries. We see a lot of clients with that kind of thing."

"I didn't injure my neck. It was just a fender bender."

He wondered why they called it that. It was the back bumper that was crumpled.

"If you want to do that, though, I could reschedule Carmichael."

"No, it's fine. If you could just let him know I'll be about half an hour late, I'd appreciate it. Hey—the police are here now. I'll talk to you later."

He finished the call and joined the police officer and the other driver, an anxious woman in her forties. She used both hands as she gave her side of the story, pointing at her car and then at Ben's Corolla, clapping her palms together to demonstrate the collision.

"It really wasn't that big a deal!" Ben protested. "We started to roll forward when the light turned green, and you must have accelerated too fast. You just ran into me. But it wasn't exactly a crash."

She turned to the police officer. "We started moving and then he braked suddenly in the middle of the intersection."

"I didn't touch the brakes," said Ben. "I was just driving normally, accelerating at a normal speed from a stopped position. She had to speed up to hit me."

The woman threw up her hands and turned away. She stalked toward her car, jabbing at her phone.

"I'll need to see your driver's license, your registration and proof of insurance." The police officer was tall and bony. He nodded at Ben's car. "It looks drivable. Do you feel okay? Any injuries? Do you want me to call an ambulance?"

"No! I'm fine!"

"Just checking."

Ben paced, watching the man take pictures and make notes. He'd wanted to be a policeman when he was a boy. This didn't look as exciting as he had imagined it. The other driver didn't stop moving. She talked to the police officer, made phone calls, and appeared to be texting. Or maybe she was posting the news of her accident on Facebook, complete with photo and angry emoticons.

"I need you to read this over and sign it," said the police officer, "and then I think we're all done."

"I insist that you see a doctor." It wasn't the first time the woman had said it.

Did he look sick? Did he have a head injury he couldn't see? He resisted the sarcasm and said, "It was just a bump. I'm not injured."

"You can't be sure there's no whiplash."

"I need to get back to work. I'm not hurt."

"Well, my husband says I shouldn't sign anything unless you see a doctor immediately." She held up her cell phone as if in proof.

Ben glanced at the patient police officer, who nodded. "Can't hurt to get checked out. Sometimes injuries don't show up right away."

"There's a walk-in clinic just over there." The woman pointed down the block.

"Maybe later. I have to go." He turned to open his car door.

"I'm not signing anything unless you get checked out now." Her obstinate statement stopped him. She had one hand on the hood of his car, preventing him from driving away, and her mulish expression made it clear that she wouldn't change her mind. He gave in.

"Fine."

The policeman shoved the clipboard toward the woman, who promptly signed it with a flourish. Ben accepted a copy.

"Thanks. My insurance agent will want to see this." His father wasn't really an agent anymore; he held a more exalted position by the time he retired a year ago, but he'd always emphasized the importance of calling the police for an accident. Once you were sure no one was dying and no cars were about to blow up, call the cops and get a police report.

Tom seemed relieved to hear that he'd see a doctor.

"I'll get hold of Carmichael and tell him you'll be there sometime before lunch. Don't hurry."

The unprecedented display of concern surprised him. Maybe he really did need to see a doctor.

Ben's patience was entirely gone by the time he got to the clinic. The woman who rear-ended him followed him to the clinic, parked next to him and got out of her car, apparently ready to accompany him inside.

"I really don't need you to come in with me."

"I just want to make sure you're all right."

"I said I'd get checked out. Please just leave."

She sat in the driver's seat and closed the door, watching him through the open window. Ben tried to ignore her as he entered the building, hoping she wouldn't try to follow him inside.

Martin Carmichael was exactly the same as he had been at Ben's last visit. There ought to have been some improvement.

"Have you been doing these exercises twice a day?"

"Every day." The man looked directly into Ben's eyes. He was lying. Ben wondered why he bothered; it wasn't like he was the rehab police. If the man didn't do the exercises, he wouldn't get better.

"Unfortunately, it doesn't look like your range of motion has improved. I'll let the therapist know, and he'll probably come out to do a reevaluation. He may want to change your program."

Mr. Carmichael didn't seem concerned. He was back on the couch picking up the remote even as Ben packed away his charts and equipment.

Back to Kendra's. He didn't know what to do about her. She turned each appointment into an intimate encounter, dressing in skimpy workout clothes, or all made up for a party. She clutched his arm when he encouraged her to step up onto the stairs and touched his hand when he showed her how to position her leg for the exercises. He tried to remain impersonal, but his was a physical job. He had to touch people.

Feminine laughter permeated the door of Kendra's apartment. A girl with long blond hair opened the door and smiled broadly at him.

"Hello! You must be Ben! Come on in. Kendra's in the bathroom. I'm Ashley." She moved aside to let him enter and closed the door behind him. "You know Vicki, and that's Megan."

The other two girls sat on the couch, legs tucked up underneath them, regarding him with interest. The redhead had brought Kendra to the clinic for her initial assessment, but he was pretty sure they hadn't been introduced. The other girl was blond and looked remarkably like Kendra and Ashley. Was there a template for college girls, with simple variations in hair and eye color?

"Hi. Yep, I'm Ben Taylor." He set down his bag and leaned across the coffee table to shake hands.

"Kendra says you're a physical therapy assistant. Do you like the work?" Ashley started the interrogation.

"Yeah. It's interesting."

Vikki spoke up before he could continue. "What do you do different from a regular physical therapist?"

Ben opened his mouth to explain, but the other girl—what was her name? —asked, "Does it pay very well? Are you going to try to get certified as a regular therapist?"

On a different day, he might enjoy the attention. Today, he wanted to get this appointment over with, get his reports written up, and go home. He had to call his dad about the accident and find out what he was supposed to do.

"It's a five-semester degree, including the internship." It had taken him longer than that; he'd taken a semester off when Anneliese died. "Then I finished the rest of the bachelor's degree, and I'm in the second year of the therapist program."

He glanced at the bathroom door. Kendra always treated his visits like social engagements, casual about the scheduled appointment time and prescribed length of his stay, but she'd never thrown a party for him before.

The girls showed no signs of leaving, even when Kendra emerged and struck a pose, booted foot in front, like a model. "I'm ready!"

Working the therapy session with an enthusiastic audience was a different kind of awkward. Kendra seemed to need more direction than usual, and when he showed her how to turn her foot, she wiggled her toes.

"I painted my toenails for you!"

She certainly had. They were a rainbow of colors. Some sparkled, and some had stripes.

"I figured you probably have to look at ugly feet every day."

Her friends spared him the need to reply. They drew closer, exclaiming, comparing their own skills to Kendra's.

He cleared his throat. "Well, time's up. It was nice meeting all of you."

They turned to stare at him in astonishment.

"We just got started!" Kendra sounded genuinely shocked.

"I have to get to my next client." He tried to sound regretful. It was partly his own fault. He'd been too flexible, too anxious to get a good start to his new job. It was easier to be firm today. He'd missed breakfast after oversleeping, and then he'd skipped lunch to get here on time. "I'll see you on

Tuesday."

It took another ten minutes to escape the babble, and by the time Ben eased into the maze of rush hour traffic, his energy drinks were burning holes in the lining of his empty stomach. If he could hold out another couple of hours, Mrs. Cooper would have dinner ready—real food, not drive-thru burgers and fries that would only make the situation worse.

He had to go back to the office. To accommodate Ben's school schedule, Tom had decided that Lauren would do the billing on Fridays instead of Mondays. That meant each week's reports had to be finished before he left the office on Thursday afternoon. He also had to appear suitably grateful whenever Tom mentioned it.

"You're back! It sounds like you had quite a day."

"Yeah, it was quite a day." Ben dropped his bag inside his office and returned to Lauren's desk. "I thought we were going paperless."

"Oh, no. I print them all out to do the billing and then shred them afterward." She pointed at the largest stack of reports. "That one is Medicare. Each of the other piles is a different insurance company, and they all have their own forms. And then there's private pay. If I have everything ready and printed out, it's not too bad."

"Is it going to be a problem to do them on Friday instead of Monday?"

Lauren leaned forward and lowered her voice. "I suggested it months ago. But, at the time, Tom needed to finish paperwork on the weekends. Now that you're here, it's a lot easier. He's not out of the office doing home visits all day."

"Well, that's good." He looked at the piles of paperwork. "Do you do this much every week?"

"This is about average. Once it's all sorted, Tom and I split it up between us, so it's not too bad. If the business keeps growing like it is, though, he's going to have to hire more help."

"It seems like you guys spend more time on billing and insurance than I do on therapy."

"We do," said Lauren. "It's time consuming, and insurance companies don't want to pay out. It takes them about two minutes to decide to reject a claim, but it takes two weeks to approve one. If you can't fix the rejected claim right away, you have to file an appeal, and that can take months!"

"So, my reports have to be really good." No wonder Tom was fussy about them.

She continued her lecture. "Insurance companies don't like therapy clinics because the care is ongoing instead of a one-time event. Every claim has to be perfect or they kick it back to us."

"I know they're always asking for updates." Before he started doing home visits, responding to the requests had been one of his main responsibilities.

"That's above my pay grade. I just pass those on to you and Tom."

"They're time-consuming, too. I'll get these last three reports finished, and then I'm going home. It's been a long day."

"Right! Are you okay? Tom said you went to the walk-in clinic."

"I only went because everyone was nagging me about it. It was just a bump, not a crash. No injuries at all, for either of us." He didn't roll his eyes or snap at her, and in his condition, that was a testimony to his amazing self-control.

He pulled the folders for the day's clients. Sorensen had gone fine, Carmichael wasn't bothering to do any of the therapy, and Kendra. . . well, she was Kendra. At least he'd got her new range-of-motion measurements before he left, even if they didn't make sense.

"Ben?"

The waiting room must be empty. He wasn't going to

shout across the room. Benjie said Mrs. Cooper didn't let them do it, and he liked to think he was at least as civilized as a seven-year-old.

"Yes?"

"The update requests can wait 'til Monday. I just need your home visit reports today."

He hadn't even seen them. "Okay, thanks."

Yep, the inbox was full. He'd been so focused on the reports that he didn't notice that. His subconscious in denial. Ben worked his way through the reports, transferring handwritten information to the computer and shredding his notes. Then Lauren would print it out, enter the information into the computer and shred the printouts. Paperless.

CHAPTER 15

"So, what do I need to do now?" Ben pressed the phone to his ear as he lifted his head so Annie could shove another pillow behind him. "It wasn't my fault, but if I turn it in to the insurance company, they'll probably just raise my rates."

"Not if it was the other driver's fault. And if you have injuries that don't show up until tomorrow, you need to get the accident on record as soon as possible."

Ben closed his eyes and then opened them again. He couldn't fall asleep until the kids were in bed. "I keep telling everyone I didn't get hurt. It doesn't take much to bust up the bumper on a small car. She had insurance, so I figured she'd take care of it."

He thought he heard a sigh in the silence that followed. "Dad? You still there?"

"I'll call the insurance company now, and they'll call you back tomorrow. Make a couple copies of the police report. Photocopies. Paper, not just on your phone."

"Okay, I will. And I need a favor."

Another silence.

"Dad? We have a really bad connection. Can you hear me?"

"Yes, son?"

"Just a second. No, Annie. Mark can use the blanket." He resumed the conversation with his dad. "Annie is trying to put me to bed. She's brought me pillows and stuffed animals to sleep with, and now she wants the blanket. Anyhow, I found Jonah Campbell—the guy who took Shari to prom. The one who might be my biological father."

"Oh."

"We sent a few emails back and forth, and I want to talk to him on Saturday. He lives in the Upper Peninsula of Michigan, in the middle of nowhere. I can leave early in the morning, and then I'd probably come back Sunday. There's a casino hotel about twenty miles south of there where I can spend the night."

"Did you tell him. . .?" The question faded out.

"No, I just said I want to talk to him about something that happened in Calumet City twenty-six years ago."

"What did he say?"

"I think he thought I was selling something at first, but then he said I could come up and have dinner with him. He seems like a nice guy. Can I just bring the kids Friday night so I can leave early Saturday? I'm not sure what time I'll be back on Sunday, but it shouldn't be late."

"Let me talk to your mom. I don't know if she has plans for the weekend or not."

Ben chuckled. "She'll be in heaven, having the whole weekend to spoil the grandkids." A banshee screech from Annie interrupted him. How could such a horrible noise come from a little girl in Hello Kitty footie pajamas? "Hey, Dad, I need to rescue Mark. I'll bring the kids over after dinner tomorrow. Thanks!"

CHAPTER 16

Jonah rubbed his shoulder. Maybe he could just toss out a few cans of salt instead of shoveling. He should have known better than to spend so much time chopping wood yesterday in this wet weather, but he enjoyed doing it. The big swings of the heavy ax felt good while he was doing it, like a stretching exercise, and he needed the wood. The electric baseboard heat wasn't as good as the wood-burning stove, especially when his shoulder was hurting.

"You gettin' old, Jonah?" Ed Koskinen dropped his duffel bag on the floor and limped over to peer outside. "Or just procrastinatin'? You gonna move dat snow or let me break d'other hip?"

"I need some coffee first." Jonah shut the door and looked at his guest. The old Finn's blue eyes were spots of color in his ashen face. "How'd you sleep?"

"Never better."

Jonah shook his head. Ed never complained about sore muscles or aching joints, even after his recent hip replacement, which had been followed by a heart attack and emergency bypass surgery. "I think I'm older than you are."

"Nah, you still have da driver's license."

"You'll get it back."

"I hope so. I 'preciate you goin' all dis trouble. Tings got complicated ven Katie's ma got sick."

"No problem. I haven't been into town for a while, and I'm running low on supplies. I'll drop you at the clinic and head towards Eagle River from there." He set a cup of coffee on the breakfast bar. "I have a mystery guest coming for dinner tomorrow."

"Mystery guest, eh?"

"Yeah. I got an email from some guy who wants to talk to me about something that happened twenty-six years ago, when I lived down by Chicago."

Ed raised his hairy eyebrows. "Vat happened twenty-six years ago?"

"I don't know. He's gonna tell me when he gets here."

"And you invited him up for dinner?"

Jonah laughed at Ed's scandalized tone. "Not right away, but after he assured me he wasn't a police officer, I couldn't resist."

"Da sins of your misspent youth, hey?"

"I wasn't a believer back then, but I wasn't any more sinful than most guys my age! I can't think of anything worth remembering."

Ed snorted. "Can't tink of anyting vert rememberin! Vat kind of childhood vas dat?"

"It was a fine childhood. Just nothing unusual enough to warrant mysterious emails. I went into the army about that time, right out of high school, and only went back a few times before my mom died. I can't think of anything unusual. Nothing exciting!"

"Ya tink he's lookin' for money?"

"Not from me!" Jonah set down his empty cup and grabbed his coat. "Even if I had done something wrong, no one would care. It's not like I'm a politician or something. I'm an artist—and a pretty boring one."

It was a nasty time of year— warm enough to make a sloppy mess during the day and then cold enough to freeze it solid overnight. Jonah scattered salt over the steps and scraped off the loose ice. He'd pull the truck right up to the door rather than risk Ed's other hip.

Was this Benjamin Taylor someone from high school? Jonah had grown up in Joliet, not Calumet City. He'd had a part-time job at a grocery store, and some friends he hung out with on the weekends, but he couldn't remember a Taylor. His life had been so ordinary! He'd played Little League when he was younger, but by the time he was in high school, he was fascinated with computers. His grades were good, but not high enough for scholarships, so the army had been his ticket out of Joliet. He'd left his yearbooks with his mom when he went to boot camp, and he couldn't remember if he'd ever got them back.

Maybe it was the Calumet City part that was the key. Maybe this guy was a P.I. and thought Jonah had witnessed some kind of criminal activity. Twenty-six years ago? Jonah hoped that wasn't the case. He couldn't even keep track of his morning coffee.

CHAPTER 17

"Are those the last reports?" Tom opened the top folder. The boy was conscientious. He hadn't decided yet if that was good or bad.

"Yep." Lauren stuck a stylus into the black curls above her ear. "I think he's getting the hang of it."

"Good. We'll see how tomorrow goes. If it works out, we'll start Mondays with a clean slate. I like that idea." He liked it a lot. It didn't matter how much money you made if you spent seven days a week working.

He pushed the door shut behind him and dropped into his chair. He needed to call Cravitz, and if the doctor wasn't in a good mood, Tom would have to sit through another "If you want to be part of this organization" lecture. He did want to be part of it. He just got off to a bad start.

He hadn't been prepared for the influx of new clients. An assistant was part of the program, but Tom hadn't had time to find and train one. He'd been sucked in, trying to do all the therapy, administration, and billing. Now that he had Ben, he was starting to dig himself out of the hole. He hoped it wasn't too late. He'd wanted to make a good impression on his new business associates—not look like an incompetent idiot.

It annoyed him that he had to talk his way past two receptionists and a nurse before Henry came on the phone. As a professional associate, he should have the doctor's direct line.

"Henry. Things are going pretty well here. Your accident rigmarole was a stroke of genius. He's rattled."

"He didn't seem rattled when he was here," said Cravitz. "He was ticked off. Just wanted to get out of here and back to work."

"It was a good idea. He's not a stupid kid. He's been asking questions about a few of the clients already. It's just a matter of time before he realizes things don't add up. If he does, and if he makes a stink about it, we can enlighten him about his own little excursion into insurance fraud. Brilliant." It didn't hurt to stroke the man's ego.

"I hope so. Wouldn't it be easier to get him on board and pay him for it?"

"I thought you didn't want to do that!" Tom flexed his free hand. What was the matter with this guy?

"He has a real Boy Scout vibe. Virtue makes me nervous."

"That's why we took precautions. It was your idea!"

"That was before I met him," said the doctor. "You didn't give us much time to check him out."

"Look—most of this year's graduates had already found jobs or were holding out for something bigger. We got Taylor because he wanted to start work right away. He has a clean driving and criminal record. And he's going to school to get his physical therapist degree, so he's thinking about his future."

"Well, then." Cravitz sounded pleased. "If he becomes a problem, we can have a chat about yesterday's little accident. You might even groom him to join us when he's fully credentialed, or maybe even take over your branch when you retire. You do want to retire someday, don't you?"

CHAPTER 18

With every mile north, Ben drove further back into winter. The suburban landscape stretched out into single houses and then farms, with the occasional modern mansion or commuter housing development sprouting out of treeless spaces. Combed rows of green spikes curved with the contours of most of the open fields. Other fields waited, their soil broken into heavy clods.

Ben found a good radio station and settled in to enjoy the drive. He couldn't remember the last time he'd taken a road trip all by himself. Maybe never. There wasn't much down time in his life right now. This felt like a vacation. He leaned the car seat back a notch and turned up the music.

He skirted Madison, annoyed at the reappearance of traffic and eager to get to his destination. When the static became louder than the music, he found a new station. This time, the music only lasted for an hour. The farms spread out and then faded away behind him as trees took over the land. Another lake appeared, filtered through the trees, and he crossed another river—or just one river snaking around—and then goggled at a series of signs for more lakes. Was there more water than land up here?

Ben wasn't sure he liked it. Black pine trees encroached on the smooth highway, kept at bay by empty ditches filled with exhaust-colored chunks of slush. The sun, if it was shining, would be directly over him, so the woods on both sides of the road darkened in their depths. There could be lakes or mountains or houses a hundred yards away, and he wouldn't even know they were there.

"It's like driving through downtown Chicago." The sound of his own voice failed to calm his jitters, probably because his statement lacked conviction. The tall buildings did cause a narrowing of the visible sky, like the pine trees, but the city streets were broken, rutted with cracks and potholes. Downtown driving was slow, with traffic lights every block or two. And there were people—more pedestrians than cars. The noise, smell, and traffic congestion were nothing like sailing through this silent wilderness on a perfectly smooth black highway.

Ben tried to tune in a radio station. He'd settle for country western music or religious programming if he had to. Even static would be good company. The few cars that passed him became a welcome activity. Some of the drivers lifted a hand in greeting. Some were actually talking on their cell phones. Ben gripped the steering wheel more tightly.

He relaxed at the sight of a gas station and assorted buildings. Civilization. Five hours ago, he would have passed it up in expectation of something bigger up the road.

He dawdled in the warm building, strolling through the aisles of overpriced groceries and tourist gifts until the scrutiny of the attendant began to unnerve him.

"Can I help you?" asked the man.

"No, I just stopped for gas and something to drink." He pulled two energy drinks from the array of beverages and walked toward the counter. "I needed to stretch my legs."

"Where ya headin'?"

"Bruce Crossing." Ben spun a rack of postcards. Some of them were raunchy, but most were pictures of lakes or animals. The animals he could identify, but the scenery pictures all looked the same to him.

The attendant reached over and plucked one from the top tier. "Bond Falls. You won't find a place to buy postcards up there this time of year."

Ben took the card and turned it over. Bruce Crossing, Michigan.

"Is there a hotel up there?"

"There's resorts, but I don't know of any open now. I think there's a couple bed 'n breakfast places, too, but probably not this time of year. You passed the big one down in Eagle River."

"I didn't see it." Eagle River looked like it might open up for tourists in the summer, but he hadn't seen a hotel. He'd stopped for a burger and fries at the Burger King, and then the town was behind him. The high school parking lot on the north edge of town was empty on Saturday. It looked as abandoned as the boarded-up strip mall on the other side of the road.

Was that only half an hour ago?

"My dad thought there might be a hotel with a casino up here."

"Oh, ya. You don't want to stay there."

"I'm not fussy. I just need a bed for tonight." Ben went back for two more energy drinks and picked up a Snickers bar.

"I guess it'll do ya then, hey? Will that be all?" The attendant nodded toward the items on the counter.

Maybe he should get some postcards for the kids. He wouldn't have time to mail them, but they'd like the animals. Would they like to come up here for a weekend in the summer? His own parents had preferred trips to the south—he'd been to Disney World three times and on a cruise once, but he'd never been camping.

"Startin' to rain," the man observed.

No camping. If they visited here, they could stay at a resort.

"I'll take these, too."

The attendant scanned the items. "You ever been there before? Bruce Crossing?"

"No."

"Pretty area. Kinda quiet this time of year."

More quiet than this town? Ben made a noncommittal sound and accepted the grocery bag.

"Be careful up there. The roads'll be slick."

"I will," Ben assured him. He'd probably be crawling.

"Have a good day!"

Ben raised a hand in farewell and let the door fall shut behind him. He still had at least an hour to drive—probably longer in this weather. Ben didn't mind the delay—his confidence had evaporated in the isolation and wet weather. What had he been thinking? No, he hadn't taken time to think. That rapid exchange of emails. . . no thinking at all. He should have written a letter.

Ben auditioned possible introductions.

"Hello, my name is Ben Taylor."

The guy would already know that much.

"Do you remember a girl named Shari?"

"A woman who knew my mother said you might be my father."

"I was adopted."

Ben groaned. He should have prepared for this. At least Linda had known there was a baby. This man, if he was Ben's father, knew nothing at all.

He cruised through the town of Watersmeet. An open sign glowed in the window of a gas station, but he didn't see movement inside. Through his mist-filmed windshield, the town looked as gray as Calumet City. Ben lowered and raised the side windows to clear away the rivulets of rainwater. Was Bruce Crossing like this? Had Jonah Campbell moved to another depressed city?

Then he saw the casino. Its colorful sign was bright in the in the drab environment. He could even hear music. It sprawled like a resort, with a hotel, restaurants, and what appeared to be a golf course. A sea of rain-washed cars reflected the brilliant security lights. Luxurious motorhomes rimmed the left edge of the parking lot, behind a sign designating the area as a campground. Ben could do that kind of camping. A scrolling marquee announced the menu specials and touted high-paying slots.

He should stop. Ben slowed the car. He should reserve a hotel room. The sign said they had vacancies, but it might fill up on a Saturday night. Maybe every resident of Eagle River and Watersmeet was here, and that's why the towns looked deserted.

No. He must get this over with. Ben concentrated on his driving. He'd printed directions from Google Maps to supplement his GPS, and after four turns onto unmarked roads, he pulled over to consult the printouts. How did people drive before GPS? If he got off track, he'd be lost forever.

He saw a few small and large houses in the distance, but there didn't seem to be many close to the road. In the summer, when there were leaves on the trees, you wouldn't even see them from the road. People probably liked the privacy here, or they'd live in town. They'd need four-wheel drive and snowplows instead of snow blowers, though, or maybe these were just summer houses. Some residents must stay all year. His father did.

His father. Ben realized he was assuming the relationship was real. Poor little Shari didn't feel like "mother", maybe because she was dead—or maybe because she had been so young. If she was right about this Jonah, Ben's search would be over. Then what? What if the man's life was full of a real family? Would his wife and children be resentful if Ben made himself known? Would Jonah be embarrassed and want to conceal the relationship? Would he deny his paternity? It would fit the pattern for the rest of his family search.

He crossed a short bridge and rounded a corner. A fat doe stood to the side of the road, indecisive and skittish. She made him feel a bit skittish, too. He'd started counting deer a couple hours ago but lost count somewhere after forty. They kept crossing in front of him or just hesitating, like this one, off to the side. What would he do if he hit one, especially if the deer didn't die right away or if the car was damaged beyond drivability? He wasn't sure that 911 was the right place to call for that kind of thing.

Something flew across the road ahead. He was already creeping, not trusting the deer to stay where she was. Was that a bird? Another one flew by, almost hitting his windshield, but it dropped to the ground on the side of the road. That wasn't a bird. Ben stopped the car. The next missile hit the side of the car. Definitely not a bird. It was too sharp. Had he been shot? Of course, there would be hunters in the woods. He ducked down, ready to accelerate away if necessary. The impact was followed by another that bounced off the back of the car. Not a gun. Someone was throwing rocks at him.

He lowered the window. "Hey! Who's out there?"

"Over here! I need help!"

If the man was throwing rocks, he probably didn't have a gun. Ben got out of the car and walked to the side of the road. "Where are you?"

"Over here! By the creek!"

Ben couldn't see a creek. "Where?"

"Over here!"

A splash of bright orange near the ground off to his left, caught his attention, and Ben pushed his way through the underbrush. The pine needles under his feet were slimy with mold and ice; he slipped and stepped into an ankle-deep puddle, grabbing a branch in time to stop himself from falling.

His canvas Chucks soaked up the water like a sponge.

He stomped a few times to shake off the water. "I see you." He picked his way more carefully this time. "Are you hurt?"

It was a stupid question. The man was reclining on a downed tree, wet and cold, his hair plastered to his forehead under the blaze orange cap. "I twisted my knee, and I can't even stand up. I knew you were coming, so I collected as much ammunition as I could reach."

Ben looked at the small pile of rocks next to the man. "You threw rocks at my car?"

"I thought you'd never get here. Someone else drove by earlier, but I missed. It's been a long time since I played ball. I thought it was you at first, and you'd be back when you found out I wasn't home. But it must have been someone else."

First Aid 101 had covered what Ben and his fellow Scouts had called "shock therapy." The man was shivering. His teeth would be chattering if they weren't clenched with pain. Ben approached and squatted next to him.

"Well, you got my car. Twice. I'd already stopped for a deer."

"Praise God. I didn't know what time you were coming."

"What time—are you Jonah Campbell?"

"That's me. You're Benjamin Taylor, right?"

"Yes!"

The man closed his eyes and didn't reopen them. "Do you think you could get me to a doctor?"

"Shouldn't I call an ambulance?" Another stupid question. "No, of course not. I'll drive you there. I have a first aid kit in my car, and I have some medical training."

"Thanks." Jonah's eyes remained closed.

"You'll have to stay conscious long enough to tell me where to go. I'm a stranger here." He knew how to handle injured limbs. He could do this. "This is a heckuva way to greet a guest. Throwing rocks at me. I'm going to get a blanket from my car. Are you with me, Jonah?" The use of the man's first name made him more of a patient and less of a person. Jonah didn't respond.

CHAPTER 19

Ben ran to the car, grabbing branches as he went to keep himself upright. The keys were still in the ignition, so he moved the car off the road and turned on the four-way flashers before popping open the trunk to get the first aid kit. Maybe someone else would come along soon.

Jonah hadn't moved. Ben draped the silver blanket over the man's chest. "Jonah, can you hear me? What happened? Are you bleeding? How did you twist your knee?" He tried to space the words and sentences, hoping for a reply, while he ran his hands down the man's body under the blanket. It wasn't hard to determine which knee was injured—it was swollen to the extent the jeans would allow. Even a light pressure made Jonah grunt. Ben couldn't find any other injuries in that leg and started on the other. Nothing on the hip or knee, but he was shocked to discover a steel animal trap clamped on the toe of Jonah's boot. It hadn't penetrated or even crushed the boot, but it was stuck.

"Did you get trapped? Is your foot hurt?"

To his vast relief, the man answered. "I was looking for moss. I guess I found one of Spargy's coyote traps. It snapped and startled me just as I was trying to step over the branch and avoid the puddle. I fell and twisted my knee. I'm so cold."

"Can you move your fingers and toes?"

Jonah wiggled his fingers.

"What about your toes?"

"I think so." He opened his eyes, focused on Ben and shut them again. "Sorry about dinner. And I hate to mess up your upholstery."

"Not a problem. Does your head hurt? Your back? Anything else?"

"No. I don't think so."

"Okay, then I am going to help you up. Right now, you need to get warm and dry. Let me get this thing off you." He tugged on the trap, dragging it over the rubber toe. It snapped shut as soon as he got it off. Startled, he dropped it. Were traps even legal anymore?

"I'm going to move your right foot over here and then pull you forward." He spoke with his most authoritative voice. "As soon as you're upright on that one leg, I'll slide over to your left, and you lean on me. Get your arm around my shoulders. Don't try to step on your left leg. Use me like a crutch. We have some rough terrain before we get to the car. We'll go slow." He shifted Jonah's body into a better position while he spoke. "Ready? Take both of my wrists. Good! Now I'm going to move. Got it. Hang on."

"Get my camera."

"I'll come back for it."

The two men made their way very slowly back to the road. It wasn't far, but every inch was a feat of balancing. Jonah kept trying to hop instead of lean, but he was too weak to make it a problem. His clothes were soaked, and he was starting to shake with cold. Ben hoped he had a drier layer underneath; the outer layers had to come off.

He would have to go in the back seat behind the driver, Ben realized. That added more steps, but they got around the car and Ben yanked the door handle. It was locked. "Can you lean on the car? I want to get it started and turn the heat on." Every second added to his worry and frustration. "We've got to get those clothes off of you."

"I'm already too cold!" He shuddered. "Right. Clothes off. They're wet."

The jeans weren't coming off, but Ben helped Jonah peel away the other outer layers. "I'll get your boots off once you're inside. And the socks, if they're wet."

After a few false starts, he got the injured man lowered to the seat, sitting sideways, with both legs outside the car. He squatted down in front of him and unlaced and removed the boots. The socks were surprisingly dry. Getting Jonah turned around and buckled in was an exercise in endurance.

"My camera."

"Where is it?"

"By me, but I pushed it further away from the creek."

"I'd rather come back for it later, once your leg is taken care of."

"No, I need it now."

He did not need it now, but it would bring him peace of mind. It took Ben a few minutes to locate the black leather camera case and get back to the car. He was pretty sure that the man wouldn't go into shock now, but even with the pain, there was every likelihood he would go to sleep now that he was getting warm and dry on a nice, comfy car seat.

"Jonah. Wake up. You have to tell me where to go."

"Ontonagon. Head north on 45."

"Get me back to Highway 45, Jonah. I've never heard of Ontonagon. How far is it?"

Jonah didn't respond.

"I have no idea where to go, Jonah. Tell me. Where do I go now? How far is it?" Ben's nerves were fraying. The GPS might get him there, if he knew how to spell it.

"'Bout an hour. Turn the car around." He got the directions piecemeal, stopping at intersections and rousing Jonah to ask for instruction. When he got on the highway, he was able to let Jonah sleep. There were signs for the hospital when he reached the city. He came to a stop in the parking lot and looked at his patient in the rearview mirror. The man was wide awake now, and Ben looked directly into bright blue eyes with dark lashes. Jonah saw those eyes, too, framed in that same mirror.

"Something personal that happened in Calumet City twenty-six years ago?"

Their eyes held. Ben tried to speak one syllable evenly. "Yes."

"How old are you, Benjamin Taylor?"

"Twenty-five."

"Oh."

After a moment, Ben broke the silence. "Let's get you inside."

Only one person occupied the waiting room. The young woman glanced up from her magazine when they entered, but the sight of Ben and Jonah, dripping and limping, didn't appear to interest her as much as the lives of celebrities.

The receptionist wasn't as casual. She rushed out from behind the counter, dragging a wheelchair with her. She shouted, "Tiffany!" over her shoulder, apparently to someone in the depths of the hospital. "Did you fall in?"

Ben was confused by that, but Jonah was fully conscious now. "No, just got rained on. I twisted my knee." He sank gratefully into the chair. "I thought I'd better get it wrapped up. I don't have any elastic bandages at home."

"You laid on the wet ground and got rained on for hours!" Ben snapped at him. "You were very close to hypothermia. And your knee is swollen like a football."

A young woman in blue floral scrubs arrived and appropriated the wheelchair handles without ceremony. Ben followed them down the hall. Under other circumstances, he would have stayed in the waiting room, but the man's cavalier attitude might cause the nurses to take his injury too lightly.

"Do you think you can get up and sit on the table?"

"Of course, I can." He pressed down on the arm rests and tried to stand on one leg. He was a foot taller and eighty pounds heavier than she was, but she caught his elbow and hip and turned him deftly to a safe position for sitting on the table.

"I'm Dr. Mendelli. You are?"

"Jonah Campbell. And he," said Jonah, gesturing to the corner where Ben waited, "is Benjamin Taylor."

The doctor didn't acknowledge the introduction. "We're going to have to cut off the jeans." She was already plying a large pair of utility shears through the muddy denim. "Violet, get some hot coffee with lots of sugar in it. Two cups." The receptionist disappeared.

Ben moved to the side to get a better look at the injured knee. The doctor was poking at it with small, blue-clad fingers. She looked like a child, with freckles on her nose and a mop of red curls. Jonah yelped, and she pressed again.

"Right there? How about here?" She prodded harder. Ben twitched.

Jonah glowered. "You sure you don't want to twist it a little more, just to make sure it's really hurt?"

She smiled at him. "The good news is that I'm pretty sure it's not broken. We'll take an x-ray anyhow, but I think it's just a bad sprain. You stretched some ligaments further than they were intended to go."

"That knee's given me trouble for years. I'm glad it wasn't the good one."

"What's the bad news?" Ben couldn't resist asking.

She transferred the smile to him. "Are you a friend?"

"I just picked him up along the roadside."

"A good Samaritan." She beamed. "The bad news is that

it hurts just as bad as a break and will take as long to heal. You'll have a hinged brace and crutches. Hopefully no surgery, but you will definitely need some physical therapy."

Jonah was frowning. "Will I be able to drive?"

"Nope, you'll have a couple weeks off work."

"I work at home, but I can't be stuck there."

"Do you live alone?"

"Yes." The answer was curt. Ben waited hopefully, but Jonah didn't elaborate.

The doctor's brow furrowed. "Do you live in town? Is there someone who can stop by periodically and run errands for you?"

"I live about five miles north of Bruce Crossing."

"Oh." She digested that. "Do you have a telephone and electricity?"

Ben stared at her, but Jonah answered matter-of-factly. "Yep. I have both feet firmly planted in the twenty-first century. I even have indoor plumbing."

"Well, then, you can just hunker down for—oh, about ten days. Then you'll need a ride to get checked out again, but you won't be able to drive for at least four weeks."

"I don't need my left leg for driving."

"Just to be on the safe side," she said obscurely. She helped Jonah back into the wheelchair as if he was a small child. She rolled him to a room at the end of the hall where she took x-rays. Ben had never seen a doctor do such a variety of jobs. In his experience, medical care involved a team of CNA's, nurses, technicians and sometimes even a doctor. When she'd developed and read the x-rays, confirming her diagnosis, Dr. Mendelli did some complex wrapping and strapped on a sophisticated brace.

"I thought you said it would be hinged."

"It is, but I locked it straight for the trip home. And just a couple days after that."

Ben listened to the familiar litany of at-home care and treatment. How odd that this should be his introduction to his father. "I'll get him settled in, but I have to go back to Chicago tomorrow."

"If you could stay with him tonight, that would be great. He's going to have some strong painkillers." She looked at Jonah. The furrow reappeared. "If that isn't convenient, I think you'd better stay here overnight."

"No." They both spoke at the same time. Jonah continued. "That will be fine. We'll both enjoy having a chance to visit. We have a lot to talk about."

Ben wasn't certain of the other man's mood. Probably, the painkillers were already making him loopy. Meaningful conversation might have to wait.

He got local directions from the receptionist. "I need to get him some sweatpants and a warm shirt." Ben glanced down at his wet feet. "And shoes for both of us." He'd already changed into clean clothes, but he hadn't packed an extra pair of shoes. "I'll get groceries when we get back to Bruce Crossing."

Violet's lips quirked. "Where?"

"Isn't there a grocery store there?"

"I think there's a gas station with snacks. I've never actually stopped in Bruce Crossing."

"Oh. Well, then, I'll get groceries here." He looked at Jonah, who was nodding in and out of sleep in the wheelchair. "Can I leave him here while I do the shopping?" Like he was a parcel, or maybe a child in need of a babysitter.

"Sure. Just push him out and he can sit with Keesha."

"Is she waiting to see the doctor?"

"No, she just stops by every so often to read the magazines."

Jonah didn't like being left behind, but they all ignored him. "Size twelve!" was the last thing Ben heard as he walked out of the building.

He grabbed a cart on the way into the store and hoped he could remember everything. Mrs. Cooper did his grocery shopping, so he wasn't accustomed to it. If Jonah was laid up, he'd need easy food. Ben loaded the cart with cereal, milk, macaroni and cheese, hot dogs, peanut butter, bread, chips, orange juice, and a lot of frozen pizzas and meals. He went back and grabbed a package of toilet paper. As he was checking out, he remembered the wet car seats and returned for a box of garbage bags. He hoped Jonah could reimburse him quickly; he hadn't planned such an expensive trip. On the other hand, it looked like he'd be saving the cost of a hotel.

CHAPTER 20

It was nearly six o'clock by the time they had Jonah dressed in new sweats and loaded into the car, on seats covered with plastic bags. Ben let him sleep. The GPS picked up his location and led him back toward Jonah's house. He passed the spot where they'd met and was relieved to know he was on the right track.

Track was the right word. He didn't have much experience with rural roads. *Was* this a road, or had he accidentally strayed onto someone's private property? If there were signs, he couldn't see them in the dark.

Ben glanced in the rearview mirror. He'd feel better if Jonah was awake to give directions, but the man was sleeping noisily under the influence of the painkillers, snoring and groaning like an old man. He decided to trust the GPS.

Jonah had been gruff about his ordeal, but it must have been agonizing. Ben had become miserably cold and wet in the brief time it had taken to get Jonah in the car. He couldn't imagine spending hours lying on the frozen ground, swathed in soaking fabric, in pain, unable to move, hanging onto the knowledge that someone would be driving by sometime in the afternoon—and hoping desperately that he could attract the driver's attention by throwing rocks at him.

Ben shied away from the fleeting idea that he might have saved his father's life. Jonah appeared to be pretty fit; he could have made it back to his house eventually. But as he drove on in the darkness, he wondered. Jonah must have been at least half a mile from home when he fell. This road seemed to go on forever.

"Your destination is on your left." The mechanized voice startled him. His destination was straight ahead of him. It had to be his destination, because the road ended there. Brilliant light flashed, illuminating the front yard as he drove forward. Motion detector lights.

It wasn't one of the large prow-fronted lodges he'd seen ringing the lakes, but it was a good-sized cabin, painted brown with a green metal roof. Like a tree. A matching, detached garage sat to his right, with a black pickup truck parked casually in front of it. Small piles and patches of snow, soft and pitted rather than fresh and white, covered most of the ground. Wherever there was no snow, there was mush and slimy vegetation.

"Home sweet home." Jonah shifted and subsided against the back seat. "It'll be cold. The fire's out."

"I'd go in and get it started for you," said Ben, "but I'd probably burn the house down. Don't you have a regular furnace?"

"Yeah, but it's all shut down, and the wood stove is better, anyhow."

"Then you'll have to show me what to do. Would it be okay to drive on the lawn so I can get you closer to the door?"

Jonah chuckled. "I did that very thing yesterday, for a friend. He stayed the night so I could take him to his doctor appointment in the morning. It worked just fine."

Once the stove was lit, Ben retrieved the groceries and started a frozen lasagna in the microwave. He tried to make light conversation as he put away the food and supplies. "I don't know if you'll like any of the food I bought, but you won't starve." He held up a box of macaroni and cheese. "My kids would live on this stuff."

Jonah's eyes grew wide. "You have kids?"

"I have four of them. Three boys and a girl." No matter how much he loved his kids, he was always a little embarrassed by their number.

"But you're only twenty-five!"

Ben busied himself folding a paper bag. "Well, we got an early start. Anneliese was pregnant when we graduated from high school. The others followed pretty quick."

"They must have. Anneliese is your wife?"

"She was." Another uncomfortable admission. "She died two years ago."

"I'm sorry."

Ben couldn't say anything. He never knew how to respond to expressions of sympathy.

After a few seconds, Jonah continued. "It must be difficult. My wife died four years ago. We. . . we didn't have children."

Ben glanced up from the bag to see Jonah watching him.

"But I do, don't I?" When Ben didn't answer, he persisted, "Why didn't I know that?"

His voice rose. "I had a right to know that!"

Taken aback by the reaction, Ben said, "My biological mother died in childbirth. Her mother gave up the baby for adoption. Me. Gave me up for adoption."

"She had no right to do that!" Jonah thumped his fist on the upholstered arm of the couch. "Why wasn't I notified?"

"No one knew." Ben walked into the living area and sat on the rocking chair. He groped for words to explain the delicate matter of his mother's promiscuity. "Everyone assumed she didn't know. . . that there were a lot of possibilities. I came prematurely, and she died." He had to swallow the lump that rose from nowhere to choke him. "No one knew who the father was. They didn't even know she was pregnant." Slowly, faltering over words and backtracking several times, Ben gave him the whole story, finishing up with an understatement. "I just wanted to learn about my biological family. It was. . . painful."

Horror carved creases in Jonah's face. "Fifteen? She was fifteen and she died?" He covered his face with both hands. "She died giving birth to my son and I didn't even know. Fifteen years old." He stared at Ben. "Why didn't her friend tell someone?"

"I don't know. She was only sixteen. I guess she was scared. Traumatized by her friend's death."

"Shari." He tested the name on his tongue. "And she lived in Calumet City."

"Connie Price said that you met at a wedding reception. She and Shari had crashed the party. And you and Shari went to a Valentine's dance."

"I do remember." Jonah spoke carefully, as much to himself as to Ben. "She had brown hair. After the prom, we went back to someone's house." He looked at Ben directly and said honestly, "But I don't remember her very well. I didn't know her very long. I think I was just waiting to graduate so I could go into the army. It's all I cared about back then. From the little I remember of our relationship, it was fast and wild and casual. I know there wasn't any commitment between us." He wiped his hands over his face again. "I had a few girlfriends during high school. That kind of relationship. . . I know it was wrong, but at the time, it seemed normal. It was that kind of generation. But, Ben, if I had known she was pregnant, I would have taken care of you. I have a lot of faults, but I would not, even at that young age, have abandoned you or her. I swear that to you."

Jonah's pain worked like a balm to Ben's. It was perverse and selfish to be glad that someone else was in pain, but after such rejection from his other relatives, he was grateful that someone did care. His father cared. He tried to find words that would bring some comfort.

"Shari wanted to protect you." It hadn't been love, of course. She wanted to protect Jonah so he'd be free to marry her—or at least support her and the baby.

Jonah shook his head. "I had a right to know."

"Yes, you did. But I was adopted by a good couple, and they raised me as their own. I love them; they are my parents."

They talked, haltingly, of less personal matters as they ate their lasagna. Ben brought down some of Jonah's clothing and toiletries from the loft so he could move into the guest room on the main floor.

"I don't know about this sleeper sofa," Ben said. "You might be better off on the couch." The thin mattress appeared to be permanently bent in the sitting position. "It doesn't look very comfortable, and it's low. It might be hard to get out of in the morning."

"A friend of mine slept on it the other night. He said it was good."

"Okay. If you want to swap beds, let me know. I'll hear you if you shout. I'm used to waking up for the kids."

"I guess I should have brought you some paper plates and cups and plastic silverware," Ben said as he washed up the dishes from the night before. "And cereal bowls."

"How do you manage with four children?"

"I don't. I have the miraculous Mrs. Cooper. Technically, she's the children's nanny, but she really runs all of our lives."

"Is that a good thing?" Jonah sounded skeptical.

"Absolutely. If she was thirty years younger, I'd marry her. The first time I met her, I called her Mary Poppins, but she makes Mary Poppins look like an amateur."

"Sounds like a treasure. How do I find one of those?"

"My mother found her for me. They're good friends." Ben changed the subject. "Yesterday, you said you were looking for moss. Did you want to take a picture of it? And wasn't there any moss closer to home?"

Jonah's unexpected grin erased some of the grim lines he'd grown the day before. "I was looking for perfect moss. But as I was lying awake last night, I realized that I was actually looking for a certain kind of lichen. I think the one I want is found closer to the lake."

He looked much better this morning, but Ben had seen him take several aspirins in addition to the prescription painkillers. Jonah had mentioned a shoulder problem that was exacerbated by strenuous exercise and bad weather, joking that he was glad it wasn't the arm he needed for the crutch. "It's my throwing arm, though, and probably why I missed on my first couple of attempts."

"I wish you had someone to stay here with you."

"There are people from church I can call if I need anything, but I'll be fine." Jonah set his coffee cup down. "Ben, what are your plans now? I wasn't prepared for all of this last night. I'd had a rough day and painkillers, and I'm sure I didn't respond as well as I'd like to. Since you sought me out, I'm hoping that means you'd like to establish a relationship. Is that true?"

Ben considered. He wanted to establish something. Not an ordinary father-son relationship, but something. While Jonah was lying awake thinking about lichens, Ben had been thinking about his family. Jonah was alone. No parents, wife, or children. Alone. Ben had never experienced that.

"Would you like to meet my children?"

Jonah nodded several times. "Yes, I would. I've never had much to do with children, though. You'd better bring their nanny."

"I think you need a nanny yourself for the next month or two." He looked around. "Is there anything else I can do before I leave?"

"No, I think everything is under control. I really appreciate all of your help. With everything."

"Okay." Ben thrust his hand forward. Was he supposed to hug the man?

Jonah shook his hand and gave him an awkward pat on the back. "Have a safe trip."

"I'll send you an email when I'm home."

"That would be great!"

"See you!" At least, Ben thought, he probably would.

"Be careful!"

Ben pondered the differences in their lifestyles as he drove home. Both of them had escaped the depressed lifestyle of that failing industrial area with its poverty and hopelessness. Ben had been removed by adoption and brought up from infancy in a loving secure home with enough money to live comfortably. He was on his way to a solid career in the suburbs. Jonah had found his own way out and never gone back. He seemed content up north. Would he still be content now that he knew he had a family? A biological family, anyhow.

He liked Jonah—a respectable and healthy new relative. Ben winced at his self-centeredness. He'd worried about how his announcement would be received—what his biological father would say to him. If he would be accepted or rejected. Not once had he considered how the news would affect Jonah.

Ben's thoughts kept returning to the man's refrain, "I had a right to know." Now what? Had he just taken on a long-term commitment?

CHAPTER 21

Teresa loved Lila Rose. The woman had been born and raised in Chicago, but her husband's military career had taken them all over the country. They spent three years in Alabama, and she'd taken the opportunity to transform herself into a southern belle. She cultivated it as she grew older, graduating to a steel magnolia—all kindness and charm, with a solid faith that sustained her through breast cancer, the death of her only son in Vietnam and the subsequent decline of her husband's health.

Lila Rose wasn't afraid to talk about the hard times in life, freely expressing both grief and joy without qualification. Teresa had never met such an honest person, or one so persistent. The woman had skillfully extracted her life history without apology or judgment, offering sympathy without syrup. She expected that the hard times had helped Teresa to grow.

"Well, I know that God put me in that shelter—not Leo. It was such a humiliating experience. I didn't know pride as a bad thing back then. Most of the women had no pride at all, and I wasn't going to be like them." Teresa picked up her cup and sipped the coffee. "It just made me more stubborn and proud, and they all thought I was looking down my nose at them."

Lila Rose raised her perfectly-groomed brows. "It does

sound like that, dear."

"I know. I was. Pride, self-esteem, gumption." She smiled at the last word. "They seemed important back then. The first time I was in there, I was busy doing what had to be done—filing the charges and getting Leo sent to prison. I wasn't there long; he was in jail the whole time, so I went home and back to work. I got a divorce and moved on. It all went fairly smoothly."

The older woman reached across the table to touch her arm. Teresa looked at the fragile hand. Though speckled with age spots, lumpy with arthritis and trembling faintly, her hands were butter-soft, with manicured fingernails that gleamed pink under the lights.

"I know it wasn't as easy as you make it sound, Teresa."

"It was a piece of cake, compared to what some of the other women were dealing with. But when I had to go back, I really was just like them, afraid, with no end in sight. I was angry, and mostly I was humiliated to be back there. . . " She realized she was getting tense and stopped to relax. Lila Rose waited without fuss.

"The volunteers were so careful to treat all of us with respect that it almost seemed phony. It wasn't phony. They were really nice ladies. I was just oversensitive. So prideful." Teresa shook her head. "Arrogant. But it was a different group of women there the second time. There were still some with the usual problems—drugs, a ghetto mentality. . . " She caught the other woman's eyebrows lifting again and hastened on. "Anyhow, there were three Christian women. They prayed before meals and had little Bible studies, even in front of the other women. One of them only wore dresses and had six kids. She wore a little scarf on her head all the time. It seemed ridiculous to me at the time, to hang onto the religious trappings. I even thought that religion was probably part of the abusive situation."

She gave a short laugh. "And, you know, that woman was the one who led me to the Lord. She was so sincere in her faith, but she didn't seem to think that God should solve all her problems or smite her husband. She didn't blame God. She blamed the man. She didn't bash him, though. She left him because she had to, but she wasn't out for revenge. I was! I hated Leo then, for ruining my life. I kept wishing he would get caught committing a crime and go back to jail. Sometimes, I wanted him to die." She bit her lip and glanced at her friend. Lila Rose didn't look shocked, so Teresa continued. "How's that for honest? I really did."

She took a sip of water, taking time to compose herself again. "But this woman—her name was Hannah. She never said so, but I got the impression that it'd been going on for years and then one day she knew she had to put an end to it. Probably for the children's sake. Something must have come to a head, and she left. She was calm about it. Oh, it's hard to explain. She just sort of rested in God and trusted that He would work things out. She wasn't stupid. She knew her world had changed. But she seemed grateful, not just for the safety of the shelter, but because she believed God had it under control. She homeschooled the kids and spent a lot of time talking to them. They were quiet but seemed to be okay."

Lila Rose sighed. "Heartbreaking. I hope she's still safe."

"I think she probably is. She was going to move back to her parents' farm when it was safe to do so. She's the one who taught me to spin! Some ladies from her church came to visit a few times. They brought some clothes and toys for the children, and one day, they brought her spinning wheel. I pestered her until she showed me how to use it. Anyhow, I think her friends even packed up things from her house and stored them for her. And there she was, glorifying God in that place, under those circumstances, and her church supported her. It was contrary to everything I knew of religion. Especially such a fundamentalist kind of religion."

"So, did she tell you about Jesus?"

"No, not directly like an evangelist. She was just a living testimony. The other women shared the specifics of salvation with me, but Hannah laid the groundwork. Before I met her, I wouldn't have even listened to them."

"That is real evangelism."

"But she didn't tell me. If God hadn't sent the other ladies to follow up with the teaching of salvation, I'd just remember her as a nice lady. I'd always see her as an exception to the usual kind of Christian. And I'd think of her husband as a typical example of a conservative Christian patriarch. So, she might have hindered me instead of being a testimony if it weren't for the other women."

"Some plant the seed, some water and some harvest," said Lila Rose. "God put it all in place for you. He's just amazing that way."

"Yes, He is. But even after I was saved, it was a bad time there the second time. I wasn't a wonderful, sanctified Christian right away."

"Oh, I am sure you were!" Lila Rose's laugh sounded throughout the emptying coffee shop, and Teresa grinned in response.

"Not even close. It took me years to attain this level of perfection."

"You do have an amazing testimony, Teresa. Have you considered sharing it with others? In shelters or other kinds of ministries, or writing a book?"

"Oh, no. Not now, anyhow. I'm still growing and learning more about God. I don't feel like He's done with me yet."

"Of course, He's not done with you!" Lila Rose rapped the table with her spoon. "And you will be growing and learning about God for the rest of your life."

Teresa tried to find the right words to express her conviction. "I don't want my testimony to be all about what God saved me from. I want a testimony of what He has done in me since then. What He has saved me *to*. Does that make sense? I'm saved, and that's all I need, but it's just the beginning of what He is doing in me."

Lila Rose nodded. "I understand what you're saying, but I still think you have a powerful testimony to share now. You think about it. God's not waiting for you to be perfect before He uses you for His glory."

CHAPTER 22

Jonah woke at noon. He'd also awakened every thirty minutes since he went to bed the previous night. He never slept well on his back—the only possible position with a bulky knee brace. He couldn't roll to his left side, and if he rolled to the right, his shoulder hurt. He'd seen the dawn before he finally fell asleep, and then he'd been jerked to wakefulness every time he shifted in his sleep and reignited the pain. Maybe he should sleep in the recliner. Anything would be more comfortable than this. How on earth had Ed managed to sleep on it? Poor guy.

He contemplated the mechanics of getting vertical. Ben had helped him yesterday. The boy was born to be a physical therapist—Jonah had practically levitated into mobility. Ben explained the process while they did it: since the left leg was straight, he'd have to put his right foot in front of him, lean forward and rise up on the one leg. It sounded simple. Jonah rose two inches before his shoulder gave way. He twisted to fall on the bed instead of the floor, and his lower back spasmed in pain.

This was ridiculous. He wasn't even fifty yet, and his body was falling apart. He worked through the process in his mind: the shoulder was fine if he wasn't putting weight on it. If he extended his left leg forward, with the crutch in his right hand, then pressing on the bed with his left hand, keeping his right leg on the floor in front of him. . . He could use his left arm to heave himself into position to stand up and balance on his right leg long enough to switch the crutch from right hand to the left and get it positioned under his left armpit. It was just like playing Twister.

The baseboard heat kept the pipes from freezing, but that was about it. Jonah curled his toes away from the cold floor. Socks. Maybe even shoes. How could one banged-up knee cause so much trouble? It wasn't even broken. Ed had broken a hip and survived a heart attack without fuss. Maybe he was just a whiner. Coffee would help.

Jonah opened the cupboard door and grinned at the row of sugar-coated cereals. Cindy used to buy him a box of marshmallow cereal on his birthday and for Christmas each year.

"It's better than candy," she always said, "but not much. And not for breakfast."

Since her death, he'd never been able to shake the Inner-Cindy long enough to buy it for himself. Ben must have picked out his own favorites. And the whole milk. . . it poured like cream over the blue and orange stars. The first spoonful was heavenly. The second was even better. He tipped the bowl to drink the remaining milk and then refilled it. Why on earth hadn't he done this before?

At least his confinement would make him more productive. He was too easily distracted by the world outside his cabin, especially this time of year. Anticipation of spring. Jonah flipped through CD's while the computer started. He wanted to work with an old picture—a doe and baby rabbit under a snow-frosted shrub—so something about winter would be appropriate. There weren't many options. Were all country western singers from the south?

The rabbits were particularly appealing displayed on the large monitor mounted in front of the drafting table. An exceptionally mild spring had let them venture from their nests earlier than usual, so the baby was small. He caught them looking directly at him, with an expression of inquisitive surprise.

Jonah settled onto the high stool—more comfortable than most of his options—and drew a few contour lines. There was little color in the photograph, so he created a gentle watercolor wash and then worked on recreating their startled expressions.

The music was wrong. Jonah slid off the stool and considered his collection. Mountain music, not country. Bluegrass. Satisfied with the creative atmosphere, he returned to his painting. Time to shut off the monitor and let instinct take over.

Dinner was frozen pizza. Ben was an excellent shopper. Jonah carried a piece into the studio and surveyed his rabbits. The painting was. . . different. Good, but it didn't really look like his usual work. He sat on the stool and regarded it. It was technically sound. Realistic. Good lighting, especially where it gleamed on the snow bending the boughs over the rabbits' heads. The colors were right. Eventually, he decided that it looked. . . cute. No, it looked whimsical. He did not do cute paintings.

He wondered if his grandchildren would like it.

CHAPTER 23

"Lauren said you want to talk to me about Kendra Moss and Martin Carmichael. Is there a problem with them?"

Ben stopped in the doorway of his office. It was Tom's business, so technically it was his computer, his desk and his chair, too, but Ben was already thinking of them as his own. Tom didn't move or apologize—just sat at Ben's desk looking at him with a cool, inquisitive expression, waiting for a response.

"Um. . . yeah. Well, not necessarily a problem." He couldn't tell his boss he felt like an incompetent failure. Tom probably shared that opinion already. "I just wanted to touch base with you."

What had Tom been looking at on the computer? Ben was fairly certain he didn't have anything personal on the computer, but he itched with the need to walk around the desk to look at the monitor.

"What's up?"

"Kendra and Martin Carmichael are similar. They're inconsistent. I don't think either of them are doing their exercises. Sometimes they seem completely healed, and other times they can barely move. They either moan and groan, or they seem to be in a hurry for me to leave." He hesitated. "I don't have much experience with assessments yet, but they just don't seem right. I wish you'd take another look at them."

"Oh, I'm sure you're doing fine."

"And about Kendra Moss. Is there any reason she can't come to the clinic instead of having me make home visits?"

Tom chuckled. "Is she flirting with you?" He leaned back in Ben's chair, grinning. "Don't worry about it. She's harmless. She doesn't drive, even when she's not injured. Besides, we make a lot more money on home visits than on office visits, even with paying you mileage."

Ben wondered why Tom had stopped by if he wasn't going to listen to anything he said. He held up the yellow folder Lauren had given him. "I've got a new client for tomorrow morning? There's no evaluation form in here."

"Yes, we can drive out there separately, and I'll introduce you. I did the initial evaluation last week. We can go over all of it together while we're there. This one's complicated because it's a minor. We have to work with the mother, and she's a little strange. After today, you'll just go there, do the exercises and assessments and come back to the office. I'll review your reports before you submit them, at least for the first few. I'm not sure how long we'll keep this one. She might be too unstable."

"Who? The mother? How old is the girl?" He glanced at the file. "Venetia?"

"I don't remember off-hand. In high school, anyhow. Not a child."

"I haven't had any practical experience with treating children," Ben warned him. "Is she fully grown?"

"Oh, I think so." Tom stood up. "We don't usually do much with children. Too risky."

"They're so little."

Tom gave a short laugh. "They're tougher than they look. Just wait until you have a few of your own. I have a nephew who can fall out of trees and down the stairs and off of his bed without even a bump. But then I have a niece who broke her arm falling off her dining room chair during breakfast."

Would it be smart to mention his family now? Wouldn't it look strange if he didn't say anything and Tom found out later? Ben opened his mouth and closed it again.

Tom clapped him on the shoulder as he passed. "You're doing fine."

Ben watched him leave. He wasn't doing fine. He'd felt well-prepared when he left the program. He'd earned good grades. His internship had been easy, but he'd done it at the nursing home where he knew everyone. Here, he felt inept. Stupid. Half the time, he couldn't understand what Tom wanted, and he didn't know how to help the clients. What if he hurt someone or failed to notice a problem?

Tom's approval didn't reassure him. His boss was a businessman. Ben knew that anyone in private practice had to watch the bottom line, but there were times when Tom seemed more concerned about reports that generated income than about healing. There were patients who continued in therapy when they seemed perfectly fine, and some people who were released when they didn't seem to have made any progress at all. Did their treatment depend on their ability to pay? That was probably standard operating procedure for all kinds of medical care—or other businesses. Costs and benefits. Maybe, as he progressed in his education, he would learn to make balanced decisions about those things.

Venetia Rood was a heavy girl with bad skin and frizzy hair. It had apparently been braided by an amateur in a hurry, and Venetia made it worse by scratching at the blobs of fuzz between the rows while her mother talked.

"She can't use her right hand very well ever since that elevator door shut on it. She was supposed to have a big test in school today, but she can't go like this. And they can't blame her, either. She's under a doctor's care. She's excused."

Tom's voice was soothing. "It must be painful."

Venetia opened her mouth to reply but was preempted by her mother. "Yes, it's very painful. That store ought to pay her for pain and suffering. An injury like that isn't going to just go away. It could stay with her for the rest of her life."

"We'll get her all fixed up." Tom smiled at the girl. "We'll give you some exercises to do every day, and Ben here will come by a couple times a week to check on you and report your progress."

"Well, she's in pain now! Look at her!"

They looked. Venetia was watching television.

"Doesn't that hurt, baby?"

"Oh, yeah. It hurts a lot. I can hardly move it."

Kandyce turned to Ben. "She needs some pain medication! I can't stand to see my baby girl suffering like that."

Venetia wasn't paying attention anymore. Ben looked at Tom for guidance.

"We don't have anything to do with medications, Mrs. Rood. You need to talk to your doctor for that. I can talk to him if he has questions, but I don't prescribe meds."

"You tell him I want those pills now." Her belligerence alarmed Ben. Was Venetia really in that much pain? She didn't seem uncomfortable.

Tom, however, appeared unusually tense. "You have his number. You'll have to call him. We need to take a look at Venetia's hand."

"Baby, come back here so these doctors can see your hand."

The girl approached, holding out her injured hand like a gift. "It hurts real bad. I can't write or play video games."

"Well, that stinks," said Ben. "I like video games."

She gave him an appraising glance and turned to Tom, who was obviously the man in charge. "Do you think it will ever get better?"

"I think you'll make a complete recovery."

Ben watched Tom go through the process of evaluation, measuring her range of motion and strength. The examination seemed rather perfunctory. His boss's grim expression darkened as the mother coached her daughter through the responses to all of his questions, reminding the girl about her pain.

'Thank you, Venetia. I think we have everything we need to get started. Come on, Ben. Let's leave these ladies in peace. I will see you back at the clinic in half an hour."

Surprised, Ben gathered up their equipment and clipboards. Apparently, he wasn't staying.

As he pulled out of the apartment complex, he saw Tom leaning on his car, talking on his cell phone. He did not look happy.

They were all asleep. Ben picked up Annie's teddy bear and put it in her crib. She'd thrown it out in a full-blown temper tantrum an hour ago. Ben couldn't remember how the meltdown had started, but it was an impressive one, and it had been contagious. At one point, all four of them had been crying.

He'd wanted to cry, too. He was frustrated by work and exhausted by fatherhood, and Dr. Wick had printed out his most recent lab report and covered it with comments and questions in red ink. He needed a vacation.

Jonah. He needed to email Jonah. He'd promised he would, and that was four days ago. Another fail.

Dear Jonah,
It was a long drive, but I made it home safely. No snow down

here. I hope you are managing alright. Do you have everything you need? Ben

He didn't know what he could do if Jonah was lacking anything, but it seemed polite to ask. The answer came so quickly that he wondered if Jonah had been waiting for him.

Hi Ben.
I'm glad you are safely home. We got more snow last night. Just a few inches. I'm doing fine here. I like your taste in cereal. I called the post office and they said they would bring the mail up to the house. I turned on the electric furnace. I hope everything is going well down there. Thanks for checking in. Jonah

Another email came almost immediately.

By the way, you left your tennis shoes here. Do you want me to mail them to you?

Ben grimaced. Those shoes had been practically new when he'd waded into that swamp to rescue the man, but he knew from experience that they'd never be the same again.

No, thanks. Throw them out. Ben

Immediately:

Will Do.

No further exchange seemed necessary. Ben pulled out the lab report and pored over it, trying to understand his professor's criticism. He needed to talk to Dr. Wick. The paper looked fine to him. A couple spelling errors that should have been picked up in spell check, but nothing worth all that red pen.
His eyelids were heavy, dropping every time he tried to focus. Enough. Ben powered off the computer and prepared for bed.

Locks, lights, appliances. . . same thing every night, but he usually made it until after eleven. He'd be better tomorrow.

Kendra Moss didn't answer the doorbell. He knocked and held his breath. No answer. Yes! Ben dropped his bag to the floor and dug out the official "we missed you" hanger. He had just hung it over the doorknob when the outer door slammed and feet pounded up the stairs. His cheerful attitude faded.

"I'm so sorry!" Kendra rounded the corner at a run, a backpack hooked over one shoulder. "I totally forgot you were coming!"

"You're really doing well!" Pleasure followed the shock. Maybe he really was doing something right. "Your leg's a lot better if you can climb the stairs like that."

She bit her lip and clutched the handrail. "Oh, no. It's throbbing. I was so worried about getting here that I probably overdid it. Can you help me get inside?"

He held out his arm and she hooked her own through it. She leaned heavily against him as she unlocked the apartment, chattering about the weather and school and her new laptop computer. Ben was silent, discouraged.

His mood must have been contagious. Kendra was subdued as they worked through the exercises. The oppressive atmosphere made him as uncomfortable as her flirting did. Part of his professional responsibility was a good "bedside manner". He should say something about the weather or maybe comment on her computer.

"Would you like to come over for dinner on Saturday night? I make a mean lasagna."

Kendra's sudden invitation surprised him. She sounded breathless. Nervous. Ben hesitated. She was pretty and vivacious, obviously attracted to him, and he was a male with the usual hormones. If things were different. . . He stopped that train of thought. His life was full, and she was a client.

He shook his head—hopefully regretfully—and said, "I think you're an amazing woman, and if I had a brother, I'd love to set the two of you up, but I'm not available."

His mother gave him that line. Mom was a stickler for the truth but said there was no need to embarrass someone or hurt their feelings when it could be avoided. It wasn't quite true in this case, though. He assumed he would be fond of this fictional brother, and Kendra was exhausting.

"No single friends?" She laughed. "I'm just kidding. Thanks for being honest."

Uh huh. He packed up his bag and escaped as politely as he could.

Tom was leaning over the reception desk when Ben entered the office, watching Lauren at the computer. He straightened and raised his brows as Ben approached. "How'd it go?"

"Carmichael and Sorensen are about the same. Mr. Sorensen's range of motion was better, but he said it hurt more." Ben set the bag on the desk and pulled out Kendra's folder. "Kendra Moss is completely recovered. You can take a look at her, but she was running up the stairs today and did just fine with her exercises. I'm pretty sure she's faking any pain or weakness. I don't know why she wants to continue in therapy." He hoped he wasn't turning red. If he was right about her reason, he'd probably put an end to it today.

Tom frowned. "If she's running around campus in perfect health while we're billing for her care, we'll get in trouble. I'll give her a call. Go ahead and continue her therapy for now until I can see her and sign off on her treatment." He tapped another folder. "So, about the Rood girl. I think she's more trouble than it's worth to us. I have a feeling the mother's just out for drugs and a lawsuit against the office building where Venetia stuck her hand in the elevator."

"Stuck her hand—you think she did it on purpose?" Could a teenage girl really do that? She might have been seriously injured.

"Oh, yeah. I think the two of them planned it together. Or the mother planned it and talked the girl into doing it."

"That's sick! Why didn't she just stick her own hand in there?"

"Because she gets more sympathy, and probably more money, if it happens to a child." Tom's sounded cynical. "At any rate, we're going to steer clear of it. I called the doctor and told him what happened. He wasn't happy, but he didn't seem real surprised, either. I just asked him to find a different therapy office."

"Do you think we should notify someone? The police or child protective services or someone?" The idea of a mother persuading a daughter to let herself be hurt for money was disturbing. Ben's stomach twisted. He wasn't a perfect dad, but he'd protect his children from accidents—not arrange them.

"No, we can't prove anything. It's not our business." Tom took Kendra's file and pushed Venetia's toward Lauren. "File that one. No charge."

She nodded. "Mothers like that should have their children taken away. There are plenty of good people waiting to adopt."

"It's too late for Venetia," said Tom. "You have to get them out when they're babies."

Ben walked into his office, their callous comments resounding in his ears. He couldn't imagine Shari or Linda—or even Rhonda—doing that to a child. Neglecting or abusing in anger was bad enough, but setting up an injury in cold blood. . . what a sick world it was.

CHAPTER 24

No one was in a hurry to leave. Jonah leaned against the back of a pew, watching the children run laps around the sides of the sanctuary and listening to the old men talk about the weather. The gentle, sing-song Finnish accent, with its V-shaped W's and blunted dipthongs, reminded him that some of these men were first-generation immigrants who found work in the copper mines or logging. Both industries were dead now, and the men bemoaned the lack of jobs. Hard jobs, and dangerous, but jobs. Their sons had moved south to Milwaukee, Chicago or beyond.

Jonah had a son in Chicago, too. And grandchildren. The oldest one was about seven. Jonah scanned the room, looking for a boy who might be that age, to help him imagine his grandson. It was a boy, right? The exhaustion and pain of the accident—and the related pain relievers, followed by Ben's revelations, left Jonah's recollections of the weekend a little fuzzy.

"You tired of telling everyone what happened?" Martin Lang, the pastor of their small congregation, pulled a chair toward him. "Sit down before you fall over."

"If I sit down, you have to help me up again." Jonah transferred to the chair without waiting for a response. "You'd be surprised how much we depend on our knees to help us stand up."

"No problem. Did Katie give you a ride today?"

"No, Katie took her mother Chicago to see a specialist."
Jonah grinned. "Took her mother *to* Chicago. I've been hanging
out with these guys too long. I'm starting to talk like a Yooper,
hey?"

Martin chuckled. "Not much. So, how'd you get here?"

"The Nordenski boy—not the oldest, but the next one—
did a senior citizen run. He collected Ed and then me, and he's
going to take us home again whenever Ed's done socializing."

"If Katie's out of town, who's staying with Ed?"

"No one. He says he can manage three days on his own.
He was doing pretty well when he spent the night at my place
two weeks ago."

"So, Jonah, what did happen?

He'd been expecting the abrupt shift but still hadn't
decided what to say. He'd never had a real pastor before. The
story of slipping, getting caught in a coyote trap and throwing
rocks at cars had entertained his audiences, but he might be
able to tell Martin the whole story—even the part about the
fifteen-year-old girl dying in childbirth—and get some
guidance.

"It was a long weekend. A long story. I'm stuck at home
for at least another two weeks, so maybe you could come out
for coffee one day."

"That would be great. How about tomorrow?"
Tomorrow? Might as well get it over with. "Tomorrow works.
Come for lunch. We can have macaroni and cheese or bologna
sandwiches on white bread or even Spaghetti-os. I haven't
opened those yet."

Eggs. Jonah held onto the counter top as he pulled out
the frying pan and set it on the stove, conscious of a desire to
slam it down in a tantrum. After he'd finished the cereal, he'd

eaten oatmeal for breakfast. The cinnamon and brown sugar was his favorite, but it took all six of the little packages to fill him up, so it hadn't lasted long. He drew the line at eating pop tarts for breakfast; they made good midmorning snacks. Eggs were certainly healthier. He'd make a stack of white bread toast with grape jelly to go with them.

Martin was coming today. Jonah had changed his mind at least six times about confiding in him. He'd rehearsed a few versions of the story, spinning them to a more acceptable scenario, but he couldn't get past the worst part. Shari's age—fifteen years old—had stuck in his throat. He tried to say it aloud.

"She was fifteen years old." The words sickened him. His subconscious offered excuses: "I didn't know at the time. She looked older. She lied to me." He'd probably never even asked her age. His memories were like snapshots instead of video. A girl with brown hair. Lots of brown hair. She wore short shorts and loose tops that slid off one shoulder, as did most other girls at that time. A yellow dress for prom, and a corsage to match. She liked him to drive fast and play loud music, and when he wasn't driving, they were in the back seat, parked someplace quiet. They hadn't talked much. It wasn't even a real relationship. Not only had he gotten a fifteen-year-old girl pregnant, he could barely remember her. If not for Ben, he would never have thought of her again. It was shameful.

"Oh, God, forgive me." He'd been repeating that prayer for the past two weeks. Yes, he needed to tell Martin.

Jonah sat down to work on a series of pen and ink winter scenes. Very stark, like having a cup of strong black coffee after a rich dessert. He needed to cleanse his palate after the cute little bunny rabbits. He drew dark strokes on the gray-white paper, shading with fine hatching. Every line mattered. You couldn't erase ink. If he made mistakes, he was stuck with them. He could throw the drawing away, or he could try to incorporate the errors into it.

He tried to extract a spiritual parallel. He didn't want to throw away a relationship with Ben. He couldn't undo the past. He hadn't engaged in any kind of sexual immorality since his salvation. Jonah set down the pen. He needed to stop the voices in his head.

He picked one of the CD's from the bottom shelf. Toby Mac's lyrics were better than the ones he remembered all too well, but the hyper-rhythmic chant and persistent beat were straight from high school. The girls had liked the sappy, emotional songs, but he and his friends rattled their car windows with Vanilla Ice.

The aggressive music drove energy into his drawing. Half an hour later, he stepped back to look at his winterscape. It was an honest drawing of a brutal winter. No bunny rabbits or soft mounds of snow. A winter to be afraid of. Was this what the Proverbs 31 woman didn't fear because her household was clothed in scarlet? Something like that. He liked winter, but he had a warm house with modern conveniences and a truck to take him into town for supplies and companionship.

The truck. It had been nearly two weeks since that cheerfully sadistic doctor had strapped him into this brace. If it wasn't so bulky, he'd have been driving a week ago. Unfortunately, the truck was in the garage. The detached garage. He was gaining confidence with the crutches, but he was old enough to have a sensible fear of falling. Jacob Nordenski had pulled his dad's SUV up to the door and shoveled the step. The slick surface had alarmed Jonah then, and it had snowed again since then. He was stuck, at least for a while yet.

What was Ben doing today? He'd revealed little about his current life except that he had four children, was a physical therapist's assistant and was in school to get certified as a full physical therapist. That must be a Monday through Friday day shift job. If he came back, it would be on the weekend. If he came back.

Jonah hobbled into the kitchen and considered lunch options. Martin might like macaroni and cheese. He probably hadn't had it since he was a kid. Jonah could slice hot dogs into it for extra protein. There might be some Twinkies left for dessert.

CHAPTER 25

Benjie charged through the crowd and into the minivan. He squirreled up into his booster seat and buckled the belt, talking all the while.

"My picture won a ribbon in the art show. See?"

Teresa glanced back to see a purple rosette ribbon swinging by its strings from his fingers.

"That's wonderful, Benjie! I didn't know you were in an art show."

"The art teacher hung everything up in the big library and everyone voted, and I got a ribbon because mine was the best!"

"In the school library?"

"No, the big one where you take the little kids." His voice was patronizing. "For story hour. We walked over there today."

"I did see that exhibit, but I didn't realize you had a picture in it."

"Yep. Can I have a granola bar? It's a picture of a cat."

"Well, I'm sorry I missed it. Where is it now?"

"Oh, it's still there. They just let us take the ribbons home."

Teresa abandoned the afternoon's schedule. "Let's go see it now."

Benjie talked all the way there and as they parked and

entered the library, explaining that the whole school had participated, and his teacher had sent a note home but he forgot it. It was probably in his desk. He'd remember next time. And it was over now, anyhow.

The picture was outstanding. Teresa dropped Annie's hand but caught her before she escaped. She picked the girl up and pointed.

"Annie, look at Benjie's picture."

"Patches!" Annie squealed and lunged toward the picture.

"You can look but not touch it."

Teresa's automatic response deflated the girl. If she couldn't touch it, it wasn't worth looking at.

Teresa couldn't stop looking at it. Why hadn't she seen his ability before? It was far above anything she might have expected from a seven-year-old. He'd used brown, orange and yellow oil pastels to create a calico cat similar to his grandparents' cat, Patches. His classmates had used a variety of media, including oil pastels, but his stood out as if he were ten years older than the rest of them. In lieu of the ribbons, little cards had been attached to the prize winners. Benjie hadn't just won the 1st grade prize; he had taken first place for the entire elementary school.

"Benjie, I wish you had told us! Your dad and your grandparents will be so proud of you!"

"I'm going to get a frame for my picture and a box of art supplies." He wasn't quite insouciant enough to conceal his excitement.

"That's wonderful!" He'd always been good at the art projects they had done together at home, but apparently having a real art teacher had made a significant difference in his skills. She hugged him.

"Can I hold your ribbon?" Jack stroked the gold lettering and purple satin and then handed it back respectfully. "I hope

I get to do art in school next year."

"You get to do kindergarten art. I will be doing second grade art." The conversation showed signs of deterioration, so Teresa herded them back out to the van.

"We'll have a special cake tomorrow night, to celebrate. I hope the pictures stay there long enough for your dad and grandparents to go see them."

"I get to bring it home when it has a frame."

"But it's nice to see it hanging there." She wanted them to see the contrast between his work and the rest of the children's. "You can call Grandma when we get home."

Knowing Eliza and Benjamin, they'd drop whatever they were doing right now and make the twenty-mile trip to see it. Maybe they could take Benjie with them. She would suggest it. Ben could take him tomorrow.

This was not a shining nanny moment. Teresa drummed her fingers on the steering wheel. She should have known about the event; there couldn't have been just one misplaced paper. She'd have a word with the teacher tomorrow.

"Where's Benjie?" Ben pried Annie's arms from his neck. "Daddy can't breathe, sweetheart."

"I hope you don't mind, but your parents took him out to dinner. You were at school, so we didn't call." Mrs. Cooper took Annie and buckled her into the booster seat. "I'll have dinner on the table as soon as you're ready."

"They just took Benjie?" Ben headed toward the bathroom. "It's not his birthday, is it?" The flash of panic subsided. Benjie was born in November. After graduation and before Christmas. He wasn't good at remembering dates, but he knew that one.

"No, but it's a special occasion. He wants to surprise you."

Intriguing. Mrs. Cooper wasn't given to cryptic comments.

"Can you give me a hint?"

Jack opened his mouth and Mrs. Cooper shook her finger at him. "No hints! This is Benjie's surprise. Sit down and wait for your daddy."

It wasn't easy to prevent the secret from spilling.

"How's the obstacle course?"

The boys looked at him without comprehension.

Mrs. Cooper cleared her throat. "The Warrior Way. You boys tell your daddy what you did today. I'll see you in the morning."

Was she blushing? Ben stared after her. No, of course not. He turned back to his family. The table looked unbalanced without Benjie.

"Patches," said Annie. She stabbed a piece of chicken with her little fork and stuck it in her mouth.

"Annie!" Her brothers shouted in unison. Jack continued, "You ruined the surprise!"

"The cat?" Now he was really curious. They weren't getting a cat, were they? "No, don't say anything else. Tell me about your Warrior Way. Did you use the slide today?"

"There it is!"

Ben winced at his son's exuberant shout, but no irritated librarians appeared to hiss at them. Libraries must have changed since he was a boy. Taking no chances and hoping to set a good example, he lowered his voice to a whisper.

"Where?"

"Right there!" Benjie pointed straight ahead. "The cat. That's my picture."

Dumbfounded, Ben walked toward the display. It was Patches. The picture was on a separate easel in front of the display panels, and it was amazing. He looked at Benjie.

"You did this?"

"Yes! I won first place for the whole school!"

"That's awesome, buddy!" He raised his hand for a high five, making the boy jump for it. "It looks exactly like Patches. Is that painted?"

Ben stared at the picture, letting Benjie's lecture on the process of working with oil pastels wash over him. Another major parenting fail. He hadn't even known Benjie was interested in art. It was like seeing your son play major league baseball and realizing you'd never played catch with him. Would he ever get this right?

"Well, let's get you some of those and some good pencils and paints, too. It's important to have the right tools for the job."

"I'm getting a lot of art supplies for winning the contest, and Mrs. Cooper said we can get frames from the store."

"Maybe you can make me a picture for my office." Not that he could hang it up there. "Or one for the living room at home."

"Can we have some ice cream? Mrs. Cooper made a cake."

"Absolutely. You can't eat cake without ice cream."

Benjie chattered as they walked toward the exit. "My art teacher said artists can do a lot of jobs. See that metal thing? An artist made that."

Ben regarded the twisted sculpture. It was artistic, all right.

"And do pictures in books, too," said Benjie. "And even that design for the library. It's a logo." He pronounced it as two words. "But I want to be an art teacher, so I can show other kids how to be artists."

Artists. Ben let go of his son's hand. "I'll be right back." He strode to the display and snapped a picture with his phone.

Jonah would like to see this.

Jonah checked his email. Again. He refused to think of it as an obsession. It was normal, when you were expecting something, to keep watching for it. Martin would turn that idea into a sermon, he thought, with the obvious parallels. He'd become quite spiritual lately.

But this time, it was there. Not just an email, but also the little paperclip icon indicating an attachment.

The message was brief:

Hi Jonah.

I thought you'd like to see the picture my son Benjie made. It took first place for the whole school, and he's only in 1st grade. It's a picture of my parents' cat. Ben

Elated, Jonah clicked on the attachment. It was a cat. The boy had used oil pastels for the fur, with pencil for whiskers and to detail the eyes. It showed great talent. He beamed at the computer monitor. Benjie was obviously a gifted child. Maybe he could use some books and good quality art supplies. Of course, that would mean asking Ben for a mailing address, and that seemed a little invasive at this point.

After he'd printed the picture, pinned it up and grinned at it for a while, he responded to Ben:

Thanks! That's a great picture. He's very talented. Thank you for sharing it with me. I appreciate it. Jonah

He hoped the redundant gratitude fell short of needy. He didn't want to scare Ben away. He wanted a relationship. He wanted pictures. Not photographs of pictures of cats, but real pictures of the children. It felt too stalker-ish to come right out and ask for them, but if he kept the lines of communication open, maybe Ben would think of it on his own.

He had a name now—Benjie. And Benjie was seven. Jonah was pretty sure there were two other boys and a girl. He'd gotten the impression that the girl was the youngest. She must be at least two years old, since Ben's wife had been gone that long. Jonah hoped she hadn't died in childbirth. How could a man bear that? And then learning about his biological mother. . . poor Ben.

It had all happened so suddenly, so long ago. Jonah wanted to be angry, but there was no one left to blame for depriving him of his only child. No one but himself. Shari was dead. Fifteen! It still made him sick. If he'd known, things would have been different. Or maybe not. He didn't know much about statutory rape. Whether or not he went to jail, she might have died anyhow. And when the baby was born, he would have gone into foster care until Jonah got out of jail. Then what? Could Jonah have taken care of him? At least this way, Ben had been raised by decent people.

Jonah looked at the cat and imagined the boy working on it, diligently blending colors, intent on drawing perfect lines. That cat wouldn't exist if things hadn't happened as they did. But here it was. . . pinned to Jonah's drawing board. The magnitude of God's gift shook him. He had to accept the mercy and be grateful for this new connection. He had to trust that this was all part of some convoluted, perfect plan. Jonah wanted the relationship. He wanted this family. He'd do whatever it took, however long it took, and try to wait for God to work it out.

CHAPTER 26

Eliza tied the ribbons under Annie's chin.

Annie pulled them free.

"Oh, sweetie." Her grandmother picked up the hat. "Look at this pretty hat! See? The blue flowers match the ones on your pretty Easter dress. And your shiny white shoes, too!"

The girl's face darkened and Eliza backpedaled. Annie had wanted to wear the Chucks that matched her daddy's.

"Let's look in the mirror. You can see how pretty you are in the hat!" She coaxed Annie to the bedroom door. "See? And we tie a pretty bow here."

"Whoa! Look at that pretty baby girl!"

Annie spun around to jump at her daddy, but her attention was caught by his shoes. Eliza followed her gaze.

"Benjamin Harris Taylor!"

"Chucks!" Annie sat on the floor and tried to tug off her shoes.

Ben lifted her up and turned to face the mirror. "Don't we look nice, Annie? Your shoes and hat match your dress!"

"Chucks."

Ben cast a guilty glance downward.

"They're new," he said. "And black. And I'm wearing a suit!"

Eliza smiled at her son's hopeful tone. She wanted him to be an independent adult, but these flashes of boyish charm were endearing.

"What's wrong with your dress shoes?"

"I forgot them at home. I thought these would be okay, but all you see is the white part, even if the rest of it's black."

"Chucks." Annie squirmed, and he let her slide to the floor.

"No, baby girl. You look pretty in those shoes."

"And the hat," said his mother. "The hat matches the dress."

"Don't you like the hat, Annie Banannie?"

Eliza sighed at Annie's vehement response. "How about a bow? Should we look and see if we can find a bow you like better than the hat?" For some reason, the girl liked the oversized flowers and bows on headbands.

"Bow," agreed Annie, "and eat."

Ben laughed. "You just ate!"

"I'll get you a cheese stick after you have a bow on," said Eliza. "Will you please check on the boys, Ben?" The request slipped out before she thought it through. They were his children, not hers. "Make sure they're ready so we can leave in ten minutes."

"We'll be ready." Ben flipped his necktie through a four-in-hand. "I told them to get their suits on and head downstairs. I'll tie their ties just before we walk out the door." He leaned closer to the mirror to examine his teeth. "They're probably already down there."

Eliza looked at him. Told the boys to get their suits on and head downstairs? They were probably still in their pajamas.

"Ben, go see if the boys have their suits on. I'll take care of Annie. We leave in ten minutes."

Teresa didn't tug on her skirt. It was normal to wear a

nice dress at Easter. No big deal. If she acted natural, no one would think anything of it. She should have practiced walking on the heels, though; she'd been wearing tennis shoes and sensible flats for the last ten years. But the dress needed heels.

"You look so pretty, Mrs. Cooper!"

Teresa smiled down—way down—at Amalie Bricker. The girl's braids were embellished with hundreds of beads in Easter egg colors to match her flowered dress and pink shoes. "So do you! I like your hair like that."

Amalie heaved a dramatic sigh. "It took six episodes of *Little House on the Prairie* to get it done."

"You enjoyed it," said Magda, "and you ate junk food the whole time you sat there."

"It was worth it," said Teresa. "I wish I could do something like that with my hair."

"I like your hair down," the girl said. "It looks reddish."

"It is pretty like that," said Magda. "You should wear it down more often. And that dress is perfect for you."

"It's really short," said Amalie. "My daddy wouldn't let me wear a dress that short."

"It would be cute with leggings," another girl contributed. "It's perfectly modest otherwise."

"Teresa! I almost didn't recognize you!"

Couldn't the woman have waited until she was closer so she didn't have to call out like that? Teresa produced a smile. It hurt her face. This was ridiculous.

"Myra! Happy Resurrection Day! I love your Easter bonnet."

The pastor's wife always wore a hat. This one was white, with a pouf of pink tulle that matched the woman's flowered dress. She wasn't easy to distract.

"That dress makes you look ten years younger!" She reached out and fingered Teresa's hair. "Have you ever thought about putting some highlights in your hair? Maybe having some long layers cut?"

"I don't know. . . " Teresa said. "It's a lot easier to pull it back."

"Nonsense," said Myra. "LaVonne, look at her hair. You could put some layers in it, couldn't you? And maybe highlights?"

The hairdresser walked around to see the back of Teresa's head. "I think so." She patted Teresa's cheek. "I can make it look perfectly natural."

She was drawing a crowd. Where was Lila Rose? She'd put a stop to it.

"Miss Lila Rose! Look at Mrs. Cooper's dress. Isn't it pretty?" Amalie touched the hem.

Why was everyone touching her today?

"It looked longer on the hanger," she muttered.

"Look at you!" said Lila Rose. "Pretty as a speckled pup."

Teresa burst out laughing. "A what?"

The girls regarded the elderly woman with disfavor. "She's not a dog," said Amalie. "She looks beautiful."

"She could even get a boyfriend in that dress."

"Hush, Sarah," said the girl's mother. "That's rude."

"She's not that old," Sarah insisted. "What about Mr. Cooke?"

All eyes swiveled toward the greeter. He noticed, nodded, and smiled pleasantly.

The girls waved. Teresa ducked behind Myra.

"Stop it," she hissed. "I'm perfectly happy as I am."

"You're a nanny," said Amalie. "Wouldn't you rather have your own kids?"

"She doesn't look like a nanny today," said Sarah.

"Yes, she does. I saw a TV show where the nanny wore short skirts and high heels. She really liked her boss. Hey!" the girl interrupted herself. "You could marry your boss. How old is he? On this show—" Amalie stopped short and glanced up at her mother. "I saw it at Grandma's house!"

"I think I need to have a word with Grandma. But you know you aren't supposed to watch that kind of show."

Teresa took advantage of the budding argument to slide away. She'd listen to the sermon online later.

Families everywhere. Large families. Large homeschooling families in matching Easter finery. Just a month ago, Jonah had thought his church would be the only family he ever had. Now he had one of his own. It probably didn't look much like this group, with even the youngest boys in suits and all of the girls in dresses, but that was okay. They could wear jeans and t-shirts to church if they wanted to.

"Don't you girls look pretty!" Jonah smiled at Emma Schenstrom and her daughters. She must be his own age, but she looked young enough to be a sister instead of the mother. "Thank you, Mr. Campbell." She looked down and asked the age-old parental question: "What do you say?"

He waited for the various expressions of gratitude and then said solemnly, "You are welcome. Happy Resurrection Day!"

"Oh!" One of the little girls jumped up and said formally, "He is risen!"

An unexpected pain checked Jonah's reply. The girl and her sisters were starting to look embarrassed when he finally responded.

"He is risen indeed!"

Cindy had loved saying that. She'd loved everything about Easter, fairly bubbling with excitement in those worship services. He is risen indeed. They were in a different church every year, but Cindy's joy was the same everywhere.

"I remember your wife saying that with our kids. She

must have spent twenty minutes with them. Even the littlest ones." Emma smiled at the girl who had spoken to Jonah. "That would have been you, Mary. You were only about three years old, and you wanted to say it over and over."

"She loved that." He was relieved to hear his voice was steady. "I'd forgotten we were here for Easter. We mostly came in the summer and fall. Easter was her favorite holiday."

"She brought Easter eggs to church for everyone." said the oldest girl. Phoebe. That was her name.

"I remember that. We must have dyed ten dozen eggs." Pleasure came with the memory. He'd suggested Peeps. Instead, they'd stayed up until after midnight coloring Easter eggs.

The irrepressible Mary looked up at him. "Mommy says she was a hero."

A hero. His Cindy. Because she had died?

"And she's in heaven now," the girl continued, "so you'll have to wait a long time to see her again."

"Mary!" Emma was turning pink.

"It's okay." He leaned on the cane he'd borrowed from Ed. "I do miss her, especially at Easter time. She liked everything about Easter, even the silly stuff like Easter bunnies. She used to make me a big Easter basket and hide it for me to find on Easter morning."

"I got an Easter basket!" the comment came from the smallest one.

"Did it have candy in it?" The chocolate on her blue-flowered dress was a clue.

"Yes."

"Well, Mrs. Campbell didn't like much sugar. She said it wasn't good for me. She put things like beef jerky, nuts, socks, and movie tickets in my baskets."

"You got socks in your Easter basket?"

"I liked them."

"Did you make a basket for her?"

"I did. I usually gave her some jewelry or perfume."

"Didn't she like beef jerky?" asked Phoebe.

Jonah chuckled. "She usually ate mine. And we went to the movies together. But she didn't wear my socks."

CHAPTER 27

Ben stopped at the foot of the stairs, his cheerful greeting fading away. What had she done to her hair? It looked like a frizzy bush.

"Look at Mrs. Cooper's hair, Daddy!" Jack pointed at the nanny's head, in case his father had missed it. So much for tact.

"You did something different." That seemed like a safe comment.

"Time for a change." She set the eggs on the table with a slight thump. "Annie already ate all her bacon, so she doesn't get any more."

The little girl wiggled in her booster seat. "Eat, Daddy!"

"Good morning to you, too, Annie Banannie. I hope you left me some bacon."

"Bacon!"

He glanced down to locate the source of a persistent squeak. "You got new shoes, too." Where had she found those? They didn't even look like women's shoes. Bulky black tennis shoes, worn over white ankle socks. Bare calves peeked out between the socks and the hem of a limp skirt.

"And her skirt has cats on it!" Jack's enthusiastic endorsement of Mrs. Cooper's fashion statement drew Mark's attention.

"Can we get a cat, Daddy?"

"No." He couldn't take his eyes off of the nanny. She

wore a beige blouse under a gray sweatshirt. Maybe he wasn't paying her enough to buy decent clothes, or maybe she just didn't have any kind of fashion sense. He'd have to talk to his mother and see if she'd be willing to give Mrs. Cooper some tips. She could even give her some of her old clothes instead of donating them to the thrift shop.

Teresa stumbled up the basement steps. Her new shoes had all the flexibility of wooden clogs. She'd overreacted. What was the matter with her? She'd decided it was okay to dress like a normal woman again, at least occasionally, but as soon as people commented on it, she freaked out and went shopping for ugly shoes and cat skirts. And her hair. . . the pin curls had done more damage than the last dye job. Maybe she should run over to Wal-Mart and get the split ends trimmed up before she colored it again. She sure wasn't going to LaVonne.

The phone rang. If Annie and Mark woke up, she'd cry. With more force that was strictly necessary, Teresa pushed the basement door shut, dropped the basket on the floor and clomped down the hallway.

"Taylor Residence."

"Is this Mrs. Taylor?"

"No, it is not. Who's calling, please?"

"This is Bill down at Acme Auto. Is Ben Taylor available?"

"No, he's not. Can I take a message?"

"Yeah, good news. I have a check for him. We made a mistake on his bill, and he has a refund coming."

"Well, that's nice news. Can you mail it?"

"I'd rather not. I'd like him to sign a receipt, acknowledging that all of the work has been completed and he received the overage."

"All right. I'll let him know."

She held her breath and listened for a minute after hanging up the phone. No noise from upstairs. As Teresa headed back toward the laundry basket, she caught sight of herself in the hallway mirror. The frizzy hair startled her; she'd become accustomed to the hairspray helmet and bobby pins at her temples.

She sighed and turned away. Looks weren't everything. Her life was good. She no longer lived in fear, was comfortable and safe, and Leo—thanks to the mercy of God—occupied a nice grave somewhere. She'd moved on. The plan had worked—now how did she undo it? Maybe this *was* the real Teresa now. She'd successfully transformed herself into a fifty-year-old frump.

No. Four more years. She'd stick it out until Annie started first grade. Ben would be a full-blown physical therapist by then, making good money and working a regular schedule. He wouldn't need her anymore, and she'd be free to do something else. Something new; she had nothing to return to.

Ben entered the clinic and stopped in front of the reception desk. "You know what today is, Lauren?"

"Your birthday?"

"Nope. Even better," said Ben.

"I can't imagine!"

"Today—all this week and next—is spring break. Kendra Moss has gone home to see her family or to Fort Lauderdale or to some other place that is not Chicago!" He pumped a fist in victory.

Annie would have shouted "score!" Lauren just sighed.

"Tell me about it. My sister has the kids this week, and she expects me to spend all my time groveling and being grateful."

"Ouch. Sorry about that. I wasn't thinking." Remorse pricked him. He had a nanny for his kids, so the school schedule didn't affect his life much. Mrs. Cooper didn't expect much from him at all.

"No problem. Not your problem, anyhow. In the absence of Kendra, you have three new clients here and your usual Tuesday home visits, plus Mrs. Melkin since we didn't go there yesterday."

"That's a busy day. Who are the three new clients?"

"You've met Mrs. Montgomery, and according to Tom, the other two are easy. Something about the treadmill." She handed him the folders. "And measurements."

"Tom won't be there?"

"Nope, he went off to Atlantic City for a long weekend. Not with Kendra Moss, I'm sure."

"I don't think I'm supposed to do that," said Ben. He was definitely not supposed to do that.

"It doesn't sound like you're really doing anything. Watching them walk on the treadmill and measuring range of motion, right?"

Ben wavered. If that was really all it was, it should be okay. Tom should have talked to him, though. They could both get in trouble.

Ben hated talking on the phone while driving, even with the car's Bluetooth, but since rush hour traffic had come to a complete stop, he might as well answer it.

"Ben Taylor." He thought the greeting sounded professional.

"Good morning. This is Randall Griggs, from Lakeland Mutual Insurance Company. I'm calling to follow up after the accident. How are you feeling?"

"I'm fine." How odd. The accident had been a month

ago.

"Glad to hear that! Therapy's going well?"

"I'm not getting therapy."

"Oh." There was a pause. "Our records show that you've been receiving regular physical therapy at Great Lakes Therapy Services. The service provider is listed as Tom Potter."

Ben chuckled. "No, I'm not receiving therapy there. That's where I work. Tom Potter's my boss."

"Hmm. . . I wonder how that got mixed up. I'll review the record again and make sure it's up to date. Thanks and have a good day."

The man disconnected without waiting for a response but called back almost immediately.

"Hello?"

"This is Randall Griggs again. Sorry to bother you, but have you received physical therapy anywhere?"

"No."

The car ahead of Ben lurched forward as traffic started to move. A semi-truck on his left—what was he doing on the left?—signaled a lane change. Ben accelerated out of his way.

"I can't talk right now. I saw a doctor at a walk-in clinic right after the accident and that was all."

Ben stabbed the disconnect button on the steering wheel. He didn't like talking on the phone while he was driving.

CHAPTER 28

Talking over the vociferous objections of his sons, Ben scooped the Legos off the table and back into their box.

"These are Jack's birthday present. If he wants to share with you, that's fine. If he doesn't, you need to back off. Jack, if you don't want to share, it needs to be put away until you have time to play with them alone."

He sounded like Mrs. Cooper.

"I was helping him," said Benjie. "He doesn't know how to do it."

"I know how to do it!"

"I was helping, too," said Mark.

Jack pushed him. "You were not. You're a baby."

Mark pushed back. Annie walked between them and got knocked down. Mark fell on top of her. Ben dropped the box and lunged to rescue his daughter, but Mark let out a howl and shook her off, kicking at her when she hung on.

Ben plucked the boy away from his sister. "What are you doing? You're going to hurt her!" He reached for Annie. "Are you okay, baby girl?"

"Ben, I don't think Annie's hurt."

His mother was probably right. Annie looked spitting mad. Mark continued to wail. Ben turned back to him in exasperation. "Stop that. You boys should all go in time out."

The last two words came out automatically before he

understood what he was looking at. Dismayed, Ben dropped to his knees in front of his youngest son. The boy had a perfect dental imprint of tiny teeth on his right cheek.

"Annie!"

"Eat, Daddy."

He stared at her, horrified.

From the doorway, his mother broke into laughter. "I just told her. . . " She had to stop, uncontrollable laughter preventing speech for several seconds. "I just told her to come and tell you it's time for the cake and ice cream." She wiped away tears and started laughing again. "If you could have seen your face."

Benjamin wiped off the sticky table while his wife took care of their sticky grandchildren. Their son leaned on the kitchen cabinet, using a rubber spatula to scrape the remaining ice cream from the bucket. He set it on the counter when his mother handed Annie to him.

"She's all clean."

"Thanks." Ben rubbed noses with his daughter.

"Will you please put that in the garbage?"

"Oh, yeah," said her son. "Sorry."

He complied with her request and set Annie on the floor. "You go watch Robin Hood with your brothers. And no biting!"

Benjamin sat down at the table and gestured to the opposite chair. Ben sat. Eliza shook out the dishrag and followed Annie into the living room.

"The caller identified himself as Randy Griggs," said Benjamin, "but you don't remember the name of the insurance company?"

"Well, I thought it might be an April Fool's joke. I mean, with a name like that, and it was April first."

"A prank call from the insurance company?" Benjamin sighed.

"I know, but I was in traffic and I didn't have time to talk."

"It doesn't make sense. This sounds like you had an ongoing personal injury claim."

"I didn't. Just the one doctor at the walk-in clinic."

"Right, and that might result in a radiology bill as well as the office visit. Two claims, both one-time events."

"Right!"

"The main damage incurred in the accident was to the car."

"Right!" Ben nodded several times. "And even that wasn't as big a deal as we thought it would be. The auto repair place overestimated it."

Benjamin eyed him. "Did you take care of that?"

"I don't know what to do about it. I haven't cashed the check."

"You let them give you a check?" asked Benjamin. "You need to call the insurance company and let them know about the refund. That's what the auto shop should have done, instead of giving it to you."

"I don't remember the name of the insurance company, but the number will be on my phone."

Benjamin tapped his fingers on the table. Auto repair claims might get mixed up, but the personal injury claims raised red flags.

"On second thought, don't call them yet. I want to see any paperwork you've received. Even though the other company was responsible for payment, the bills would have passed through your own health insurance first. Bring me copies of the explanations of benefits and anything else you have related to the accident."

"I'll try to find them," Ben said. "When the first few

arrived, I checked to make sure I wasn't being billed for the doctor visit. They all said I wasn't responsible for any part of it, so I ignored them."

"Did they list charges for physical therapy?"

"I don't know! I just looked at the bottom line. Those things are hard to understand."

"You do still have them, though?" asked Benjamin.

"I don't know. Probably. I put some in a folder, and I think there's a pile of them on my desk. Mrs. Cooper puts all the mail in there."

"Are there a lot of them?"

"Not too many," said his son. "Some. There's nothing to it! It was a minor accident!"

"They don't seem to think so. Your answers surprised this Griggs guy. Their next step will be to make other calls or send letters asking for verification. That's why it's so important to get the auto repair reimbursement taken care of."

"So, should I call them or not?"

"No. In fact, don't even answer their calls," said Benjamin. "If you do get trapped into talking to them, tell them you are consulting your own insurance agent and can't answer questions yet."

Ben stood up. "In other words, you don't want me to do anything."

"I want you to bring me every bit of information you have about the accident, including the original police report. Everything. If it's okay with you, I'm going to take it to Dick Harpin and see what he says. He's the head of the fraud and auditing division at Mariners Mutual. He'll be willing to start with the assumption that you're innocent. Dumb, but innocent."

"Fraud!" Ben sat down again. "What do you mean, fraud? I didn't even file any claims."

"Someone did," said Benjamin, "and we need to find out

who it was. Don't mention it to anyone. Especially your boss."

No matter how exasperating, his son's irresponsibility never failed to induce guilt and remorse in Benjamin Taylor. He'd enabled it—was still enabling it, and he planned to continue doing so for at least two more years. He didn't know what else to do.

He and Eliza had fully intended to push Ben out of the nest at the appropriate time. He'd been a bright boy, earning good grades at school, reasonably athletic, with good friends and a desire to be a doctor when he grew up. Then Anneliese Martin moved in next door. Sixteen-year-old Ben took one look at her and dropped everything else.

And the time for pushing Ben out of the nest never arrived. When he and Anneliese announced their pregnancy and wedding plans, Benjamin and Eliza said they would help out financially so Ben could take classes at the community college. Maybe, thought Benjamin, if they'd withheld their support at that point, Ben would have been forced into maturity, but they wanted him to get an education, and they didn't want to lose him.

If he'd gone away to college, they'd have paid for his tuition, room and board, health and auto insurance, and cell phone. They might even have provided him with a decent car. It was easy to justify continuing to support him while he was in community college, working and starting a family.

Ben and Anneliese assured them that it was a temporary situation. As soon as little Benjie was old enough, he could go to the college day care center and Anneliese would get a job. Instead, more babies came. Anneliese didn't cope well with Ben's long hours at work and school. Eliza helped with the children, but none of them could stop the inevitable. Anneliese's death was devastating, emotionally and financially. While Ben struggled with the loss, Benjamin bought a house in a new town, to give them a clean start, and Eliza hired Teresa Cooper to care for all of them.

They built Ben a new nest.

Kendra perched on the edge of the table as Ben packed to leave.

"Do you think I'll have to do this much longer?"

"I don't know. The regular therapist will come out in a week or two and evaluate your progress." Or not. So far, Tom had ignored all of Ben's reports and requests for a follow-up visit.

"Because I'm running late for my classes every Tuesday and Thursday. The professors were nice about it at first, but they're getting kind of snotty. We'll be having finals in a couple weeks, and I'm getting C's and D's in those two classes. If we're going to do this much longer, could we switch days, or do it at night?"

"You'll have to call the office and talk to them about scheduling." He showed her the telephone number on the folder that contained her exercise plan. "I just go where I'm told."

Martin Carmichael actually rolled his eyes when he opened the door and saw Ben. "Do we really have to go through this again?"

Ben blinked. "Only if you want to get well! Therapy can be painful, but you have to think long-term." He hoped he sounded professional as he trotted out the stock phrase, but he felt more annoyed than patient. Was there a full moon or what?

"Fine." Martin dug through a stack of unopened mail

and junk newspapers until he found his folder. "I'm ready."

He went through the routine and just grunted as Ben left.

His phone rang just as Ben sat down in his car, and his father started talking as soon as he answered. "Ben, did the doctor at that clinic give you a prescription for pain killers?"

"No. It was nothing." Ben didn't usually get impatient with his father, but this was getting ridiculous. "I didn't need anything. There was no pain whatsoever. Not even a stiff neck. I never even took an aspirin!"

"But, Ben, according to the insurance paperwork, you had a prescription for Oxycodone and even refilled it twice."

"I did not! I've never taken Oxycodone in my life!"

"Didn't you read any of this paperwork?"

Ben hadn't even opened most of the envelopes until he turned them over to his dad. "I just checked the bottom line," he admitted, "but I think I would have noticed that."

"You can usually figure out the codes if you read it carefully, and it always lists the service provider and date. You're in a medical field! You should know these things."

"Well, one visit can yield a lot of paperwork," Ben said. He resented being put on the defensive. "When Jack had his tonsils out, we had bills from the regular doctor, the surgeon, the hospital, the anesthesiologist, and the radiology place. Oh, and the lab, too."

"You said you just saw one doctor and left," his father said, "but the insurance company has also been paying for regular therapy at Great Lakes Therapy Services."

"Yeah, that's what the guy said when he called. I told him it was a mix-up—that Great Lakes was just my employer, and I wasn't getting therapy."

"Ben, this is bad! Dick Harpin looked through your

paperwork and did some checking. He wants you to meet with a team of fraud investigators."

"Why?" Ben leaned back and closed his eyes. He didn't have time for this.

"Because, according to Dick, all this paperwork indicates that you're committing insurance fraud."

"Me?" Ben sat up, voice squeaking on the word.

"Yes. I told him about the car repair bill. He says that's a common form of soft fraud. The garage sends a bill to the insurance company for a certain amount, the insurance company pays it, and the garage gives you a kickback. You get your car fixed, the garage makes a profit, and so do you. Sometimes, the garage doesn't even do the work, or they bill for new parts and use cheaper ones. The insurance company doesn't even know that one yet, of course."

Ben opened his mouth to argue, but his father rushed on.

"That's pretty minor at this point. The real problem is the drugs. The assumption will be that you're using them recreationally or selling them. Plus, they're paying your own company to provide therapy for you. There are some other bills, too, for x-rays and follow-up visits, that may implicate the doctor. Or—"

Ben broke in, aghast. "But none of that's true! I didn't even cash the garage's check. I didn't go back to the doctor or get medications at all!"

"According to Dick," his father said, "this looks like a classic case of hard fraud."

"What's hard fraud?"

"That's when an event is created specifically to collect insurance money. Soft fraud would be having a real accident and padding bills or making false statements on insurance applications. Like the car repair business. Allowing yourself to be rear-ended in order to collect insurance is the number one kind of hard fraud. And it can be a felony."

"I didn't do it, Dad. I swear I didn't do any of that."

"I know that." His father's voice was testy. "I wasn't accusing you. Someone is using that accident to make a lot of money, though. Dick says the fact that you have a doctor and your employer involved is interesting. You said you'd never been to this clinic before?"

"No, it was just convenient! The doctor was a total stranger."

"How about your boss? Do you think he'd be involved with something like this? Is there any way you can create bills and collect on them through his accounting system without him knowing about it?"

"I don't think so. I don't have access to financial matters. But Tom's very careful about insurance. He's mentioned fraud several times, and just a couple weeks ago, he turned down a potential client for that. He thinks she set up the accident to get pain pills and might even file a lawsuit for pain and suffering as well. He said she's too unstable." Ben took a deep breath to stop the babbling. "He had a fit a while ago because I told him I'd been working on some of the paperwork at home and then emailing it to myself at work. He said we had to be careful because of the insurance."

"Dick wants you to meet with the investigation team soon. He suggested Saturday morning, and I told him they could come to our house. Your mom can watch the kids."

In other words, his dad would be sitting in on the meeting. Probably a good idea.

"Okay, I don't see how I can help, but I'll meet with them."

"Good." His dad was clearly relieved. "You need to get on the right side of this problem, Ben. Dick seemed awfully excited."

CHAPTER 29

"Hello, Ben. Nice to meet you. I've known your dad longer than you have! I believe he gave me a cigar the day they brought you home."

Ben shook the man's hand. "I understand he passed them out for months."

"He was pretty happy. Everyone got cigars, from the boy in the mail room to the cleaning lady. She sold hers to me for a dollar." Dick Harpin's blue eyes, under a thatch of steel-gray hair, narrowed with laughter. "After I moved to Mariner's Mutual, your dad and I lost touch. We can't let that happen again."

Dick slapped his old friend on the back and drew them both closer to the group standing by the dining room table. "Let me introduce you to everyone. This is Marcus Franks from the Illinois Licensing and Registrations Board. He's the go-to person for suspected insurance fraud in Illinois. There's another person who deals specifically with Medicare and Medicaid issues, and we can get him if we need him." They shook hands, and Dick moved on to the next member of the team. "Pete Collins is a state prosecutor from the Attorney General's office. He's responsible for determining whether or not there's a prosecutable case. And this is Mary Reid. She's a representative from the National Insurance Oversight Commission, an officially-recognized non-governmental agency that coordinates efforts to stop insurance fraud."

The woman smiled as she shook Ben's hand. "Sounds impressive, doesn't it? Thanks for meeting us." She had the darkest skin Ben had ever seen, and wide open black eyes. Her olive green blouse looked expensive, and she was tall enough to look good in the wide-leg black slacks she wore. The three men looked like insurance agents.

Dick motioned them to sit down and distributed thick folders to everyone before launching into speech.

"I read the papers your dad brought to me, Ben, and did a little research to cross-reference the service providers. I would expect to find them listed in other insurance claims, because that's the nature of their business—they get paid by insurance, either health or liability. What I was looking for was a pattern, and there *is* a pattern, because they're networked professionals."

Ben tried to look intelligent. Were his eyes glazing over?

Dick went on. "You see a certain doctor, and he recommends a certain therapist, chiropractor, or other treatment. Sometimes it's a personal injury lawyer who recommends specific doctors." His mouth twisted in distaste. "So, you're going to have the same people showing up, associated like that, in any number of claims. But since insurance companies are individual entities, their databases and other records aren't linked. Those service providers could be spreading claims out over a variety of insurance companies. And if one insurance company is investigating a service provider for potential fraud, none of the others would know about it, so they couldn't contribute helpful information. That's what Mary works on. Her group is trying to connect the companies so they can share information about fraud, but they're a trade organization and not a law enforcement agency."

Pete Collins interrupted the monolog. "The problem is,

medical records are legally protected as confidential. They can be released under certain circumstances, but not shared. That means that a person's doctor can bill that person's insurance company with details of the care received, but that insurance company can't tell other insurance companies about it or share vague suspicions with law enforcement agencies. Marcus, here, is the person who you would report to if you suspect insurance fraud, but that's generally done by individuals."

Apparently, Pete liked to lecture, too. Ben nodded as if he was paying attention.

"Some fraud is committed by individuals, often in collusion with service providers. Look at your car repair bill. The shop gave you an estimate of $2400, and that's what the insurance company paid them. But maybe the repair didn't really cost that much in parts and labor, especially if the shop owner did the work instead of paying someone else. He could have bought used parts, or maybe he didn't fix things at all."

His dad had already explained all that. "Okay. But I don't understand why they gave me a check. I wasn't in collusion with them."

Dick leaned forward and spoke with satisfaction. "That's why we're here today, Ben. If you'd been working together, he might have given you cash for your share of the profit. In this case, he gave you a check, which could be traced. They want a record of your involvement. Proof that you profited from the transaction." The insurance man sounded quite pleased.

"*Who* wants a record? Why? Are you saying someone's trying to frame me for insurance fraud?"

"Someone *did* frame you for insurance fraud." The irritated comment came from his father, of course.

Ben flared up, angry to be treated like a child in front of other people. "Well, how was I supposed to know that?"

Dick Harpin jumped in. "Right. The auto repair shop

could have committed fraud and you'd never have known anything about it. Health care service providers don't always need the participation of the insured, either. Most people don't understand their explanations of benefits if they bother to read them at all."

Ben hadn't bothered to read them, of course. "It was just nothing! No injury. I didn't have any reason to suspect something was wrong." Except that the explanations of benefits had kept coming. He should have opened them.

"If you know how to read them there's a series of claims that tells the story." Dick pointed at line items on the paper in front of him. "The first one is from Dr. Cravitz—an urgent care visit with charges for two x-rays. That same day, you had a prescription for Oxycodone filled at a local pharmacy. Two more claims for the same drug and dosage. Then another office visit and more x-rays. That day, you picked up a heavier dose of Oxycodone from the same pharmacy. You refilled it. That's when the bills from Great Lakes Therapy Services started coming in. After a few weeks of service there, you had another office visit and got another prescription at the original dosage. You filled it that day at a chain pharmacy. Then there are more bills for physical therapy."

"But I never picked up any drugs! They can't prove I did!" Ben's head hurt. How could this be happening?

"The pharmacy could be another involved service provider, but I'm inclined to think that they were picked up in your name."

"Why?" The question came from his dad. Ben would have asked "who?"

"Because this isn't about money. Their objective is to implicate you as the crook. Aside from the profit on the car, you had the meds. You had eighty-four pills in the first prescription. Twenty milligram pills. You refilled that twice. Then you had eighty-four of a stronger dose and refilled it once. Then you had forty-two of the lower dose again." He glanced at his notes. "That's four hundred and sixty-one pills, two different doses. At a conservative estimate of forty dollars each, you could have sold them on the street for over eighteen thousand dollars. Tax free."

Ben sprang up, pushing his chair into the hutch behind him. "I did NOT do that!"

"We really don't think you did, Ben. That's why we are talking to you." Mary's voice was soothing. "We're hoping you can help us track down the people responsible. We need an insider."

"I don't know anything, and I don't have a way to know anything. I'm just an assistant. I don't have anything to do with billing or insurance."

"Sit down, Ben." His father sounded resigned. "No one is accusing you of anything."

Ben pulled the chair forward and sat down but kept both hands flat on the table, tension stinging his muscles. "I don't understand any of this."

"What would your boss say if insurance investigators asked him about your therapy sessions?" Marcus Franks's gravelly voice cut into the strained moment.

"I don't know." He'd never particularly liked Tom Potter, but he had no reason to distrust him.

His father answered for him. Again. "Potter would claim that Ben was embezzling. And he would have a way for that to be plausible."

Dick reclaimed the conversation. "Let's back up and talk about automobiles. It used to be a quick way to make a little money or pay off a car loan that's become a problem. The con artist sets himself up to get rear-ended. In your case, the idea is that you stomped on your brakes unexpectedly, and the woman behind you couldn't stop in time. Rear-ending someone is always your fault. Anyhow, if you were an individual, instead of part of a ring, you would get a check for repairing the damage or the value of the totaled car. End of story."

"But we think we're looking at something bigger," said Mary. "We think—"

The intense atmosphere was shattered by a squealing pink fluff ball that hurtled into the dining room and flung itself at Ben's legs.

"Whoa, Annie!"

Jack and Mark raced into the room and grabbed their sister. Ben separated them and lifted Annie to his lap. "What's going on?"

"She 'scaped! We had her tied to a chair with Grandma's apron, but she got away and then she climbed over the gate." Jack grasped Annie's hand. "We'll take her back in the kitchen."

Annie bared her teeth at him, and Jack let go. Ben pretended he hadn't noticed.

"Where's your grandma?"

"She's in the bathroom."

Ben's mother hastened into the dining room as he asked the question. "I'm sorry, Ben. I thought they'd be okay for just one minute, with the gates up. Come on, kids." Annie reached up, but her grandmother set her on the floor. "You'll have to walk, sweetie. You're getting too heavy for Grandma to carry."

Before they were out of the room, Benjie stomped in. "Where is everyone? The cookies are done. I took them out."

"You took them out of the oven?" Ben stood up and strode to the kitchen. Sure enough, there was a pan of cookies on the stove top. The oven door was closed. "Did you use potholders?"

"I used the mittens."

"Good boy. Never do that again. Take things out of the oven, I mean."

"They were done. The timer went off."

Ben turned around to see his mother shepherding the other three children back into the kitchen. She bent to re-lock the gate and straightened with a hand to her back and a sigh. When she saw Ben, she smiled brightly. "You'd better get back in there, dear. We'll be fine. I think we'll put a movie on pretty soon."

An awkward silence hung in the dining room. Dick Harpin's enthusiasm had disappeared, and Pete Collins had stacked up his paperwork and rested his folded hands on top of it, as if ready to leave.

"I didn't know you have a family, Ben," said Dick. "Your dad tells me your wife passed away a couple years ago. My condolences."

"Thanks." He tried to soften the curt response. "Where were we?"

No one answered. Before Annie's entrance, they'd all been engrossed in the discussion, hopeful of progress in their investigation. No one looked hopeful now.

Pete Collins looked especially grim. "The thing is, Ben, we had another guy in a similar situation about a year ago—he was an RN at a private urgent care clinic like Cravitz's. He came to us with suspicions that the clinic was involved with insurance fraud, and he agreed to collect evidence for us. We hadn't gotten very far when he called me at the office and said he quit. He said he wouldn't put his wife and children in danger. We don't know what kind of danger, or what made him feel threatened, but he packed up and moved across the country within the month. A few days after they left, their house here burned down. Further back, there was a pharmacist who committed suicide. We were pretty sure he had help. We'd had a man watching him, and we got a doctor to write some prescriptions for him to fill. We were just trying to see how good he counted and how fussy he was about who picked up the prescriptions."

"In other words, you want me to put my family in danger."

"No, we don't." Collins was adamant. "Forget it."

"How can I forget it? They've already set me up for insurance fraud. I can't just quit my job and walk away."

"Actually, yes, you could." His father hadn't known about this part.

"Well," Martin Franks said apologetically, "they might be a bit nervous about letting him go. Right now, they think they have a leash on him. They don't know he's talking to us, so they'll expect him to be afraid of exposure or prosecution. They might offer him a piece of the action. But if that doesn't work, they'll be worried he might turn them in to save himself. And," he continued, "they might realize they made a mistake in his case. They connected several of the principals in this puzzle. He could take down a lot of people—the Kirson Center Clinic, the Acme garage, possibly the pharmacist, and Potter and Great Lakes Therapy Services. And the woman who rear-ended him, although she's probably low-level."

"I'm not convinced they are the principals," put in Mary. "I think it's much bigger than you think it is. My associates and I believe that we're looking at a highly sophisticated organized crime ring. It's beyond Illinois."

"Tom doesn't even know I have a family. He could find out pretty easily, though, and I'm not willing to let this gang terrorize me or burn down my house." said Ben with asperity. "Why do they want me, anyhow? They could just pretend to have provided services like they did for me. Why bother paying me to actually do the therapy?"

"Insurance companies look a little more closely at ongoing treatment than they do short-term office visits and tests," said Dick. "Clinics like yours have to be able to prove they have the qualified staff and actually make visits and have reports on file. Assistants and technicians are relatively cheap. You don't even have to be in on the fraud. You're just a paid employee. For some reason, though, they thought it was worth framing you. Were you asking a lot of questions?"

"I don't think so. Look, I'd like to get safely out of this. I didn't know what was going on and I don't want to get involved."

There was quiet at the table. Ben's father finally spoke up. "He can't do this. I didn't know it would be dangerous. I thought you just wanted him to take notes on what was going on there."

"We do have a sort of safe house program, but it's not really set up for children." Pete Collins tilted his head to the side and considered Ben. "Are you sure Potter doesn't know you have a family? You've been there a few months now. It would be hard to avoid that coming up in conversation. Even if you just mentioned it to a client, it could get back to him."

"And he could find out at any time. Is there someone who can take care of the children for a while?" asked Dick. "Relatives in another state?"

"No. There's not." Ben was getting angry.

"Your mother and I will take care of them." His father sounded pugnacious.

"Not here," Dick cut in. "If they are in danger—and I don't say they are—they won't be any safer here than at Ben's own house."

"We'll take them somewhere. Disney World. The Grand Canyon. Paris."

"That might work." Franks acted as if the matter was settled.

"No, it's not going to work," said Ben. "With all due respect, Dad, four children is a lot of work for you and Mom. They'd run you ragged on a vacation like that."

"Nonsense. We'd do just fine. They'd love it."

"I'd feel more comfortable if the children were gone," said Dick Harpin.

"I don't care if you're comfortable or not. And even if the kids had fun, they're still too much work for the two of you. Great kids, but there are four of them under the age of eight, and Annie isn't completely potty-trained yet. You'd need help."

Matching expressions of hope dawned on their countenances. It was his dad who spoke triumphantly. "We don't have to do it alone. We'll take their nanny with us!"

CHAPTER 30

"Good morning, Ben." Lauren stood up behind her desk to hand him a stack of folders. "Three new clients today. Tom wants to talk to you about them before they get here."

"Is he in his office?"

"He's around here somewhere," she said.

Ben stepped into his own office to drop his bag and then returned. "Hey! I like your hair like that. That scarf thing matches your shirt."

She looked up, as if she might be able to see it, and then leaned close to him and whispered. "I cut it out of one of my work shirts."

"That would explain it," said Ben.

"My four-year-old wanted me to braid her hair, but I didn't have time to do it this weekend. So, we got matching headwraps instead.

"Does she look like you?" Ben hadn't realized how hard it was to listen to someone talk about their children without mentioning your own.

Lauren picked up her phone and showed him the lock screen. It was a posed picture of her and the children. Everyone was smiling.

"Cute." Panic flickered in him. He needed to delete all the pictures off his phone. Now.

"Are you people having fun?" Tom stood behind Ben,

loud and irritated.

Ben didn't feel like backing down. It wasn't quite 8:00, so they weren't visiting on company time. Lauren had retreated, however, so he held up the folders.

"New clients?"

"Three of them. Come to my office and I'll fill you in." Tom closed the door behind them. "Have a seat."

Ben sat.

"The first two new clients are brothers. They were rear-ended by a semi."

"Ow!" Ben cringed.

"They have similar injuries to the cervical vertebrae. I'll introduce you and get you started, but it's pretty standard treatment."

"What about the other one?"

"Jerry's only eight. He fell wrong on the neighbor's trampoline. Bent up his neck and back. We'll probably work with a chiropractor."

"Eight? I've never worked with a child that age before."

Except for Benjie, of course, and Ben had to remember he was supposed to be a childless bachelor. "Isn't pediatric physical therapy a specialized field?"

"Usually. His mother was a client a few years ago, and she asked us to do the therapy."

"The neighbors have insurance on their trampoline?"

"It's a good thing they do. Jerry's mom will probably sue them for every penny she can get." Tom leaned back in his chair and took a sip of coffee. "We just want our bills paid."

"So, all three of these new people are neck injuries," said Ben. "We seem to have a lot of that here. More injury than geriatric or medical."

"We're picking up more post-operative clients. Hip and knee replacements. That sort of thing," Tom said. "But treating accident victims is a more reliably profitable line because it's paid for by someone else's insurance. Easy to bill and recover. When you bill private pay or people's own health insurance, they tend to delay or avoid payment."

Well, that was frank.

He saw the brothers in consecutive sessions. They were middle aged men with standard injuries and standard treatment plans. Ben's head was so full of insurance fraud that he saw it everywhere.

When the second brother arrived, Ben pulled up his record on the computer. The x-ray looked a lot like the first one — typical of a neck injury incurred in a car accident of the type described.

He ran his fingers up the vertebrae, mentally counting and naming them. When he got to the top, he continued up the back of the head. "Ouch. That's quite a bump you've got there."

"Yeah. But that's not from the accident. I got hit in the head with a baseball bat when I was a kid. It actually cracked the skull."

Ben scrutinized the x-ray. Last semester had been heavy on spinal study. He wasn't an expert, but as far as he could tell, the image revealed no skull fracture or damage at all. The only visible fault was a compression of the cervical vertebrae. He looked and felt again, but the man was starting to fidget. Ben closed out the x-ray image and returned to the treatment plan. It felt as if he had chills running up and down his own spine.

He wasn't actually supposed to report to his father, but he had to tell someone immediately. "Those weren't his x-rays," Ben hissed into his phone. "I think they were copies of the ones in his brother's chart."

"Hang up, Ben. We're just leaving for vacation, remember?"

Affronted, Ben hung up. He'd felt rather dashing, going

outside to make the call to his father. The walls had ears and all that. He knew they were leaving on vacation. He'd waved goodbye to his entire family just this morning.

Jerry wasn't an innocent little child. Ben had trouble believing this foul-mouthed kid, dressed in expensive jeans and a gray t-shirt featuring a heavy metal rock band, was only a year older than Benjie. The boy ignored his mother, who bleated encouragement and praise at him, and followed Ben's directions with an arrogant boredom that Mrs. Cooper would never tolerate in his own sons. She'd make short work of this brat.

"That's really good, Mrs. Piper. Much better than last week." He held the elderly woman's arm as she pivoted to transfer back into her wheelchair. He wished all of his patients took their therapy so seriously. Ben admired her determination to be mobile and independent as long as possible. Her broken hip had been pinned, not replaced, and at her age, healing could be a slow and painful process. She worked harder than any of their other clients, diligently following the care plan Tom had prepared for her.

Ben bent over to unlock her wheels. Before he could straighten up, she put her hands on both sides of his face and pulled him down so she could look into his eyes. "I am going to get back on my feet."

He swallowed a lump in his throat. "I don't doubt it for a minute."

Another dark and stormy night. Ben rolled along with

the traffic. On all sides, headlights and taillights glared in the rain and reflected off wet glass. He hated driving in this weather, especially after dark, but Kendra had persuaded Tom to change her appointments to five o'clock. When Ben objected, Tom pointed out that he let him leave "early" three days a week, so Ben let it drop. He wasn't in a hurry to get home to an empty house, anyhow.

His parents, the kids, and Mrs. Cooper left for Florida on Tuesday. He missed them already. A temporary diet of convenience foods—the kind he'd purchased for Jonah—wouldn't hurt him, but the house was a mess and he couldn't find any clean socks. He couldn't even find many dirty ones.

Ben signaled the turn onto his street and waited for an opening in traffic. Between work, school, and home, the Corolla was getting a workout. Fraud or not, Acme Auto had done a good job restoring alignment to the rear end.

Why would people participate in these schemes, with such risk of serious personal injury? Money? Drugs? Ms. Rood's insistence that Venetia needed more pain pills took on a new significance after Dick Harpin's math lecture. And she would probably sue for pain and suffering. If a "victim" received ongoing therapy and medical care, it would lend credibility to their claims. Was Kendra doing that? She wasn't in it for the therapy. It would explain Martin Carmichael's attitude. Mrs. Piper and Mrs. Melkin, with their recent surgeries, had to be genuine patients.

Was he becoming paranoid? Ben hoped his acting skills were up to the job. He must be doing okay so far; Tom continued to load his days with new clients and tightly-scheduled appointments. Some seemed to be legitimate clients, and some fit the increasingly obvious pattern of fraud. He liked the home visits best. They got him out of the clinic, away from Tom's watchful eyes.

Ben parked the car in the garage and pulled up the collar

of his coat before sprinting through the rain to the back door of his house. He shouldn't grumble about the miserably cold spring in Chicago; the Upper Peninsula probably still had snow.

He needed to email Jonah tonight, to give him the new, clean email address.

Hi Jonah.

I hope you're staying warm up there. It's cold and wet here, but at least we don't have snow. My parents, Mrs. Cooper and the kids have gone to Disney World for a week or two, leaving me alone here. How are you feeling? Is the doctor letting you drive yet? Sorry I haven't been in touch. Work is a little stressful right now. Ben

The response came about an hour later:

Hello Ben.

Yes, we still have some snow here. Florida sounds great. I just got cleared to drive again. It's nice to not be dependent on other people for everything. I'm sorry your work is stressful. It's meaningful work, and that always brings pressure as well as reward. Will it ease up soon? Jonah

Before he stopped to think about it, Ben typed back:

It doesn't feel like meaningful work right now. It's difficult and I can't talk about it. That's part of the reason I've sent everyone away. I am hoping to get it all cleared up and bring them home soon. It's kind of lonely here. Ben

He hit the send button and then re-read the email. He winced. Much too dramatic. Jonah's reply arrived ten minutes later.

Dear Ben,

To be having trouble at work and loneliness at home must be very difficult. I don't understand why the children are gone, but I trust you have made that decision carefully, so you can be encouraged that they are having a good time down south, safe in the care of your parents and their nanny. I hope you are able to use this time effectively and accomplish your goals. Jonah

Another email arrived almost immediately.

Ben, I don't know the names and ages of your children, except for Benjie who is 7. Would you mind telling me about them? Jonah

Ben didn't know how to respond to the first email. The second was easier.

Sorry—I didn't realize you didn't know. Jack just turned 6, Mark is four and a half, and Annie is two. They're quite a handful. I couldn't have sent them with my parents without Mrs. Cooper. She's a bit younger than they are, and she does a good job with the kids. They obey her better than me or their grandparents. I don't know how she does it. Ben

He added a postscript with his telephone number "in case of emergency".

Thanks, Ben! Those are great names. Nice, traditional, manly names. Being named "Jonah" was a great trial to me in my childhood. I made everyone call me Joe, forcibly if necessary, but now I like Jonah. Is Annie "Anneliese" like your wife? That's a pretty name. Jonah

And he'd added his phone number.

Ten days. Eight days of arriving at the office and trying to act natural. Ben took a deep breath, pushed open the door, and walked inside as if he owned the place.

"There you are, Ben." Tom spoke as if he'd been waiting

for hours.

Ben cast a reflexive glance at the clock behind the desk. He was five minutes early.

"Here I am. What's up?"

"I want you to learn how to operate the accounting software."

Ben experienced a rush of affection and gratitude toward his father. The man was a genius.

"I'm not very good at accounting," he said.

"It's good software. Very simple," said Tom. "Lauren says you don't have any appointments until nine. This won't take more than half an hour. We can do it in your office."

Tom waited, his eyes on Ben's, until Ben acquiesced. "Okay. Now?"

"It works for me." And he was the boss.

Ben led the way into his office. "Have a seat."

Tom took the chair behind the desk. Ben pulled a client chair around so he could see the computer.

"I can walk you through it now, and you can explore it more later, until you're comfortable with it," said Tom. "You need to know how to do this, in case someone wants to make a payment and no one else is around, or if someone has balance inquiries, or if they want an invoice or receipt. I really should have shown you before, but we've been so busy."

He rolled the chair aside to give Ben access the computer. "Click on that icon."

Ben's stomach cramped. That icon hadn't been there yesterday. He clicked. He tried to focus as Tom walked him through the simple accounting program. The fraud squad would probably love this, but the ache in Ben's stomach grew worse.

"There's a help button up there, and the manual's on your bookshelf."

Sure enough. . . there it sat, where it hadn't been

yesterday.

"Great. I think I've got it." Ben forced a smile and willed Tom to leave.

His attempt at mind control failed. Tom leaned over to show him a log in button. "I set up an administrative user ID for you a few weeks ago, but that's only used for secure financial information. You don't actually have to sign in that way."

A man may smile and smile and still be a villain. Of course, Tom smiled. He was the villain and not the innocent dupe. Ben didn't remember a lot of the Shakespeare he'd read in high school, but Tom's pleasantly bland expression brought that bit to mind. Thank God, he was already on the side of the angels.

Hi Jonah. Yes, I am missing the kids, as well as home-cooked meals and clean laundry. I hadn't realized how much Mrs. Cooper does around here. Anneliese wasn't much of a housekeeper, but we were a lot younger then and didn't know any better. I guess I've gotten used to having an orderly home. Take care of yourself. Ben

After he hit the send button, Ben realized he hadn't felt the usual surge of emotion that accompanied thoughts of Anneliese. Was that good or bad?

Dear Ben,

I'm sure it's quiet there. I picked up the habit of being neat in the army, and there's only one of me, so it's not hard now. Cindy and I never had children. We were both busy with our military careers. She was an army veterinarian, and I worked with computer graphics. She was killed in Afghanistan, while delivering a pack of working dogs. I retired and moved here two years later.

So far, I've kept busy with different projects, so I haven't been too lonely. Maybe when things settle down there, you'd like to bring the children up here for a visit. It's very nice in summer. I only have a canoe, but we could rent a boat and take the children fishing. You wouldn't have to explain our relationship to them. No pressure, though. Just keep it in mind. Jonah

Jonah's wife had been killed in Afghanistan! His. . . his step-mother had been killed in Afghanistan. In military action. Ben pressed both hands against his face—against the tears. How unlike Anneliese. He shut down the bitterness and opened a reply window.

Dear Jonah, I am very sorry for the loss of your wife. That must have been

Ben stopped. He wouldn't imagine what it would be like to lose a wife like that. Not like that. And not alone. A new awareness of his importance in Jonah's life rocked him. Ben had never been alone. When Anneliese died, he still had parents and children and even a few aunts, uncles, and cousins. Then he'd gained a nanny/housekeeper who kept his daily life running more smoothly than it ever had before. Jonah had just been alone.

And now Jonah knew he wasn't really alone. He had a son and grandchildren. Could Ben, in good conscience, keep a distance from him? It wasn't Jonah's fault that Shari died and their baby was put up for adoption. Ben remembered Jonah's cry that he had a right to know he had a son. Did he have a right to know his grandchildren?

Ben had embarked on the search for his biological family thinking only of himself. He'd never considered how it would affect those family members; he wanted to connect on his own terms. But family came with responsibility.

He backspaced and started over.

Dear Jonah,
I am sorry about your wife. That must have been terrible for
you. I think the kids would love to visit the Upper Peninsula and go
fishing, even in a canoe. I think it would be best if they just call you
Grandpa Campbell right from the start. Ben

And now he needed to call and check on Linda.

CHAPTER 31

Teresa ignored the stares and rude comments; Annie was perfectly happy in her sparkly purple harness. She could move around freely within a certain radius, without having to reach up to hold an adult's hand all the time. Teresa only wished she could keep all of them on leashes. Benjamin and Eliza were drooping, and the boys, like young wolves, were quick to sense weakness and take advantage of it.

"Time to head back to the hotel!" She spoke abruptly, surprising the grandparents as well as her charges.

"But, Mrs. Cooper, we want to see the pirates."

"You can see them tomorrow." Since she had all of their attention, she continued. "This is a very fun place, and it was nice of your grandparents to bring you here. But when you whine and beg and run away when you are supposed to stay close to us, or when you don't obey us, it isn't fun for us anymore. At that point, we go back to the hotel. Tomorrow, let's see if you can keep it fun for all of us, all day."

Eliza looked apprehensive. Her husband snorted. Teresa hoped they had the sense to keep quiet. Drawing on dwindling reserves of patience, she remained calm and pleasant with the children, encouraging them to talk about their favorite experiences of the day while they waited for the monorail. If any of them started whining or objecting to the abrupt end to their day, she might lose it. She'd wanted to see the pirates, too.

Annie and Mark fell asleep while she was running their bath water, so she left them grubby and bathed the other two instead. Benjie and Jack took longer to succumb to sleep, whispering and poking until she separated them so Jack slept with Annie and Benjie with Mark.

After a quick shower of her own, she joined the Taylors in the sitting room of their suite.

"I wasn't sure you two would still be awake."

"We were feeling guilty about leaving you to take care of all the kids. This is supposed to be fun for you, too." Benjamin held up a tumbler. "I'm having a drink. Do you want one?"

"No, thanks. I am having fun! This place is fantastic. I really appreciate you including me in your vacation."

"My dear," said Eliza, "we couldn't do it without you."

Teresa agreed with her. It was a working vacation, but she'd never been to Disney World before, and she was having a wonderful time. Benjamin and Eliza had fond memories of family vacations at Disney World, but they only had one child. They'd been in their late forties when they adopted Ben, and their last trip had been twelve years ago. This time, in their seventies, they were trying to manage four highly energetic and overexcited children. They needed her.

"It's too bad Ben couldn't have come," said Teresa. "I bet he would have liked it."

"Oh, yes, we used to bring him here." Eliza gave a nervous laugh. "It was certainly easier with just three of us."

"Eliza, you mustn't let them run over you." Teresa spoke as gently as she could. "They will have just as much fun if you make them follow the rules and obey you."

"I suppose so." Eliza leaned toward her confidentially, "I have to admit, I'm finding it a little stressful."

A *little* stressful? The woman looked like she was ten

minutes from a heart attack. Teresa helped the older couple get settled in their room before heading back to her own bed. She propped herself up on the pillows and sent a note to Ben on his new email account. As usual, she shared the day's events but not the boys' behavior or his parents' exhaustion.

Why hadn't they just waited until Ben could join them, or at least until the school year was over? Part of this trip would overlap with Benjie's spring break, but he'd still miss at least one week of school. It was odd. The idea for the Disney trip had come up suddenly, and the Taylors wanted to leave immediately. Ben had seemed willing. . . no, glad to have them go. He'd practically shoved them out the door as soon as his parents arrived, loaded up the minivan and waved them off as if they were leaving for a year. Very odd.

She closed up the laptop computer and fell asleep almost immediately. She was tired, too.

Didn't they have round trip tickets? Teresa couldn't pin Benjamin or Eliza down to an itinerary. She'd never known them to be spontaneous people, but now, whenever she broached the subject of leaving, one of them came up with another must-do activity. After ten days of lavish entertainment, even the boys were ready to go home.

"I can't thank you enough for bringing me with you. It's been so much fun. We must have seen every tourist attraction in this part of Florida!"

"We should take the children out to Sanibel Island. I don't think they've ever seen the ocean before, and the beach is famous for shell-collecting."

Teresa stared at the elderly woman. The boys would drown. Seriously. What was the matter with Eliza?

"It's been a wonderful vacation, but I think we're all ready to sleep in our own beds again." she said gently.

To her consternation, Eliza burst into tears. "Oh, Teresa, I would love to sleep in my own bed!"

Teresa sat down and pulled her close for a hug. "Then let's go home."

"Not yet," said Benjamin from the doorway. "We need to stay down here a little longer. Ben's working on a special project, and we promised him we'd keep the children out of the way."

"Ben asked you to keep the children out of the way?" He'd been responding to all of Teresa's email updates without any such indication.

"Yes." The old man spoke staunchly. "Sanibel Island sounds like a good idea."

"It's a lousy idea!" Teresa said. "Can you imagine trying to control Benjie, Jack and Mark on a long stretch of beach like that? Not to mention Annie, who will take off running the minute you take her out of her stroller."

"Then where?" Eliza sounded hopeful.

"Home! I've always kept the children out of the way so Ben could work or do his school."

Benjamin came into the room and sat down. "We can't go home yet."

Teresa bit her lip and waited, instead of shrieking at him, but the stubborn silence continued. "Fine." She stood up and walked past them. "I'll go pack and prepare the children for a trip to the beach."

"No." The quiet word came from Eliza. "Even if we can't go home, we have to go somewhere manageable."

"How about something closer to home?" She had to persuade them. "It doesn't have to be a vacation. We can stay at your house or even in a hotel if necessary. Benjie wants to go back to school."

"He can't do that."

"Are we talking Witness Protection here?" asked Teresa,

startled.

Benjamin fidgeted. "More like taking protective measures."

"Where's Ben?"

"He's at home. Going to work and school. But there's a situation at work, and he doesn't want the kids involved."

"It must be a pretty serious situation."

"It is."

"Wisconsin Dells!" Eliza sat up triumphantly. "The Craigmoors took their grandchildren there over Christmas. She said there are some very comfortable hotels there with indoor water parks and other attractions for children."

An indoor water park sounded infinitely better than a long stretch of ocean beach. Teresa was growing concerned about the Taylors. They looked tired. A nice hotel with an indoor water park would allow them to rest while she took the children swimming.

"I think that sounds good," she said. "We must have walked a hundred miles in the past week. I didn't know Disney World was so big. The boys will enjoy the water parks. They're more confined, too. I'll pick up some more books and maybe some educational games to play in the hotel room."

Benjamin looked vastly relieved. "I'll email Ben to double-check, but the Dells should be fine. We can fly back to Chicago tomorrow and take the van from there."

"Ask him if it's okay if we stop home and get different clothes. I didn't pack for winter. I can leave the kids with you and do it myself if he's worried about them."

"No, I'll give you a credit card and you can pick up new things for yourself and the kids when we get to Wisconsin. We're not supposed to go near the house or anywhere near him."

She checked on the children before pulling out her suitcase. Annie was awake in her portable crib, watching the cartoon through glassy eyes. Benjie was reading, and Mark and Jack had fallen asleep. Poor, exhausted kids.

When they were in their pajamas and tucked into bed, she leaned back on the couch and prayed instead of letting her mind wander. She wasn't frightened, but the situation was alarming. If she couldn't even go near the house for a brief visit, things must be more serious than Benjamin let on.

By the time they landed in Chicago, Teresa's "keep me sweet" prayer had become an endless litany. "I'm hanging on by my fingernails, God. Way past sweet. Please get us through this soon, or I'm going to say and do things I shouldn't."

The trip to Florida had been her first airport experience, and the Taylors were still fresh then. Now, they looked ghastly. Mark's ears hurt from the changes in air pressure, and his crying upset Annie.

"God, walk me through this." This was her job. She was the nanny. Right now, she needed to nanny all of them.

Teresa twisted around to talk to Benjamin in the row behind her. His eyes were shut. Eliza was gazing out the window, probably thinking about how close they were to home.

"Let's wait until everyone else is off the airplane before we get up. It'll be easier to keep track of the kids if there aren't so many other people around."

In a younger person, Benjamin's grunt might have been interpreted as "whatever". Eliza just nodded.

Teresa conscripted a flight attendant to help with the removal of their carry-on bags and car seats. The woman seemed more than willing to assist them with their exit. Mark's wails had made the last ten minutes of the flight hideous for everyone.

Teresa took her time. They'd paid a lot of money for this

flight, and she wasn't going to be rushed. When she had all the children's backpacks buckled in place, she handed Annie's leash to Eliza.

"You go ahead. Mark, you hold Annie's hand and don't let go. Jack, you hold Mark's other hand. Do not let go. Benjie, you carry this bag and hold onto my jacket. Benjamin, you take these and go flag down a courtesy cart."

At the baggage claim area, she sat everyone but Benjamin on a bench.

"Don't get up."

Had they really brought this much luggage with them? Benjamin went in search of another porter, and Teresa walked out of the airport into cold crisp air. It tasted delicious. She ignored the noisome clouds of car and airplane exhaust — after a long day in airports and planes, even that was a relief.

And she was alone. How far was it to the long-term parking lot? After consulting a porter, she gave up the idea of a brisk walk and boarded the crowded shuttle bus. Holding onto the overhead railing for balance, she closed her eyes and pretended she was on her way home. Her snug little apartment would need to be aired out. She'd stripped the bed before she left, so she'd make it up with fresh linens and take a nice, long bath before wiggling down between the sheets. Tomorrow, she'd dust the furniture, make a pot of mint tea and settle at her spinning wheel with the wool roving she'd picked up in Orlando. Which audiobook should she listen to? There were so many.

"Hey, lady!" The words shocked her awake. A young man was gripping her arm. "Long flight?"

A few of the other passengers smiled sympathetically.

"With four children under the age of eight."

Her wry comment elicited laughter, and Teresa enjoyed the brief moment of adult interaction.

She caught a glimpse of herself in the rear-view mirror

as she started the van. Ugh.

"No disguise needed today." She already looked like a dumpy fifty.

"On the Road Again." The song was stuck in Teresa's head. The kids looked out the windows at the city lights. Benjamin and Eliza both sighed audibly as they passed the freeway exits that would have taken them home in fifteen minutes. The morose atmosphere was better than bickering, though. On the road, again, away from home.

Teresa started to wilt as she drove into the setting sun. Everyone else in the van had fallen asleep, and she was starting to be frightened of her own drowsiness when she spotted the resort.

It took nearly an hour to get settled into their suite, and Teresa was so tired she could have cried. She'd shower in the morning. Hopefully, the children would sleep late.

CHAPTER 32

"Tom, Dr. Henry Cravitz called. He said he couldn't reach you on your cell phone and needs to talk to you as soon as possible."

Tom patted his pockets. Where was it? "Thanks. I'll call him."

He sat down at his desk and looked at the phone. The fact that he still didn't have the doctor's cell phone number rankled.

"Henry! How are you?" His genial tone was just right. He wasn't going to apologize for not being reachable by cell phone.

"That boy—Ben Taylor—how's he doing?"

Okay. . . no friendly chit chat. Tom leaned back in his chair and contemplated the painting of palm trees on the opposite wall. "He's fine. Doing his job. He—"

"I called to tell you that I'm discontinuing his care. I got a letter from the insurance company about the pain pills. You know they're cracking down on opioids. We're going to have to reevaluate that situation."

"I was wondering about that."

"So, I'm signing off on his care," said Cravitz. "Have you received anything from the insurance company?"

"Payments. No inquiries. Do you think I should discharge him?"

"Might not hurt." Cravitz changed the subject. "Have you ever heard of a chiropractor named Hanks?"

"I don't think so. Why?"

"Kent mentioned him to me. Said he might be a good fit, but doctors don't often recommend chiros. It seems to me that it might be better coming from you."

"Who's Kent?"

"Oh—you didn't hear that."

Kent. He'd come back to it later. Knowledge was power. "Is Hanks a local guy?"

"He has a website, but it says his office is in Gurnee."

"Not many of my clients would drive to Gurnee for a chiropractor, and I'd prefer to keep a client with me than send him to someone else."

"Business is booming. It might be a good idea to get selective. Keep the clients you want and pass on the others to someone else," commented Cravitz. "So about this boy—Ben."

"What about him? He just does his work and goes home. He's asked about a couple clients, but that's what I would expect a PTA to do under normal circumstances. I set him up with the accounting software and showed him how to use it, but I don't quite understand how framing him is going to protect me—or you or anyone else. It'll drag us right into the investigation."

"So maybe he'll keep his mouth shut and not stir up trouble in the first place," said Cravitz with asperity. "That's the danger of involving someone innocent. It's better to just pay them. The accident was probably a mistake."

"Then why did you think we should do it? If there's an investigation, it's my clinic and I'll be sunk."

"No," said Cravitz. Exaggerated patience drawled out with the words. "You can look stupid and outraged. A trusted employee betrays his boss. Happens all the time. And if it hurts your business, so what? PT is a lucrative field. Start a new clinic in a new town. You'll be fine."

Tom pulled the phone away from his ear and stared at it. Really? "That's easy for you to say!"

"I've done it twice," said Cravitz. "It happens."

"So if he does start asking too many questions, I show him how he's committed fraud. What if he doesn't care? You said he was a Boy Scout."

"Maybe Ben will have an accident. I heard that happens sometimes."

"Another accident?" Tom drew his brows together.

"No, an accident. A real accident."

"What do you mean?" Tom heard the shrill in his voice and changed his question. "Do you think that's likely? I mean, he's not any trouble. He's fine."

"That's good so far. See that it stays that way. Seriously, Potter, the network is big. These guys aren't going to sit back and let one assistant therapist mess up their whole plan. So, tell me about the woman who answered the phone."

"Lauren? She's just a receptionist." Tom stopped. "She's been doing some of the billing, too, but just the Medicare and private pay. I do the rest."

"What about payments? Doesn't she see those?"

"I take care of those."

Cravitz's sigh was audible. "Is she going to be a problem?"

"Oh, no. She's the easy one. She's afraid of losing her job. A single mom with a bunch of kids and no daddy in sight. I hired her when no one else would. She has a record."

"What kind of record?" Cravitz's voice was sharp.

"Petty theft of some kind, years ago. She's not going anywhere."

"Do you think it would be best to just tell her the truth?"

"And pay her more?" Tom snapped.

"I would. Do the cost-benefit analysis." Cravitz was

disinterested. "Anyhow, I wanted to let you know about Ben Taylor. Give me a call if there's any trouble."

"Lauren!"

The woman materialized in his doorway. Her long, black skirt dragged on the floor, but she wore the Great Lakes polo shirt, which was all he'd written into the short employee handbook. The scarf tied above her smooth, dark forehead looked suspiciously like a uniform shirt, too. She raised her eyebrows in inquiry, not speaking.

"Come in and have a seat." Best to follow Cravitz's advice. He could pass the buck if it blew up.

She slid onto the edge of a client chair.

"You've been here a while now, haven't you?"

"Two years."

Tom was startled. "Really? I didn't realize it had been that long."

She nodded, and Tom resented her reserved composure. He couldn't replace her at this point. How irritating that she had that power.

"You're doing a fine job."

She didn't relax. He tried again. "You're a valued member of the Great Lakes team."

Her eyes widened at that. He groaned inwardly. He sounded like he'd just come back from a management seminar.

"It's time you move up."

Unexpectedly, her lips quirked. "There are only three of us. Where am I going?"

He should have thought this through ahead of time. "As you know, our billing is taking more and more time each week."

"That's for sure."

"And you've been doing great with it."

"Thanks." She still sounded cautious. Was it really so out of character for him to pay compliments and appreciate his employees?

"I'm going to give you a raise."

"Really?" Her face lit up in a brilliant smile. "That would be awesome! Thank you!"

So now what? Just jump in and tell her about the billing processes? Maybe she knew already. She wasn't stupid. He leaned forward, clasped his hands on the table and looked at her with sincerity.

"Lauren, I'm sure you've noticed that our business is growing rapidly. Even with Ben on board, we can barely keep up with the workload."

"Are you thinking of hiring another assistant?"

"No!" That was the last thing he wanted to do. This one was trouble enough. "I would like to see if we can streamline our process, though. Moving the billing to Friday was a great idea. It's been much easier."

"Thank you."

"The thing is, medical insurance billing is getting more complicated all the time. And, as you know, the insurance company's object is to avoid paying us."

She nodded.

"We need to streamline this process and make it work to our benefit. We shouldn't be put in the position of having to beg to be paid for the work we've already done."

"No!"

"So," said Tom, "we're going to change our billing policies. And I need you to spearhead the changes. It would mean a bump in pay, to go with the increased responsibilities. Do you think you could take it on?"

"I'd be happy to!" She beamed.

So easy to manipulate. Why hadn't he tried it before?

CHAPTER 33

"Magnusen looks good. He's got full range of motion in that shoulder now."

"He has eight sessions left," said Tom. "Just do the plan."

"But he looks fine!"

"Ben! Just keep doing the plan. I am the therapist, remember? I think he needs a course of twelve sessions, and his insurance will pay for that many."

Ben shrugged, "Okay. I noticed Molly Hearns isn't on my schedule this week. Is she out of insurance?"

Tom darted a suspicious look at him. "Her insurance company sent a letter requesting copies of her x-rays and treatment plan. It seemed wisest to sign off on her care."

"Miraculously healed." Ben hoped his voice sounded sarcastic instead of scared. This was supposed to be a turning point in his relationship with Tom, if he didn't mess it up.

The therapist slammed his hand on the desk. "What's that supposed to mean, Ben? Is there a problem here?"

"Now that you mention it. . . " Ben tried to keep air flowing normally through his speech, but his chest and throat were tight. "It seems to me that people's therapy treatment is based on their insurance company's willingness to pay."

Tom broke in. "It's a sad fact of life, Ben. You know that. We'd all love to run medical care as a charity project, but it's just not happening. This is a business. I have bills, one of which is your salary!"

Ben went on doggedly, "But some of the people with good insurance don't seem to have real injuries." It was out.

"What are you implying, Ben?"

Tom's measured, quiet statement was terrifying. Pete and Marcus told him it was okay to backpedal and seem nervous now. Good thing.

"Well, I feel like I'm treating people who haven't really been injured. If there really was an accident, they couldn't have been hurt very much, or they healed really fast. And even when I think they are healed, we keep treating them. I know I'm not the expert here, so maybe I'm just not reading the signs right."

"No, you aren't the expert." Tom tapped his pen on the desktop. "But you aren't stupid, Ben. Insurance companies control medical care these days."

"Maybe I'm hyper-sensitive to it because my dad was in insurance when I was growing up." They had told him to say that; if Tom didn't know already, he could easily find out. "He talked a lot about that kind of thing."

"What kind of thing?"

"You know. . . " Ben turned up his hand in a shrug. "People getting more than they should in insurance compensation. But all they're getting here is more therapy than they need."

Tom continued to watch him silently, and Ben made a meaningless excuse before leaving the office. He wasn't cut out to be a spy.

He couldn't decide if the conversation had gone well or not. At least insurance fraud had finally been mentioned, so they had a starting point.

Ben pulled the blue folder off the top of the stack in the

inbox. Mrs. Melkin. He read the question on Lauren's sticky note and started looking through the reports. The name of the service provider caught his attention. Had Tom been out to see her, too? Ben scrolled through his calendar. That was his visit. Why did it have Tom's name on it? He found the information Lauren needed and set the folder aside. He'd ask her about it later.

The cell phone—the new one—buzzed in his pocket. It was Mrs. Cooper's number, not his father's. He slid his finger across the screen to accept the call.

"Hello."

"Hello, Ben. I'm calling to let you know that your mom slipped and fell today. She's okay, but the paramedics think she may have broken her hip. Your dad's gone with her to the hospital. He told me that you should wait an hour or two to call, because he won't have any news until then."

His father must have given her a script.

"An accident?" A giant lump in his throat obstructed the words. He coughed. "It was an accident?"

"Yes, we were all there. It was one of those freak accidents. She was stepping off the curb, and a bird swooped down really close to us. She turned to look and fell hard. It was very painful, of course, and frightening for everyone."

Ben closed his eyes. Those poor kids. "I'll call you at lunchtime. Will you be okay until then?"

"Oh, yes. I'm staying pretty busy here at the hotel."

No doubt. "You're at the Riverview, right? Stay there." He heard her exhale. "Thanks for letting me know. I'll call you back."

Tom's shocked and supportive reaction surprised Ben. He must like old people better than kids.

"You go. Don't worry about anything here. It's going to take you almost four hours to get there, and then you'll need time to find out what's going on." Tom clapped Ben on the shoulder. "We won't expect you tomorrow, either. They'll need you there. They're pretty elderly, aren't they?"

"Yes, but they're very active," said Ben. "They just got back from Florida and decided to run up to the Dells for a few days."

"The Riverview is a good place."

A coppery taste filled Ben's mouth. He hadn't said anything about the hotel. Had Tom been eavesdropping?

Ben made it back to his car before he called Mrs. Cooper back.

"How's Mom?"

"I haven't heard anything yet. Your dad's still at the hospital with her. I doubt he'll leave her alone there. He'll call when he has some news, Ben."

"And you're okay with the kids?"

"Of course, I am. They're fine now, but it was upsetting when it happened. I'm keeping them in the hotel room until we have some word from your dad."

"So, what really happened?"

"Just what I told you. It's most likely a broken hip, and she's at the local hospital. I don't know the name of it, but I can't imagine that there's more than one hospital in this town."

"And it really was an accident?"

"Yes! I saw it!" The familiar nanny voice made Ben wince. "Ben, what is going on?"

He blew out a long breath. If his dad stayed at the hospital, someone else would have to watch out for the kids. Who better than their nanny? She could probably protect them better than anyone else—better than all the rest of them put together.

"There's something going on here at work—something illegal—and we think they might use the kids as leverage if they think I'm not cooperative. I'm so sorry you've been put in this position. I know we're asking a lot of you, but it's really important."

He waited through a moment of silence. She wouldn't abandon them in an emergency, but he didn't know how long the situation would last.

"Who is 'we'?"

Relieved, Ben said, "A group of insurance investigators—law enforcement people—including Dad. He knows all about it. Look—only use this phone number and the new Gmail address." He rushed on. Might as well get it all out. "Don't call the office or answer phone calls from anonymous numbers or the clinic. If you get a message that I've been hit by a car or am sick, ignore it. Call Dad."

"Ben!"

"Pack everything." Frightening scenarios played through his head. He'd wondered if all the precautions were overkill, but Tom's casual mention of the hotel's name sent red flags waving all around him. Even if Tom didn't know about the kids— Ben dropped his head onto the steering wheel. "Don't go near the hospital."

"Ben!"

"I'll find a safe place for them. Probably not Disney World again. Tell the kids I love them." He disconnected. Mrs. Cooper would probably quit as soon as the children were out of danger. If they were in danger.

After a rapid trip through Walmart for clean socks and underwear, Ben headed north. He jabbed the Bluetooth button repeatedly, panic rising with each unanswered call. He was halfway to the Dells before his father responded.

"Ben. Your mom is going to be fine. It turns out that the femur is broken, too, in addition to the hip. It was such a small step to do so much damage!"

Ben could barely hear his father's exhausted voice.

"And they've given her medications, so the leg shouldn't be so painful, but she just keeps crying that she wants to go home." His father sounded on the verge of tears, too.

Guilt and helplessness settled on Ben like a blanket, not assuaged by the knowledge that this particular incident wasn't his fault. At least not directly. But she wouldn't have been at that place at all if it weren't for him.

"Can she go home?"

"Not yet. They want a specialist to take a look at her. They're talking about pins and a nursing home for rehab."

"I'm going to send the kids somewhere else. Somehow, my boss found out that you were at the Riverview. I think I mentioned it when I talked to Mrs. Cooper the first time, and he could have overheard it. I'm sure I didn't say anything about the kids though; I was careful." He paused. "They can't go back to Disney World. What do you think about uncle Stan? He's got that big house out in Oshkosh with the tree house and swing set."

"He's still in Arizona. I can call him there." His father faded out and then came back stronger. "I have to go. The doctor's here."

Ben staggered under the children's assault. If they hadn't seen him first, he might not have found them. The humid, cavernous water park, noisy and crowded, swarmed with sleek, otter-like swimmers and frazzled adults.

Even Annie splashed in a shallow pool. Mrs. Cooper—not at all frazzled—lifted the girl out of the water.

"Walk, Annie."

Despite the hubbub, Ben was momentarily distracted by the sight of Mrs. Cooper before she pulled on a thick toweling robe. She looked good for a middle-aged woman. The fleeting thought vanished in the onslaught of the boys and Annie—

who had indeed walked most of the way. She threw herself against him when she got close enough, though, and he scooped her up before she slipped on the wet tiles.

The kids all talked at once, shouting to be heard over their siblings in the echoing structure. His wet work clothes made them laugh, and they wanted to squirm against him, to soak any fabric they might have missed.

"Hey, you guys! I didn't bring any other clothes, and it's cold outside!"

The boys found that hilarious, too.

Mrs. Cooper fished a keycard from her pocket. "You can get something from your dad's luggage. Bring it back when you're dressed, and I'll take the kids upstairs to shower and dress."

Somehow, her nanny voice restored Ben's calm and erased the anxiety of the past three weeks. He handed Annie to her and detached his sons.

"I'm going to see how Grandma's doing and then we'll all have dinner together! My treat." They laughed again, not understanding the joke but enjoying the tone of voice and his presence. He hugged each of them and told them to be good for Mrs. Cooper.

He hadn't expected the hospital to be so small and friendly. The staff knew his parents by name, and a tall, skinny man wearing a stethoscope around his neck escorted him to her room.

"Your mom's leg can be stabilized enough for an ambulance ride to Chicago, even as it is, but I'd rather go ahead and pin it and put a plate on the femur first." He stopped outside an open door. "She'll go through the surgery and recover better if you can get her calmed down first. She's very agitated, and your father is distressed because she's distressed."

"I'll see what I can do. When would you do the

surgery?"

"If she's ready, I can do it early tomorrow morning." He didn't enter the room with Ben but waved as he continued down the hall. "I'll be back later."

His mother was in a flat bed, weeping while her husband rubbed her hand and talked to her. Ben couldn't hear his father's words, but they were probably an attempt to reassure her about the kids.

He coughed to let them know he was in the room. "Hey! The doctor says you're being uncooperative."

His attempt at levity failed. Eliza let out a fresh wail of lament.

"Mom! Don't do that! How are you?" He stepped around Benjamin to drop a kiss on her forehead. "You stop that. Everything's under control. They're going to fix you up with some pins and plates and then you're going home."

"Well, she's going to have to spend some time rehabilitating," his father interposed. "She's not doing it here. She's going to a nice place close to home. You can visit her every day and annoy the nurses, and all of her friends will come by to play bridge and gossip."

His mother wasn't weeping anymore, but she looked like she didn't believe him, or as if he had foolishly forgotten something. "But, Ben, what about the children?"

"The mighty Mrs. Cooper, super nanny, has everything under control. She's taking them to your brother's, in Oshkosh. Stan's still in Arizona, but they'll be fine there."

Hope flickered in his mother's eyes and then winked out. "No, he's leased it to some foreign teachers until the end of the school year."

"Well, then, we'll go to plan B. Mrs. Cooper has some relatives near Baraboo. They have a farm with chickens and goats and baby lambs. The kids will love it." The lies tripped off his tongue with shocking ease. Lambs? Really?

His father regarded him with narrowed eyes. "That sounds great. And these people are willing to feed and house five extra people for an indefinite period of time?"

"Happy to do it."

"Good." He turned back to his wife. "Once again, the amazing Mrs. Cooper has everything under control. We're no longer needed here."

Eliza lay back and closed her eyes. "I'm so glad."

His dad jerked his head toward the door. Ben kissed his mother again and joined his father in the hallway.

"Um. . . speaking of feeding and housing, Dad. . . "

"I've given Teresa enough cash to get by for a week or two and a credit card for hotels. What's your plan?"

"It'll have to be another hotel," said Ben. "The kids are loving the water park. We could just do another one around here."

His father frowned. "Teresa's an amazing woman, but she can't take care of all four of them in a water park. We took turns, watching movies and playing games with two of them in the hotel room while she took the other two to the pool."

"Okay. Look, Dad, you take care of Mom, and I'll figure out what to do with the kids. I really appreciate the money. Thank you."

CHAPTER 34

Mrs. Cooper and the children were waiting in the hotel restaurant, dressed and hungry.

"I thought this was a family restaurant."

Ben looked up at the nanny's frosty comment in time to see their waitress whirl around and stalk toward the kitchen. Her pirate costume did seem a bit skimpy for the setting.

The children talked over each other, not noticing his preoccupation as they told him about airplanes, Disney and the water park. Each had noticed and preferred different parts of their trip, except for Annie, who wanted to sit in his lap and pat his cheek. He squeezed her and sniffed loudly at the enormous silk flower adorning her head.

"Annie, your flower smells so good. Is it a daisy?"

She pointed at the menu. "Eat, Daddy."

He laughed and squeezed her again. "Good idea."

What was he going to do with them? A tentative question revealed that Mrs. Cooper had no relatives in the area, with or without lambs. It would have to be another hotel, even if they were bored. He glanced at the nanny's face. She'd give notice as soon as this was over.

Forcibly collecting his wits, he gave the boys his full attention, responding appropriately, until Benjie broke in on Jack's description of the Monorail.

"They've got a river here, Dad, that goes all around the

water park. I got a canoe all to myself and I paddled around the whole thing three times! Can we get a canoe?"

Ben dropped his glass. A sheet of water arced across the table, and the kids squealed, drawing back into the seats. Mrs. Cooper waved a hand to command the hostess's assistance. Ben stared at Benjie.

As soon as he was alone, Ben pulled up his new email account and scrolled back until he found the email with Jonah's phone number.

"Answer, answer, answer," Ben muttered. The guy should be home at this time of night. "Come on, answer the phone."

He disconnected and punched the number in again. The phone rang a dozen times before Ben gave up. He composed a hurried email. Jonah always answered those quickly.

Dear Jonah. I need your help with something. Can you please call me? Thanks, Ben

He followed it immediately with another that included his phone number and changed into his dad's pajama bottoms while he waited for a response. Jonah might be online even if he wasn't answering his phone.

Ben could hear the kids through the suite's connecting door. He didn't have much time. Mrs. Cooper had the children in their pajamas, ready for him to read them a story, just like at home. She probably needed a break.

He tapped the redial button on his phone. Again. A third time. The man had a bum leg! He wasn't supposed to go anywhere. Ben did some calculations and decided that maybe Jonah was getting around just fine now. He should be home, though. It wasn't as if there was a night life in Bruce Crossing.

Ben started to worry that something might have happened to him and rapidly shut down the idea. He had enough to worry about already.

The children all wanted to sleep with him tonight, so he moved into their room. Mrs. Cooper shut her door. Was that snick the lock?

Ben stayed awake until the children were asleep, calling Jonah every few minutes. He fell asleep at some point, because daylight blazed through the edges of the heavy curtains when the sounds of bickering children awakened him. He picked up the phone and glanced at the list of missed calls. There were none. Apparently, Jonah hadn't checked his email.

A small body hurled itself on top of him, quickly followed by others. Annie bounced in her portable crib, wanting to join the fray. Ben wrestled with them, enjoying the normalcy of it for a while.

"Time to get dressed, guys!" Their clothes for the day were laid on top of their suitcases. His were draped over the radiator. At least his socks and underwear were dry.

Had the kids been this hyper when they left home, or were their high spirits a result of seeing him? He brought them downstairs for a continental breakfast of donuts and orange juice, wondering if Mrs. Cooper was still asleep. Her door remained closed. Ben checked his email. Nothing. No phone calls. Maybe Jonah had given him the wrong telephone number. He had to be there.

Dear Jonah, Please, call me. Thanks, Ben

He ate a donut without tasting it—or maybe it didn't have a taste—and listened to the kids' stories of their vacation. Disney and the Dells had inspired ideas for expansion of their Warrior Way. They wanted to go home. Benjie wanted to go back to school. Ben wanted to go back to the hospital to check on his parents.

Where was Mrs. Cooper? Maybe he should go upstairs and knock on her door, just to make sure she was okay. Or maybe she was enjoying a break from the kids, expecting him to take care of them. She hadn't been off-duty in weeks. Still, he felt unreasonably indignant when he caught sight of her across the hotel lobby, sitting on a leather couch, with her feet up on the ottoman, knitting while she watched a daytime talk show.

As if sensing his stare, she rolled up whatever she was working on—knitting? He'd never seen her knit before—and came over to meet them.

"Ben, your mother will be going into surgery in an hour. Why don't you go over to the hospital, and I'll take the kids swimming for a while?"

She had them sorted out in no time, but before he left for the hospital, Ben found the hotel's business center and opened MapQuest.

"This is where I want you to go," said Ben. "The man who lives there is Jonah Campbell. I've been trying to get hold of him, but he's not answering his phone or email."

"Maybe he's not there!" Teresa accepted the sheaf of papers he was thrusting at her. "He doesn't know we're coming?"

"No, not yet, but I'm going to keep trying. I'm sure he can't have gone far."

"Ben, this is way up north. It'll take at least five hours, and what if he's not home when we get there?"

"Then wait for him. If he's not there by dark, go back to Watersmeet to the casino hotel for the night and try again in the morning. This is an absolutely safe place for the kids. Jonah will protect them with his life."

Teresa opened her mouth, but Ben hurried on. "Not that

it will be necessary; I just mean that you can rely on him."

"Who is he?"

A strange look passed over Ben's face. "The kids can call him Grandpa Campbell. He'll like that."

"So, he's an elderly man?"

"Oh, no. He's a few years younger than you, I think."

She ignored the annoying comment and continued her interrogation. "Is he prepared for guests? Is his house child-proof?"

Ben actually chuckled. She wanted to slap him.

"I'm sure it's not proof against four Taylor children. And he's not prepared for guests, so stop at Walmart on your way and pick up bedding and pillows and groceries. It would be best if you leave now, so you get there early in the day. You have the GPS in the van, but you may not have a strong satellite signal, so you'll want to take these with you, too." He nodded at the papers she held. "The directions are good. Even if it looks like you're in the middle of nowhere, just keep going. It's a great place. The kids will love it. Boating, swimming, fishing."

Teresa set the directions on the table. "Ben. I am going to leave the children here with you and go to Walmart now. When I get back, you can load up the minivan, and the children and I will make the trip up north. I hope your friend is a patient man, because they're going to be wild hooligans by the time we get there. They've been away from home for three weeks, to Disney and water parks and traveling in airplanes. Their grandma was taken away in.. . . oh, never mind. I'll be back in about an hour."

It took longer than an hour. Ben jumped up when she knocked and entered their room. The children gazed mindlessly at a movie they had seen several times.

"I picked up everything we'll need for a vacation in the Northwoods. The salesperson said I should bring everything from mittens to sunscreen and lots of mosquito repellent. I got life jackets and other things for outdoor activities, so I think we're all set. I got the bedding and some groceries, but we'll have to get milk and other perishables once we're closer."

"Don't wait too long. There aren't any real stores in the last 50 or 60 miles. Try Eagle River."

Teresa decided she could be charitable instead of strangling him. He was cheerful because he felt relieved. His mother was doing well, and he'd found a safe and interesting solution for the kids. He didn't know what it was like to shop with four little children, even when you just needed a few gallons of milk. She had obviously made his life too comfortable.

CHAPTER 35

The first half of the drive was long and horrible. Teresa thought the world outside might be rather pretty, but she didn't have time to admire the scenery. She stayed fully occupied with driving and the children. The children stayed occupied with driving her crazy.

As Rhinelander faded into the distance behind her, Teresa fought the urge to turn around. Ben said there was a grocery store in Eagle River, but he also said the population was fifteen hundred. What did Ben consider a grocery store? A gas station that sold milk and bread?

"Keep me sweet, God. We have a long way to go."

The kids settled down to watch movies on their tablets. How did parents survive family vacations before portable movies? It wasn't that the children were bad, but they'd been away from home for weeks. The excitement of airplanes, Disney, and the water park—followed by their grandmother's accident and the arrival of their father—had them off balance. And now this flight up north to a stranger's house. They didn't see it as a flight, of course. Ben had whipped them up to a frenzy of excitement with talk of canoes and fishing. To her knowledge, Ben had never been fishing in his life.

"Oh!" Teresa slowed the van. "Look at that!"

The deer stood at the edge of the pavement, skittish, watching them.

Teresa brought the van to a stop. She had never seen a deer before, except in the zoo. "Can you all see that? Be very quiet so we don't scare it away."

"It's a deer!" said Benjie, not quietly.

"It doesn't have antlers, so it must be a doe," said Teresa. She kept her voice low.

"Is it lost?" Jack's voice wasn't low.

"Hush! No, I think it lives here, in the woods." Teresa was mesmerized by the animal's stare. Its head was like a horse, but blunted, with remarkably long ears. Its gray-brown, oval body looked too heavy for the slender legs. Top-heavy. Could it really run like that?

They watched it for a while, and it watched them back.

"Okay, guys, we'd better get moving again." Teresa put the van in gear, inching forward to avoid startling the deer. Without any warning, the animal leaped in front of them and raced across the highway.

Teresa screamed and slammed on the brakes. Before she had time to recover, two small deer followed the first.

"She had babies," exclaimed Jack. "You almost hit her babies!"

Teresa rested her head on the steering wheel. She'd never have forgiven herself, and the children would have been scarred for life.

"I need all of you to keep your eyes open. Tell me if you see any more." Teresa crept forward, her knuckles prominent as she gripped the wheel. At this rate, they wouldn't arrive until tomorrow.

"There's one!"

Teresa slowed and swiveled her head at Jack's shout. "Where?" She located two of them, standing a few yards back in the woods. They sprang away, further into the shrubbery. She pointed. "Over there?"

"No," said Jack. "On that side."

Another doe stood, not looking up from whatever she was eating, on the edge of a creek.

Teresa started driving again, afraid to blink. She relaxed after a few false alarms. The boys saw deer in every rock and tree. They got bored after a while, and then started doing it just for fun, finding entertainment in their nanny's reactions to their calls.

Teresa pulled over. She didn't believe in asking if the children wanted her to stop the car. She just did it. The van fell silent as she unbuckled her seat belt and opened her door. As she was exiting, a flash of brown crossed behind her. More deer followed.

"Six of them," said Benjie. "How many does that make so far?"

Teresa quieted her heart and climbed back into the van as the children bickered about the math. She turned around to face them. "Boys, I cannot drive safely, without hitting deer, if you distract me. If you really see deer, let me know. Count them! At this rate, you should hit a hundred before we get to Grandpa Campbell's house. Not hit," she corrected herself hastily. "Just count. Quietly. And you both have to see it before it counts."

As she drove farther north along the smooth highway, the landscape changed. The farm fields dwindled away as trees spread over the available land. They were driving on a wide road in the middle of a forest. It filled her with awe. The privacy settled over her like a blanket. She couldn't see any buildings or other cars. Even the deer were absent. Had she ever, in her life, been in a place like this? God had created this place. Teresa wondered why. Just because it was beautiful?

Black birds wheeled in circles ahead of her, swooping down and flying up again. They were bigger birds than she'd ever seen in town. Would she see eagles up here? What other wildlife was there?

"Oh, no!" The cry was wrenched from her. Teresa slowed down, but the deer was obviously dead. The birds—nasty things—swooped overhead, waiting for her to drive on. She did.

Eagle River. Last bastion of civilization. Teresa stopped the van and leaned back against the headrest. "Thank you, God."

She squeezed her eyes shut and wiggled her fingers to loosen up the joints. Why didn't they put up fences along the roads? How high could a deer jump, anyhow, with that bulky body on such spindly legs?

The wide, glossy aisles of the grocery store inspired the boys with the apparently-irresistible desire to run and slide. How had two years of training been undone so quickly? In her own defiant act of rebellion, Teresa popped Annie into the seat and Mark into the basket, contrary to the diagrams on the grocery cart.

"Benjie and Jack. You two stay right next to us. I want you to keep one hand on the cart at all times. Do not talk to each other. Do not ask for anything. Do not touch any of your siblings. Do you understand me?"

The boys mumbled responses.

At the sound of a snicker—or maybe it was a snort—behind her, Teresa whirled to confront an eavesdropper. An elderly man, leaning on a cane, grinned broadly.

"Dere ain't no vay you aren't a school teacher, eh? Ven I vas a boy, my teacher said dat all da time: 'do not, do not.'"

"Did it work?" Teresa felt her tension ebbing away under his friendly gaze.

He held out a hand and waggled it back and forth. "Sometimes, sometimes not."

"Well, I'll keep trying," said Teresa. "Have a good day."

The exchange relaxed her. They'd make it through here, get some food and be on the road. Next stop, Bruce Crossing.

Highway 45 disappeared into the forest. On both sides of the road, as far as Teresa could see, bare trees rose above misty green undergrowth, fighting for branch space among the pines and firs. She drove in rapt fascination, thrilled by the sensation of being absorbed by the forest whenever the highway curved away to one side and woods closed in around them, ahead and behind.

Puffs of white clouds shifted in the swath of sky over them, filtering the sun. What did it look like from above? A ravine? A river? On the map, it was just a line cut through a green splotch. When she wasn't driving, Teresa thought, she'd look at the satellite images on her map software.

What would it be like to call this home? To go into the city for a vacation and then return here, instead of living in the city and going up north for vacations? Why hadn't she known about this place ten years ago, when she needed to run and hide?

Teresa pulled herself back to the present time and place. She couldn't have come here without a job or a place to live, and she was a city girl, anyhow. Another green sign—the kind that marred the scenery she was trying to enjoy—informed her that Watersmeet was only ten miles ahead and she was entering Land O'Lakes. Wasn't there a butter company by that name?

Several cars flew past her as she proceeded north. So much traffic! No wonder that deer had died. People should be more careful. After passing her third dead animal—this one had been fat and furry—Teresa slowed the minivan. They weren't in a hurry, and she wasn't going to be responsible for dead wildlife if she could prevent it.

Watersmeet was a small town, drab in April, and empty. The children watched through the open side door as Teresa filled the gas tank.

"I thought we weren't going to stop anymore," said Jack.

"Keep me sweet, God," Teresa said under her breath, "and please help him stop whining." He'd been doing better until they got in the van this morning. Teresa didn't blame him; she just wanted it to stop.

"After I get gas, we're all going to use the bathroom, and then we'll be on our way again."

"Again?"

Teresa replaced the nozzle in the gas pump and leaned into the van. "Jack, I don't want to hear any more complaints. It's a long trip, but we're almost there. No more whining."

He didn't look at her. At home, she may have insisted on a response. Now, she just wanted to get to Bruce Crossing and unload the kids on another adult for a little while.

No one was waiting for the gas pump, so they left the van where it was and entered the store. This was what she had expected to find in Eagle River: an expanded convenience store that also sold live bait and beer. The elderly woman behind the counter smiled at Teresa.

"Are dey all yours?"

Teresa couldn't help laughing. "There are only four of them!"

"It alvays seems like more when dey're cooped up in de car for vacation, hey?" The woman's friendly voice reminded Teresa of the man in the grocery store. Was that a regional dialect?

"It has been a long day," agreed Teresa. "But we're almost there."

CHAPTER 36

Ben said she should trust the van's GPS and the printed maps. Teresa prayed he was right, because she would never find her way out again. The GPS told her she was getting closer, but nothing looked different.

"There are a lot of trees here," said Benjie.

"There are, and they're very pretty, but I'd like to find Grandpa Campbell's house soon."

Teresa's comment was interrupted by the GPS: "You have reached your destination."

The road curved twice and ended in front of the most perfect house she had ever seen. Teresa, not usually given to whimsy, thought of Goldilocks: The house wasn't too big and it wasn't too small. It was just right. The brown house, with its sage trim and front door, looked as if it might have grown there instead of having been built.

It also looked deserted.

"Oh, no," said Teresa. There had to be someone home. "You kids stay in here while I go knock on the door."

She trod across the soggy grass and stepped onto the porch. Through the front windows, she could see shapes of furniture, but it was dark inside. She rapped on the door.

"Hello!" It was like knocking on an empty box. She walked over to the detached garage and knocked on the side door. Nothing. Teresa headed back to the van to let the children know she was going to check out the back yard, but she could hear Annie crying as she grew close. Maybe they should all get out. They needed to run, and there was plenty of space for that here.

The boys tumbled from the van like eager puppies, but Annie's crying had matured into full-blown hysteria by the time Teresa released her from her car seat. All her people kept leaving; she didn't want to let Mrs. Cooper out of her sight.

They all stood still for a minute, looking at the forest around them, intimidated by its depth and silence. Then the birds and cicadas, briefly startled by their arrival, resumed their chatter, and the woods became comfortable.

"Stay close, guys." Teresa walked around the back of the house, holding Annie's hand. A deck ran the length of the house and wrapped around the corner, with steps leading down to the grass. Teresa considered going up to peer through the glass doors, but that would just be nosy. No one was home.

"What should I do, God?"

"Eat," said Annie.

"We need to work on your vocabulary." She lifted Annie to her hip. "And I wasn't talking to you. Let's go check on your brothers. It's getting cold out here."

The boys roamed too wide for her comfort, so Teresa led them on a nature hike around the edges of the front yard and driveway. She didn't know what they were looking at, most of the time, but none of them cared. They just wanted to be outside as long as they could, because if no one came home soon, they'd have to go to another hotel.

"I think we should go ahead and eat now," said Teresa. "We can sit in the van and warm up while we have peanut butter and jelly sandwiches, or we can go back to the hotel and eat in the restaurant. What do you want to do?" If she hadn't known the answer, she wouldn't have asked the question. This way, they made the choice and enjoyed the meal. And they stayed here longer.

Teresa was cleaning up their mess when the shouting erupted. She slammed the hatch door and rounded the van to find all of them wrestling. She pulled Annie off first and then untangled the rest of them.

"Stop it! What's the matter?"

The boys pointed at their sister. "She knocked over the stick house I was building," said Benjie. "She did it on purpose. And she bit Mark."

"Annie," said Teresa, "let's read a story."

She continued to rock Annie long after the girl fell asleep. They'd have to leave soon and drive back to that hotel in Watersmeet. She didn't want to navigate that maze of roads in the dark with no streetlights.

"Mrs. Cooper!" All three boys raced toward her. "There's a car coming!" A black truck came into view and jerked to a sudden stop behind the minivan. The driver stared through the window for a few seconds before opening the door. He emerged slowly, dragging a crutch out with him and using it for balance as he stepped down. He looked at the group of them, confused.

"Hello." His friendly voice encouraged her.

Teresa rose from the rocking chair with some difficulty, clutching the sleeping Annie with one arm. "Hello. I'm Teresa Cooper."

He stopped walking. His stillness began to worry her, and Teresa prepared to start the introduction again.

"Benjie," said the man. "Jack. Mark." He looked up at Teresa. "Annie." He moved to the foot of the stairs and reached up to shake Teresa's hand. "And you must be Mary Poppins."

She frowned and retrieved her hand. "I'm Teresa Cooper. I assume you're Jonah Campbell?"

"Yes, I am. Where's Ben?"

"He's back in Chicago." Her heart sank. "Didn't he

reach you?"

"No." The man seemed perplexed. "I didn't know he was trying. The power was out for a couple days. I spent last night at the hotel in Watersmeet so I could get a hot shower and meal." He peered around her. "It looks pretty dark in there. It's probably still out."

Teresa sighed. "I think that's what we'd better do then."

"No!" His urgent response startled her.

She regarded him warily. "But you won't be prepared for guests."

"That's okay. You're probably hungry. I have peanut butter and jelly. I understand it's a real favorite with these guys." He watched the boys in fascination. They were hanging back, letting the grownups talk.

Annie hadn't awakened. When the girl slept, she gave it her full attention. Teresa set her in the rocking chair and descended the steps.

"Boys, come and say hello to Grandpa Campbell." Grandpa? This man couldn't be more than forty.

He squatted down with a little awkwardness, dropping the crutch and using one hand on the ground to help him balance. His voice was husky. "Benjie. Your dad sent me a photograph of the picture you made for the art show. It was very good." He shook hands with Jack and Mark, telling them that he was happy to meet them. "Did your daddy really tell you to call me Grandpa Campbell?" They nodded. "That's wonderful. I am so glad you are here."

Bewildered, Teresa asked, "Mr. Campbell, have you ever met the children before?"

"Jonah."

"Jonah. Please call me Teresa."

"Ben said you're an angel."

She blinked at his unexpectedly charming smile. "He said you were a grandpa!"

A crease formed between his brows and he looked at her for several seconds. "Did he? What else did he say?"

"Not much. He never mentioned you until this morning, and then he just printed out a map and told me to drive here." She thought about Ben's words. "He said you would protect the children with your life."

"I will."

The simplicity of his words—all two of them—irritated her. Enough. She'd spent quite enough time feeling confused and stupid lately. "Well, Jonah, here we are. Ben has been trying to call you and email you to let you know we were coming. You can use my phone to call him if yours is out." She pulled it out of her coat pocket and looked at it blankly.

"You won't get a reliable signal out here. I have an old wall-mount phone that might be working. We can try it once everyone gets inside." He raised his voice. "Come on, guys!"

"That will be nice," she admitted. "We warmed up in the van for a while, but it's cold out here! We actually saw some piles of snow in the woods."

"Oh, it'll be cold inside," he said, "but I'll have a fire going in no time. I have some battery-operated lamps, too."

Teresa pondered logistics. She had to make up beds for all of them, and she'd rather not do it by the light of a few lamps. Their bedding, luggage and groceries were all in the van, and this man was limping and using a crutch. It fell to her to do the heavy work, but she didn't want the children to go into the house without her. She needed to reconnoiter and make sure the house was reasonably safe for and from children.

She was still thinking when Jonah started doing.

"Benjie!" Jonah spoke to the boy as if he were seventeen instead of seven. "Would you grab one of those big chunks of wood over there by the side of the garage? Those are especially dry and will catch fire quickly. We'll put some other lightweight stuff in there to get it hot fast and then add bigger logs."

Without waiting for permission from Teresa, Benjie ran off to do his bidding.

"Mark, can you carry this inside?" He handed his cane to the little boy.

Mark took the cane by the handle and dragged it behind him toward the house. Jack followed like a lemming as Jonah walked to the van and opened the passenger door. He accepted two plastic grocery bags and turned to carry them inside.

Teresa bit her tongue. The children were her responsibility, but he had them working helpfully with no effort at all. Jack reached the front door before Mark. He turned the knob and pushed the door open.

"It's unlocked?" Teresa asked. "I was getting so desperate I was considering using. . . well, never mind." She grabbed her purse and an armful of pillows.

He seemed to enjoy watching her incredulity. "The bathroom is at the end of the hall to your left. There's a bucket of water for flushing."

"A what?"

"When the electricity is out," said Jonah, "the pump to the well doesn't work. We don't have running water in the house, but there's an old-fashioned hand pump outside, so we'll just bring buckets inside. The boys will love it."

"So, how do you flush a toilet with a bucket of water?" Teresa asked. Did it really work or was he making fun of her because she was a city girl?

"When you are done, pour the bucket of water right into the toilet bowl. It will flush. Honest." He smiled at her as he pushed open the door.

"I can't believe you leave your door unlocked when you're going to be out of town overnight," said Teresa.

"Well," Jonah said, "you never know when an angel will come by and need to use the bathroom."

CHAPTER 37

The phone worked fine. For some reason, telephone lines survived ice and blizzards better than power lines did. Jonah watched Teresa from the porch as he waited for the call to connect. That was Mary Poppins? He'd been expecting a much older tyrant, in black.

Ben answered on the first ring. "Hello! Did they make it up there?"

"Oh, yes. I was in Watersmeet overnight, and they were sitting on the porch when I got home."

"They're all okay? How's Mrs. Cooper? She's probably wiped out. She's in good shape for her age, but we've been pushing her hard lately, and she wasn't happy with me when she left the Dells."

Jonah raised his eyebrows. In good shape for her age? "She's fine. Looks a little tired, but that's only to be expected. Listen, she's going to be back inside soon. Does she know I'm your father?"

Your father, what an amazing thought. Through the window, he could see the children sitting on the floor where Teresa Cooper had left them. Not just a son, but a whole family. God was good.

"No, I haven't told her anything. I was so desperate to come up with somewhere to send the kids. She'll give notice when things are under control again. I just know it."

"Do you care if she knows?" Jonah asked.

Ben was quiet for a minute and then said, "No, I suppose not, but I don't want to explain the family tree to Benjie yet. Is he calling you Grandpa Campbell?"

"They all are, about every two seconds." He smiled. "So, tell me what's going on." Jonah watched Teresa wrestle with bags and suitcases while Ben explained, and when the tale ended, he said, "That's fine. You do what you have to do. Nothing will happen to your children or their nanny. I have to go now. Bye."

A shadow fell across Teresa as she continued unloading the van. He sure moved quietly for a man with an injured leg. Jonah reached over, picked up the handles of several plastic bags with one sweep of his hand and used the other hand to pick up a suitcase. Teresa dragged out two more suitcases and lugged them back to the cabin. It was warm now, and the boys were curled up on the couch. Annie had a chair to herself and used every inch of it.

They left the suitcases on the living room floor, and Teresa followed Jonah into the kitchen. She couldn't see details in the twilight, but the house appeared clean enough, simple in design, with comfortable furniture. The kitchen had an island with stools, but the table in the dining area could seat eight on benches and chairs.

"This is a nice place."

"Thanks. I like it."

She led the way outside again.

"How long did you say you're staying?"

She glanced up at him, startled. "I don't know."

He waved an arm at the still-full van. "You look like you're moving in permanently. Not that I mind, of course," he added quickly.

"Well, this is everything we took to Florida and then the Dells, and I bought more warm clothing, bedding and food to come here."

He peered into a bulky bag. "And bug spray and life jackets."

"Ben said you'd be taking the boys fishing and swimming." Did Jonah know that or was it just an invention of Ben's, to get the kids excited? "Really, I do get frustrated with him. I need to keep reminding myself that he's only twenty-five." She stopped herself, not wanting to gossip about her employer. "So, there should be plenty of everything."

It took several more trips to empty the van. Teresa was embarrassed at the state of the floorboards. "I don't usually let them eat in the van, but it was a long day, and I didn't want them to arrive here hungry."

"We can leave the doors open and let the squirrels clean it out. They like french fries." He sounded so matter of fact that she looked up, startled. His teeth gleamed white in the moonlight. "Or we can lock it up for now and vacuum it out when the power comes back on."

"Do you have any idea when that might be?" She hoped she didn't sound like she was complaining. "I'm just wondering because I bought a lot of milk and other refrigerated and frozen stuff, and I don't want it to go bad."

He pointed toward the garage. "I have a big locked box in the garage that I use for a refrigerator or freezer, depending on the weather. We've been pretty borderline lately, so I've been throwing a blanket over it and using that for a refrigerator and keeping the frozen things tightly packed together in this smaller box. If they stay frozen and the garage door is locked up, they won't attract critters."

"You lock up the garage and leave your house open?"

"Our local predators are more interested in food than anything in the house."

The children were all asleep. Jonah turned on a battery-powered lantern. "I would have reorganized things if I had known you were coming. Can we make them pallets out here for tonight and set up better beds tomorrow? I have two guest rooms, and I can get the bed cleaned off for you." He winced. "It's a terrible bed."

"Thanks," said Teresa, "but for tonight, I'd rather stay out here in case they wake up in the middle of the night. Is there a lamp like that one we can leave on in the bathroom?"

Twenty minutes later, Teresa sank gratefully onto the couch. She hoped Ben knew what he was doing. Jonah Campbell didn't look like a grandpa to her.

A siren—no, a scream—shredded the night and swelled through the house. After a few seconds, it receded a little and transformed into gulps and loud sobs. Jonah remembered to favor his knee just in time to prevent himself from falling as he swung down the stairs.

"What's the matter?"

The awful noise stopped. Teresa's soothing murmur was the only sound for a minute, and then the baby started whimpering again. The nanny shifted in the darkness, probably trying to calm Annie so she wouldn't wake up her brothers. It didn't work. The boys woke up, confused by their surroundings.

"Mrs. Cooper? I need to use the bathroom."

"Me, too."

"See where the light is? That's the bathroom. Don't worry about flushing the toilet or washing your hands," Teresa said. "How are you doing, Mark? Do you need to change clothes?"

Why did she want the boy to get dressed in the middle of the night? It occurred to Jonah that Mark might have wet his bed. He was just a little guy, after all, and it had been a long day. He could see Teresa trying to detach the baby so she could help Mark.

"Jonah? Do you see that red suitcase by the coat rack? Could you please get it for me?"

He handed it to her and then turned on a battery-powered lamp. "Is there anything I can do to help?"

"Yes." She thrust the baby at him. "You can hold Annie."

Jonah's arms were suddenly full of pink. A very pink, very soft, squirmy girl. They regarded each other in surprise and then relaxed into interested observation.

"I don't think I've ever held a baby before," he said conversationally.

"You're doing just fine." Teresa's voice was distracted. "Where do you put laundry?"

"There's a washer and dryer in the mudroom, just off the kitchen. I'll take care of it." His leg ached, after hurtling down the stairs, but he carried Annie with him. He tossed the bag into a corner and nearly dropped his granddaughter when she shouted "Score!" into his ear. He smiled at her. If she liked that, they could throw things all day tomorrow.

CHAPTER 38

Jonah pushed more firewood into the stove.

"No showers?" asked Teresa. She was sitting on the edge of the couch, rubbing her face with both hands. "I could really use a hot shower."

"Heat up some water in a pan on the stove."

He grinned when she inadvertently glanced toward the kitchen before realizing he meant the wood stove.

She straightened her shoulders and asked in a no-nonsense tone: "Just where is that water pump you mentioned?"

"I already got a few buckets," he said. "I require coffee in the morning. What do you want for breakfast?"

"How about cereal and milk and bananas?"

"Sounds good. I already brought the milk inside."

Jonah got out bowls, spoons, and napkins, enjoying the noises of the waking children. Teresa Cooper did seem a little Mary Poppins-y today, getting all the children dressed and cleaned up. Without going overboard, she made it all seem fun. Jonah heard them exclaiming over the novelty of using a communal soapy washcloth and brushing their teeth without running water.

"We need to straighten up the living room before

breakfast."

Jonah wished they would wait until after breakfast, but he wasn't going to undermine the work of a good nanny. She was raising future houseguests. He joined them in folding up the bed linens and stacking suitcases.

"Later today, we'll clean out the two bedrooms, but let's eat first."

"Eat." Annie slipped her hand into his.

He gave it a gentle squeeze. "Are you hungry, sweetheart? Do you like cereal and bananas?"

She made agreeable noises, and Jonah led her into the kitchen.

Teresa and the boys were standing at the sliding glass doors that opened to the wraparound deck. Beyond the deck and small yard, was forest—thousands of acres of forest, lakes and rivers. The boys pressed their hands and faces against the glass door, as if they wanted to pass through it. Annie pushed her way through them and licked the glass. He would never wash that door again.

Teresa turned to face him. Her eyes were wide. "I've never seen anything like that." She picked up Annie so the girl could see better.

"Like?" Jonah prompted. "Like what?"

"Like that!" Teresa gestured past the doors. "All that. . . woods. It's incredible."

"It certainly is. Nothing like it in the world." Jonah felt a sense of satisfaction at their wonder, as if he was personally responsible. He cast up a quick prayer of apology to the true Creator. At least Jonah would have the pleasure of showing it to them.

Breakfast was a loud and cheerful meal. Teresa and the boys told him about the deer on the road. When was the last time he was so excited about deer by the road? Mostly, he just prayed he wouldn't hit one and damage his truck. They weren't particularly attractive animals, until they moved, but few animals could equal the grace of a deer in motion.

"Sixty-eight of them? That's a lot. I only saw forty-one last time I went into town, and most of those were between here and Watersmeet."

The boys puffed up, pleased with their superior accomplishment.

"I stopped to report the dead one at the police department in Eagle River, and they laughed at me," said Teresa. "I guess it was silly, and I had all the kids in tow, but I couldn't bear to just leave it there, being picked over by those vultures."

Maybe someday he'd deliver a cycle of life homily, but today he just nodded. Jonah caught himself on that thought. Someday? He might never see this woman again. Watching her describe the beauty of the drive north, he thought that would be a great shame.

He was impressed at the children's manners. They thanked Teresa and asked to be excused before they left the table, carrying their dishes to the sink. She looked at him. "Is there enough hot water to wash dishes?"

Jonah had underestimated the water needed to make coffee and wash six people. "I'll get some more and put it on the stove."

"Can we go out on the porch?" Jack had already put his shoes on.

Teresa raised her eyebrows at Jonah. "I don't know what's out there. Is it safe for kids?"

Jonah laid a hand on Jack's shoulder. "Let's go see what's out there, Jack. I think it's okay, but it's always a good idea to check first."

It only took a minute. He smiled hopefully at Teresa. "Jack says Mark will fall down the stairs. Did I see a gate in that stuff we brought in from the car?"

"Actually," she said, "I brought three of them. I wasn't sure if you had stairs here." She looked askance at the spiral staircase. "I don't know what to do about that one. But you can take a gate out on the deck and see if it will work there."

Soon, all four children were running back and forth on the long deck. Jonah watched them for a few minutes and then went back inside to help clean up.

"This kitchen is beautiful," said Teresa. "Bigger than I would have expected for a bachelor."

"My wife and I planned it together," Jonah said, "but she died before it was finished."

He regretted the explanation as soon as it was out, because Teresa's pleased smile vanished.

"I'm sorry."

"Thank you."

The meaningless exchange didn't improve the sudden discomfort. Jonah sought a topic that would open conversation. He gestured at the terra cotta floor.

"I did the tiling myself, with a guy from church. He was the expert, I was the grunt labor."

"I like the black grout. It makes it look modern without losing the cabin feel."

"That's what I thought," said Jonah. A brief silence fell between them.

"And the benches at the dining room table. . . what made you decide on benches?"

Jonah smiled. "My grandma had six kids, and she had benches. My mother had them, too, because it was what her mother had. That's how she put it, anyhow. Unfortunately, I was an only child, so Mom's benches didn't get filled up. And then. . . well. . . "

He'd brought himself full circle to the topic of Cindy's death. It was a conversation stopper.

Jonah's attention was caught by the sight of Jack

climbing the railing. He dropped the handful of spoons he was drying and sprinted outside. He hauled the boy down and set him on his feet. The others stood and gaped.

"What happened?"

Jonah turned to Teresa apologetically. "I thought it would be safe out here. I didn't realize they might use the benches as stepping stools to get up higher."

He squatted awkwardly in front of Jack. "You can't do that, buddy. You scared me nearly to death."

"Is that what you did, Jack?"

"Yes, Mrs. Cooper." The boy didn't look up from the deck flooring.

"Is that something you're allowed to do?"

"No, Mrs. Cooper."

"Apologize to Grandpa Campbell."

Horrified, Jonah said, "No, really. I should have realized."

Teresa speared him with a steely gaze and then turned back to Jack. "Apologize."

Jack didn't raise his eyes, but he said, "I'm sorry, Grandpa."

Teresa rounded up the children. "This is the same kind of deck that your other grandparents have. The same rules apply. You know you may not stand up on the benches or climb on the railings. Don't drop things off the sides or through the floor boards. Do you remember those rules?"

There was a subdued chorus of assent. Annie smiled angelically. Teresa eyed her. "Benjie, keep an eye on Annie."

The children returned to their play. Jonah ushered Teresa back into the house.

As soon as they were out of earshot, Jonah said, "He didn't need to apologize to me."

"Oh, yes, he did. Just because what he did was scary and life-threatening doesn't absolve him of the consequences of disobedience. In fact, it's most important then." She must have noticed his unhappy expression. "Children are much happier when they have rules and they know responsible adults are watching them. If we adults don't live up to our responsibilities in the training process, they can't live up to theirs."

"Training process?" asked Jonah. "Like a dog?"

"Sure. You wouldn't let a dog run wild. Think how much more important it is to train up a human. You start with a baby and raise him up into a mature man. It doesn't just happen, you know."

"If you say so." It wasn't at all the same thing.

"Or," she elaborated, "it's like a soldier. You couldn't just take him out of high school, give him a haircut and a gun and send him off to war. You have to train him. Prepare him for battle. That's what training children is all about: preparing them to handle life well."

"You have some interesting theories about raising children," said Jonah. Iron fist in a velvet glove. She might look like Mary Poppins, but she sounded like a drill sergeant.

"I've had a lot of practical experience."

"Won't Jack be upset with both of us now?" He wanted the children to like him, and she'd made him look like the bad guy.

"Not at all."

Jonah didn't share her confidence, but his anxiety lightened when Jack was at the front of the group trying to force open the door. He stepped over to slide it aside and moved out of the way as the kids tumbled in.

"There was something moving out in the woods!" Benjie's excitement warmed Jonah's heart. This was going to be fun.

"How about if we all go out together and I can show you around." He turned to Teresa. "You, too."

"Yes!" She looked as eager as the kids did. "We need to

find all the winter gear."

Jonah stoked the fire and went out for water while Teresa rummaged through Walmart bags. Benjie dressed quickly, eager to help Jonah with pumping and bringing water into the house while the nanny assisted the younger children. Jonah watched the boy laboring over the pump handle and remembered his own enjoyment of that job when he'd visited his uncle. Here was this grandson, doing the same thing. God was so good, dumping this blessing on him all at once, without notice. Amazing. Incredible. Humbling.

The others were ready, bundled up for a blizzard. It was thirty-eight degrees out. They would roast. Jonah opened his mouth, looked at Teresa in her puffy, knee-length coat and snapped it shut again. Her green eyes were alight with anticipation, and she looked. . . cute in that striped hat. She'd figure it out.

Jonah beamed at Annie in her pretty pink snowsuit. She smiled at him.

"She won't walk for long," warned Teresa, "and she's heavier than she looks. I might have to bring her back to the house while you guys finish exploring."

Jonah brought a walking stick instead of the crutch. It worked better than the crutch outdoors on the uneven ground, and it looked less pathetic than the cane.

"How about if we just cover the basics this morning?" They wouldn't have time for much before the rain started. The heavy cloud cover hung low, with a taupe hue that usually presaged snow. They could come out again later.

Teresa praised everything, but she drew close to him periodically to point out hazards. Her voice was too low to be overheard by the rambunctious children.

"That branch over there—" she indicated the one she meant. "Jack will jump up to swing on it, and it looks like it might be heavy enough to do damage when it falls on him."

Jonah hadn't expected to enjoy the nanny's commentary, but her frank assessments made him chuckle, even if she did tend to overreact. It wasn't likely that Jack would climb on the wood blocks he used as a ladder to reach the old deer stand.

Twice, she stopped to make rules. "Boys, you may never go into that building. It stores dangerous chemicals Grandpa Campbell uses, like I keep bleach and toilet bowl cleaner under the sink. Stay away from it." And: "If you see a sick or dead animal, or any animal that's not moving, come and get Grandpa Campbell immediately. He'll take care of it. Do not touch it or poke it with a stick or throw things at it or even get close to it. Stay back until Grandpa looks at it."

His fuzzy memories of summers with Uncle Jake consisted mainly of the wood stove, the outhouse, the water pump, and fishing. The adult Jonah had never looked at his land through the eyes of a careful nanny. It delighted him.

Teresa lifted Annie when the girl started whining—not that Jonah thought of it as whining. The poor little girl was tired. He wanted to carry her himself, but he couldn't pack Annie safely when he needed his stick for balance and support. "I think I'll take Annie back to the house and get lunch going. Can you manage the three boys on your own?"

He hoped the question wasn't a discreet inquiry about his handicap. He wasn't crippled.

"Of course!" He grinned at the boys, who were doing their best to look harmless. "We'll get along just fine. I want to show them an eagle's nest."

He watched Teresa drift down the path toward the house. She didn't appear to be in a hurry. Did she like it here?

Benjie tugged on his sleeve. "What's a neagle?"

CHAPTER 39

Teresa cut up carrots and apples and made peanut butter sandwiches for lunch. No dishes to wash, and it would be ready whenever Jonah and the boys returned. What were they doing out there? Was there really an eagle's nest? Would they see a real eagle? She'd never seen one of those, even in a zoo.

Teresa checked on Annie and found her nodding over Dora the Explorer.

"Oh, no, sweetie. No naps yet."

The girl rolled over onto her side, dropping the tablet on the couch. Teresa shut it off. If necessary, she could charge electronics in the car later, but she might need them yet this afternoon.

"Come on, Annie. Let's get organized. We don't want to camp out in the living room forever." Or even one more night. She took Annie's hand and walked through the house. In addition to the main living area and bathroom, there was a sort of mudroom off the kitchen, with laundry facilities and a door that must lead outside. She found the two bedrooms Jonah had mentioned. It wouldn't take long to fix them up for use. A third door opened to what must be Jonah's office. If that door couldn't be locked, they would need a gate.

Jonah slept upstairs in the loft. Teresa contemplated the open spiral staircase with trepidation. The children would find the metal contraption irresistible. As if in confirmation, Annie ducked away from her and scrambled up three steps. Teresa caught her as she fell off the side.

"No, Annie! Don't touch that!" Right. Hopefully Jonah would have some ideas.

The male people returned and devoured everything she'd prepared. Like a swarm of locusts, she thought. Did they have locusts up here?

"I love this milk," said Jonah as he tossed his paper cup into the trash can. "I'd been using skim milk until Ben bought me the good stuff."

Teresa raised her brows. "Ben brought you milk?"

"After I hurt my leg, he picked up groceries to tide me over a couple weeks."

"Ben went grocery shopping?" Jonah must be joking. There was no way Ben actually went grocery shopping. If she didn't do that chore, he and the kids would live on fast food and frozen pizza. Or maybe they'd show up at Benjamin and Eliza's house at dinnertime several days a week.

"He did a good job. I had several kinds of sugar-coated breakfast cereal, macaroni and cheese, ramen noodle soup, hot dogs, potato chips, Twinkies. . . and the whole milk, of course. I think I gained five pounds in two weeks."

"Did he buy butter to make the macaroni and cheese?" Teresa asked.

"Well, no," admitted Jonah, "but I had some in my freezer."

"Toilet paper?"

"Yep."

"Bread?"

"Three big, fluffy, white loaves." Jonah grinned. "It was like eating cake."

"Amazing," said Teresa. "I've been underestimating the boy."

"I could move around the house—just not get outside.

And some people from church came by to help a few times."

That was the second time he'd mentioned his church. Was he a Christian, or was church the only available social activity up here?

"Are you ready to go back outside?" asked Jonah.

Teresa shook her head. "I can't. Annie and Mark both need to take naps, and I'd like to get our things cleaned up. But you and the older boys go ahead."

She watched them leave, going down the driveway—or was it just a road that happened to end at his front door?— instead of along the path they had used earlier. They really were surrounded.

Mark and Annie were asleep in minutes. Teresa set up the two bedrooms and moved all of their belongings into them. She could sort it out later, but Jonah shouldn't have to trip over plastic bags in his living room. He was remarkably good-natured under the circumstances. Who was he?

Teresa eyed the stove dubiously. She'd heated pans of water on it, so theoretically she could cook on it like a normal stove, right? With a sigh, she opened several cans of soup and poured them into a large pot. If she put a lid on the pot, it might get warm enough by supper time. She'd intended the soups for lunches, but her options were limited. If they were still without power tomorrow, she'd try to be more creative.

A little canned soup wouldn't fill up a man like Jonah, though, even with salad and rolls. Teresa cut up some cheese and summer sausage and put it on a plate. What else? Canned soup didn't have any real nutritional value. Its sole benefit came from its heat. After a day in the cold, damp woods, they all needed a hot meal.

She wasn't counting iceberg lettuce as a vegetable. Teresa cut up more carrots and some celery. At home, with a real stove, she'd add them to the soup. She pulled open a sleeve of saltine crackers and put them on another plate.

It was a good thing she'd been so annoyed with Ben, she reflected. Teresa had pushed her cart through the store, grumbling, recklessly tossing in convenience foods of every kind. Not sugar-coated cereal or Twinkies, of course, but enough to feed a family under even these conditions. She added a jar of pickles to the table and stepped back to evaluate. Butter for the rolls. Salad dressing.

It still looked more like a spread of snacks than supper. Dessert would jazz it up. Teresa caught herself humming as she strolled out to the garage. She took a minute to pin down the song and then laughed. This is my Father's World. Indeed. A sense of well-being filled her.

"Thank you, God. For everything."

Teresa pulled a carton of ice cream from the freezer. Peach? She would never have taken Jonah for a peach ice cream kind of guy. He probably wouldn't mind if she used it for dinner. If the power didn't come on soon, he'd lose a lot of food. Humming her new favorite hymn, Teresa returned to the house. Peach ice cream with canned peaches. It would stay cold if she left it on the deck until supper time. Peaches and cream. The boys would love it. Would Jonah?

She left the soup on the stove until she saw them coming, but by the time Jonah and the boys blew into the house, everything was ready. They pulled off gloves and jackets as they entered, eager to tell Teresa about their explorations. Jack clutched a feathery branch with tiny pine cones on the end of it. When she tried to take it, so she could help him out of his warm clothes, it stuck to his gloves. He grabbed it with his free hand and then wiped his nose, smearing the sap across his face. "At least you smell good," said Teresa. "Everyone needs to get washed up right away. The soup is hot."

They didn't waste any time. "That's a lot of food, Mrs. Cooper!" Benjie announced, awestruck. "I'm hungry!"

She glanced at Jonah. He surveyed the table with wonder. "Do you guys eat like this every day? I haven't seen a spread this nice since I was a boy and we had Thanksgiving dinner at my grandma's house." He looked at Annie. "Hi there. Did you have a good nap?"

"Eat."

"That's her favorite word," said Jack.

"Well it's a good one." Jonah sat down at the head of the table. "At my house, we say grace."

The children folded their hands and bent their heads. Teresa followed suit and waited.

"Oh, God, Father in Heaven, holy is Your name. Thank You, God, for this family, for this meal, and bless the hands that prepared it for us. In Jesus' name, Amen."

The ending of Jonah's prayer came out in a rush, possibly because of Annie, who was dropping carrots into her milk, but it answered Teresa's question. Jonah Campbell was a believer. Interesting.

Annie got bored after she ate her soup, some crackers, carrots, cheese, and sausage. "She does like to eat," said Jonah. "Can I take her out of her seat?"

"Yes, but don't let her down until I wipe off her face."

He unbuckled the little girl and sat her on his lap. She twisted around to stare at him and pat his cheek while he talked to her.

"May I be excused?" asked Benjie.

"No! I have dessert, but I have to wash up the soup bowls first!"

Jonah looked up. "Can I help?"

"No, thanks. You hold Annie." She collected the bowls and washed them quickly. The dessert was perfect - the ice cream was soft but not melted, covered with chunks of fragrant peaches. She set the first bowls in front of Benjie and Jack.

"I'm sorry," she said to Jonah, "but I used all your ice cream. We can replace it later."

Irritation made his voice sharp. "You are my guests. You can eat or use anything you want. I will buy the groceries next time."

Teresa bit her lip. "I'm sorry. I just thought it might be something special you bought for a treat."

He regarded her seriously, "If it was the most special treat I had, you would still be welcome to it. I mean that." The boys had fallen silent, uncertain of the atmosphere. Without taking his eyes off of Teresa, Jonah reached out a long arm and snatched Jack's bowl, dipping a spoon in it and opening his mouth to eat.

Jack's eyes grew round. "Hey!"

Jonah looked at him, all innocence. "Hay is for horses."

The other boys thought that was hysterical, but Jack was outraged. "That's mine!"

Jonah gave an exaggerated sigh. "Fine."

He pushed the bowl back toward the boy. "Your Mrs. Cooper sure is a good cook. Maybe I should marry her."

"You can't marry her. She lives with us." Benjie's logic made Jonah smile.

"Enough of that." Teresa knew she was turning pink. "When you're done with dessert, go find some books to read while I clean up."

"No. The boys and I will clean up while you and Annie go read a book." Jonah stood up. "Thank you, Mrs. Cooper. That was a delicious meal." The boys quickly imitated him, their youthful voices raised in chorus. They used good manners at home, but it was different today. They were emulating Jonah here instead of just being obedient.

Teresa smiled and took Annie from Jonah's arms. "Thank you. Annie and I will await you in the living room."

Jonah showed them a few of his drawings after dinner. He described how he worked, but the computer wasn't working, of course, and it was getting dark. Benjie was fascinated. Teresa would have liked to see more, too, but the younger kids were bored. She took them to the living room to play games. Maybe Jonah would show it to her later.

They still didn't have power when they went to bed. Jonah set flashlights by each boy so they wouldn't be afraid of the dark. When it became clear the boys weren't going to drift off to sleep as long as they had such fun toys, Teresa took them away and handed them to Jonah. "There's moonlight shining right into their room. They're not afraid."

He held them in one hand for a minute and then set one on the floor outside their door. "Just in case."

Teresa thought it was charming.

CHAPTER 40

Ben took a deep breath and hauled himself out of the car. Show time. Act normal.

"Good morning!"

"Hi, Ben," said Lauren.

"Morning." Tom passed him, heading toward his own office.

"Hey. You remember that car accident I was in?"

Tom stopped. Lauren looked up.

Ben kept his head down, pretending to look for something in his bag, and continued his speech.

"I got a check from the repair place. They said I overpaid them! How often does that happen?" He walked into his office, glad to turn his back.

Tom followed him. "Nice bonus."

Ben sat down and started the computer. "I didn't get to keep it, of course. I called the insurance company and got their mailing address." He shook his head. "That company's not very organized. I could have kept it, and they would never have known. You wouldn't believe. . . I got a call from some guy there last month. He wanted to know how my therapy was going. It turned out they saw my place of employment and listed you as a service provider."

Ben let the words hang in the air, waiting for his boss to laugh at the joke, play dumb, or confess to the crime. He could feel his heart pounding. This was the point of no return—if there had ever been a choice. They were forcing Tom to respond now, instead of doing it on his own terms. He couldn't ignore Ben's comment.

Tom sat down in the client chair and rested his elbows on the table. When he spoke, he sounded confused.

"But, Ben, we've been providing therapy as well as a paycheck."

So, it was going to be confession. Good. Ben looked up and raised his brows, as if expecting a punchline. Tom didn't provide one, and he didn't elaborate.

"What are you talking about? What kind of therapy?"

Tom leaned back in the chair, stretching his legs ahead of him. He looked comfortable, and his voice was admonishing, as if reminding Ben of something he already knew.

"I've been meeting with you twice a week for a couple months now, trying to get those neck and shoulder muscles back in order."

Ben gave a bark of laughter and turned back to his desk, opening his drawer and taking out a pen. He needed something to do with his hands. "You don't miss an opportunity, do you?"

"Seriously, Ben," said Tom. "That insurance company has paid every invoice for therapy. I think there've been fourteen or fifteen sessions so far, plus evaluations."

The man's condescending, placid tone sliced through Ben's nervousness. He dropped the pen, put both hands on his desk and leaned across, genuinely angry. "What do you mean by that?"

"Just what I said."

"I see. And how did you get the referral for that?" He didn't wait for Tom to reply. "Oh, that convenient urgent care clinic doctor. A friend of yours?"

"A business associate. He thought you'd heal quickly, because the x-rays didn't show much damage, but when the pain continued, he wisely passed you on to me for treatment."

"I didn't have any x-rays." Ben kept his voice level, not accusatory.

"You had an x-ray when you first came in," said Tom, "suffering so much pain. The doctor tried to treat it with Oxycodone and some other muscle relaxants, but no matter how many times you refilled the prescription, you kept coming back to him. He decided you'd had enough drugs and sent you to me. You're still getting the meds, but in lower doses."

Ben regarded him silently for a while before saying, "How nice of me to provide the two of you with another income stream."

"Well, it wasn't just us, Ben. Those pills were worth a lot of money on the street. You made a nice profit, too. As for the therapy, it's possible that you fooled me into thinking you were in pain so that you could keep getting medication. Doctor Cravitz and I just look a bit stupid. We can live with that. Another possibility is that there was no therapy treatment. Any man capable of such complex insurance fraud is capable of simple embezzlement, especially when he's had access to the accounting records since he started work here."

"You just set me up with that account last week." Ben narrowed his eyes. "No, you set me up a long time ago, didn't you, Tom? Why?"

"I'm just pointing out how kind it is of Doctor Cravitz and me to cover for you, Ben."

Was that a waver in his boss's voice? Ben pressed. "What do you mean—cover for me?"

"Naturally, I'm a little hurt that you abused our employer/employee relationship, but you probably needed the money. After all, you have a large family to provide for." Tom paused, obviously wanting to let that sink in. "That big house and the nanny must cost you a fortune. It's hard to maintain that lifestyle on what you make as a therapy assistant. Really, you should have just kept that check." Tom rose and walked to the doorway. "We can discuss this later."

Ben jumped up, sending his chair rolling away behind him. "No, we're going to discuss it now."

That wasn't in the script. They hadn't really given him a follow-up script except telling him that it was okay to storm out of the office if he needed to. No. The only storming Ben wanted to do would be happening here and now, face to face.

He caught up with Tom as the man tried to close the door behind him. Ben pushed it open, clipping Tom's heel, and strode inside. He kicked it shut behind him.

"You don't get to drop a bombshell and run away, Tom. Tell me why you went to so much trouble for a few thousand dollars you had to split with the doctor."

Tom hastened to put the desk between them. He didn't sit down. "You're not stupid, Ben. You've seen how the insurance companies control everything from how much care a client gets to how much we get paid for what we do."

"I don't care what the insurance company does. This is my life you're destroying!" Ben didn't have to feign outrage. This part of the program was real. He'd be explaining it to employers and certification boards for years. Shouting at Tom kept the fear at bay. He wanted to smash something— preferably Tom.

"Not destroying it, Ben. Ensuring it." Tom put his hands on his desk and leaned forward. He retreated when Ben advanced.

"I don't see that, Tom. I see you making a lot of money and setting me up to take the fall if you get caught!" Ben slammed his own hands on the desk and snarled, "It's all about you getting paid. You and that quack."

Tom raised his voice over Ben's attack. "If we don't get

paid enough, we can't afford to pay employees."

"Oh, no," said Ben. "You just wanted a scapegoat. I'm not playing." He swept a cup of ink pens off the desk. They skittered across the floor.

"Ben! It doesn't have to be like this. Right now, you've got a good job. A secure job, doing work you like."

Tom's attempt at soothing him had the opposite effect. As Ben drew a breath to annihilate him, the reason for this encounter flooded back to him. He'd almost blown the whole thing. The shock dashed Ben's rage and left him weak enough to make his anxiety convincing.

Tom continued, taking advantage of Ben's apparent confusion. "You'll finish school with a solid track record as a PTA that'll make it easy for you to get a good job anywhere."

Ben shook his head as if to clear it. "I can't have this hanging over my head."

"I'm not asking you to do anything but show up for work and do your job," said Tom. "We'll even flex your schedule to accommodate your school when the next semester starts. You're doing a fine job here, and I don't want to lose you."

Ben squashed his rising ire and the urge to tell Tom he wouldn't submit to blackmail. He couldn't do that now. But he couldn't produce words of submission or fear, either, so he wrenched open the door and left Tom's office.

It took all the resolution he could muster to enter his own office and close the door behind him. He took the phone from his pocket and whispered into it.

"End recording, April twenty-eighth, nine o'clock a.m."

CHAPTER 41

Teresa sat on the bed with Benjie on her lap, crooning in his ear and rocking him. His crying broke her heart, great gulping sobs, wailing, "I want Mama." She held him close, murmuring wordless comfort, and he wrapped his arms and legs around her, clutching as if she might escape.

A change in the light made her glance up to see Jonah in the doorway. He took a step into the room, and she waved him back. Benjie needed to be comforted. That's what the counselor said, "Don't try to reason with him in the middle of the night." It was short this time. When Benjie settled into a restless sleep, Teresa covered him with a blanket and stroked his damp cheek. It shouldn't be this way.

Jonah was waiting for her.

"I'm sorry we woke you up. Benjie has these nightmares every so often. The other boys usually sleep right through them, even when he wakes up every adult in the house."

"Why are you angry at Benjie for missing his mother?"

"I'm not angry with him. Did it look like I was?" She was angry, but not at Benjie. These sessions left her exhausted. Angry and sad and tired.

"No," he said slowly. "Maybe. Not so he could see it."

"Good." She nodded and headed toward the room she shared with Annie.

"Do you want to see the forest by moonlight?"

Teresa stopped at the unexpected question.

"I can't leave the house while the children are sleeping!"

"Just on the back deck."

She paused. She would like to see the stars shining out of total darkness, and the idea of an adult conversation was appealing.

"As charming as that outfit is, though, I think you'd better put on slippers and a warm robe."

Teresa realized that she'd run out to Benjie in a red silk pajama set. The cropped top was sleeveless and the bottoms, while wide-legged, were low-waisted and fit smoothly over the hips. Not at all indecent, but not exactly modest, either.

"It stays so nice and warm in here," she said brightly, "that I forget it's still winter outside!"

She emerged from her bedroom a few minutes later, bundled into a shapeless fuzzy robe and fluffy slippers, wearing glasses and with her hair in a tight ponytail. In the dim light, she nearly bumped into Jonah, who still leaned casually against the wall opposite her door.

His lips twitched, but he didn't comment on the transformation. He picked up the conversation where they'd left off. "It's not winter anymore. This is spring."

"Are you sure?" She followed him through the kitchen and onto the deck, sliding the door closed behind her.

The moon gleamed above the night world. The cold, pure air slid smoothly over her face and throat, like her red silk pajamas. Teresa leaned over the railing, reveling in the touch. She inhaled deeply. The air smelled spicy.

"I love this." The words were just a whisper between her and God, nearly inaudible in the great, silent night. It was a discovery, a gift. "Thank You, God."

Her beautiful moment was interrupted by Jonah's voice. "Can I ask you a question?"

Teresa hedged. "What?"

"How old are you?"

"Fifty-five." She used her most nanny-like voice, firm and pleasant. "How old are you?"

"Sixty-five."

She spun around to face him. "You are not!"

"Well, I must be, because I think you're about ten years younger than me, so if you're fifty-five, that makes me sixty-five."

She glowered at him. "Fifty."

"Thirty."

"Forty-eight."

"Thirty." In the moonlight, the humor lines at the corners of his eyes were clearly visible.

Teresa persisted. "Forty-eight!"

"Liar."

She narrowed her eyes in speculation. "If I tell you the truth, will you answer a question for me?"

"Maybe." But he was still smiling. She could hear it.

"I'm thirty-four."

"You look younger."

"No, I don't." At least, she tried not to.

"What's your question?" He sounded casual, relaxed.

"Why are we here?"

He sighed. "I don't suppose you mean that in an existential way."

"I mean, why are the children and I here with you?"

Jonah took her arm and pulled her toward a chair. "Let's sit down."

"Is it that bad?"

"No, but it's a long story. Can I get you a blanket?"

"No, I'm fine. Thanks."

"Did you know that Ben was adopted?"

Teresa nodded.

"I'm his father."

"Oh." She hadn't expected that, but it made sense.

"It came as a complete surprise to me."

Teresa watched his expressive face in the moonlight as he talked. He was obviously deeply moved by their meeting, but he made it an amusing tale.

The implications of his story struck her. "Wait! You've only known him for six weeks?" She sat up straight. "Do you mean you've only met Ben one time and then he dumped four kids on you? That's outrageous!"

"No, no. It's amazing. Six weeks ago, I didn't know I had a son. Now I have a whole family."

She stared at him. "You didn't know you had a son at all? How could that happen? Didn't you have to sign papers for the adoption?"

"His mother didn't tell me she was pregnant. She only told one person, and that person didn't really believe her, so she never told anyone, either. I mean, the baby came early. Shari died in childbirth. I was away at boot camp." His voice wavered. It wasn't as simple as he made it sound. "I never even knew. Not until six weeks ago."

"No one told you you had a child? Oh, Jonah, I am so sorry." Teresa reached out and laid a hand on his arm. She used her other hand to wipe away her tears. "That was so wrong."

"Yeah," said Jonah. "It was. But there's no one to blame. She was just a kid, without a stable family. I wasn't around. They had to put the baby—Ben—up for adoption. But then Ben found me."

"And then Ben sent his children to stay with you." She shook her head.

"Well, he is only twenty-five," Jonah said with a grin. "And, really, I couldn't be happier. Of course, I'm awfully glad he sent you along with them, because I don't know anything about taking care of kids."

"You never had any other children?" No wonder he was

glad to find Ben.

"My wife and I didn't have any children. We talked about it, but we were both in the army and kept moving around."

Teresa pulled up the collar of her robe, suddenly cold. This story did not have a happy ending.

"She was a veterinarian, responsible for escorting groups of working dogs to and from the Mideast. On the last trip to Afghanistan, she stepped outside the kennels and someone shot her. A sniper. He took out two other people and disappeared."

"I'm sorry," said Teresa.

"What about Mr. Cooper?"

She knew what he meant. When she didn't respond right away, Jonah said, "None of my business. Sorry."

"No, it's fine. It's just an ugly story. It was a long time ago, and he's dead now."

Jonah waited.

"Leo was physically abusive. I pressed charges and he went to jail. While he was in jail, he joined a gang. When he got out, he threatened me. I ran. I got a job as a nanny, and, eventually, I went to work for Ben."

"Are you still in danger?"

"Oh, no." She smiled faintly. "Although I'm sure you could protect me as well as the children."

"I would." He wasn't smiling. "You said he was dead."

"It was a gang-related killing."

"I'm sorry. Well, not sorry he's dead, but sorry you had to go through that."

"Thank you." An unexpected, peaceful silence rested between them. Eventually, she stood up. "I'm going to bed. I'll see you in the morning."

"Me, too. Good night, Teresa."

CHAPTER 42

They woke to the musical sounds of appliances. Teresa made scrambled eggs and pancakes for breakfast, while Jonah checked the pump, plugged in the computers and reset clocks.

"It was fun for a few days," she said, "as long as we had heat and water, but I'm grateful for electricity."

"Especially the coffeemaker." Jonah pushed the syrup bottle beyond Annie's reach.

"I liked the way you did it with the pour-over cone," said Teresa. "It just didn't get hot enough."

"Yeah, it's better if the water boils. You did great putting together meals. I haven't eaten so well in a long time, even with electricity."

"I'm not doing anything fancy, and I'm still using paper plates and cups," Teresa warned him.

He gave her an exasperated look. "I told you, you're guests here. I appreciate what you do, but you don't have to do it unless you want to. We can eat peanut butter sandwiches as far as I'm concerned."

"I like peanut butter sandwiches," said Benjie. He used the last bit of his pancake to mop the remaining syrup on his plate. "I wish the electricity hadn't come back on. We were having fun."

Jack nodded. "It was fun using flashlights and pouring water in the toilet. Can we still do that?"

"Let's just flush them now, guys," said Jonah. "I turned the pump back on."

"It was more fun without electricity," repeated Benjie. "It was an adventure."

"I don't see what difference electricity can possibly make to you," Teresa said. "You've hardly been inside at all. I am very glad to have it back. I'm going to start some laundry and make sure all the food is put away." She turned to Jonah. "I don't suppose you have a crockpot, do you?"

"Actually, I do!" Jonah got up and went into the mudroom. When he came out, he was carrying a box. "I don't think it's ever been used. Cindy wanted it, but she wasn't much of a cook. We usually just grilled burgers or steaks when we were here."

"Why didn't we have burgers or steaks?" demanded Benjie.

"Sorry, buddy. I was out of propane. Bad timing. I wasn't expecting company."

"Can we go outside now?" Mark climbed over the bench. "Thank you, Mrs. Cooper. May I be excused?"

"You can be excused from the table and start K.P. duty," said Jonah. "That's the procedure around here, remember?"

"What's K.P. duty?" asked Benjie.

"Kitchen Patrol. We clean up."

"Do we have to?"

Jonah started to respond to Jack's question, but Teresa interrupted.

"Jack, you will stay inside and do all of the K.P. while Grandpa Campbell and Benjie and Mark go outside." She turned to Jonah. "Jack will be out when he's finished."

Jonah snapped his mouth shut and looked at the other two boys. "You heard the lady. Let's go."

When Jack was finished, Teresa sat down and patted the bench next to her. "Come sit down by me, Jack. Just for a minute."

He slid in but didn't say anything.

"It's been a busy few weeks. It's fun being on vacation, but I miss home, too. Do you miss home?"

He nodded.

"What do you miss most?"

"Daddy." The little boy shuddered and then started sobbing.

Teresa held him close until his crying slowed. "It's hard to be away from your dad. He misses you, too, but he has to do this special thing for work right now. As soon as it's over, he'll be back, and we'll go home."

Jack's sobs dwindled to hiccups. Teresa continued. "He thought this would be a fun place for us to visit until we go home. Are you having fun?"

Jack nodded.

"Me, too!" She ruffled his hair. "Are you ready to go outside, or would you like to hang out with me for a little while?"

"I'll go outside." Jack dressed quickly and ran out the door. Teresa watched him join the others and disappear around the corner of the garage. He'd be okay. He just needed a few minutes by himself.

"Okay, Annie. Let's get this place cleaned up and get outside. We don't want to be stuck in here while everyone else is outside, do we?"

It didn't take long to get things in order and dinner started. Teresa stepped outside holding Annie's hand and breathed deeply.

"Can you taste that air, Annie? That's clean air. God made that air and man hasn't messed it up yet."

Teresa surveyed the land. The shrubbery and smaller trees were misty green. The grass was soggy but definitely green. She imagined it as it must be when all the trees were leafed out. Incredible. Jonah's house would be even more isolated, hidden behind walls of green foliage. It was like being in your own apartment with all the curtains drawn, but in a living environment. A big, private, secret living environment. No, it wasn't anything like being in her apartment with the curtains drawn. It would be magical. In a nice, non-supernatural kind of way, of course. And in the winter, would they be snowed in, inaccessible? Teresa laughed and squeezed Annie's hand.

"I think I must be feeling crowded lately, Annie, if being snowbound sounds appealing. Let's go find those boys."

Annie babbled and hopped and stopped to examine things. Teresa found some pink flowers, and they made a bouquet. Wildflowers, just free to pick. Teresa marveled at the abundance. She'd seen beautiful places, mostly from the road or on television, but she'd never been in one, close to the ground, able to touch everything.

She and Annie walked slowly, following the path as it curved to the right and up an incline. From the top, they saw the male people squatting down behind a shrub.

Annie squealed. Teresa called out, "Hi there!"

A doe and two fawns bolted away at the sound of her voice, and a chorus of disappointment rose from the boys.

"Oh, I am sorry!"

"Grandpa Campbell was going to take a picture!" Mark was so excited that Teresa couldn't imagine any sensible deer coming within one hundred feet of him.

Jonah rested a hand on the boy's head. "We'll take a picture of something else. You guys keep your eyes open and remember to walk vewy, vewy quietly."

Teresa laughed. "They've seen all the Elmer Fudd cartoons! Ben has a large collection of what he calls 'classics'."

"A chip off the old block. I have them, too. I'm glad you brought me some kids so I have an excuse to sit down and watch them again."

"Do you need an excuse?"

He grinned. "No. Now that I'm a grown up and not in the army anymore, I can do whatever I want. Can you?"

"Within reason," she said cautiously. "Right now, I'm responsible for these children. I'll probably be responsible for them for at least four or five more years."

"What then?" asked Jonah. "Do you just disappear from their lives?" He looked appalled.

Teresa glanced at the kids. Assured of their privacy, she said, "This is an odd situation. In my previous jobs—for most nanny positions—the nanny is just a sort of full-time babysitter. They still have two parents, usually, or maybe the parents are divorced but both still see the kids. When all the kids are old enough to go to school, there's really no reason to have a nanny anymore." She stopped to accept a bunch of flowers from Annie, and the girl ran back to her brothers. "This is kind of different. For one thing, Ben is a very young, single father, working full-time and also in school to become a physical therapist."

"Ben will probably be unemployed and considering a career goal change in another few weeks," said Jonah wryly.

"Probably. Unlike other nannying jobs, this one has been more like having my own home and family," said Teresa. "I know he's your son, but really. . . Ben can be clueless sometimes. His parents tended to overindulge him. Not terribly. I get the impression he was an easy-going boy, and they enjoyed providing things for him. And then, when he would normally have moved on to college and adulthood, things kept happening and they had to bail him out. Now they're stuck doing it until he graduates."

"You were talking about this job being like having your own home and family," Jonah prompted.

"I do absolutely everything that a wife and mother

would do in that home—except being Ben's wife, of course--from cooking three meals a day to choosing clothes and furniture, scheduling children's appointments and activities, cleaning and running errands. . . as if it's my own home. I can't really imagine leaving it. The children don't regard me as a babysitter, and there's no way I could have kept my distance anyhow. Just look at them!"

The children were sitting in a row, astride a downed tree. Annie kept falling off, and the boys helped her up again each time.

"I think they're playing train, or maybe Monorail. Or maybe that flume ride from the water park," said Teresa. "Anyhow, I was looking for a job in a school when Eliza found me. I didn't even want to do nannying anymore. She promised me an apartment of my own over the garage, insurance, a good paycheck. . . and she started crying when I said I wasn't interested. So, I agreed to meet Ben."

Teresa fell silent, remembering that day. She'd walked in the door with the intention of turning down the job, but one look at the shell-shocked young man melted her heart. She would have stayed for whatever wages he could provide. He tried to talk details of employment, but he kept getting distracted. His grief was so raw, and he was so overwhelmed by the magnitude of his new responsibilities, that he couldn't focus on anything. Finally, she reached across the table and touched his hand.

"If the apartment's ready, I'll move in on Saturday. Your mother will teach me everything I need to know."

Ben let out a ragged breath. "Just like Mary Poppins, huh? I'm glad we found someone older, someone who already knows the ropes." He looked at her anxiously. "You do realize that there are four of them, right? And none of them are in school yet. The baby's only six months old."

"Yes," she said gently. "I know."

He persisted. "That's two in diapers, and Jack's been having a lot of accidents, too. We thought he was almost trained, but not lately."

"That's very normal in times of stress." She spoke soothingly. This man needed comfort as much as his children did, but he was still pouring himself out for them. He was so young. "I'll take care of it." And she had.

Jonah was watching her. "And Ben talked you into it?"

"Pretty much. He needed help, and I was available."

"What happened to Anneliese?"

Teresa broke a twig off a branch. "That's not my story."

"Is she still alive? Did she abandon them?"

"Oh, no!" She shot him a startled glance. "Wherever did you get that idea?"

"Neither you nor Ben like to talk about her. You both seem angry. I don't even know how she died."

"Well, she's dead. She was killed by a drunk driver."

"That's awful. What happened?"

She turned to him. "I try to avoid gossiping about my employers, and I have already said more than I ought, especially about Ben and his parents. And with you being Ben's biological father. . . I shouldn't have said as much as I did. Please forget it."

"You know I can't forget it. They sound like very loving parents. I really would like to know more about Ben's wife, though. He said she was pregnant when they graduated from high school. Childhood sweethearts. It must have broken his heart to lose her that way. See! You were angry again. I could see it in your eyes."

She turned her face away. "Maybe we can talk about it later. I think Annie's fallen off the train again. I'll take her inside and make lunch."

CHAPTER 43

"It's not admissible?" Benjamin slumped in his chair. The steak in front of him might as well have been shoe leather. He'd lost his appetite.

Pete Collins shrugged. "Maybe. Even trained investigators seldom get an admissible recording. It all depends on the judge. Ben got a little out of control there, and Potter could claim he felt intimidated and confused. Even if we can use it, it can't be a large part of the case. We need physical evidence." He paused while the waitress refilled their water glasses and then continued, "But it gives us a good foothold for the investigation. We're sure that Potter and Cravitz are involved."

"We knew that already," snapped Benjamin. "What about the woman who hit him? It's her insurance."

"She doesn't know anything. She told us a man gave her five hundred dollars to bump into Ben and make sure he went to that clinic. They told her where to wait so she could get behind him at the light. Can you hand me a roll, please?" Pete went on talking as he broke and buttered the bread. "She had to try three times before she got into position."

"But what about her insurance company? Why aren't they checking it out?" asked Benjamin.

"They are now. She had a clean driving record until this, and good insurance. It sounds to me," said Pete, "like the man gave her more than money. Apparently, she's addicted to opioids. She's actually in jail now, for trying to break into a pharmacy."

"But she'll be charged with insurance fraud, right?"

"Why bother? We'll see if we can get her to identify the man who approached her, but it's not likely. She remembers the money and trying to get behind Ben's car. According to the corrections people, she's in bad shape."

"You don't think Dr. Cravitz is the head of the ring?"

"No," said Pete. "He's one doctor in a strategic location, but they can't go on having accidents at that particular intersection. I think the head of this is going to be in regular family practice. That would give him a broader spectrum of people and service providers. But we also hope to net a few personal injury lawyers."

"It should be challenging to prosecute personal injury lawyers," Benjamin grinned.

Pete stabbed a carrot. "Not at all. Judges hate 'em. Public opinion's usually negative, too, until they need one." He looked at Benjamin. "Your boy should be in the clear, but if I were you, I'd get him a good lawyer, just in case."

CHAPTER 44

Jonah stopped to watch Teresa as he entered the living room. Ben had implied the nanny was older and rather commanding. Was the boy blind?

Teresa propped her feet on the ottoman and squirmed her way into a snug position in the corner of the leather couch. After a few seconds, she tucked her feet underneath her and grabbed one of the throw pillows to shove behind her back.

"Comfortable?" he asked. "I made two cups of that tea you brought with you." He set one on the coffee table in front of her and then moved it to the end table where she could reach it.

"Your couch is very big," said Teresa. "When I sat down, my feet didn't reach the floor."

"I like it," said Jonah, "but usually I sit in the recliner, anyhow. Would you like to try it?"

"No, thanks. I think I'm settled in for the night. This is comfortable." She glanced up. "Is that rain on the roof?"

"Sleet. Freezing rain. It's not supposed to be an ice storm, though, so we shouldn't lose power again."

"That's good. I like electricity."

"I had a generator when I first moved here permanently, but it went out, and I never got it fixed." He nodded at her Kindle. "What are you reading?"

She held it up for his inspection. "My Bible."

"You're a Christian?" Pleased, Jonah reached under the table next to the recliner and pulled out his own Bible. "Me, too."

"I thought you might be," she said. "You prayed at dinner."

"Lots of people pray at dinner." He opened the door of the stove and fed it more wood. "I go to the community church in town. Do you want to come with me on Sunday morning?" He hastened to make himself clear. "All of you, I mean."

"Maybe. Let's play it by ear." She scooted a little higher on the couch. "I thought about it all afternoon, Jonah, and I'm going to tell you about Anneliese. I don't want you asking Ben, and I don't want you to say something tactless just because you didn't know. Eliza told me for the same reasons."

"I don't want to pry into sensitive matters."

Teresa looked amused. "Yes, you do, and it's okay. I think we just made too big a mystery of it."

"So, was she killed by a drunk driver or not?"

"She was. It was a bad accident. Two other people died, too." Teresa stopped talking and looked down at her mug.

Jonah watched her struggle for composure, wishing he knew what to say. He saw her swallow, and suddenly he knew. The truth rocked him back and made him sick.

"Anneliese was the drunk driver," he whispered.

"It was raining." She glanced up toward the ceiling. "A night like this one. Witnesses say she approached the intersection without slowing down and slammed on her brakes too late. She hit a car and killed the two passengers—a mom and a nine-year-old girl. Both cars spun sideways, and Anneliese was killed when she hit a telephone pole."

Teresa raised her cup to her mouth but appeared to change her mind. She continued, "The publicity was vicious. Ben and the kids lost Anneliese and then had to survive a blood-thirsty media attack."

"And Annie was a baby then? How could she do that?" Jonah knew there was no good answer to that question. "Poor Ben."

"He and Anneliese started 'going together' in their junior year of high school. Anneliese's father moved out and got a divorce about that time." Teresa rubbed her forehead with one hand. "Eliza thinks Anneliese started drinking then. Ben stuck to her like glue. Like Sir Galahad, in my opinion. It was noble of him, but. . . " Teresa sighed. "Benjamin and Eliza expected the relationship to die a natural death when Ben went away to college, but Anneliese got pregnant. They insisted on getting married."

Jonah had a fleeting thought of his own "relationship" with Shari. His parents would have hit the roof.

"The Taylors were heartbroken. They thought their son's life was all mapped out and on track for an independent adulthood, and then he got his girlfriend pregnant. But they helped out financially so he could go to the technical college and get his physical therapist assistant degree. Then he could work at that until he got his doctorate in physical therapy."

"I get the feeling things didn't work out that smoothly," said Jonah.

"No. Apparently, she did okay through the pregnancy, but she kept sliding back into it," said Teresa. "I only got it third-hand, so it's really gossip, but it sounds like Ben was in denial for a long time. Once, he caught her drinking and driving with Benjie and Jack in the car, coming home from an afternoon play date. She said she only had one drink, but he suspected it was more, and he didn't know how to stop her. He did the usual things—taking away money and the car keys, and throwing out any bottles he found in the house, but you know that won't stop a determined drinker. She got angry when he confronted her, and Ben doesn't like conflict. He was even younger then."

"No one likes conflict, at any age," said Jonah.

"I don't know about that," said Teresa. "It seems to me there are plenty of quarrelsome people in the world. Anyhow, the Taylors knew some of it. Eliza tried to help out with the kids, to give Anneliese a break, but, well, it just kept getting worse. Once, she got stopped, but she was below the legal limit, and the police officer just brought her home. Eventually, she got caught way over the limit, and she was arrested and charged with drunk driving. Ben's parents posted bail. The judge suspended her license and let her go, on condition that she attend AA meetings. A week later, she took the car while Ben was sleeping, got drunk and. . . had that accident."

Silence hung in the air until Jonah stirred. "Thank you for telling me. Poor Ben. And those poor children. No wonder Benjie has nightmares."

"Yes, and I'm a little worried about Jack, too. I'm keeping an eye on him."

"They're lucky to have you," said Jonah.

"No, they're lucky to have Benjamin and Eliza. They bought a house in another suburb and rent it out to Ben. I'm pretty sure they cover a lot of the bills, including his tuition and insurance." She cast him an impish grin. "And they provided him with a perfect nanny—a housekeeper who makes his life run more smoothly than it ever has before."

Jonah remembered Ben's comments about running out of clean laundry. "I can see that. I think he knows how good he's got it."

"Ben's a nice kid. He just got a rocky start on adulthood. I think he's becoming more assertive as he works through this situation at work. I have great hopes for him."

"So, you're Ben's nanny, too?" asked Jonah.

"It feels like it, sometimes, but that's okay. I really do like my life very much. It'll change in a few years, but for now I just go on here."

Jonah considered her in the dim room. "What kind of life do you think you'd like to have long-term?"

"I don't know, at least not right now. It's been an emotional evening, and emotions give me a headache. Thank you for listening and understanding." Teresa climbed out of her nest and stood up. "I do have some pity for Anneliese, you know. I never met her, but she obviously had her own family problems. The thing is, lots of people have problems and get over it. She had every opportunity to get over it, with supportive family to help her. Maybe she would have been able to stop drinking after a while. And it's only been a couple of years. We'll all probably be able to view it with more compassion over time. Goodnight, Jonah."

CHAPTER 45

Meeting at the restaurant was a sensible option. Neither of them had eaten a home-cooked meal in weeks. At least his dad could afford good restaurants—Ben had been living on fast food.

His father opened with the most important question. "What's going on with the kids?"

"They're with Jonah Campbell, up in the U.P."

"Where?" His dad's voice could probably be heard throughout the restaurant.

"It's a good place for them. No one will find them, because no one knows he exists. And Mrs. Cooper's with them." Ben opened the menu. Anything but beef.

His dad stared at him, eyebrows drawn together. "I understand your thinking, Ben, and I agree that it's a good, safe place, but you've only met the man once. For that matter, it's a bit presumptuous to expect him to keep four children."

"Yes, but they have their nanny, so they won't be any trouble," said Ben. "He wanted to meet them."

"Teresa is a very competent woman, Ben, but you can't just keep sending her around the country, expecting her to watch your children."

"You and Mom took them to Disney and the Dells. This is the first place she's had to go on her own." Ben forced confidence into his voice, as much for his own sake as his dad's.

It was the perfect solution. It had to be.

"Tom knew you had children and a nanny," his father said, "and he mentioned them to demonstrate his power."

"Well, he doesn't have any power if he can't find them. I'm going to have the fettuccine Alfredo."

"I'm having the snapper." His dad set the menu aside and regarded him. "I listened to the recording of your conversation with Potter. You were pretty upset."

"Well, yeah! Wouldn't you have been upset?" Ben scowled. "And I'm pretty upset with Pete Collins, too. I gave him exactly what he wanted, and he says they 'might' be able to use it."

"Your recording was good. Even if it's not admissible as evidence in court, it goes a long way in clearing up your personal issues."

"I don't see why it wouldn't be admissible. Tom confessed to everything," said Ben, "and went into detail about it. I'd think it would be exactly what they want."

"Well, until there's a prosecutable case, no one can tell. Pete said it'll be up to the judge."

Ben eyed his father. The man looked exhausted and ten years older. "How's Mom?"

"Okay. Worried about you and the kids. It'll be easier once we find a good rehab facility. I checked out two places this morning and have three more later today. You worked in a nursing home. You know how they can be."

Ben nodded, his mouth full of salad. He swallowed. "But there are some good rehab places that aren't nursing homes. That's what you're looking for, right?"

"Yes, definitely. You know, it occurred to me this morning that it's mostly the small, independently-owned operations than can profit from this kind of insurance fraud. In a larger company, there's too much bureaucracy. Too many people would have to be involved. Something like a nursing home, especially with Medicaid clients, is subject to continual inspections and audits."

"Right," said Ben.

"They can't just make up imaginary patients or claim that the patients are receiving additional services," said his father, "because it has to be documented every step of the way." He snorted. "They don't need to commit fraud. They're committing highway robbery. I can't believe how much these places charge."

"A setup like Great Lakes is perfect," agreed Ben. "There are only two employees—Lauren Windel and me. I provide his documentation." He grimaced. "I've probably signed a hundred fraudulent records."

"And if he was taken to court right now, he could produce those records to show that you were providing continuing care, and you would have to admit that you did the therapy. You wouldn't be allowed to give your opinion on whether or not that care was necessary."

"I do have some training and experience," said Ben.

"Legally, not enough to diagnose. That's why Potter needs you." His dad nodded. "You'll get that degree eventually, if we can keep you alive and out of jail."

CHAPTER 46

"The van's warming up, but I'll let you drive." Teresa closed the door behind her, enjoying the warmth of the house after dashing through the cold rain.

"Okay, I can do that." Jonah looked harried. "Annie and I have been talking about the importance of wearing coats in bad weather." The girl was sitting on her coat, clutching it to her bottom with both hands.

"She'll be fine, Jonah. The van will be warm, and it's not safe for them to wear coats in the car seats."

"Really? Are you sure?"

She raised her brows, and he chuckled.

"I know. . . my parenting skills are sadly lacking. I'd make a terrible nanny."

"You'd be a 'manny'." She laughed at his expression. "Yes, I know. What a revolting term. It's hard enough for a woman to get a job as a nanny. I'm pretty sure you'd be unemployed." She looked around. Benjie was sitting at the dining room table reading a book.

"Where are Mark and Jack?"

"They're in the bedroom getting dressed," said Jonah. "They're excited about not having to wear suits to church."

"Well, they only go on Easter, and most people dress up then. Even me." The memory made her wince. She was wearing her least ugly dress today, with all of her "old nanny" makeup. She'd scraped her hair back into a tight twist and hung her reading glasses chain around her neck. She wanted to cry.

Jonah rubbed his chin. "You don't have to dress up. Most of the people in our church do, but they don't think it's a symbol of righteousness or anything. You could have worn your jeans." He waggled his brows. "Then I could have worn mine."

Was his comment an oblique reference to her appearance? She'd hardly considered her appearance at all since arriving. She'd been comfortable with her "natural" look until today, but even the best church might find their situation irregular. Four children did not count as a chaperon, and it would be unfair to Jonah if his reputation was affected by this visit.

"Ben and the kids don't go to church?" asked Jonah.

She shook her head. "No. I wish they did, but I have to let Ben and his parents be in charge of that. The problem is, I'm pretty sure they would let me take the kids with me to my church, but I like having the weekends off and going to church on my own. Then I feel like a heathen monster for not taking them."

He considered that. "Does your church have evening programs for the kids? Or VBS? Even our little church has those."

"Yes, but that's when Ben's home, and it would have to be his choice," said Teresa. She walked to the bedroom door and looked inside. "We're leaving in five minutes, boys. Do you need help?" At their negative response, she returned to Jonah.

"It's hard to back off and let him be in control, sometimes, especially since he's so willing to *not* be in control. His parents have the same problem. They didn't have much choice but to step in, and now they're stuck with it."

"You mean financially?" Jonah sat down to tie his shoes. "Or in general?"

"You can't really separate them. Without financial responsibilities, it's hard for a young man to feel like an adult. They've tried to make sure he has some of that. He buys gas and groceries, and he pays rent and utilities, too."

"And your wages?" Jonah reached under the table to get his Bible.

"Oh, no. That's Eliza's brainchild. Ben pays me $300 a week, and his parents bring that up to an appropriate salary without him even knowing. They pay for my insurance, too, and I have an apartment over the garage. It's a good deal for me, for now."

He stopped. "What do you mean—for now?"

"Like I said before, I'm not their mother. Eventually, the kids will all be in school, so they won't need a full-time babysitter."

"What will you do? Find a new nanny gig?"

"Nanny gig!" Teresa laughed. "I like that. I don't know yet. I have four more years. I've thought about working on a master's degree online, but I just don't know. I'm a certified preschool teacher. I'd have to renew my license, but that's not a big deal."

"Do you want to be a preschool teacher?"

"I don't know, Jonah. I don't know what I want to do. Mostly, I don't want to get stuck in the wrong job. I need to pray about it more than I do."

As Teresa slid her Kindle into her purse, she caught sight of Annie trying to stuff her coat under the couch. "Sorry, kiddo, but the coat has to come with us. And you can carry it." She only had four years left with this girl, and Teresa had a feeling she would be a challenge.

"I thought your church was in town," said Teresa.

"It's almost in town. Just half a mile down this road." He signaled and turned onto a narrow, paved road. "See? There's the sign. I designed that."

"You did? It's beautiful!" The simple wooden sign showed a cross surrounded by and rising above pine trees. The name of the church was spelled out in cream-colored, elegant block lettering. The sign could be seen, but it fit into its environment.

"I wish you'd show me more of your work," said Teresa.

"I'd be happy to. Maybe this evening?" Jonah looked across at her and smiled.

Teresa didn't have time to analyze the elation that ruffled through her before the church came into sight. The one-story building was made of logs and boulders, with red double doors. A large wooden cross was planted next to it, instead of on the roof. To one side of the building, she could see a cemetery with an ironwork fence.

The parking lot was full. Anxiety rose in Teresa as she shepherded the children toward the door. When Jonah held the door open and put a hand on her back to usher her inside, she jumped and tried to move aside inconspicuously.

"Are you okay?" Jonah asked. "Teresa, nobody here bites." He paused. "Well, except for Annie, but I told her she can't bite anyone here."

"You told her. . . " Teresa couldn't help laughing. "It's *never* okay to bite people."

"She's only two. We have to start small. You know. . . in bite-size pieces."

His teasing did the trick—Teresa was smiling when they entered the fellowship hall. The room was crowded and noisy. Where did all these people come from, in such an isolated region? Dozens of children played and ran in circles. They were more formally dressed than at Teresa's church, but that didn't slow them down.

Every introduction was a variation of the same formula. Ben introduced the children by name, saying they were "young friends come to visit while their father was busy with a big project at work." She was introduced as their nanny, of course.

Annie enjoyed the attention, but the boys stuck close to Teresa with an unprecedented shyness.

A pretty blond woman walked through the crowd and extended a hand to Jonah. "Hello, Jonah."

He enfolded her hands in both of his own. "Emma. You're looking good. All over the flu?"

"Oh, yes. I still don't think it was the flu. Just a cold. Introduce me to your friends!" She bestowed a ravishing smile on Teresa. "I'm Emma Schenstrom. Welcome!"

"I thought you wanted me to introduce you," complained Jonah. "Emma, this is Teresa Cooper. She and her young charges are visiting me for a while."

"It's nice to meet you," said Emma. She shook hands briskly and continued. "Where are you from?"

"Near Chicago." Teresa tried to use her formal nanny voice, but she was out of practice.

"Are you glad to get out of the city, or do you miss it?"

Teresa looked at the woman. She didn't appear to be making small talk. Maybe she really wanted to know. "I think I could stay here forever." The words came out of Teresa's mouth before they filtered through her brain. She tried to temper her response. "It's very beautiful."

"Actually," said the other woman, "this is the ugliest season. Just wait until you see it later this spring, or summer, or fall, or winter!"

Her words hit Teresa like a bucket of cold water. She wouldn't be here for those times. She might have a few more days or a week here, but surely it couldn't go on longer than that. She smiled politely at Emma and brought the boys out from behind her.

"Mrs. Schenstrom, this is Benjie, Jack and Mark. Boys, this is Mrs. Schenstrom." They shook hands politely and tried to withdraw. Teresa didn't let them.

"You boys must be about the same age as my two youngest girls. Lizzie is seven and Naomi's five." Emma turned back to Teresa. "Would you like to keep your little girl with you during the worship service, or have her visit our nursery? My third son is in there, now. I was just about to go check on him. Can I take you over there?"

Teresa hesitated. She did *not* want to keep Annie with her. And how many children did this woman have? She looked at Jonah. "I think Annie might do better in the nursery. Can I leave the boys with you?"

As if in reaction, the boys pressed closer to her. Exasperated, she said, "All three of you need to stay with Grandpa Campbell while I take care of Annie. I'll be back."

"You are definitely a nanny," said Emma. She turned to Jonah. "Grandpa Campbell?"

He just grinned.

Emma lifted Annie and led Teresa across the room. "We have a baby nursery and a toddler nursery. Some people use them and some don't. She stopped at a Dutch door. "Hi, Tim. We have another customer for you."

Teresa looked at the young man in alarm. He couldn't be the only attendant. In the opposite corner of the bright room, three little girls stacked oversized cardboard blocks to build a tower. Annie wiggled, and before Teresa could stop her, Emma handed her to the young man, who set her on the floor. Annie marched across the floor and kicked down the cardboard tower.

Tim handled the ensuing melee efficiently. When he had restored order, he returned to the doorway. "Don't worry, two of my sisters will be here soon. I'm just filling in until they get here."

Teresa looked at the girls on the floor. Emma had said her third son was in the nursery. "This is your third son?"

Tim rolled his eyes. "She likes to refer to us by number."

Emma reach over and pinched his arm. "You're being very disrespectful." She was smiling, though, and Teresa had a feeling it was a family joke. "Yes, and daughters number 2 and 3 will be here soon. Any minute. Do you want to wait until they get here?"

Each of the girls had a doll now, and they were making beds out of the blocks. "I think she's fine." She called across the nursery. "I'm leaving now, Annie. I'll be back soon. Have fun." Annie looked up briefly and returned to her play.

Emma walked her back toward Jonah and the boys. "I like the way you let her know you were leaving. Too many parents don't. They bring their child and sneak off while he's distracted. Then he panics later. Children like to know where their parents are and when they'll be back, just like parents want to know about their children."

"Very true," said Teresa. "I never thought about it that way. It just seems impolite to disappear."

"You'll have to meet my oldest daughter." Emma chuckled. "Phoebe. She worked as a nanny for a couple years, for a family near Madison. She liked it, mostly, but I missed her."

"How many children do you have?" It would be impolite to ask Emma how old she was, too.

"Nine," said Emma. "Five girls and four boys. Phoebe's twenty-two, and they're all about two years apart, ending with Jacob, who's three." She cast a sidelong glance at Teresa. "See what I did there? *Ending* with Jacob?"

"Do people keep asking you if you're going to have more?" Teresa asked.

"It happens to all large families. First, they ask you, "Do

you know what causes that?" — as if you're going to stop doing it — and then they want to know if you plan to have more. I used to tell them I was hoping for twelve."

"You're back," Jonah spoke from behind her. "We have about five minutes before the service begins." The boys stood close to him.

Teresa hadn't heard him coming. More disturbing, she hadn't heard the boys coming, either. She regarded them briefly and then said, "We need to go outside for a minute."

CHAPTER 47

"So, are you going to say anything to Ben about what the boys told you?" Jonah accepted a cup of tea and sat down at the breakfast bar. "About church?"

"I don't know," said Teresa. "He probably feels the same way the boys do. Benjamin and Eliza are very nice people—"

Jonah interrupted her. "You keep saying that, but it's not nice to tell children that you have to wear your best clothes and be quiet in God's house."

"They do seem to have taken it to an extreme." Teresa snapped a seal on the container of chopped apples and put it in the refrigerator. "I think their church is mostly older people, and more formal than mine or yours. And today, the other children were dressed up, but they weren't at all quiet. Our boys were in jeans, and they were too nervous to make a sound." She scratched her ear. "I wonder how Eliza accomplished that."

"Our boys. I like the sound of that," said Jonah. "They seem to have accepted what you told them."

"I hope so. They said they liked the worship service. I'm sorry about Sunday school, though. I would have enjoyed that."

Jonah shrugged. "Maybe they'll be more comfortable next weekend. If they want to wear suits, we could order some online."

Teresa didn't say anything. Would they still be here next weekend? What about Benjie's school? Benjamin had taken care of that, according to Eliza. For a large donation, the school would probably be willing to be flexible with their attendance policy. Maybe he'd be back in school by the end of this week. They'd all be back home, back to their normal lives, in the city, where all the trees were domestic ones, planted by people instead of God.

The kids would be back, of course. Jonah was already in love with all of his grandchildren. If Ben thought he was going to be able to whisk them away at the end of this situation, without continuing the relationship, he was seriously mistaken. Jonah was good for the boys. Benjamin was loving and generous, but he was an old man without energy or interest in the kinds of things that fascinated little boys.

Jonah cleared his throat. "Are you still interested in seeing my work?"

"Yes, I would like that."

Teresa had glimpsed the studio when Jonah had the boys in there. She'd been surprised at how modern it looked, with multiple computers and high-tech light arrangements. Now, at night, in the quiet house, it felt like a private space. A pleasing fragrance—oil paints?—wafted out as he opened the door.

Jonah sniffed. "Normally, the door is left open and the smell dissipates."

"It's not bad." Teresa moved into the studio. Light wood cabinets and racks for hanging canvases lined two walls. In addition to the large drafting table with its overhead computer monitors, the spacious room held a butcher-block island and a long, adjustable table. The table held a portable easel, empty now, with a bar stool in front of it.

Teresa stopped and stared in bemusement. This was where Jonah felt creative? A stainless steel and glass computer desk, laden with modern equipment and two printers, rounded the corner next to the door. The rolling office chair would slide easily on the laminate floor.

Jonah flipped lights off and on. "I can create different lighting in here, for different kinds of projects. I have special blinds for the windows, too, to control the natural light. I do sketching outside, and photography, of course, but I paint in here." He pointed at the monitors. "Sometimes I project a photo or copy of my drawing up there and then recreate it at the drafting table."

"It's not at all what I associate with an artist's studio. I knew some artists in college. Their studios were a mess. This is more Swedish Modern than Jonah Campbell."

"I don't work well in a mess," said Jonah. "It's the Army in me. I like clean, open spaces where nothing distracts. I focus better."

Teresa wandered around the immaculate—nearly sterile—studio until she came to a case of music CD's and an old-fashioned stereo. "But you listen to music while you work?"

"Most of the time." Jonah joined her and ran his finger along the rows of CD's. "Country, jazz, folk music, contemporary Christian in different genres. . . I choose the music to fit the project."

"Rap?" Teresa pulled out two discs and held them up in laughing accusation. "What kind of artwork does rap music inspire?"

"It's Toby Mac," said Jonah. "Christian rap. I can show you what I did with it last time."

She continued to browse the shelves. You could tell a lot about a person by the kind of music they listened to. The problem was, none of it meshed. Bluegrass music in this clinical setting?

"No hard rock or classical?"

"Not usually. If I want something, I can stream it." He opened a cabinet door and drew a folder from one of the horizontal shelves. "This was a Toby Mac special."

She joined him at the drafting table. Jonah sold his artwork locally and online, and he did commercial art, too, but somehow, this felt like an intimate occasion. Possibly too intimate, under the circumstances. Teresa took a deep breath and then choked on a gasp.

She coughed self-consciously. "Excuse me. That isn't what I was expecting." She leaned in and studied the black and white drawing.

After a moment of silence, Jonah asked, "What do you see?"

Teresa didn't look up. "Is this what winter looks like here?"

"Oh, no!" said Jonah. "It's the bones of winter. What winter would look like if you didn't *look* at it. Look into it."

"Like a shell?"

"A shell or a crust. Or just a very cold winter day under the influence of pain, anger, and rap music."

"Is that what you were feeling when you drew it?" Compassion stirred in Teresa. She didn't like the drawing. It might be fine art, but it hurt to look at.

Jonah gazed at the picture. "I had just learned about Ben, and how I'd had a son and never even known. The guilt still kills me. Getting a fifteen-year-old girl pregnant and she dies in childbirth? I barely remember her, but what I do remember was. . . lively. She thought I'd come back from the army and marry her. Unfortunately, she never told me or anyone else."

He scanned Teresa's face. "I did not know she was that young."

Was he seeking some kind of absolution from her? Teresa bit her lip. She wasn't good with this kind of thing.

Jonah continued while she was still trying to find words.

"I know God's forgiven me. The problem is, I can't seem to forgive myself. It keeps coming back to me." He shoved his hands in his pockets and looked out the window. "If I heard this story about another man, I would be disgusted with him."

Using her fingertips on the edges, Teresa straightened the winter scene. "I'm not an expert, Jonah. Far from it. I think. . . a couple things do occur to me, though. One, you haven't known about this for very long, and, at the same time, you've gained a son and grandchildren, which has brought you joy."

Jonah nodded without looking at her.

"I don't think you've had time to process those extremes and really work it out with God. He knew all about it a long time ago, but it's fresh for you. It's natural for you to feel that disgust. Sin should disgust us. But when you've had a little time—time without four little kids climbing on you—I think it'll be easier to work out."

He turned back to her. "Thank you. That's true, and it helps. What's your other thought?"

"It's a little more preachy," Teresa said. "But God declared you clean. You say you believe that, but you think He's wrong." She wrinkled her nose. "I don't think you should do that."

That made him laugh. "Yeah. It's probably a bad idea to tell God He's wrong."

"But," said Teresa, "my first point is important, too."

"Thank you," he said again. "I will remember that."

Ben had the same bright blue eyes and dark lashes, Teresa reflected, but Jonah's were. . . different. How could blue eyes be warm? Maybe they just made her feel warm. Teresa shut down that train of thought and brought her attention back to the artwork.

"What else do you have to show me?"

His other work was more "Jonah," with all the facets and vitality of the man. Teresa listened as he narrated each piece, paintings and photographs.

"It's all so beautiful, especially the way you show it in your art. It would be easy to miss all those details." She tucked a strand of hair behind her ear. "You'd have to live here a long time to see it all."

"You'll never see all of it," said Jonah. "And it never gets old."

Teresa turned to look at him. "Do you like living out here all by yourself?"

He took a minute to answer. "I've been very content here. I joined the army right out of high school, and you're never alone in the army. After Cindy died, I wanted to be somewhere quiet and peaceful, and then I realized that I like being peaceful."

Teresa went back to looking at the images on the large computer monitor. "Do you think you like winter because it wraps around you like a cocoon, and you can't do anything else, so it's okay to do whatever you want? There's a freedom in that."

"Yes, I can see that. It's possible. I do have that feeling sometimes. But since I retired, I don't have to be snowed in to do what I want."

Teresa glanced at him. He was watching her.

"Do you think," asked Jonah, "that winter would appeal to you like that? You're responsible for so many people, all the time. You're very tied down. Do you ever get to do what you want to do?"

"It hasn't been an issue. I have weekends off, and most evenings. I have my own apartment. That's more than I've had before. In my other nanny jobs, I just had a bedroom, sitting room and private bathroom in someone else's house. This," said Teresa with a sweep of her arm that encompassed the great outdoors, "is amazing. I've seen it, but I've never been *in* it."

He nodded.

Teresa drew figure-eights on the table with one finger. Would Jonah think she was crazy? Would she get eaten by a bear? The kids were asleep, though, and it wasn't raining. She slanted a glance up at him. He regarded her with something like compassion, but he didn't speak.

"Do you think," said Teresa, "that I could go outside for a little while? I mean, would you stay in here with the kids? And lend me a flashlight." Her words came out in a rush.

"Why?" His voice was curious. She drew courage from the fact that he didn't say, "Why on earth would you want to go outside in the forest after dark, you crazy city girl?"

"I. . . well, you probably think it's crazy, or just not a big deal, but. . . "

"No," said Jonah. "I don't think you're crazy, and you don't need to justify it to me. I'll get a flashlight."

The moon followed her, teasing and displaying itself through nettings of bare branches as Teresa walked along the path between trees. Thin cirrus wisps played like veils over the moon's silver face, blurring its edges, making it soft.

Teresa kept her flashlight trained on the path. It would be humiliating to stumble and have to wait for Jonah to come looking for her, and it would ruin her night. This might be the only chance she'd get to be out here alone. Excitement jittered along her shoulder blades. It might be silly to most people—maybe everyone else—but she didn't care. She didn't need to be like anyone else.

When the lights of the house were completely out of sight, Teresa stopped. She clicked off the flashlight and stood silently, alone. It was everything she'd thought it might be. The air smelled of dirt and mold and pine pitch. She breathed it in, filling her lungs, holding it for a few seconds, exhaling, and then inhaling again. She'd never felt so peaceful. . . so private, where she couldn't see any other building, cars, or people. No fences or roads, no airplanes overhead. And no one could see her. No traffic or human noises. Nighttime woods sounds were natural and welcome. If she spoke, no one would hear her.

"Be still and know that I am God." Had she ever been still? Even when she could have been still, she occupied her mind with clutter—details, lists, reading, listening to audio books. She read Scripture and prayed, and maybe listened briefly to see if God had anything to say, but was she ever absolutely still?

Teresa turned her face upward. The moonlight silhouetted the treetops without illuminating their depths.

"Behold." Just a husky whisper. She tried again. "The heavens declare the glory of God, and the sky above proclaims his handiwork."

Teresa absorbed the peace. She should be able to find this—this stillness and glory of God—in the city or anywhere else. Could she, once she got back to her apartment, be alone like this, when everything distracted her? She supposed she could knit or spin, the rhythmic movements occupying her eyes and hands but leaving her soul at rest.

You could do that here. Teresa chased away the errant thought. God had her in the city. *Four more years.* Then what? Teresa drooped. She wasn't out here to make plans. The fiery arrows of discontent did not coexist with stillness.

"Keep me sweet, God."

CHAPTER 48

Ben threw his bag into the passenger seat and slid into the car. He tried to be civil and helpful to the clients, but this one, with all the eye-rolling and impatience, had frayed his temper. He wondered if the man would complain to Tom. Ben didn't care. He wanted to go home. Maybe Tom would let him do the reports at home now. He wasn't in a position to refuse Ben a few concessions.

Tom had spent Friday in his office, doing the billing, and today, Ben sneaked out of the clinic while Tom met with a new client in the therapy room. Lauren had stuffed his schedule with clients, which meant he spent too much time driving around the city for fraudulent sessions. Cold humidity had been heavy in the air all day, and as Ben drove out of the apartment complex, sprinkles of rain splattered on his windshield.

He twisted the knob for the windshield wipers and slammed his hand on the steering wheel when the one in front of him failed to clear the glass. How had it become bent? He couldn't think of any reason for Tom to do it, but he blamed him anyhow.

Ben stayed in the right lane, nursing a foul attitude and navigating by following the tail lights of the car ahead of him. He hit the curb when he turned into the clinic's parking lot. The rain changed to a downpour then, plastering his hair to his head and soaking his clothing.

His irritation had graduated to wrath by the time he made it inside. If he worked fast, he could finish the computer work in an hour, and then he could go home. That was his only objective now, and Tom was standing in his way.

"Hi, Ben! How is your mom?"

Ben had to play the game.

"She's fine. Moved on to a rehab center."

"That's good news." Tom appeared to be waiting for a response.

Ben didn't have one and didn't feel like making small talk. Tom had been lying in wait for him. If he had something to say, he could say it.

"I'm in a hurry, Tom. Got a lot of school to do tonight."

Tom stepped aside but didn't leave. "And a big family, too." He shook his head in apparent admiration. "I don't know how you do it."

"Neither do I."

"You don't have any pictures of them here."

"I try to keep my work and family separated."

Tom didn't seem to object to Ben's short answers. "How many kids do you have again?"

"A lot." Ben clicked on the icon for the therapy reports. "Why?"

"Just wondering. It's hard being a single dad. So, are you divorced?"

Ben was getting angrier with each question, and he needed to stay in control. He was stuck in this job for now, even though he knew it would come to an end and leave him unemployed eventually. Tom must know all about Anneliese if he knew about the children.

"I'm really busy, Tom. I have to get this done and get out of here."

"You're lucky to have a nanny. Does she do housework,

too?"

"Yeah, she's great."

Tom repeated his earlier phrase: "I don't know how you do it." He shook his head. "My sister pays five hundred dollars a week for a nanny, and she only has two kids. She has to pay for the woman's health insurance, too, and she doesn't do anything outside of watching the children. And her nanny doesn't get vacations in Florida."

Ben looked at him. No one could find the kids. No one knew about Jonah.

"I really have to get this done, Tom. You know the documentation is important if we expect to get paid." He didn't give his employer a chance to speak before he continued, "Speaking of which, I need that raise. I think I've been doing a good job for you, really helping to make your business profitable. In fact, I've been thinking about that a lot. A raise is good, but a bonus system would be an even stronger incentive system. On top of the raise, of course. I think I'm a valuable employee here, and a bonus system would give me motivation to help you make as much money as possible."

That was bold. Ben kept his breathing steady and watched Tom through hard eyes—at least, he hoped they looked hard. His words could be interpreted as blackmail, or as a sign that he was willing to be bribed into full cooperation. Either way, it was a turning point.

Tom contemplated him for a few seconds. "I think that's an idea worth considering. It's in both of our best interests for Great Lakes Therapy Services to be a thriving and profitable business. I'll think about it."

Ben's mind wasn't on the raise as he started the reports. He was wondering about Mrs. Cooper. He paid her three hundred dollars a week. His parents had added her along with him and the children to their health insurance policy. On an impulse—the same kind of impulse that had inspired him to research Jonah online—he did some searching for the going rate for nanny/housekeepers in the Chicago area. The results were staggering. According to his research, Mrs. Cooper should be making as much money as he did.

The more he considered the situation, the more certain he was of the likely answer. He picked up the phone to call his father, and then he stopped. What could he do? He'd be job-hunting soon, and he wouldn't be able to pay her at all. With a pained grimace, he began researching day care costs. That was even worse. And his house would be trashed. He decided to let it go until this was all over. He'd deal with it later.

After the casual meeting at his parents' house, Ben had regarded the investigation as a relatively small affair. This was big. The conference room on the thirtieth-floor overlooked Lake Michigan, cutting off most of the rest of the city. Pete Collins and Marcus Franks were the only familiar faces. A dozen men in business suits sat around the oval table waiting for Pete to start the meeting. Extra chairs were set up for Ben and others giving testimony.

Pete continued his conversation with the man next to him, and the others grew restless. When he shoved back the chair and stood up, he looked pleased.

"Most of you know that the structure of this investigation has changed. We've connected the initial case against private insurance with an ongoing case of suspected Medicare and Medicaid fraud. The Board of Licensing and Regulations has a special division for that, so we're now an expanded joint task force. Because Medicare is a federally-funded program, we have access to some very useful resources."

Ben tuned out the details and didn't listen to the introductions. What were the kids doing now? Canoeing?

Fishing? Jonah seemed to be having a good time. Maybe they had better weather up there. And what was he going to do about Mrs. Cooper? Ben started at the sound of his name.

"Benjamin Taylor, a physical therapy assistant at a small, private physical therapy practice, has been instrumental in linking up some of the participants in this ring," intoned Pete. "He made a recording in which the business owner confessed to insurance fraud, which may or may not be useful evidence. In addition, he's submitted client lists and insurance and billing information when he could get it. He's been providing lists of legitimate clients, as well as the suspicious ones. As it turns out, a few of those legitimate clients were on Medicare or Medicaid. His employer has had Ben making home visits for these people, noncompliant with Medicare policy, which states that this service must be provided by the physical therapist and not an assistant.

Pete referred to a separate piece of paper. "A woman named Irene Melkin was surprised to hear that Medicare had been billed for therapy three times a week, when, in reality, she was only going twice a week. We interviewed each client on his legitimate list, and about half of them were government pay. Almost all of those had 'errors' in their bills. The difference with those clients was that most of them were innocent victims. We don't believe they were involved in the fraud."

Really? Tom had been using Mrs. Melkin, too? Was there no limit to Tom's greed?

A man from the far side of the table spoke up, "Are we clean on the HIPAA rules?"

Pete looked at him impassively. "Yes, all of the evidence we will produce in court was obtained by legal methods, Jansson."

"What about the methods used in collecting information that won't end up in court?"

"Are you accusing us of something illegal?"

"I'm just worried that the case will be thrown out of court because of fault on the side of the prosecution." Jansson sounded defensive. "The insurance companies might have been willing to share inappropriate information because it was in their best financial interest to stop the fraud."

A man from the same agency Mary Reid had represented rose from the table. "It is in our best interest to stop the fraud, but there are ways to check these things without violating HIPAA laws."

"Okay," said Collins. "Melkin and the majority of the government-pay clients were patients of a group of clinics registered to what appears to be a holding company. Those ownerships have to be traced by forensics accountants and lawyers, but we are pretty confident that they will all be owned by a small group of men living in the Chicago area. One is a representative for an association of personal injury lawyers, and the other two are reputable physicians. Our best plan of attack is to investigate their top level employees. They might be a little spooked right now, because one of them just died in a house fire. Chances are, anything below that tier is just corporate bureaucracy. They just do business and think they work for a legitimate company."

Like me, thought Ben. He'd just been doing his job, assuming Great Lakes was a reputable clinic, and now he was stuck here while his kids were up north having a good time. Unfair.

Ben loitered in the wide, carpeted hallway, waiting for Pete Collins to come out of the conference room.

"Is my family out of danger now? It seems like I'm a pretty minor player in this huge investigation."

"Maybe not yet, Ben," said Pete, "because Potter and Cravitz don't know anything about the investigation. You're their only concern at this time. Do you think your children are safe?"

"Yeah. They're safe. But are they in more danger now? I mean, now that it's a federal case? Or doesn't that really make a difference?"

Pete shook his head. "Ben, if you have them in a safe place, out of town, just leave them there for now. Do you think Potter is worried? Is he doing anything different?"

"He took on a lot of new people all at once," said Ben. "As an assistant, he is supposed to do a therapy session with me and the new client before I see them alone. I've had several lately where I just get a therapy plan. Not even an introduction."

"But you actually do the complete plan with each client?" asked Pete.

"Yeah. Whether they like it or not."

Pete considered that. "You really are providing the services he bills for."

"For what it's worth."

"It's worth a lot to Potter," said Pete. "But you don't think he's suspicious of you?"

"I don't know. I haven't seen much of him this week. He hasn't said anything about the raise or bonuses. He seems to think I'm under his thumb, and I've just been going along with it. Do you still want me to ramp it up a bit and ask for a raise again?"

Collins thought about it. "Can't hurt, as long as that's all you do. You got pretty close to blackmail last time. Maybe emphasize your need for more money—for your personal expenses. If he refuses, back off."

"Okay," said Ben. "What has to happen before I can bring my family home?"

"I think," said Collins slowly, "that once we make the top-level charges, we can pick up the mid-level players like

Potter and Cravitz. And the guy at the garage. We'll make sure they know you're cooperating with the police - and that you're just one of many people testifying. They're only interested in intimidation to protect themselves; they won't come looking for revenge later. Once they've been arrested and charged and know you've made statements, you can go back to life as usual."

Unemployed and unemployable. Not trusting himself to speak, Ben nodded and walked away.

"I think it would be easier to understand if it came from you, Dad. Then she'd know you're okay with it."

"Oh, no. You did it on your own, and you can tell your mother all about it." His dad wore the familiar exasperated expression. "I'm okay with it, but I'm not doing your dirty work."

"It's not dirty work," Ben protested. "It's just. . . this is a rough time for her, and I don't want her to worry."

"She will worry less if she knows what's going on."

They made light of the danger to the children, emphasizing the holiday aspect of their stay up north. Ben described the scenery and Jonah's schemes for the children's entertainment.

"Is Teresa comfortable with it?"

"Well, she'll probably dump us when she gets back," said Ben, "but she's holding everything together up there for now." Suddenly recalling that he wasn't ready to discuss Mrs. Cooper's wages with his parents, he rushed into a new topic, "How long will you have to stay here?"

"Too long," his mother said aggrievedly. "I could go to therapy just as easily from home. I could even have a visiting therapist, like you."

"You probably will, once you get home, but really,

Mom, this place is more like a hotel or spa than any nursing home I've ever seen."

"It's not bad," she said, "but it's not home. I have things to do."

The men listened sympathetically until she laughed. "I'm sorry. It's a fine place. I just can't believe I was stupid enough to do all this damage stepping off a curb. And I have been worried about the kids."

"Well, they are safe, and Teresa is probably enjoying herself, too," said Benjamin. "She doesn't get out much. Maybe she's enjoying a nice flirtation with this Jonah."

"Dad!" Ben's voice indicated his scandalized revulsion. "She's way too old for him!"

His mother looked at him oddly but didn't pursue the topic. They chatted about the entertainment possibilities for the children until an aide came in to take Eliza to therapy.

"I'll see you two later. Be safe, Ben! And next time you talk to Teresa, say hello for me." She paused and continued with some difficulty. "I'm glad you took them there, Ben, and I look forward to meeting Jonah. It sounds like he's a fine man."

CHAPTER 49

Teresa stood next to Jonah, trying not to look like a couple. He didn't appear to notice the speculative glances. She followed the children around for a while, looking ridiculous. She was a nanny, not a mother hen. She'd taken Annie to the nursery and checked on her a few minutes later. Was it really necessary to come so early?

"Da teacher!" Teresa turned to see an elderly man approaching. His cane appeared to be superfluous; he swung it slightly with each tap on the floor and stepped nimbly without regard for its timing.

"Ed! Have you met Teresa?" Jonah reached out to grip the man's hand. "You're looking good."

Teresa extended her hand. "We met in Eagle River. I was having some trouble with the children. But we weren't introduced. I'm Teresa Cooper."

"Ed Konskinen." He beamed at her. "I didn't know you vere a friend of Jonah's."

"Oh, I'm not!"

Both men looked at her, and she could feel herself blushing. "I mean, I brought the children up here to visit him. I'm just the nanny."

"Just da nanny?" Ed seemed to find that funny.

Jonah's brows were drawn together over his nose. Teresa winced.

"I mean, we are friends now, but I came up with the children." She sought a new topic of conversation. "Your accent. I hear it in a few people up here. Not everyone. Is it a Finnish accent? I understand the area was settled by Finns and Italians."

Ed waggled his hand in the same motion he'd used at their last meeting. "It vas Finnish vhen I vas a boy. Now it's just leftovers. Da next generation von't know it at all."

"That would be a shame," said Teresa. "It's very pleasant to listen to."

"T'ank you."

That brief comment might mean she had offended him, or it might mean "thank you." She smiled brightly and turned in relief to respond to Emma Schenstrom's greeting.

"Good morning!"

"Hello, Teresa! I want to introduce my daughter, Phoebe."

Teresa shook the girl's hand. "Would you be her first daughter?"

The young woman laughed. "First or oldest. Mom said you're a nanny."

"Yes, I am. I was a preschool teacher first, but I've been a nanny for about ten years now."

"Do you like it?"

"Most of the time," said Teresa.

"Me, too, but I was glad to come home. I missed everyone. Now I just babysit part time and do odd jobs."

"I bet your mom appreciates the help."

Phoebe nodded. "It's a crazy time of year at our house. All the kids are in 4H, so we have lambs and goats and a pig. And that's on top of the animals we already have."

"You have sheep?" asked Teresa.

"Several. A few kinds of sheep and goats, and even two alpacas someone gave us when they moved away."

"You have alpacas?" A few heads turned toward them at her exclamation, and Teresa dropped her voice. "So, what do you do with the fleece?"

"Nothing, yet," said Emma. "Someday, I'd like to learn to make it into yarn and knit with it."

"I could help you with that!" Except that she wouldn't be there. "Well, I could talk you through it on the phone or by email if you want, but I'm sure I'll be back in Chicago again. I have some good online resources I could send you."

"Maybe you can come up and stay with us sometime," said Phoebe. "I'd like to learn how to spin, and I bet other people around here would, too."

Come and stay with the Schenstroms? Like real friends? Teresa was still trying to come up with a response when Emma said, "We'd have to know how to clean it and everything."

Teresa had never done that part before, but how hard could it be? There were probably videos on YouTube.

"Could I buy some from you? I'd love to experiment with it."

Emma laughed. "You can have it. We had to shear one of the sheep early this year, because it was injured, and I don't have time to do anything with it right now. But it smells like a sheep!"

"I love that lanolin smell," said Teresa. "I even have hand cream with lanolin in it."

"No," said Phoebe. "This smells like a sheep."

"If you want it," said her mother, "you can have it. We'll be shearing the rest of them soon, so if I decide to take up spinning, I'll have plenty of raw materials."

"Thank you!"

"We'll bring it to church next Sunday."

Teresa wanted it now. She wanted to skip church and go home and spin. Home to Jonah's house. No, she didn't really want to skip church. She could wait. She needed time to research what to do with a fleece.

"Thank you," she repeated. "If we have to leave before then, could I come over and get it?"

"Sure," said Emma. "I didn't realize you might leave so soon. But I second Phoebe's invitation. We have room. I'd love to have you show us how to spin."

A wave of self-pity washed over Teresa. She hadn't experienced that emotion in a long time, but the mood was unmistakable. She didn't want to leave. She liked it here. Liked Emma and Phoebe. And Jonah? She shied away from the thought. If she came on the weekend, she'd be able to visit this church.

"There's a lot to be said for a fenced yard," Teresa muttered. When would Jonah be back? "Annie! Stop!" The girl stopped and sat on the ground. In a wet puddle. Teresa had hoped the dense underbrush on this side of the house would make a kind of psychological fence to keep the girl close, but Annie gravitated toward it like a scared rabbit.

"You need to stay on this side of the trees." Teresa held Annie's hand and walked her back toward the house. She wasn't about to carry her, and it was pointless to change her clothes until they were inside for her nap. "Play here by me or over there by your brothers."

"Eat."

"Not yet, kiddo. We'll eat when Grandpa Campbell gets back."

Teresa still wasn't convinced a boat was a good idea. She'd picked up the life jackets without giving much thought to the actual logistics of confining four active children to a boat in the middle of a lake. Maybe Jonah would take each of them out individually.

No, he wouldn't. He'd take all of them—or at least the

boys—and they'd fall out the back while he jetted across the lake. Teresa stopped the stray grumbling. Jonah was more cautious than she was about the kids' safety. She had to trust him.

As if to prove the point, the van's horn beeped in warning before Jonah rounded the corner. The boys joined Teresa and Annie near the porch, waiting impatiently for him to stop.

"He drives really slow," said Benjie.

"He drives carefully," Teresa said. "He knows that you boys sometimes play in the driveway, and he doesn't want to hit one of you."

"He doesn't have a boat!"

Jack was right. Teresa's disappointment surprised her. She hadn't wanted a boat, had she?

"We have a new plan," Jonah made the announcement as he closed the door behind him.

She followed the children—even Annie—as they raced to greet him. He smiled at her over their heads, and she stopped moving. The boys bombarded him while she tried to regain her composure. What was the matter with her today?

"Why didn't you get a boat?" asked Benjie.

"Aren't we gonna go fishing?"

Teresa ignored the whiney note in Jack's question. She wanted to know, too.

"Yes, but I got a bigger boat, and we're keeping it on the lake at someone else's house. We can drive there when we want to use it. Is it okay to go after naptime, or should we plan on tomorrow?" He directed the question at Teresa.

"It should be fine." She hesitated. "Did you want everyone at once?"

"Oh, yes. That's why I decided on a bigger boat. It's a pontoon boat, so it's more comfortable. The boys can fish, and you can lie around looking glamorous."

"Glamorous?" Teresa chuckled. "That's a word not often used to describe me."

He considered her, his head tilted to one side. "No, not glamorous. More of an earthy beauty. You fit in this environment." Without waiting for a response, he began issuing orders to his young recruits in preparation for their adventure.

Teresa didn't hear a word of it.

CHAPTER 50

Ben jerked to wakefulness and sat upright on the edge of the bed. The phone. He tried to compose himself enough to answer. His nerves, already frayed, threatened to snap. Middle-of-the-night phone calls never brought good news. He breathed in and out several times before touching the screen to connect the call.

"Hello?"

"Hello, Ben. This is Pete Collins. We have some bad news. I wanted to let you know that the body of Bill Hansen was just recovered from the ashes of his garage."

"What?" It took Ben a minute to realize what the man was saying. The auto mechanic. Acme. "Oh. What does that mean?"

He really just wanted to know how it affected him and his family. They had warned him of the danger, but it hadn't seemed real at the time. Ben's stomach hurt.

"Someone is stopping leaks," said Pete. "We're watching both Tom Potter and Henry Cravitz, as well as a few others right now. They might be next on the leaks list."

"You don't think they set the fire?"

"It's possible, but it's more likely to be their boss-the next man up the chain of command."

"Stopping leaks means they intend to stay in business, right? They wouldn't stop leaks if they were just going to run."

Ben tried to grasp the idea. "What if they see me as a leak?"

"They might," said Pete, "but I don't think so. The garage mechanic would be easier to replace, and they think you're working out fine. I can't make guarantees, though."

"Thanks!"

Pete ignored Ben's hostility. "What I want you to do is go to work tomorrow. Ask about your raise. Take care of your patients. Go home. I just called to let you know about Hansen, because, yes, there is a remote possibility they will see you as a threat. If you want to get out now and disappear for a while, I can't stop you. Just tell me what you're going to do, so we can make plans."

"Is that a choice? Run away, or go to work and pretend nothing has happened?"

"Those are the only options I can think of. Do you have any others?" The man probably hadn't had any sleep; he wasn't usually sarcastic.

Ben considered. "How about if I know about it? Not about the body." He swallowed. "Just the fire. I could tell Tom about it and see what he says. Just casually. I could say I heard it on the news."

"Not for a few hours yet. Only a couple news crews showed up, and they weren't live."

"Well, what if a friend called to tell me about the fire because he knew that's where I had had my car repaired."

There was a moment of silence on the other end of the call. "Okay, go with that. Call me when you get a chance."

Ben's body wanted to go back to sleep, but his mind wanted to look for things to worry about. It created a series of scenarios so dire that Ben decided he might as well get up. If he did manage to fall asleep, he would have nightmares.

He picked up his cell phone to look at the time. Not even

five o'clock. Weeks ago, before Tom Potter had ruined his life, Ben would have slept until seven, dressed, and been downstairs in time to eat a good, hot breakfast with his children. Mrs. Cooper would have them ready for the day. The dishes would be done, he'd have clean laundry and there would be food in the refrigerator.

He threw back the covers and rolled out of bed. He'd bought cereal and milk a few days ago, and the dishwasher was clean. He must have a bowl and spoon in there. He made a pot of coffee—the energy drinks were getting expensive—and started up the computer. Jonah had been slow in responding to emails lately. Were they without power again? Maybe the kids were just keeping him busy outside. To his relief, there were emails from both Jonah and Mrs. Cooper.

Jonah's was short:

Hi Ben.

Everything is good here. We went into town a few days ago and rented a pontoon boat. The boys and I went fishing while Teresa stayed on the beach with Annie. We didn't catch anything, but it was fun. When the weather warms up, I'll take them swimming. I hope things are getting straightened out there. Jonah

Ben read the email three times, indignation growing in his breast. Jonah was having a grand time playing with the kids while Ben was in danger. Mrs. Cooper had sent more:

Hello, Ben.

I hope that your business is progressing and that you are staying safe. Jonah says your mother is recovering. Please tell her I said hello. The children are doing quite well, enjoying playing outside whenever the weather permits. Jonah has been teaching them about living in the woods. During rainy weather, they have been drawing pictures for you and your parents. Benjie has been experimenting with Jonah's art supplies. Jonah says he has real talent. Jack and Mark mostly like to dig in the dirt and mud. Annie is as charming as ever. Jonah loves her. They are all quite healthy, eating and sleeping well. They have been asking if you will come up here, too. Jonah tells them that you are very busy on a special work project right now but he hopes you will come up as soon as you can. We are all looking forward to seeing you. Teresa

Astounded, Ben reread the email and then read it out loud, under his breath, counting on his fingers. Mrs. Cooper had used Jonah's name six times in one paragraph. It sounded like he was helping her with the children, though. She was probably grateful for his help. She must be getting tired. Ben drummed on the keyboard before coming up with an appropriate response.

Dear Mrs. Cooper,
It sounds like everyone is having fun. I'm glad Jonah is able to help out with the kids. I know it's a lot of work for you, and I really appreciate it. I hope I can come up there soon, but it's not a good idea yet. Tell the kids I love them.
Thank you, Ben

Hi Jonah.
Sounds like everything is going well. Thanks for helping Mrs. Cooper with the kids. She's been great about this whole thing, but I think she's getting tired. At home, she only has them during the daytimes, five days a week, and has her evenings and weekends to relax. At her age, it's got to be hard to keep up with them 24/7. I hope I get to do some fishing, too, eventually.
Ben

Ben rehearsed his story while he drove to work. He didn't want to think about Bill Hansen or the significance of the fire. His job was to get Tom stirred up and see what he'd do next.

Tom wasn't a killer. A weasel and con artist, but not a killer. Ben didn't know about Doctor Cravitz. Throughout their only encounter, Ben had been annoyed, impatient to get back to work. He didn't remember the man being unusually menacing.

Show time. Ben entered the office and greeted Lauren before turning to Tom. "Hey. Did you hear about the fire at Acme garage? I have a friend who lives over there. He said it was a real fireworks display, with all the oil and chemicals they keep there."

Tom went rigid. Ben pretended not to notice. "My friend said there were at least a hundred people out watching it, but the police were trying to keep them back."

"Were there any injuries?" Tom asked.

"I wouldn't think so. No one got close enough." Ben enjoyed the malicious satisfaction of being deliberately obtuse.

Tom glared at him. "Was anyone in the garage when it happened?"

"Oh, I don't know that. I'm sure it's on the news." He walked away before Tom could mention the insurance issues. He had to act natural, and lately that meant avoiding Tom.

By the time Cravitz came on the line, Tom was spitting mad. "What's going on over at Acme? Do you know anything about that?"

Cravitz was silent as Tom related Ben's news. When he spoke again, the doctor's voice was pensive. "I'm thinking it may be time to retire. Someplace warm, in South America."

"I'm not ready to retire," Tom snapped. "And I can't afford it. Was that really necessary?"

The doctor's sigh was audible over the telephone. "Tom, I didn't torch the garage."

"Maybe Hansen did it, for the insurance."

"It's possible." Cravitz's tone was non-committal. He didn't believe it any more than Tom did.

"If he didn't do it, who did? Could it be an accident?" Tom tried to sound calm instead of jittery.

"That seems unlikely." The gentle response made Tom shiver. "Goodbye, Tom."

Tom sat quietly for a few minutes, considering the organizational structure of their recent enterprise. They were just branches of something bigger, separate from any other branches. If Cravitz quit and Hansen was dead, Tom's referral network was gone. Would someone contact him to connect him with other doctors and mechanics?

He wondered if Cravitz would really retire, or if he would go to the police. Perhaps the mechanic had threatened to do so, or maybe someone else had simply decided the man posed a risk. In Tom's opinion, Ben was a more likely police informant than the mechanic. He was a weak link, in spite of his recent displays of a more mercenary attitude.

Actually, mused Tom, Ben wasn't a link at all. The trail ended with him. He was easily disposed of, and he'd make a convenient scapegoat if things got dicey. If the higher-ups began to get suspicious, he could blame Ben. If they thought Ben would talk to the police, they would find a way to scare him off. Tom refused to entertain any other possibilities until he knew the fate of the mechanic.

CHAPTER 51

Teresa surveyed the muddy, shivering crew approaching the house. Jonah cradled Mark in his arms. Even from a distance, she could see the grim set of his mouth. If the other boys hadn't been skipping and chattering, she might have been worried.

"Mark slid down the bank and into the creek. He didn't go under, but he's soaked through, and he's freezing."

She reached out for the boy, but Jonah held onto him. "I've got him. I'm already covered with muck. I'll get him undressed while you start a bath. Warm but not hot."

"Is he in danger of frostbite?" asked Teresa. She'd never dealt with frostbite. That was probably a necessary skill up here.

"No, he'll be fine. Benjie, please bring in a few more pieces of wood. We'll get it nice and warm in here."

While they finished bathing and redressing Mark, Jonah gave Teresa a rough outline of their adventures. "He just got overexcited. I should have realized the danger. It's a lot like what happened to me when Ben found me."

Teresa shrugged. "It doesn't look like any harm was done. Accidents happen. It wasn't like you left them unattended."

"Do you think we should take him into town and have the doctor check him out?"

"For what?" Teresa squeezed Mark and rubbed his hair.

"No more playing in the creek, Mark. It's still too cold out. You can go watch cartoons with Jack and Benjie for a while."

The boy wriggled away and ran out of the bathroom in search of his brothers.

Jonah watched with a worried frown as she collected the wet towels. "Do you think Ben will be upset? I want him to trust me with the kids, and this accident was so much like my own. Not a good way to demonstrate my ability to protect all of you."

"Jonah, Ben isn't going to be mad about Mark falling into a shallow creek. He'll probably never even hear about it. The boys have so many new adventures each day that it will be forgotten." Teresa draped the towels over the shower curtain.

"I can't not tell him!"

"Jonah. It's no big deal. You were right there with him. You pulled him out and brought him in to get cleaned up. Sounds like protection to me." Teresa carried the muddy clothing out to the laundry room.

Jonah followed her. "No, that's rescue. Protection would have been not letting him fall in."

"It's fine!" Teresa pushed the clothes into the washing machine. "If you go change clothes, I'll put your stuff in here, too. Look. . . right now, Ben has his hands full with other things and he's not the most over-protective parent at the best of times. It's not his fault. He just doesn't realize how much work *ought* to be involved in parenting."

"Are you saying he's a negligent parent?"

"No, not at all. Well," she considered, "he's just never had to do it alone. He was going to school and working while Anneliese was alive, and his parents have always supported them, and now he has me. He doesn't know much about raising kids." She hastened to add, "He's learning."

Jonah was silent for a minute and then asked, "How does a man learn to be a good parent?"

"The same way a mother does. You can read a few books if you want to, or ask questions of experienced parents, but mostly it's just being there. Being involved. Not letting someone else do it all. Take responsibility for your children. Know them. Change diapers. Read to them. Listen to them. Take them for walks. Rock them. Play with blocks and throw a ball."

"Having a good father probably helps," Jonah said.

"Or mother. Or grandmother." Teresa led the way out of the laundry room and into the kitchen. "I thought we'd have hamburgers tomorrow, since you got a new propane tank. Does that work for you?"

"Yes, of course," said Jonah. "Unless it makes more work for you. I feel like all you've done is cook and clean since you got here."

"No more than usual, and here, I don't have to drive Benjie to school and pick him up every day. You entertain the kids most of the time, too." She pulled packages of ground beef from the freezer.

"I had a good dad," said Jonah, reverting to their previous topic of conversation, "but he died when I was young. He was sick for a long time, with COPD. Mom died a few years ago, of a heart attack."

"You don't have to learn to be a good dad, Jonah," said Teresa. "At this point, you can just be a good friend."

"I guess so." He didn't sound convinced. "Are your parents still alive?"

"No. At least, I never really knew my father. My mom and I lived with my grandma, and when Mom died, I stayed with Grandma. Later, she couldn't take care of me, so I went into foster care when I was sixteen."

"Your grandma couldn't take care of you?" asked Jonah.

He was shocked. Teresa bit her lip, wondering how to explain it. She hadn't shared the story with anyone except Lila

Rose, and that lady had extracted it with questions and sympathy. It wasn't a secret—just private. But she knew a lot of private things about Jonah. It would be good to share it with him.

"Neither my mom or my grandma graduated from high school. Mom worked as a waitress, and Grandma had a couple different jobs while I was growing up. She babysat other kids sometimes, and once we even had someone else living with us, renting our bedroom, so Mom slept on the couch and I moved into Grandma's room with her."

She smiled at Jonah's expression. "It wasn't as bad as it sounds. I wasn't abused or hungry, or anything like that, and they didn't leave me home alone. They took good care of me. Mom died when I was ten, and it was pretty hard for a while. I was able to keep living with Grandma, though, and we made ends meet. Sometimes we rented out the second bedroom, and that helped. I did babysitting in our apartment. Grandma didn't want me going to other people's homes."

"So, what happened?" Jonah asked. "Did she get sick?"

"No, actually, she didn't. And we got along pretty well. But our neighborhood and my school were going downhill. Some of my friends quit school. Some of them had babies. One day I came home and told Grandma I wanted to drop out of school and get a regular job. We had our first real fight that day. Like I said, neither she nor my mom had finished high school. Grandma was determined that I would graduate. She went down to the school to talk to a counselor, and she came home madder than a wet hen. Apparently, the man told her I might as well drop out because I'd just get pregnant or start using drugs if I stayed there."

Teresa filled a glass from the tap and walked over to sit at the table. The boys were still watching television. Jonah joined her and followed her gaze. She slid her attention back to him. How could this man be a grandfather to four children?

Despite the limp, he played as energetically as the boys, and she couldn't detect any gray in his dark hair. His eyes—almost a cobalt blue—had those laugh line creases that men sometimes got when women got wrinkles. At his age, he could still have children of his own.

He turned to face her. "Then what happened?" He prompted.

"Well, she started looking for a way to make sure I stayed in school or even find a better one for me. One of her friends talked to a different friend who talked to a sister. . . something like that, and one day, Grandma told me she had a plan to get me into a different high school and even through college. Those words changed my world. I hadn't really cared about finishing high school because I didn't see a different life ahead of me. But the possibility of going to college seemed to open up all kinds of opportunities."

Teresa sipped her water, remembering that day. "Still, we had a really big fight over that, and I nearly left, but she talked me around. She said she was going to tell the county people that she couldn't take care of me anymore and get them to put me into foster care."

"How could putting you in foster care help?"

"In Illinois," said Teresa, "the state would support me as a foster child until I was twenty-one, instead of eighteen like most states, and there were programs to pay all my expenses while I was in college. I was an orphan and had never been in trouble with the law, so they were able to place me in a good transitional living group home. I still saw Grandma regularly. She came to my high school graduation and cried through the whole thing, but she died before I finished college."

"She must have been very proud of you."

"She was," said Teresa, "and even back then, I knew she did it because she loved me, so I wasn't going to let her down by not going to school."

"What an amazing woman," said Jonah.

"That she was. So even though it sounds like I had a rough childhood, it wasn't bad. Without Grandma's drastic measures, I probably would have fulfilled that counselor's prophecy. Instead, by the grace of God and Grandma's determination, I have a good life right now and options for the future."

Teresa looked out though the glass doors. "And right now, I'm having a vacation in a wonderful, peaceful place. Life is good."

"Do you really like it here? I mean, as a place to live, not just visit?"

She didn't look away from the forest. "I don't know. It's easy to say yes after just one month, living as a guest in a comfortable home and not having to support myself. I know that actually living here wouldn't be so easy."

Jonah remained silent, and after a minute she continued. "I have a commitment to the Taylors for four more years. You wouldn't want me to leave them."

Was that enough to open an honest conversation? Did she want to talk about the elephant, or let it go until they were ready to leave? It seemed silly, at their age, to continue the pretense of disinterested friendliness. They weren't dramatic teenagers. Once the attraction came out in the open, though, living together like this might become awkward. Teresa realized she was holding her breath. Maybe she did have some teenage angst after all.

She sneaked a peek at him. He was looking at the boys again.

"No, I don't want that." Jonah stood up. "Do you want to go out on the deck?"

Well, she'd started it. Benjie would come out to get her if Annie woke up. Teresa rose and waited for Jonah to come around the table and open the door. Crossroads. Point of no return. Rubicon.

She walked through the door.

"Look!" Jonah's whisper stopped her. "See that?"

"I don't see anything." Teresa joined him at the railing and searched the shrubbery.

Jonah put an arm around her shoulder and pointed upward. "There. At the top of that broken pine tree."

"Oh." She squinted at the dark shape. "Is that an eagle?"

"Yes. Or as Benjie says, a neagle. There are more of them near the lakes, but I see them here once in a while. And look at that moving water on the swampy patch. Along the edge, can you see how the small, new leaves make the bushes look misty?"

She glanced up at him and caught him looking at her instead of the scenery. "It looks like it's coming alive for summer."

"I wish I could show it to you in winter. It's amazing in winter. Almost everything is shades of bright white or gray, so you notice the colors more. Cardinals are the brightest splash, of course, and there are some red berries. One of my favorite sights is the weeping willow. Its branches are yellow, and they whip around in winter, free from the leaves that weigh it down in the summer. The yellow branches stand out against the cold blue winter skies. And the evenings are blue, too, but I think you see that in the city."

His rich, poetic words painted a picture in her mind. She'd never met a man who saw creation so intimately. His intensity moved her.

"I see all of that in the city," Teresa said, "but I imagine it's different out here. So much of the shades of gray there are buildings, streets, smog, and dirt. The lake is a steel gray, never blue in the winter. And the sky isn't nearly as clean as this."

She tried to keep her voice light, pretending he wasn't holding her in his arms. It was only one arm, more of a hug than an embrace. Not even a hug, really.

"You wouldn't want to leave it," she said. It wasn't a question. How could he? God had put this man in a garden, like Adam. He belonged here as much as the trees and eagles.

"I don't know. I've only lived here full-time for a few years. It's been a good way of life for me." His gaze strayed toward the door, through which they could see the boys lying on their stomachs and watching a Bugs Bunny cartoon. "Are you asking me if I could give it up?"

She didn't answer, and he went on. "I would, if I had to. But do I have to?"

"I wouldn't want you to."

Jonah took her hand and turned her to face him, waiting for her to meet his eye before he spoke. "This situation has created a rapid sort of intimacy, but I don't think it will fade once the crisis is over. I know it won't, on my part, and I think you must be feeling something similar. I'd like to know. I don't expect you to fall into my arms." He quirked a grin. "I would like it, but I don't expect it. Do you think we could continue to see each other after this is over?"

"Where?" She didn't have the freedom he did, and she was pretty sure that Jonah wouldn't want her to leave the children.

"Here. There. Where ever you want. I like my home here, but I'm not afraid to leave it. I lived in cities with the Army. I can work anywhere."

"No, you can't. You love it here, and this is your art." She gestured at the woods. "I've never been out of the city until this year."

"Tell me what you are feeling."

"Stressed." She held his eyes. "But I wouldn't feel stressed if I weren't interested. I'd just go away. But I can't see you wanting to live in my garage apartment and sending me off to be a nanny/housekeeper for Ben every day. And I can't imagine that you want me badly enough to deprive those children of their nanny."

Too fast. Teresa winced. She'd leaped to a whole new level.

"I do want you that badly, but you're right. I don't want to do that to them. Do you have any ideas for making it work out?"

"Not yet. But as you said, we haven't known each other that long. When this is over, I'll go back to Lombard and get Ben's life reorganized. Maybe you can come and visit all of us."

His brows drew together in a frown. "I don't see you as part of a package deal, Teresa. I hope you aren't thinking that."

"No, but it's convenient."

"It's not at all convenient," he snapped, annoyed. "It's extremely inconvenient. If you weren't tied up with my family, I could just. . . well, we could do things differently. Have a few dates, get married, live happily ever after."

Wow. Talk about leaping levels. . . Teresa laughed. "That does sound like a simpler approach, but I think we'd better go more slowly while we work out the details. I would like to see you again, when we're back in the city, and since I'm living in a place that might be convenient to you as you start visiting your grandchildren, perhaps we can spend time together there. I like you very much, Jonah Campbell."

"Oh, Teresa," He leaned his forehead on her hair. "I like you, too. Four more years? There must be another way."

"Let's see what happens after this," said Teresa. "And pray about it. Definitely pray about it. It's complicated."

He lifted his head and looked into her eyes. "It's not complicated. It's just the nanny commitment. Other than that, it looks pretty straightforward to me."

He stroked her cheek, and she swayed closer to him,

captivated by his expression and touch.

"May I kiss you?" Jonah's voice, low and smooth, stirred a new yearning in her.

"Oh, yes." She breathed the words and wrapped her arms around his neck. "Yes."

CHAPTER 52

Phoebe was waiting for them outside the church, sunshine reflecting on the length of her blond hair. The skirt of her blue dress billowed in the warm wind.

"Hello, Teresa! I brought you some fleeces. Can we put them in your van now, so we don't miss each other after church?"

"Oh, yes. Thank you!" Teresa turned to Jonah. "Could you take the kids inside, please, and get Annie into the nursery?"

"Of course," said Jonah. "You ladies go enjoy your fleece."

Teresa squealed at the row of pillowcases in the back of the truck. "Thank you! I didn't expect so much!"

Phoebe pulled one over to show her the pinned label. "This one is alpaca. That one is angora goat, and the other two are wool. We ended up shearing a couple of the others early, and Mom didn't want to keep all of it. We're just glad to have someone who will use it."

"I will! It might take me a while, but I will. I'll send you some of the yarn."

"Okay," said Phoebe, "but we really want to learn how to do it ourselves."

"If I can, I'll come back and show you." Teresa sniffed. "It does smell a little like sheep. Or rather, what I imagine sheep smell like. I've never actually smelled one. I'll get it all cleaned up before I spin it."

"We're keeping ours in the barn," said Phoebe.

Teresa laughed. She'd done that a lot lately, she realized. She felt happy. Not just excited and romantic, but happy all over. "I don't have a barn, so I'll just clean it as soon as we get home."

"Back to Chicago?"

"I meant back to Jonah's house," said Teresa. She busied herself with pushing the bags further into the minivan. "I need to look it up online, but it can't be too hard. I just wish I had some carding combs with me."

"Maybe he can make you some," said Phoebe. She waited for Teresa to close up the van and walked with her toward the church. "Where you live in Chicago—is that near Maly Park?"

"Pretty close," said Teresa. "I. . . lived there for a little while. It's about an hour from Lombard, where I live now. Do you have friends there?"

Phoebe nodded. "Some of our missionaries live there. They run a shelter for abused women. Hope House."

Teresa caught her breath. Impossible. No way. "I don't know many people there anymore. What's their name?"

"Betty and John Mitchell. They're really nice."

"Do they come up here often?" Teresa asked. She hoped Phoebe didn't notice the evasion. She didn't know Betty well. The woman mostly did the administrative work, but she sometimes had lunch with the residents and was always kind.

"At least once a year. We have a little respite house where missionaries can have a vacation, and I've watched their kids a few times so they can go out alone together."

"That's nice of you!" Teresa hoped her hearty enthusiasm concealed her dismay. She would rather not run into Betty Mitchell here. The woman might pretend they had never met, but that would be awkward for both of them. Someday, if Teresa became a real part of this church, she would share her testimony. It would be a blessing, in light of their support for the Mitchells, but she didn't want to do it now, while she was passing through and they were still strangers.

"I'd better go rescue Jonah," Teresa opened the door and held it for the younger woman. "He does fine with the boys, but Annie wraps him around her little finger."

"He's really good with kids," said Phoebe. "Maybe someday he'll remarry and have some of his own."

Teresa watched Phoebe's back as the girl disappeared into the crowd of people. Really? Betty Mitchell and now this? And it wasn't quite ten o'clock.

The worship service glorified God, and glorifying God always made Teresa feel more peaceful. Phoebe's little bombshells didn't matter today. Today, they were going out on the boat again, and she'd discovered she loved being on the water as much as she did being in the woods.

"Being on the water on a lake in the woods."

"Vhat?" Ed Koskinen stood in front of her. She hadn't even noticed him. "Vere you talking to yourself or to me?"

Teresa groaned. If this morning was any indication of how the rest of the day would go, she'd better make sure to wear her lifejacket, because she'd probably fall off the boat. "Just talking to myself, Ed, and it was just silliness."

She headed toward the nursery, her happiness returning as people greeted her. She hoped she would be able to come back to this friendly church someday.

Teresa looked over the Dutch door into the nursery. Annie and another little girl were squeezed into a corner, clutching dolls and looking at books.

"Hi, Annie! Did you have fun?"

Annie looked up and marred the idyllic scene with a ferocious scowl. "Stay."

Stay? That was a new one.

"We have to go, Annie. Grandpa Campbell's going to take us for a boat ride." She didn't feel up to discipline and training today; bribery and manipulation would have to suffice.

"Are you her nanny?"

The nursery attendant's hesitant voice made Teresa wary. Her response came out as a question. "Yes?"

"I'm afraid Annie and Esther had a little spat today."

A spat? *O God, please don't let Annie have bitten Esther.*

"Annie bit Esther. She wanted the doll Esther had, and Esther wouldn't let her have it. Annie bit her on the arm, and. . . um. . . Esther bit her back."

"Oh!" Well, that was good news. Teresa smiled at the woman. "I am sorry Annie did that. Is Esther okay?"

The woman gestured at Annie and her friend. "They're both fine now." She opened the door to let Teresa into the room. "They made up in about two minutes and have been inseparable since."

Teresa squatted down in front of the girls. "Did you two have a problem today?"

They looked at her without comprehension. She pointed at Esther's arm, which showed the all-too-familiar impression of Annie's little teeth. Annie bore a similar wound.

Teresa shook her head and looked at the worried nursery attendant. "Would you think I'm a terrible nanny if I just pick her up and leave instead of waiting for Esther's mother?"

"Oh, I'm sorry. I should have introduced myself. I'm Debbie Nurmi. Esther is my youngest daughter."

Of course, she was. Teresa should have expected it. "Well, I am sorry, and I will talk to Annie."

"I just feel bad that Esther bit her back." The woman looked as if she might cry. "None of my other children were biters, but Esther is so bad!"

Teresa patted her arm. "I think Esther is a delightful child, and I don't blame her for biting Annie. Maybe it will cure both of them. They look pretty happy now."

Annie pressed further back into the corner, squashing her friend behind her. "Stay."

Teresa stayed in the nursery to outlast Annie's tantrum. Jonah found her just as the girl's angry sobs were receding. Esther had taken one look at her mother and gone quietly.

"Is she okay? I heard her all the way across the basement." He didn't look worried; not even a childless man could have mistaken Annie's howls of rage for heartbreak or pain.

"Yes, she's fine. She bit a little girl in the nursery, and guess what!"

Jonah raised his eyebrows. "What?"

Teresa leaned toward him and whispered, "The girl bit her back. Look!" She displayed Annie's arm.

Jonah looked at Teresa instead, and his lips twitched. She giggled. Actually giggled. Jonah burst into laughter and she joined him.

"What kind of a nanny gets so excited when her child gets bitten?" he asked. "Shame on you!" He grinned. "You look so pretty when you laugh."

Teresa got herself under control, but Annie's offended glare nearly set her off again. "Would you like to carry her out to the van? I'm ready to leave."

Jonah teased Annie into a happier mood as they tracked down her brothers. "We're going on the boat today! You like the boat, don't you? And it's going to be nice and warm today."

"It's already warm," said Teresa. "I'll have to get out the kids' shorts and swimsuits."

When they reached the van, Teresa reached around the boys to slide the van door open.

"Okay, everybody, let's go home and eat. Then we can go out on the boat." She'd just finished the sentence when the boys recoiled against her. Even Jonah took two steps back, holding Annie against him.

"What is that smell?" Benjie and Jack asked the question at the same time.

"Pee-you!" said Jack.

A horrible, pungent odor oozed from the car's warm interior. Teresa clapped her hand over her mouth. She shouldn't laugh. She'd been on the brink of hysteria all morning, though, and she wasn't sure she could stop herself.

Jonah opened the hatch. "The fleece." He shifted Annie to his other arm. "Not much we can do about it now. We'll put the windows down and be home in half an hour. Maybe twenty-five minutes."

CHAPTER 53

The woman was scarier than the man, and she didn't seem to be impressed by Tom. He'd thought he was ready when they arrived. He'd been expecting something of the sort, and when Lauren told him that Dr. Cravitz had referred a new client, he recognized the name Kent from a previous conversation. Henry had told him to forget he'd heard that name.

And Henry had disappeared. Retired. Tom had called the clinic three times before the receptionist told him that the doctor had a family emergency. She didn't have a record of a Kent Gebel.

Mrs. Gebel—if that's who she was—pushed the new client folder toward him. "We don't need to fill out paperwork," she said, "until we know what we want to do. We're here for a consultation. Nothing else."

So far, it was more of an interview than a consultation or discussion. The woman did most of the talking. Without defining the purpose of their visit, she asked about his business structure, his staff, his client base and bookkeeping practices. The man watched Tom from hooded eyes, as if waiting for a wrong answer or a lie.

Tom fidgeted under the polite interrogation. He'd become dependent on this stream of income, and he didn't want to lose it. The alarm bells were deafening, though. He'd been insulated by Cravitz, and while a closer connection to the core of the organization might be even more profitable, recent incidents had highlighted the danger of knowing too much.

Tom had no ambition to become powerful; it was all about the money. He didn't even like the responsibility-the risk-of having employees. The Gebels didn't seem bothered by Lauren, but they grilled him about Ben.

"He knows the clients are getting services according to what the insurance company will pay, but he's doing the visits, so he thinks it's all right. He doesn't know whether or not the billing matches the schedule," said Tom. "He's got an expensive lifestyle and likes his job. He makes good money here, and he's due for a raise and maybe some bonuses. When he learned about the insurance claims for his accident," Tom stressed the last word, "he just wanted a cut of the profits. He's not stupid; he realized pretty quickly that if there was any investigation, he would look like the guilty party, especially since he had easy access to the accounting systems."

They didn't look convinced, so he rushed on, "He's got four kids and is taking classes to become a physical therapist. He's out for every penny he can squeeze from me."

"But he has nothing invested," the woman said. "He's not going to lose his business or go to jail. If he got cold feet and went to the insurance commissioner, he'd be a hero. They'd probably give him a reward."

"He'd have a hard time getting another job with that 'whistle blower' label, though," Tom said. He tried to sound as cool as she did, but his voice sounded nervous even to himself.

"Unless he just opened his own private practice, like you did," said Kent Gebel. The words came out slow and measured, as if he thought through each sentence before he said it.

"We didn't expect Doctor Cravitz to retire so soon," snapped the woman, "so we weren't prepared to replace him. You are, of course, a valued member of our organization."

The obvious afterthought didn't sound sincere, but Tom

jumped on it.

"I am anxious to continue our association. I believe we can work well together."

"It's a matter of structure," said the man apologetically. "We know you have some other referrals—private and Medicare clients—but the most profitable clients were the ones referred to you by Cravitz. You just aren't much good to us on your own. You need a referring physician."

A fleeting thought of his shiny new Goldwing passed through Tom's mind. He'd made enough money for the motorcycle's down payment and financed the rest. His apartment and car were much nicer than he'd been able to afford a year ago. He wasn't buying diamonds or luxury yachts, but after pinching pennies to pay back student loans and start his business, it was nice to be able to impress women with his generosity, eat out whenever he wanted to and otherwise live without a budget. He couldn't lose this income.

"I'm sure you can channel some referrals my way until you find a permanent replacement for Cravitz." They needed him. He went on with more confidence. "We actually don't have a lot going on with him at the moment. We just declined two of his referrals and finished two ongoing cases."

The woman's lips compressed, as if she refused to comment, but her husband nodded. "We had a run of losers, not worth the risk. Usually, they get weeded out pretty quickly, but we had a change in our managerial staff and things got messy for a little while. It was perceptive of you and Cravitz to recognize the danger."

Before Tom could preen, the woman spoke sharply, "There are three more patients of Doctor Cravitz's already in the system, and they'll be calling for appointments soon. We'll see if there are any other projects at the moment, but otherwise you'll have to wait until we replace him. His practice on Kirson Street is already on the market. We plan to buy it and operate without interruption."

Tom absorbed that information, tying it to what Gebel had said earlier about Ben. This group would buy the business and give it to the doctor in exchange for his cooperation. It had to be licensed by the physician or a medical group, not by these people, so it would be a gift. A gift with strings, but they wouldn't have any trouble recruiting a doctor with that kind of sign-on bonus.

Gebel mentioned that Ben might go into business for himself, with his own clinic, once he was a fully-licensed physical therapist. Would they offer to pay for that? Was that good or bad? Short-term, it would be good for Tom. Ben had a few years of school left, and if they saw Ben as an investment, they would keep him safe with Tom, under their eye. Long-term, of course, they might use him to replace Tom. They didn't need to have a lot of therapists; one therapist could oversee a lot of assistants, who did the bulk of the actual work.

He tried to focus as Mrs. Gebel fired blunt questions about the receptionist and Tom's other professional and personal associations. They scrutinized his face as he stumbled through answers. His brain hurt, pressing on his skull and spine. She asked more questions about Ben, too, and Tom began to think he'd been wrong. They weren't happy about Ben's involvement.

"But you need an assistant," she said, "and it would take a while to get a new one." She pushed a business card and sheet of paper across the table. "These numbers are for contacting us. Don't call unless it's necessary." She pointed at the paper. "And those are a few doctors who might send clients to you. Don't call them at all. We'll establish a new permanent workflow system as soon as possible. For this interim period, until we have that in place, we're sending you a new employee. You'll find it most useful to call her a business consultant, specializing in small medical practices. She'll advise you on how to streamline your operations and be more profitable. You do want more profit, right?"

His visitors stood up, ending the meeting and departing without ceremony. Tom didn't know whether to feel exultant or sick. He'd committed to a larger role in a very unstable set-up, and neither of his new associates seemed enthusiastic to have him on board.

He'd have to find a way to keep Ben under control. He could be an asset, if he'd keep his mouth shut and do the work. He'd have that raise he was after and a handful of promises for the future. Maybe it would help to know a little more about Ben's family. He was probably very fond of them.

CHAPTER 54

Entrapment. Pete said it wasn't, because they weren't collecting evidence to use in court. It felt like entrapment to Ben, but he was fine with that. He wanted his life back.

"We can't find Cravitz—at least, not yet—and Potter might be feeling jumpy. If we can shake him up and threaten him with criminal charges of fraud—especially the federal charges—I think we can get him to tell us about his bosses. If he doesn't know enough yet, we can use him as an inside man to collect information." Pete smiled at Ben. "Like you. Either way, Potter will be helpful."

"More helpful than me! Will I be done then, once you have him?"

"I think so. The only other people you know about are the dead mechanic and the doctor, who's disappeared. Once we've brought in Potter, there's no reason for you to worry. You can go on with your life."

"Awesome."

"Your desk looks as bad as mine does."

Tom looked up at Lauren's voice. "We've had a busy week. Did you need me?"

"Yeah, I have two clients for you. They're Medicare, and it looks like we've provided services this week, but I don't have any reports for them, and they're not on Ben's schedule. Did you see them?" She came around the desk and clicked through to the client list. "This one," she said, pointing, "and this one. I'm sorry, but I don't even remember these names. We've been so busy."

Tom's brows drew together. He hadn't provided services for these people. He'd never heard of them. There was only one other person who could have added them. Lauren was waiting, and Tom made a quick decision.

"Yes, I'm sorry. I did put them in there." He glanced at the information. "I saw them on Tuesday, one after another. It was probably when you were at lunch. I'll get the reports done." His rueful chuckle must have been convincing.

"Okay, good." Lauren turned to leave the room.

"Hey," said Tom, "is Ben in his office?"

"No, he's gone. He was going to a client visit and straight to school from there."

"Thanks."

Tom sat at his desk, staring at the computer monitor without seeing it. What was he going to do? His initial impulse was to call Ben and tell him he was fired. But he couldn't fire Ben. Ben might go to the police. Gebel and his wife had been right. Ben wasn't invested. He didn't have anything to lose.

Would it be better to call the Gebels and tell them about it? Tom swallowed. They could "take care of" Ben. They wouldn't like it, though. Tom would look like a fool and probably a risk to them. They might "take care of" him, too. He had to get this under control without letting them find out. But what if they found out he'd kept it from them?

Tom propped his elbows on his desk and pressed his hands against his temples. His head still hurt from Wednesday's visit with the Gebels, and he needed to think. What was Ben trying to do? That was the question. Adding clients to the list didn't bring in more money unless they had referrals and billed. It didn't make sense. He needed to talk to Ben.

Ben strolled from the client's front door back to his car, soaking in the long-absent sunshine. No one had answered the door, so he had an extra hour before he had to be at school. He whistled cheerfully as he started the car and moved into traffic. Entering the Medicare patients—real people, according to Pete, with real social security numbers—had been easy. They were there now, ready for the fraud squad to find and use to pressure Tom into cooperating with them.

And when that happened, Ben would be free. He'd be able to drive up north and get his kids back. Get his life back. Pete was going to have everything in place by Monday. Ben grinned. This might be his last full day of work. Of course, he'd be unemployed then. He wasn't going to worry about it now. Something else would come up.

His text tone sounded, and Ben tapped the Bluetooth button to have the message read to him. As if to crown the perfect day, the mechanical reader informed him that the afternoon's lab was canceled. Ben whooped and pumped a fist. It was a great day.

Traffic was light and his favorite music was on the radio. By the time Ben parked in the garage and entered his house, he felt happier than he had in months. At the sight of the kitchen, some of the sparkle dimmed. He really missed Mrs. Cooper. She was up north enjoying the sunshine, playing with Annie on the beach, while the boys jetted around in a boat with Jonah. It was so unfair.

He pulled off his Great Lakes polo shirt as he climbed the stairs. It was clean enough for one more day, and hopefully, that would be the last day he'd need it. He hummed as he undressed. He had the whole weekend ahead of him with nothing to do. A nice, long weekend.

Ben dropped the shoe he was holding and stared at the alarm clock. He had time to make a trip up north, just for a quick visit. He'd go back again next week, when Pete said it was all over, to pick up the kids, but he could go now, too. If he left right now, he'd get to Bruce Crossing at about bedtime. Mrs. Cooper was a stickler for bedtime. But they were his kids, he thought with a flash of rebellion. If he wanted them to stay up late, they could. But it wouldn't be just a few minutes. It would take hours to get them settled down again. Maybe he'd better wait 'til morning. He didn't want to annoy Mrs. Cooper at this point.

He mulled over his options. If he waited until morning, he wouldn't arrive until afternoon. If he left now and stopped in Watersmeet for the night, he could drive the last hour early in the morning. That would work. He'd have all day Saturday there and then come back on Sunday night. He looked forward to seeing the boys' faces and having Annie jump at him. Mrs. Cooper might be glad to have a break from full-time babysitting. Maybe Jonah would take them all out on the boat.

Thirty minutes later, Ben tossed his overnight bag in the back seat of his car. He put a CD into the player and drove away.

CHAPTER 55

The boys' breakfast conversation, loud and enthusiastic, made any private exchange impossible. Jonah loved his grandchildren, but courting Teresa around four small chaperons required ingenuity. He wished she and Annie had come with them this morning. Teresa would like the sunrise on the lake. It had been a fun expedition, though, and if the boys hadn't quite appreciated the aesthetic glory of the sunrise, they did enjoy hiking in the pre-dawn darkness and throwing rocks into the water.

They continued to chatter as they did the kitchen chores, heedless of Jonah's distraction. He'd made arrangements on Sunday, without consulting Teresa, and without a fully-formed plan, but he'd spent all week in preparation, dreaming up and discarding ideas. Now, only an hour before he unveiled his grand plan, Jonah wished he'd talked to her ahead of time. But she might have refused, and that would have been awkward. Better to surprise her, and she couldn't fault the arrangements he'd made for the kids.

Benjie brought him back to full attention by snapping him with a towel.

"Hey. . . you're getting pretty good at that." Jonah took the towel and draped it over the oven handle.

"You can't put that there," Jack told him. "Babies can pull on it, and the oven door will come open and hit them on the head."

"Good point." Jonah shook it out and then tucked it through a drawer pull. "I hadn't thought of that. I think we're all done here. Good work, guys."

They charged out of the kitchen. Jonah followed them, amazed as always at their boundless energy, even after getting up at four a.m..

"KP duty done."

He smiled at the domestic scene in the living room. Teresa and Annie sat on the floor, folding laundry. Teresa looked up at his announcement, and Jonah had an unexpected vision of her sitting there with another little girl. One of their own. Maybe a boy and a girl. Not four. His grandsons bounced at his heels, ready for new adventure now that the dishes were done. He did some mental math. If he married Teresa tomorrow and they started a baby right away and had one every year. . . no, not four.

"What are you smiling at, Grandpa Campbell?"

He liked the way she read his mind. Jonah open his mouth to respond with a teasing comment but stopped when he saw what she was folding.

"Why are you doing my laundry?"

"It was dirty. Besides, you do the kitchen chores and a lot of the other work."

"You're not my housekeeper," Jonah said. "You're a guest here. You shouldn't be working at all."

"Uninvited guests, for an extended visit and there are five of us. The boys are always with you, so the housework's easy."

"You're doing more than your fair share." He turned to the little girl. "Are you helping Mrs. Cooper?"

Annie stood up, knocking over a stack of neatly-folded t-shirts and wading through a pile of socks as she brought him a folded washcloth.

"Excellent." He beamed at her, scooped her up and carried her to the linen closet so she could put it away. "You're going to make some man a good wife."

Teresa threw a balled-up pair of socks at him.

"What?" he asked in mock innocence. He smirked. She could hardly call him a chauvinist when he'd just told her to stop doing all the house work.

"I have to admit," she said, "you've been a good influence on the boys. They're never so helpful or tidy at home. Maybe Ben should come to stay with you for a while. He's a slob."

"It may be too late for Ben. You have to start them young." He set Annie on the floor by Teresa. "Or send them to the army to train, and I don't think Ben would be a good fit for that."

The sound of a car engine startled Teresa. The fact that it startled her made her laugh. She wasn't in Chicago anymore, and company here was. . . well, unprecedented. She lifted Annie and walked around to the front of the house in time to see Phoebe hop down from a large white van. Two of her brothers followed. They were definitely Schenstroms—well over six feet tall and solidly built, with cheerful smiles and blue eyes under closely-cut blonde hair. Their t-shirts were tucked into jeans. Phoebe wore a denim skirt with a pink blouse and cardigan sweater.

Teresa waved as she approached. "Hello! How nice to see you!"

"Hi," said Phoebe. "We're glad to be here. I don't think you've met Peter and Noah."

Teresa set Annie on the ground so she could shake hands. "Nice to meet you." Were they just here to visit?

The male members of the household emerged from the

garage, and Jonah called out a welcome. "I'm glad you guys could come!"

Benjie jumped up and down. "Surprise, Mrs. Cooper! They're going to stay with us so you and Grandpa Campbell can go to town!"

"Oh!" Teresa's gaze flew to Jonah. Into town? Alone?

"Not just to town," said Jonah. "I have a whole day planned." He took advantage of her speechlessness to address the Schenstroms. "We'll show you around before we go."

"Why don't you show the guys," asked Phoebe, "while I get dinner out of the van?"

"You brought dinner?" Confused, Teresa followed her.

Phoebe opened the back of the van and handed her a basket. "Mom said Mr. Campbell might not have thought about that."

"She's probably right." said Teresa. "I don't think I saw anything in the kitchen. We just had sandwiches for lunch, and I was planning on pork chops for supper. I only took six out, though."

She couldn't seem to stop babbling. What did Jonah have in mind?

"That's okay. We brought our own." said Phoebe. She pulled forward a wooden box and lifted out a crockpot. "Can you close the doors, please?"

Teresa complied and led the way back to the house. Annie skipped ahead of them.

"Eat!"

"I have no idea what he has in mind," admitted Teresa. "I didn't even know you were coming!"

"He said it was a surprise." Phoebe set the crockpot on the counter and plugged it in. "He just said you'd be home by ten."

Teresa glanced at Annie, who had climbed on the bench to investigate the basket. Phoebe reached over and removed it before the girl could open it.

"I don't think the kids have ever stayed with a babysitter before," said Teresa. She hastened on, not wanting to hurt Phoebe's feelings. "I mean, I know you're very competent. I can't imagine anyone better. We've just never done it."

"Mom and Dad said they could come to our house, but he wanted us to come here instead, so the kids would be more comfortable."

Teresa froze. At some point, she'd stopped thinking about the reason for their visit to Jonah. They were in hiding. She and Jonah were supposed to be protecting the children, not leaving them with strangers. Phoebe and her brothers were trustworthy, but it wasn't fair to leave them in harm's way.

"Would you excuse me for a minute? I need to ask Jonah something. Come on, Annie."

The girl scooted behind Phoebe's skirt. "Stay."

Teresa couldn't help but laugh. "I'm glad you're expanding your vocabulary, sweetie. Is it okay if she stays with you, Phoebe?"

"Sure!" The younger woman smiled at her. "I know it's not my place, but I think it's nice that you and Mr. Campbell are going out. And you look really pretty today."

Teresa hoped her cheeks weren't turning pink. Increasingly conscious of the irregularity of their situation, she'd continued to dress in character for church, makeup and all. At home, she didn't bother. Her freckles were coming out in the sunshine, and strands of copper lit her drab hair. Her jeans and green plaid shirt were perfectly appropriate for a thirty-four-year-old woman. She made a meaningless response to Phoebe's compliment and hurried from the room.

"Can I speak to you for a moment, Jonah?" Teresa used her most nannyish voice, which appeared to amuse him. He nodded at Peter and Noah and walked toward her, male assurance obvious in every step. What was there about men in groups that brought out the testosterone?

She turned her back to the visitors and hissed at him, "What is this all about, Jonah? We can't leave the kids!"

"Just for a few hours," he said in a maddeningly soothing voice. "We'll be home by ten o'clock."

Teresa wavered. "What are we going to do?" She didn't have anything to wear if they were going to have a real date.

"Well, we're going to hike and go for a canoe ride and then go out to dinner at the casino. I wanted to take you to a nicer restaurant, but on Friday, you only get fish fry at the local places. And I wanted to stay closer to home."

"Have you talked to the Schenstroms about why the kids are here?"

"They'll be fine. We'll come back here to change clothes before we go to the casino, and we can call from there to check on them as many times as you want. Now go get dressed for hiking." He patted her shoulder and turned back to the young people.

Infuriating man. Teresa stared after him. What would she wear?

She'd only been outside for five minutes, but she wasn't at all surprised to see Phoebe reading to Annie in the big recliner. Annie would be asleep in five minutes.

Teresa took advantage of the opportunity to change clothes. Hiking and canoeing. Jeans and sturdy shoes. That was easy. She brushed her hair and put it in a ponytail. She took the ponytail out and brushed it again.

There was a soft rap on the door. Teresa opened it to find Phoebe cradling Annie. The little girl was fast asleep.

"Should I lay her in her crib?"

"Yes, thank you." Teresa watched Phoebe. "I know the three of you will be able to manage. It's awfully isolated out here, though. Are you sure you're comfortable with it?"

The girl looked surprised. "Oh, yes. Our place is a lot

like this. Not quite as far out as this one, but not in town." She pulled the blanket up over Annie, who turned over and curled into her usual sleeping position. "We go camping out here in the summer. The guys spent a week at Paulding Creek this winter, doing some sort of survival training. It's just down the road about ten miles. They were excited when Mr. Campbell told us where he lives. He said there's a van here if we need to go anywhere, and he has a telephone for emergencies. And he's paying us a lot of money!"

Teresa beat down the urge to ask how much. It was sweet that Jonah had gone to so much trouble and expense just for one afternoon alone together. It would be all right. Phoebe was a born mother, and two strapping young men who did winter survival training in the Upper Peninsula should be able to keep track of the three Taylor boys. She was going to be alone with Jonah.

CHAPTER 56

Teresa watched Jonah run his finger up over the curved fern. He was so gentle, she thought, but very masculine. She'd never met a man like him before. He saw things.

"You can eat these."

"They look like snails." Teresa said. "Or green cinnamon rolls."

"You cook them like asparagus. They're good with morel mushrooms." He glanced around and then walked over to a cluster of trees and stirred the wet leaves at their base. "None here. I bet we could find some, though."

"You pick mushrooms? And eat them?" Her voice squeaked on the last phrase.

"Sure. You just have to make sure you get the true morels and not the false ones. Those are toxic." He prodded at the leaves for a few minutes and then rose. "We can hunt for mushrooms some other time. I want to go out in the canoe. It's on the other side of those rocks."

They scrambled over the wet rocks. Teresa slipped, and Jonah caught her before she fell. The quick incident shouldn't have brought a rush of joy, but it did, and Teresa reveled in it.

"Why is it upside down?"

"It keeps rainwater and other things out of it." Jonah heaved the canoe over, and she helped him push it to the edge of the creek.

The narrow craft reminded her of the flume ride at the water park. Despite the final downward slide that soaked everyone, that had felt pretty stable. This one wasn't attached to a track, though.

Jonah handed her a cushion. "Don't tell the boys, but you can just sit on this. I make them wear their life jackets even before they get in the boat. We have inspection."

He shoved the canoe out further into the creek. "Go ahead and get in. Sit on that bench there." With one final push, he stepped into the canoe and sat down on the last seat.

"It's a little different from the pontoon boat." She hoped her voice didn't betray her anxiety. She sat as still as possible.

"Relax!" Jonah pulled them through the water with alternate strokes of an oar—no, a paddle. "It's steadier than it seems. It's like the Weebles that wobble."

She smiled ruefully. "I'm sorry. I've just never done this before. It's so. . . wild. It's all larger than life."

"It is life," he said. He made it sound simple. "Everything is alive. At this time of year, it's all growing fast. Six weeks ago, it was frozen solid, and everything was buried in snow. In another six weeks, it will be greener than you could ever imagine. You won't be able to move through the underbrush. It will be warm. Baby animals and birds will grow enough to multiply and survive the next winter, which will start all over again in about five months. The miracle isn't just the cycle—it's that the cycle is so extreme and so fast."

"Is that why you don't get bored up here, all alone?"

"I. . . " He stopped, feeling his way through the question. "I don't get bored, wherever I am. The seasonal changes are fascinating, though, and I never get tired of photographing and sketching them. I want to do a sort of time-lapse series of paintings featuring one small piece of land, probably near the edge of the lake. I started it shortly before you arrived, but I got distracted." He gave her a slow, rich smile that warmed her from the toes up.

"In the winter, the air is so cold it frosts up the hairs in your nostrils. Ever felt that?" He continued pointing out wildlife and amazing beauty that she would have missed if he had not shown it to her. His voice was smooth and calming, and soon she was enjoying the movement of the canoe in the water. She'd never felt so relaxed.

"This is sun bathing!"

He raised his brows. "You need a bikini for that."

"No, really. It's like a bath. Like bathing in sunshine. It's so warm and wonderful. I could stay right here all day."

"Okay."

She laughed at his serious tone. "Well, not today."

"Another day," he promised. "It's good now, and fall is the best. Midsummer is great as long as you bathe in DEET before you do the sunbathing. Up here, mosquito repellent is sold by the gallon at gas stations and grocery stores."

It was hard to imagine being pestered by mosquitos on such a golden day. As if on cue, one flew into her face. "Does that mean summer is coming?"

"Yes, it is."

"You sound as if summer's a bad time of year," Teresa said in surprise. "I would think it would be the best."

"Tourists," he said succinctly. "It's a different place in summer. It's not bad this far north, but some of the other towns get crazy. I like summer, but there's something special about the other seasons."

They hiked after their canoe ride. Jonah helped her up some of the rocky places, and sometimes he didn't let go of her hand afterward.

"I think I must be out of shape," Teresa said. "All we've done is walk, but I feel like I've run a marathon."

"There's a lot of difference between walking and hiking," said Jonah. "We haven't been strolling on a boulevard.

Shall we head back to the house? I don't know about you, but I've worked up an appetite, and the casino's half an hour away."

Everything was under control at the house. Peter and Noah were showing the little boys how to play soccer, while Phoebe and Annie sat on the grass playing with the violets growing at the edge of the woods.

"It looks idyllic," Teresa commented. "I wonder if their home life is like this. I don't know how Emma manages to keep nine children clean and fed."

"And educated," said Jonah. "They're all homeschooled."

"Of course, they are." Teresa chuckled. "I'll change clothes and be right out."

Jonah had assured her that jeans would be fine, which was a good thing, since she didn't want to put on one of her frumpy dresses. In the bathroom mirror, she saw a light sunburn on her nose and a mosquito bite on her forehead, but even to her own eyes, she looked younger and happier than she had in years.

They bade farewell to the Schenstroms and the children, who didn't seem at all upset by their departure, and climbed into the truck for the trip to town.

"Peter and Noah want to take the two older boys fishing at their favorite camping spot," said Jonah. "I told them they could go, just for an hour or two, after dinner, and they had to be home by nine o'clock."

"I don't know if they should be on the lake without you!"

"It's not on the lake. It's just a creek."

"The one people keep falling into?"

He grinned. "No, a different one. They'll be fine."

"Was Phoebe okay with being left alone?"

"She was fine with it, but I told them they have to stay

at the house until Annie and Jack go down for the night. That's why I'm letting them stay out late. It'll still be fairly light out at nine. It will be okay." Without taking his eyes off the road, he reached over to take her hand. His fingers were long and warm, his clasp comfortable. She didn't pull away.

The hostess tried to place them at a table near the entrance, but Jonah shook his head.

"We would like to sit in the back." He pointed. "Over there would be fine."

The girl shrugged and led them to a booth. She recited a list of specials and soup options, dropped menus on the table, and left. It wasn't a romantic setting, in the garish lights and noise of the casino, but the high backs of the booth gave it privacy.

"What would you like to eat?" he asked her.

"Fish fry!"

He stared at her, dumbfounded. "Fish fry?"

"Yes! I understand it's a local specialty." At his expression, she burst into a peal of laughter. "Really," she insisted, "I've never had that."

He shook his head. "It's not as exciting as you think. I'm having steak."

Teresa felt wonderful. They talked about their interests and hopes and even a little bit about their pasts. They did *not* discuss Ben or the children. It was their own night out.

When they ran out of excuses to linger over the remains of their meal, Jonah came around the table and extended a hand to help her out of the booth. She scooted over to the edge of the seat and took his hand. He caught her off-guard, pulling her to her feet and hard up against him in one motion. Without giving her an opportunity to escape—as if she might try—he wrapped his arms around her and kissed her soundly, until she broke away from him, laughing. In her happiness, she nearly giggled at the sight of a man staring at her from over Jonah's shoulder. At first, she thought their public display of affection had shocked him, and then she recognized him.

The young man was certainly shocked. His mouth opened and closed twice before he blurted out, "Mrs. Cooper!"

CHAPTER 57

Tom rehearsed the lines in his head until Mrs. Gebel answered the phone.

"Why are you calling me at this time of night? What's wrong?" Her voice, even over the airwaves, conveyed irritation and contempt.

Tom ignored it. "I thought about what you said about Ben Taylor—that he had nothing to lose—and decided to keep an eye on him. He skipped school and left town after work today."

"And why is that important to me?"

"I followed him. I thought he was heading to wherever he's stashed the kids, but he's at a casino in the U.P. If we're looking for leverage—something to keep him working—a gambling problem might do it. Don't you think?"

Mrs. Gebel didn't respond right away, and Tom wondered if she'd hung up on him. When she finally spoke, her tone was more thoughtful. "If he wanted to gamble, there are places closer to home. You were probably right the first time. How long has he been there?"

"He just arrived. He carried a suitcase, so he must be staying at the hotel."

"You followed him? And he never noticed you?"

"I stayed back." Tom tried to sound off-handed, but he was afraid his pride was obvious.

The woman sighed. "Okay, well, stay there in your car and follow him when he leaves."

"Shouldn't I go in and get a room?" asked Tom. "I'm getting hungry and I have to use the bathroom."

"What if he leaves while you're in your room?"

Her exaggerated patience irked him. "Then I'll just eat and use the bathroom, so I can keep an eye on him if he's gambling. I'll find out what room he's in."

"No!" Her voice was loud and sharp. "You can go inside, but don't make any effort to find his room number. Stay out of sight and be prepared to follow him when he leaves. Just don't let him see you."

"No problem." He disconnected the call and scowled at the phone. He wasn't as incompetent as she made him out to be, and he didn't deserve to be treated like some kind of minion who couldn't be trusted to think for himself. He'd show them he could take the initiative and stop this potential leak.

Tom left his car and strolled casually through the lot until he found Ben's car. As inconspicuously as possible, he tried the doors. Locked. The Corolla was clean and empty, except for a sheet of paper on the passenger seat. He was starting to walk away when its significance hit him. A MapQuest printout. He could see it through the window, but he couldn't memorize the long list of turns or get his phone into a good position to take a clear picture. He'd look suspicious if he fetched the notebook from his car and stood here copying the directions through the window.

A glance around reassured him that no one was watching. There had to be another way in. Anyone as flaky as Ben needed a back-up plan in case he locked his keys in the car. He'd done it once, at work, and his father had come out with a spare set. The man's acerbic comments made it clear that it wasn't the first time it had happened. After the father left, Lauren had suggested that Ben get a magnetic key safe. Had Ben taken her advice?

Tom squatted and ran his fingers along the underside of the car. It had to be secure, where velocity wouldn't blow it off. He stood up again, surveying the car through narrowed eyes. The hood wouldn't open without unlatching it from the inside. He walked around the car, trying to appear nonchalant when an older couple walked by him, staring curiously. He nodded. They smiled and said hello.

Perhaps it was in the metal casing around the back window, or near the latch for the trunk. He reached under the handle and pulled up. The trunk sprang open, startling Tom so he staggered backward. He fought for composure as another car drove into the lot, leaning into the trunk as if he was looking for something. The new couple went inside without even glancing at him.

He stared. There were straps on the back wall. It would fold down, he realized, and he could reach into the back seat. All he had to do was get to the door handle. No. They'd have child proof locks. He'd have to reach one of the front doors. Tom glanced around again. His heart beat rapidly against his ribcage. It would be hard to be inconspicuous climbing into a car through the trunk. It would be a tight fit, too, in such a small car. He didn't have a choice. He took a good look at his goal, dove in and wiggled through. He didn't have to climb up front after all; he could reach the lock from the back seat. He pulled it up.

Tom was astonished at his own effectiveness. In a matter of seconds he was out again. He shut the trunk, opened the car door and slid inside. He sat for a minute, head back and breathing hard. When his heartbeat was back to normal, he picked up the map and studied it. Ben was going somewhere in a town called Bruce Crossing, apparently about 20 miles north of Watersmeet. Ben had been carrying an overnight bag when he entered the casino, though, so he must be staying here. Would he go to Bruce Crossing this evening and then come back here, or did he plan to stay here and finish his journey in the morning?

Tom programmed the address into his cell phone's GPS, returned the sheet of paper to the passenger seat and headed toward the casino. He'd try to get there before Ben did and be in position to see what was going on, but he had to find a bathroom first. He'd skip dinner. This opportunity was too good to miss.

CHAPTER 58

"Have a good time! Be careful!" Her brothers waved back, but the little boys were too excited to hear her.

Phoebe closed the door and peeked into the bedrooms before returning to the living room. Teresa seemed to think this house was too isolated, but Phoebe loved it. She'd like to have a house like this one someday—just the right size, a good distance from town, and in a beautiful setting.

She pulled her book out of her bag and curled up in a corner of the couch. Noah had stoked the fire before they left, but it was still cool in the house. Phoebe decided to check on the babies again, to make sure they were warm enough. Annie had kicked off her blanket. Mark had wound his around him like a cocoon.

Well, *she* was cold. Phoebe sat in the recliner this time and covered up with a crocheted afghan. She let the book rest in her lap and gazed out the window. The late afternoon sun filtered through the trees, dappling the ground with light. She watched the shadows play as a breeze swayed the treetops.

Without warning, a car drove around the pile of rocks where the road curved. She couldn't see the driver's face, and she didn't know the car; he must be lost. Sure enough, he turned the car around and drove away.

Phoebe picked up her book, but it didn't hold her attention. She wondered how the boys were doing. Peter and

Noah were as thrilled as the children. They'd camp and fish all the time if they could.

Still restless, Phoebe stood up and walked to the kitchen to get a glass of water. They didn't have a deck at their house. This one had a table and chairs overlooking the woods and an open space where children might play. Yes, someday she'd have a house just like this one.

A movement at the edge of the yard caught her attention. She loved to see deer in the woods. Her dad claimed that most deer hung out on the roads instead of staying in the woods where he could shoot them. Her mom teased him, saying that he was always talking about "the one that got away," as if he was telling a fish story.

That flash of color didn't look like a deer, though. It might have been dark red. Phoebe leaned across the sink to squint out the window. Was there a barn back there? She couldn't see anything. Uneasy for the first time, she checked on the sleepers again and returned to the couch. She heard a noise and drew in a sharp breath.

"Stop it!" The bracing words failed to reassure her. "You're acting like a big baby." That didn't help, either.

Phoebe jumped up and started tidying up the living room. She carried some of the boys' clothes into the bathroom and threw them in the hamper. She looked out the window again. Nothing moved. She wandered through the main floor of the house, peeking out windows and listening. She couldn't seem to relax.

A louder sound made her jump, and then she saw him. A man was moving behind the trees, just outside the yard. He wore slacks, not jeans, and a red shirt. Phoebe stepped back from the windows, breathing quickly, unable to stop the tremors in her hands. When she peeked out the window again, she didn't see anything.

He couldn't have any excuse for being out there. She

wondered if she should call Mr. Campbell. Even if the man had permission to be on the property, Mr. Campbell would want to know. She pulled her phone from her purse, but there was no signal. She'd have to use the one on the kitchen wall. She looked out again. No sign of the man.

Phoebe ran up the spiral staircase and through Mr. Campbell's room to look out that window. From the higher elevation, she saw the man sneaking along the garage toward the small back door.

Phoebe spun around. She needed to call 911. Or maybe her dad. She couldn't let fear confuse her. She stopped, pressing her fingertips to her temples. She didn't have enough time to sit and wait for the police.

Turning back to the bedroom, she flung open the closet doors and groped around on the shelf above the clothes rod. Five seconds later, she held a shotgun.

"Men are so predictable!" Her voice held a trace of hysteria, and she forced herself to be calm. The shells weren't in his nightstand, where her father kept his; she found them in the dresser.

Clutching the shotgun by its barrel in one hand and the box of shells in the other, she made her way downstairs. She closed the bedroom doors and wondered what to do next. With fingers made clumsy by agitation, she loaded the gun while calling 911. The woman at the dispatch center was efficient at first, but then her questions became foolish.

"Can you get out of the house?"

"No, I have two babies here. The man is not in the house. He's outside."

"Do you have a car?"

She didn't have time for this. "I have to go. I'll expect the police in about 30 minutes."

Phoebe cradled the phone and collected her thoughts. She had a weapon and could defend herself and the children.

Actually, she was hoping that the mere sight of the gun would be an effective deterrent.

She opened and closed drawers in search of more resources. Was there anything else she could use? Her eyes lit on a package of zip ties. Her cousin Jake had told her that those were often used in place of handcuffs. She laughed out loud. She was all set, just in case she needed to handcuff anyone. She snatched them up and carried them into the living room.

If the man was going to come inside through the back door, he'd go through the mud room first. It was too late to lock it. Phoebe stilled herself, waiting silently, ready.

CHAPTER 59

Jonah turned around, already dreading the anger he'd see on Ben's face. His son had trusted him with his children—his greatest treasures—and he'd casually left them behind to go out on a date. He'd ruined it all. The grandchildren, Ben, his new hopes for a family. Jonah shook off the overreaction and made a valiant attempt at a smile.

"Hello, Ben."

Ben hadn't moved but stood staring at them. "What are you two doing here?"

Teresa spoke before Jonah could, her nannying voice firmly in control. "We're having dinner. We just finished."

"Are you. . . " Ben sought for a suitable word. "Together? Like dating?"

It took Jonah a few seconds to understand the words. Unbelievable. Ben was shocked because he and Teresa were here together, not because the children weren't with them.

"Yes." Like a comedy routine, he spoke just as Teresa said "No."

She looked up at him, and Jonah smiled at her. He could tell by her pink cheeks that she'd suddenly remembered the kiss.

"Yes, Jonah and I are pursuing a relationship."

Ben gazed at her in obvious confusion, but all he said was, "Oh."

Jonah took mercy on her and changed the subject. "The kids will be glad to see you. They're at home with a babysitter this evening. Actually, three babysitters, and we told them we'd be home by ten." He thought he saw Teresa roll her eyes.

"Three babysitters?" Ben laughed. "I was going to spend the night here so I didn't arrive at bedtime. I figured they'd all be asleep by now."

"You may as well come home with us now," said Jonah. "I'm sure the younger two are asleep, but Benjie and Jack will still be awake."

"Okay, that sounds good. I've gotta have some food first, though."

Jonah and Teresa sat down with him and shared anecdotes of the children's recent activities. As Teresa had predicted, he didn't seem at all concerned about Mark's plunge into the creek, merely laughing at the coincidence between that and Jonah's accident.

Ben pushed his empty plate to the middle of the table and stood up. "I feel a lot better now. I missed breakfast and lunch." He eyed Teresa uncertainly. "Things are kind of a mess at home." She didn't respond, and he continued hastily, "I'll get someone to come in and give it a good cleaning before you come home."

Jonah remembered Teresa's description of Ben as a slob. It might be a pretty bad mess after a month on his own. He leaned toward Teresa and whispered, "Don't let him skate out of that."

She shook her head and whispered back, "I'll hire someone myself." Aloud, in her nannying voice, she said, "Ben, you can follow us back to the house."

"That works." The boy loped off toward his car. Jonah watched him go and then turned back to Teresa. "So much for staying out until ten o'clock."

"Maybe next time."

That was encouraging. Ben hadn't said much about the ongoing investigation, except that it would all be over soon. Jonah had mixed emotions about that. He didn't want any of them in danger, but Ben would want to take the children — and Teresa — home with him as soon as it was safe. Jonah wanted to make sure there *was* a "next time" with Teresa. A "next time" with all of them.

"I didn't think Ben was going to come up here until the investigation was over." Teresa sounded thoughtful.

Jonah hadn't liked to mention it. "I'm sure he wouldn't have come unless he thought it was safe."

"I hope not."

The disquieting idea hung in the air between them. Ben had achieved perfect security for his children by bringing them to the one person who would protect them with his life but had no discoverable connection to them. It had probably never occurred to him that he might undo that by driving up for a visit.

CHAPTER 60

She'd forgotten to call her father. Both fathers, she thought with another shaky giggle. "Oh, dear God, dear God, dear God. . . " She whispered the litany under her breath. "Keep him outside. Don't let the babies wake up. Get the police here fast. Get Mr. Campbell. Oh God. . ." She made herself stop. She couldn't afford to panic. She needed to listen. With one more desperate, "Oh God," she shut her eyes so she could hear.

Into the silence came a light tap on the door. Phoebe hesitated. If the man was well-intentioned, he wouldn't have been sneaking around, but maybe it was someone else. Maybe a neighbor had come to help her. No, as far as she knew, there were no neighbors. If someone was knocking on the door, it had to be the man she'd seen hiding in the woods and skulking around the garage. Even if it was an honest visitor, she didn't have to answer the door.

The man knocked again, and after what seemed like an eternity, he must have opened the door, because she heard a tentative male voice say, "Hello? Anyone home?" Torn between fear and relief, she let the gun drop to her side. Her dramatic overreaction had been foolish. No one bent on mischief would have come while it was still daylight; they would have waited until it was dark outside.

Phoebe decided to answer, but then she heard the voice again, closer now, and the tone made her stop. It wasn't a hearty call for the occupant. It was secretive. Low. "Helloooo.. .?" The man didn't expect an answer. He thought the house was empty, and he was still coming in. Phoebe drew in a breath and held it. He wouldn't see her when he entered the room. She might get into one of the bedrooms, but Annie and Mark were in separate rooms. She couldn't be with both.

And then he was walking through from the kitchen, and she was behind him. Speaking as loudly and firmly as she could, she commanded, "Stop." And she ratcheted the gun.

It was wonderfully effective. The man froze.

"Hey."

She didn't allow him to speak. Not yet. He probably had his own gun. "Put your hands up."

He complied but kept talking. "I'm a friend of Ben's. I wanted to surprise him."

Phoebe knew several Bens, and then there was little Benjie, but that didn't make sense. She decided to ignore it. He started to turn around, and she actually poked him with the end of the shotgun. He stopped with gratifying promptness, and she felt a measure of power. She was in control.

She prodded him again. "Keep your hands up and sit in the rocking chair."

He shuffled sideways and sat hard in the chair, unable to use his hands to help him.

"Really, I'm sorry. I didn't mean to startle you."

Another hysterical giggle threatened in spite of the tense situation. Startled her? Yeah, he'd startled her. He looked silly sitting in that chair, too. Was he really a threat, or was she overreacting? Phoebe walked around in front of him, to see his face, keeping the shotgun pointed at his body. He didn't look scary. He looked a little scared. Of course, she thought reasonably, he was bound to be nervous.

Bound. The word reminded her of the zip ties. She could tie his hands and feet together and wait for the police. She didn't know how long she could keep the heavy gun pointed at him.

He was still trying to explain his presence. She found it distracting.

"Stop talking!"

"But I need to explain!"

"No!" Phoebe had to concentrate. She couldn't afford mistakes. Her current problem was getting him secured. Zip ties required the use of two hands, and she needed at least one — probably both — of her own to control the shotgun.

"Do you have a gun?"

"No! I don't carry a gun when I go to visit a friend!"

She tossed a zip tie into his lap. "Tie one of your ankles to the chair leg."

"Oh, come on. . . I'm just here to see Ben and his kids."

That stopped her. Could it be true? Ben could be Benjie's dad. And some men had a strange sense of humor. Parking out of sight and sneaking into the house to surprise his friend might be normal behavior for them. But Ben didn't live here, and the man's behavior at the door didn't fit that. It must be a lie.

"What's your name?"

The man paused. His reluctance put an end to her qualms. "Tie up your ankle." Phoebe emphasized the order with a jerk of the shotgun, and he obeyed. "Now tie the other one to the same leg." He considered the logistics of that while she waited. Finally, he got the other ankle hooked above the first and hooked the plastic. She looked at him with scorn. "Pull them tight."

The man chuckled. It wasn't convincing. "Ben is never going to let me live this one down. My name's Steve Cravitz. We work together. He must've mentioned me." He flashed a white grin at her. "He told me about you. He got quite poetic about those pretty blue eyes and dimples."

Phoebe drew a deep breath, steadied the gun and took a step backward. She felt more confident now that her suspicions had been confirmed.

"I've never met this Ben." She didn't think the man had a gun under those snug clothes, but he was big enough to overpower her if she didn't get him tied up. She moved around him again, wondering if she could knock him unconscious by hitting him on the head with the gun. Even with her renewed resolve, the thought made her queasy. She just wanted to keep him tied up until the police arrived.

"Tie one of your hands to the chair."

"No!" He'd realized her dilemma. "I can't! Look, I don't know who you are, and I shouldn't have tried to snow you like that, but I really am a friend of Ben's. Is he visiting you?"

"I said I've never met him." Phoebe heard her voice rise in pitch.

The man kept talking. "He's on his way here, isn't he? You must be the nanny. He's going to fire you when he finds out you tried to kill his best friend."

A wail from the boys' bedroom interrupted him, but he persisted. "That's one of the kids, isn't it? A good nanny never lets the baby cry."

The danger, she knew, wasn't that the baby would keep crying. It was more likely that Mark would get out of bed and come in search of her.

She didn't know what to do. If she was right about him being a threat, he'd attack her or Mark as soon as he got a chance. She didn't think he had a gun, but he might be able to get the shotgun away from her. If he was innocent, she would just look like a fool. She could live with that, but she couldn't risk the children in her care. Inspiration came to her. She let her voice quaver.

"Oh, don't hurt Billy! He's only two. I'll let you go if you promise to leave and never come back."

"I will. You'll never see me again."

"You won't hurt Billy?"

"No. I'll leave. I swear it."

She brought the stock of the shotgun down on his head.

CHAPTER 61

Jonah slowed when they saw the car.

"This part of the road is national forest, so the car might belong to an innocent tourist, but at this time of year it seems unlikely."

His comments sounded light, but Teresa wasn't fooled. She tried to match his steady tone. "Can you see the license plate?"

"No, and I don't think we'll stop to investigate," Jonah said. "There's a gun in the glove compartment. Will you get it out, please?"

She didn't argue. The heavy gun felt hard and awkward in her hands.

"Is it on safety?"

"The safety's on." He accelerated, nearly losing Ben. "Do you know how to use that?"

"I've never touched one before," she confessed, "and never wanted to."

"I'll take it when we get home." He reached over to touch her knee. "I'm sure everything's fine. The boys won't even be back from fishing yet."

That made it worse, of course. Phoebe would be alone there, without her brothers to protect her.

Ben caught up with them and was on their heels as they walked to the door, but they were moving too quickly for explanations. Jonah's jeans didn't have a pocket big enough for the gun, so he held it down, close to his leg as they entered the house.

He didn't stride forward as Teresa had expected, so she bumped into him from behind. It was like running into a tree. Ben managed to avoid a collision, peering around them to see into the living room.

Unable to see anything and afraid to interfere with whatever was going on, Teresa hissed, "What is it?"

Jonah moved into the room, the gun hanging loosely at his side, and they all stared at the tableaux. Phoebe sat in the recliner reading to Annie, a shotgun on the table next to them. Opposite them was a sheet-covered person, grunting and struggling in the unstable rocking chair.

Before anyone could speak, Annie shrieked "Daddy!" and clambered out of Phoebe's lap.

Ben scooped her up and hugged her tightly. "Where are the rest of them?"

"Benjie and Jack are out fishing with Peter and Noah," said Phoebe, "but they'll be back soon. Mark is sleeping." She smiled at him. "Are you Ben?"

"Yes. What's going on here?"

She gestured at the shrouded figure. "That man came into the house. I saw him sneaking around, so I got Mr. Campbell's gun." They all looked. The man's feet were visible under the edge of the sheet.

"You tied him up?" Ben's voice held wonder.

Teresa, exasperated, asked instead, "Who is he?"

"He said he's a friend of Ben's," said Phoebe, "but he was acting so oddly, and he said Ben had told him about my blue eyes and he thought I was the nanny and didn't know that Annie was a girl!"

Teresa thought Phoebe might break down, but the girl collected herself and went on. "I called 911, but they take forever to get out here, and he was behind the garage, so I couldn't take the children and run. Then he came into the house, and I had to protect them. And they were in separate rooms."

She stopped to take a few deep breaths. No one interrupted. "I made him tie up his legs, but he couldn't do his hands, and I was afraid to get too close to him. I thought I could just stay behind him with the gun until the police came, but then Mark started crying, and I was afraid he'd come out of the room."

Phoebe looked at Ben. "He kept saying he was a friend of yours, but I didn't believe him, so I asked a trick question and he got it wrong. So, I hit him on the head with the shotgun so I could finish tying him up and take care of Mark."

She primmed her mouth. "Mark went back to sleep, but the man woke up and started swearing. Really bad words. So I stuffed a washcloth into his mouth and tied it in place. Then Annie woke up, and I threw a sheet over him so she wouldn't see him and be scared." She looked at Ben with worried eyes. "I do hope he's not really a friend of yours."

Jonah and Teresa were speechless, but Ben responded with enthusiastic praise. "Wow! That's amazing! I can't believe you did that. You saved my kids' lives!"

She blushed, her cheeks as pink as her blouse. "I just did the best I could. I am so glad you are here now."

Jonah walked up and pulled the sheet away with a flourish. "Anyone you know, Ben?"

The younger man's attention was recalled to the immediate situation. "Tom! What are you doing here?" He turned to Jonah. "He's my boss."

"Oh, no!" The wail came from Phoebe.

Ben hastened to reassure her. "No, it's fine. You were amazing. You did exactly the right thing. He had no business here."

"He said his name was Cravitz."

A knock on the door interrupted them, and Teresa saw Jonah slide his handgun out of sight on top of the tall bookshelf as she went to admit the police. Two deputies followed her back into the room, pursued by the rest of the babysitting team and their charges. The younger boys' awe of the policemen evaporated at the sight of their father, and they charged him, whooping loudly. He staggered under the attack, and Phoebe prudently removed Annie from his grasp.

All of the newcomers fell into stunned silence at the sight of the trussed-up man. Teresa watched with amusement as Phoebe related the evening's events. Both policemen and the Taylor boys listened with open-mouthed astonishment, passing from surprise to admiration to adoration of the sweet girl holding the baby.

Peter reached over and thumped his sister on the back. "Good job!" The other men's extravagant compliments seemed to make Phoebe uncomfortable, so Teresa collected everyone except Jonah, Ben, the policemen and the captive, and swept them into the kitchen for a snack.

Peter and Noah wanted to know all about the intruder, but Teresa didn't want Benjie and Jack to be frightened. She asked about their fishing trip and let them talk. The boys could talk about fishing for hours.

Ben came in and went straight to Phoebe. "The police would like to ask you some questions. There's nothing to be afraid of. They just have to go through the routine, you know. I'll stay with you." She rose and let him escort her from the room without a word to anyone else.

"Who's that?" Peter demanded.

"That's my dad." Benjie spoke through a mouthful of ice cream.

"Isn't he married?"

"No, my mom's dead."

Teresa marveled at Benjie's matter-of-fact statement. Children were resilient. She finished picking up the ice cream bowls, hoping that the policemen would remove their prisoner soon so she could get the children to bed. The babysitters needed to get home, too.

Another knock sounded on the door, and Teresa peeked out of the kitchen in time to see Jonah greet a man who could only be the senior Schenstrom. They joined the rest of the men and talked briefly before Jonah led the new guest into the kitchen. Neither man looked happy.

"Come on, guys. It's time to go." In response to their father's curt words, they stood up, said goodbye to the boys and headed for the door.

Jonah stopped them and handed each boy a folded bill. "Thank you."

He returned to the kitchen when they were gone. "Bill's pretty ticked off. The police wouldn't let him take Phoebe home. They want her and Ben to go to the sheriff's office to make statements and get hold of the insurance investigators. So, then there was the issue of how she would get back and forth. Her father is the protective type."

Jonah's eyes were shut, his head leaning against the back of the couch when Teresa returned to the living room, but he unerringly reached out a hand to pull her down next to him.

Teresa sat. "You do know how to show a girl a fun time. That was the most interesting date I have ever been on."

"It's not exactly what I had planned," he admitted, "but maybe it will work out for the best."

"Except that you have one outraged neighbor. I get the impression that Mr. Schenstrom won't be letting his children babysit for us anymore."

"Probably not. I'll let Ben deal with that. They're his

kids."

Teresa smiled. "Did you learn to delegate in the army?"

"They usually called it 'passing the buck,' but it is an important skill. Chain of command."

They sat in companionable silence for a few minutes before he spoke again. "Are all the kids asleep?"

"Yes, finally."

"Do you think Benjie and Jack will have nightmares? Post-traumatic stress disorder?"

"I don't know. They didn't seem too stressed to me. They really didn't see much." She chuckled. "Benjie said he's going to marry Phoebe when he grows up."

Jonah slid his arm along the back of the couch behind her. "I was thinking maybe Ben could marry Phoebe."

Teresa wrinkled her nose. "Mr. Schenstrom was pretty mad."

"But think about it. She's used to a lot of children, she's smart and courageous, very pretty, and her family is right here, so holidays would be convenient."

"Apparently, you've given this some thought."

"Seems like the perfect solution to me." His arm dropped around her shoulders and he pulled her close against him. "Do you think he'll realize that on his own, or should I mention it to him?"

Teresa remembered the fascinated expression on Ben's face when he beheld the young woman reading calmly to his baby girl in the presence of the housebreaker she'd captured, shotgun at her side.

"I think we can leave it to him."

"I guess he's unemployed now, huh?"

"Oh. Yes, I suppose so," said Teresa. "I hadn't really thought about that."

"He won't be back until late. He has to take Phoebe home."

But he was wrong. It wasn't yet midnight when they heard a light tap on the door. Jonah called out for him to enter.

"You're back earlier than I expected."

"They said they can't do anything tonight." He sat down and gazed moodily at the stove.

"Did you take Phoebe home?" asked Teresa.

Ben burst out resentfully, "No! Her father came and took her home. He acted like the whole thing was my fault."

He flushed under Jonah's steady regard. "I know in a way it was, but I didn't mean it. I didn't realize anyone was following me, and I only went as far as Watersmeet. Tom is still saying he just wanted to surprise me. He said I left the directions to your house on the seat of my car, so he thought it would be funny to get there ahead of me. The police weren't even sure they could hold him, until I got hold of my dad and he called someone from the insurance commission. It's hard to say what they can do over the weekend, but he's locked up for now."

Teresa stood up. "You should probably get some sleep, Ben. The boys will want to show you all their favorite places tomorrow. Unless you want to share a single bed with Mark, you'll have to take the couch. We're a little crowded here."

She went out to find some more blankets and sheets, leaving father and son alone together.

Jonah looked at Ben. "Long day, huh?"

"Yeah. I'll sure be glad when Mrs. Cooper and the kids can come back home." It would have sounded like a non-sequitur if he hadn't been so studiously casual.

Jonah decided to pursue it. "It's been great having the kids here. I hope you will bring them up here frequently. And you and I haven't had much time to get to know each other. I'd like to remedy that."

"It's been crazy. My life used to be so simple."

"Simple?" Jonah raised his brows. "As a single dad with

four preschool children?"

"I have Mrs. Cooper." The sentence ended uncertainly. "At least, I've had her for a while now."

"Have you ever thought of remarriage?"

Ben gave a short laugh. "I haven't had time. And who would marry a man with four children, who's not even done with school?"

Jonah didn't meet his eyes but spoke pensively, "You'd have to find a girl who likes children. Perhaps one with several younger siblings."

"You think so?"

"Definitely," Jonah said. "Of course, you'd have to marry her because you love her, not just to get a mother for your children."

"Well, of course!"

"Jonah!" Teresa's voice held as much laughter as warning. "Ben is probably exhausted. Let him go to bed."

Jonah grinned. "Your nanny is pretty bossy sometimes."

Ben looked at him uncertainly. "So, you two. . ."

Teresa answered. "It's late, Ben. The children will be up early and climbing all over you. Go to bed."

CHAPTER 62

The common area of the nursing home—rehabilitation center—was as elegant as any five-star hotel. Ben sat in the rich leather chair and flipped through a gardening magazine. Did the residents here really want to read about gardens when they couldn't even get out of their beds or wheelchairs?

"Ben!" He sprang to his feet at the sound of his mother's happy exclamation.

She looked back at his father. "This was your surprise?" She returned Ben's hug and held his shoulders so she could look into his face. "It's over, isn't it?"

"Almost," he said. "My part's done."

"Thank God. So, will the children be home soon? I've missed them!"

"Pretty soon. I'm not sure I can persuade them to leave. They spend all their time fishing and playing in the woods. Annie's new favorite pastime is playing in mud puddles. Mrs. Cooper lets them get as dirty as they want and just gives them a bath every night. Jonah's really good with them."

His parents were silent. Ben regretted his enthusiastic description. He'd hurt their feelings.

"It's all still a novelty," he said. "They're on vacation. You know they love you."

His mother reached out from her wheelchair and took his hand. "We know that, and we're happy for them. For you."

"Thanks." He squeezed her hand. "I love you, too. Jonah's a great guy, but you're my parents." He cleared his throat, which seemed to have grown a lump. "You're stuck with me."

His dad clapped him on the shoulder—the Benjamin Taylor equivalent of a warm embrace—and said, "Sit down. I told your mom about Tom Potter breaking into Jonah's house and the girl who caught him."

The girl who caught Tom. The unfairness of that inadequate description irked Ben. Phoebe deserved medals for her heroism. Her ingenuity and bravery. He opened his mouth to enlarge on the subject, but his mother spoke first.

"Did you say Teresa and Jonah were out on a date?"

"Yeah, that's why they had a babysitter. And it would have been fine," he said honestly, "but I led Tom right to them, on the one night Jonah wasn't there. He actually hired three people to babysit the four kids. Phoebe said he paid them fifty dollars each."

"That's a lot of money for one evening." His mother raised her perfectly arched brows. "It must have been very important to him."

"I guess so," said Ben. "They seemed to be enjoying themselves when I saw them at the casino."

If his parents noticed any change in his inflection, they didn't mention it.

"Is Tom still in jail?" asked his father. "Pete Collins said they weren't expecting to bring him in until Monday, so they had to scramble to get him held."

"Yeah," said Ben, "and that was my fault, too. I was supposed to put some extra files in the client records—and I did—but I forgot they were doing billing on Fridays. Tom caught it, or Lauren did. Pete says that's why Tom followed me."

"Will they be able to hold him much longer?"

"Pete said no. He's already got a lawyer."

"Would it help if Jonah pressed charges for trespassing?" asked his mother.

His dad responded before Ben could reply. "Maybe for another day, but then it would bring Tom back up for court, and the girl would be the only witness for the prosecution. She'd come under fire for her own actions."

"Oh, that would be bad." Ben said, aghast.

His father looked at him. "Phoebe sounds like quite a girl. Don't you think she could handle herself in court?"

"Her father would kill me. He's pretty protective." Excessively so, in Ben's opinion.

He returned to their original topic. "Pete says it doesn't matter if Tom's in jail or not. He's willing to cooperate, but he doesn't know much. He met some higher-up people once, and they gave him a fake name and a cell phone number. He had a list of other doctors who might be involved, but he doesn't have any proof."

His mother looked disappointed. "All that trouble, and nothing happened?"

"Well, putting him out of business gets me and the kids out of danger, and he's cooperating with what he does have. Pete says they'll find clues in the books, and if they do make an arrest, he'll be able to identify the people he talked to." Ben shook his head. "In exchange for that, they're letting him keep his PT certification. He won't be in private practice again, though. No insurance company is going to accept him as a service provider."

"Did they find that doctor?" asked his father.

"Yes. He's cooperating, too, from some South American country, and he knows a lot more than Tom does, but it's still bits and pieces. According to Pete," Ben said, "and I'm not real clear on all the details, this is like a franchise organization."

"A what?" His father's brow furrowed.

"Or like one of those multi-level marketing setups. The people at the top are probably lawyers—especially those personal injury lawyers who advertise on TV—and medical CEO's. They run perfectly legal businesses, but they hire people to set up accidents, make connections. . . not just car accidents, but things that are filed on homeowner's or business insurance. We had a kid who hurt his back on a neighbor's trampoline and a girl who stuck her hand in the elevator."

"Stuck her hand. . ." his mother's exclamation faded out. After a second, she asked, "But how is that profitable for the people at the top?"

"I can see that," replied her husband. "They get a small percentage of everyone's income, and then they can sue for personal injury, lost wages, and a variety of other things. They have a convenient medical history of the accident from day one."

"Something like that," said Ben. "It sounded to me like Pete and his crew plan to blackmail Tom and Cravitz into cooperation and hope they have enough to get the higher-up guys." He stood up. "That leaves me free and clear, because they know I've already told the investigators everything I know—which wasn't much—and I'm not a threat to anyone."

CHAPTER 63

"It's over." Jonah set the handset back in its cradle and made the announcement as if she didn't already know. She should have been able to hear everything; he'd used the phone call as an excuse to put an arm around her waist and pull her close so she could listen to Ben's description of the legal proceedings.

"It's safe to go home." Teresa moved away from him and gazed out the door.

He understood her mood. She didn't want to leave, any more than he wanted her to, but the danger was over. That was a good thing. The children would be going home, and she had to go with them. Four more years.

"I guess so. Ben's coming up this evening and staying overnight. He didn't say anything about taking you home right away."

"You didn't ask him," Teresa said drily.

It had been a pointed omission. Jonah had avoided the topic and ended the phone call before they got around to making plans.

"I think I'd better start collecting our gear."

Jonah watched her helplessly. She didn't seem to be achieving much—just shuffling things around. If he offered to help, it would look like he wanted her to leave, and he didn't want that at all.

"There's no hurry, is there? Ben's unemployed, and the

school year's just about over. He could stay up here for a while. Take a vacation."

"That's true! There's no reason to hurry back. He'd enjoy it!" Teresa promptly abandoned any effort to pack.

Jonah grinned.

Teresa let Ben into the house.

"Shh. . . the boys are in bed."

She stepped back so he could enter. Jonah sat in the rocking chair, crooning to Annie as she resisted sleep.

"She's almost asleep. Do you want to hold her?" Jonah handed Annie to Ben before rising stiffly from the chair and moving to the couch. Ben sat down and rocked Annie, who hadn't appeared to notice the transition.

"We were expecting you earlier," said Jonah. "The boys wanted to show you the woods at night."

"They can show me tomorrow. That is, if you're willing to have me for a while. I brought an air mattress so I can bunk with the boys in their room."

"Glad to have you."

Teresa smiled at the restraint in Jonah's voice. How could Ben be so blind? Jonah wanted nothing more than to keep all of them right here forever.

"I stopped by the Schenstroms' on the way here," Ben blurted.

"Yeah?" Jonah waited.

"Her father wouldn't let me see her, even just to say thank you."

Jonah grimaced. "Sorry about that."

"He came out on the porch and talked to me. He told me I need Jesus."

Teresa hid a smile at Ben's dejected tone.

"Well," said Jonah, "you really do."

"Anyhow," said Ben, "I told him all about it. I said it was all my fault, and I didn't make excuses. I didn't use the word 'but'."

This time, Teresa couldn't stop a choke of laughter.

Jonah frowned at her. "He did a good job of apologizing."

Ben grinned. "Yeah, she taught me how."

"So, how did he respond?"

"He still won't let me talk to her, but at least he knows I don't normally live like this, in dangerous situations."

"It was an abnormal situation," agreed Jonah.

"Right!" Ben's voice was eager. "One of those freak accidents. But he's still mad. He thinks you and I should have realized it was a dangerous situation."

"We should have known better," Jonah admitted, "and I'll apologize to him as soon as I get a chance."

"Why apologize to Mr. Schenstrom?" asked Teresa. "An apology to Phoebe would be more appropriate."

The men both looked at her, and she saw the family resemblance in their faces.

"Well, yes, but she didn't really mind. It's her father who was upset," Ben explained. "He seems to think we put her in a dangerous situation." He paused and squared his shoulders. "And he's right. You two couldn't have known I would come up here, but I should've thought about it. I led Tom right up here. I put her in harm's way."

"I'll share some of that responsibility," Jonah said. "I was thoughtless. I just wanted Teresa to myself for a few hours."

Ben looked at them for a minute and then returned to the more interesting subject of his own problems. "I did get a few points for devotion to my children. Mr. Schenstrom said he understood my need to come see them. But then he pointed out that I have a daughter and asked how I would feel if she was put in that situation?"

Jonah shook his head. "Sorry about that. Phoebe seems like a nice girl, but I'm afraid your goose is cooked."

"I'm not giving up." He looked at Jonah. "I told him you're my father, Jonah. I hope you don't mind. And about Anneliese, since I have four kids."

Teresa wondered what Bill Schenstrom—the man with the perfect family—had thought of that. She hoped the man realized how little of that baggage was really Ben's fault. This situation had matured him, and he'd be a fine man someday. Benjamin and Jonah were both good role models. Maybe Phoebe would be a good wife for him. They might even have four or five more children!

"What are you smiling at?" Jonah pulled her down next to him.

"I was thinking that Phoebe is a very nice girl. I hope you can talk him around, Ben."

"Me, too." He looked down at his sleeping daughter. "I guess I'd be pretty protective of my daughter in that situation, too."

He rocked forward and rose to his feet. "Is she sleeping in the bedroom on the left?"

Teresa stood up. "I'll put her in her crib."

Ben handed Annie to her. "Thanks. I really appreciate you." He gave her an awkward hug around the baby.

She kissed his cheek. "Go to bed, Ben. We can talk it all through in the morning."

Jonah leaned on the railing, watching the boys chase their dad in some intricate version of tag. Ben let them catch him and rolled over onto his back, pretending to be dead, and the boys jumped and gave each other high fives before starting a new game. Ben excused himself and came up to stand by

Jonah.

"I can't believe how green everything is. It was all so icy and cold last time I was here."

"Early spring isn't the U.P.'s best season," Jonah admitted. "At least the winter is pretty, even if it's too cold for most people."

"The Chicago winters are pretty rough, too. Mom and Dad are looking for a winter place down in Florida. Dad thinks a warmer climate would be easier on Mom's bones. They've been talking about it a long time, but they've been too busy to leave town. Dad never completely retired, and Mom was busy with every do-gooder committee in town. And," Ben said, "they didn't want to leave me and the kids."

Jonah nodded.

"They were finally ready to do it, though, but then I told them that you and Mrs. Cooper—"

"Ben, can you please call her Teresa?"

"I have been trying," said the younger man earnestly, "but it's a hard habit to break. And when I think I have it, she says something in that nanny voice."

Jonah chuckled. "I know what you mean. So, they're afraid you'll be left alone with the kids?"

"They're worried about all of it: me, the kids, my school, work. . . and especially losing Teresa."

"But you'd be okay, wouldn't you, Ben?"

There was confidence in Jonah's voice as he said it, as if it were a statement instead of a question, and his son responded with gratitude.

"Yes! I think I would! Dad and I talked for a long time. He thinks maybe I should wait a few years to go back to school, until all the kids are in school. I can support a family on what I make as a PTA—if I get a job, that is. They'd still let us live in our current house rent-free and pay for the kids' school, so that would save a lot of money. I'd just have to figure out babysitting. I know I can't afford a nanny. Apparently, Mom and Dad were subsidizing that, too. He said they'd keep doing that, but I don't know. . . if I'm just working and not even paying rent, I should be able to pay for childcare."

Ben looked at his sons, who had moved into the edge of the woods and were crouching to examine something on the ground. "I'd like to come up here sometimes."

Jonah swallowed. "Ben, I hope you'll come here frequently. As often as you like. I've been thinking, too. . . maybe your parents would come up for a visit, or I could go down there, if they'd prefer. I'd like to meet the people who did such a fine job of raising the son I never knew about."

He turned to face Ben. "When you first came here and told me who you were, I was upset that I hadn't known about you. And then I felt guilty—terrible guilt—for what happened to Shari. I can't go back and change that. But I've come to realize that God gave you the right parents—gave you to them. It wasn't an accident or my sins that arranged your family. Before you were conceived, He made those plans for you. And then, after He had done that, when the time was right, He brought you to me, too. That's the kind of planning God does, Ben. It's big. It's perfect."

Teresa and Annie walked around the corner of the house. Teresa had a long-handled shovel over one shoulder and the little girl carried a bucket. They waved at the men but didn't stop.

Jonah and Ben watched them disappear down the forest path. The boys scrambled out of the shrubbery and followed.

"What about her?" asked Ben. "Do you think God brought her to you, too?"

Jonah nodded. "I think so. I hope so." He chuckled. "You know, Ben, I do hope you and the kids can break yourselves of the habit of calling her Mrs. Cooper."

Ben gave a shout of laughter, and pleasure washed over

Jonah at the sound. He hadn't been dissatisfied with his life before he knew this family, but nothing could compare to this gladness, this abundant blessing.

"Come on, Ben. Let's go see what they're up to. We don't want to miss out on all the fun."

If you enjoyed *Baggage Claim*, don't miss the rest of the Hope Again series!

Follow some of the *Baggage Claim* characters back to Chicago, to the Unity Plenkiss Community Center. The Unity Plenkiss is a Christian ministry serving an eccentric community of elderly people, homeless vets, needy families, and other all-too-real fictional characters. They come for meals and fellowship, but the Unity Plenkiss is so much more…

Snow Angels, book 2 in the Hope Again series, is a mistaken-identity romance sure to make you laugh and make you cry… and then make you laugh again.

Snow Angels
Chapter One Excerpt

It was the worst facial hair she had ever seen. Most of the men in the Unity Plenkiss Community Center's gymnasium had beards. Some were attractive. Most looked like birds' nests. This one was exceptional.

A large red hand waved between them. "Hello?"

Lisa plastered on a bright smile. "Happy Thanksgiving! Would you like white meat or dark?"

"Hey!" A slight man pushed the newcomer aside and shoved his plate at Lisa. "I was next. I want both. Pete can wait in line just like everyone else."

"Yeah, you go to the back of the line." An enormous teenager, dressed entirely in black, slid in front of Pete. "White meat."

"Sorry, Damarius. You go ahead."

"Just did."

As soon as the boy walked away, Pete stepped close to the table.

"Happy Thanksgiving!" She couldn't take her eyes off his face. An irregular beard obscured the shape of his jaw. Dark hair bristled in three clusters on one side of his mouth, but his mustache was sparse on that side and thick on the other. One of his sideburns grew along his cheekbone instead of down along the jaw, and his chin had sprouted a crop of long straight hairs that nearly hid a round cleft. The skin revealed between the clumps of dark hair was pink and white with cold. He looked like a monkey with mange.

"White or dark?"

"I have enough turkey. I'm here for the potatoes."

Lisa hoped she was smiling helpfully. "Potatoes are over there." She used the meat fork to indicate the twin lines of servers. "First stop that way."

"I'm supposed to get them from you." He scowled. "A lot of potatoes. Like twenty servings. Mashed potatoes, in Styrofoam containers. And some butter."

Her smile became fixed. "Sorry." Lisa looked for one of the more experienced volunteers. She could see several of the official purple T-shirts across the room, but no one was paying attention to the turkey table. "We have plenty of potatoes, but I don't think we have Styrofoam containers. We offer free delivery but no takeout."

"I know that." Pete staggered as an underdressed blonde hip-checked him.

"Are you back for seconds, Pete?" The woman batted sticky eyelashes at him and rolled her eyes toward Lisa. "You'll have to watch this guy."

"Didn't you get enough the first time?" Another woman stepped between him and the table.

"I'm a growing boy." Pete was pushed back further by the invasion of a third woman, and Lisa smirked at his futile efforts to escape his increasingly friendly admirers. Maybe they'd carry him away.

An air horn blasted the hollow clamor of the gymnasium. Lisa had been rattled the first two times it happened, dropping her meat fork into the pan on both occasions. This time, the Thanksgiving prayer was brief and business-like, a welcome contrast to the previous one, offered by the preacher of The Blessed Church of the Sacred Lamb and Holy Lion. That man clearly enjoyed long talks with God. After five minutes of responsive amens and hallelujahs, most people had gone back to eating and serving. Quietly, of course.

Pete spoke as soon as the prayer ended. "So, you don't have the potatoes?"

He looked under the table and behind her as if she might have missed them, and Lisa sighed. She shouldn't have been left alone. At least he wasn't as alarming as some of the other men here. The smell of cheap perfume—probably a recent addition—was better than the pervasive odor of smoke, alcohol and unwashed clothing. Except for the peculiar facial hair, he looked like the rest of them in jeans and a stained tan canvas barn coat over a black sweatshirt. A knit stocking cap was pulled down to cover his ears, pressing damp strings of dark hair down over his eyebrows. With a shave and a shower, a haircut, clean clothes, and a better attitude, he'd look fairly respectable. He could probably even get a job if he tried. His dark blue eyes were attractive.

Lisa shook herself. Where did that thought come from? She wasn't in the habit of noticing men's eyes. "Potatoes are over there." She pointed again.

"They're probably in the kitchen. I'll get them myself." He turned around and bumped into a woman whose head didn't reach his shoulder. "Well, hello, Mary."

"I want dark meat, in small pieces." The tiny woman wore at least two long wool coats, her head perched on a nest of multicolored scarves. Her toothless smile explained the request.

"Certainly!" Lisa's smile was genuine now. She'd seen too many elderly people today—people who should be enjoying family celebrations in warm houses with plenty of food. None of them should be lonely or living in poverty, forced to get a free Thanksgiving dinner at the community center. "Is this okay?"

"Perfect, dearie. I just love having Thanksgiving here. You all are so nice. Maybe just a little more?" She wedged herself in front of Pete, and he stepped back, bumping into a child and causing him to drop his plate. When the boy bent over to retrieve it, his mother yanked him up, and his wails drowned out the soft voice of the old woman.

"I'm sorry." Lisa leaned forward. "I didn't hear you."

"I just want a bit of the white meat, too. Not much. And cut the pieces a little smaller than the dark, because it's usually drier."

Lisa bit her lip. Mr. Strough had instructed the volunteers to be careful with portion size, but this poor little woman looked like she could use the calories.

"That's a lot of food, Mary."

Lisa gasped at the man's hypocrisy. This sweet old lady was just asking for a few more pieces of meat—not massive amounts of potatoes.

The woman glowered up at him. "That's Mrs. Henders to you, Pete. I saw you knock down that little boy."

He opened his mouth, probably to argue, but others took up the complaint.

"You're a big ox, Pete."

"What a klutz."

"And you're butting in line. Wait your turn."

Pete ignored the comments and waggled his finger at the small woman. "Mrs. Henders, are you trying to take food home for Bill?"

She huffed. "No, it's for me. I'm hungry."

He looked at her plate. "That's a lot of turkey. Are you sure you weren't planning to take some home with you?"

"Bill deserves to have Thanksgiving, too!" She clutched the plate fiercely in both hands, as if afraid he might snatch it away. "You know he can't get outside anymore. He has such bad arthritis, and it's so cold out."

Her voice quavered pathetically, but Pete shook his head. "No, Mary. No turkey for Bill."

What was the matter with this brute? Lisa wondered if they had bouncers at the Community Center. "We do have a home delivery service."

"Not for Bill," Pete said.

Lisa watched them as they moved away, still bickering. She was never doing this again, under any circumstances. According to the news reports, people signed up years in advance to serve Thanksgiving dinner at homeless shelters. Why didn't they keep a waiting list? Lisa had been roped into it at the last minute, when half of the church's service team got strep throat, and even then, she would have slid out of the "opportunity" if her sister-in-law hadn't made the request in the same conversation as her announcement that they were canceling the family dinner.

"So, really, the timing is perfect. I was feeling guilty about abandoning you on Thanksgiving, and now you won't be alone!" Lisa had protested, but Claire ignored her with the ease of long practice. "Pastor Keller was so relieved when I told him you already had the background check! He said to thank you and just be there at ten."

Lisa had been there at ten, squashing a craven impulse to send a nice donation and cancel at the last minute. What kind of heartless person didn't want to serve Thanksgiving dinner at a shelter? An introverted person with anxiety issues, of course. At least she hadn't stabbed anyone with the meat fork yet or spilled the pans of turkey on the floor.

***

Buy *Snow Angels* now to continue the Hope Again series!

CATHE SWANSON

After 40 years of wandering (but always in lovely places and not in a desert), Cathe Swanson has recently returned to her childhood home and family in Minnesota.

In the summer, she and her husband enjoy spending time with their grandchildren and being outdoors, gardening, hiking, birdwatching, and kayaking. The long winters are perfect for playing games, reading, and indoor hobbies. Cathe's been a quilter and teacher of quiltmaking for over 25 years and enjoys just about any kind of creative work, especially those involving fiber or paper.

Everything inspires new books! A lifelong love of quilting, Cathe's Swedish heritage and an interest in genealogy led to The Glory Quilts series, and the Hope Again series is inspired by her life in the Midwest and experiences with the elderly, the military, and inner-city ministry. As a child of the 60's, she's having fun writing about hippies and the Jesus People movement in the Serenity Hill series.

Cathe writes books with creative plots and engaging characters of all ages, to glorify God and entertain and bless readers. Her heartwarming stories will make you laugh and make you cry — and then make you laugh again.

Visit catheswanson.com and sign up to receive monthly updates, special offers, giveaways and more!

MORE BOOKS BY CATHE SWANSON

The Hope Again Series
Baggage Claim
Snow Angels
Long Shadows
Hope for the Holidays
Home Run
The Road Home

The Glory Quilts Series
Always and Forever
Matched Hearts

The Serenity Hill Series
Season of Change
Starting Now (2022)

Potato Flake Christmas
Murder at the Empire

Made in the USA
Columbia, SC
20 June 2022